Wreckage River

By Barbara J. Barker

Dedication: For Helen, whose soul speaks fluently in the language of dogs.

Your bond with them inspired these pages.

Contents

Chapter One
Columbus, KY: Friday, August 15, 6:51 p.m.

In the far distance, way on the west side of the Mississippi River, Vic could see the sky bruising, the stain of a coming storm blotting out the evening's setting sun. He muttered under his breath, wiping a layer of sweat from under his tangled, crimson-dyed hair, irritation mounting.

"Just my luck," he grumbled.

"Maybe we should postpone until the storm passes. Some dangerous storms have come through this summer," the skinny little guy beside him offered.

When they arrived at the outdoor concert venue, the scrawny guy introduced himself as Ted. Ted owned and operated the facility where they were to play tonight. Ted was a strange little dude. Long strings of brown hair crossed his bald pate, slipping over his forehead every time he bobbed his head. He wore a bright red T-shirt over faded jeans with *The Kentucky Ravine* embroidered on the pocket in big, fat letters.

"The Kentucky Ravine is an all-around extreme music venue," he bragged as he showed them around the space. Ase, their drummer, rolled his heavily mascaraed eyes and flicked his fingers in the talk, talk, talk motion behind Ted's back. Clearly, this corn cob never visited LA, where the real music venues were located.

Well, at least this place stood up modest market stalls to sell their shirts, plastic porta-potties, a concession stand, and most importantly, a bar. A wide-open stage backed up to a dope river view, and the afternoon's glow on the water's surface earlier today was awesome. Even now with the clouds bringing an early twilight, the Mississippi, lined with giant, long green levees in this stretch, was magnificent. But Vic wasn't here to sightsee.

His fingers drummed against the side of his van as he stared at the storm. He didn't need this right now. Vic didn't want to deal with the wind, rain, or whatever the hell was about to come tearing through. He just wanted to get through the show, grab a beer, and then head out with the farm girl they had met earlier at the dinky town diner.

Vic ignored the weather. Let the locals like Ted worry about it. He'd promised himself that tonight he was going to enjoy himself. He wasn't about to let some storm ruin his shot at a good time with the one hot girl he'd met since they started this tour. Vic was going to score. He was sure of it.

Ase and Neil were grumbling in the background. The two shared his disdain for the cycle of small towns, hot, miserable days, and endless talk about the weather. They'd been stuck in the Midwest too long.

After disaster consumed the West Coast, they knew it would be a long dry stretch before their band —BROKEN HEADS! — would get to open again in LA or anywhere in California. It'd been pure luck that they'd been playing in Chicago when disaster struck the West Coast; they'd missed everything. Indo Fleming, their manager and agent, wasn't so lucky. He was wiped out with the rest of LA, leaving the guys looking for new representation.

Three months later, the new manager they snagged—some kid out of Wicker Park—was all about country music, not rock. So here they were, slogging through gig after gig in the heartland, with no end in sight. California felt like a lifetime away.

He pushed off the side of their van and ran a hand through his long hair. Time to make music. He headed for the stage, sliding out of the spiked leather jacket covering his band shirt and hiking up his ripped jeans. Rousing up his partners, he ran on stage, with a big smile, shouting out hellos to the crowd of a few thousand. The band's studded boots stomped the boards as they took their places. The sooner they started, the sooner they'd be done.

Amplifiers and speakers boomed into the night as Ase dropped behind the drums and Vic and Neil grabbed their guitars. Their newest sound man, Rolo from South Chicago, who'd only been with them this summer, was already behind the mixing desk, hammering through recordings of previous concerts to get the crowd in the mood.

Sudden feedback screeched. Vic glared at Rolo, and with a dufus grin, the mixer started up the first set. Hicks. Vic hated the Midwest.

Vic started the first song without missing a beat, belting out tunes like he was standing on stage at The Hollywood Bowl. The crowd went wild, stamping feet, singing and chanting along, and waving arms excitedly.

Ted ignored the concert and continued to watch as the storm approached. He fidgeted, wondering if he should do something now or wait until the storm arrived. The risk of customer complaints if he interrupted the concert for nothing stayed his hand. Besides, the bar was doing great business, and that's where he made the most of his profits.

The base of the storm was a low, ominous, inky blackness, while the upper clouds spiraled upwards like a monstrous skyscraper of vapor. The top of the supercell was almost an anvil shape, a violent, turbulent cap that glowed faintly with flashes of lightning dancing within.

Ted had seen his share of storms over the years, but this was next level. The atmosphere felt electric, and he glanced back at the stage, debating whether it was the storm or the concert that was making him feel this way. Gusts of wind picked up, raking his clothes, and the air felt heavy, saturated with moisture.

He guessed the storm was still miles away, but took it seriously when the thunder rolled in fifteen minutes later with a low, deep growl. Backing up a few steps, he turned, trying to decide where to start. He didn't have a basement or shelter on the property. The best bet was for people to get to their cars. But first, he'd have to interrupt the concert.

The sky flickered with lightning, and the storm sent a jagged streak of bright light cutting through the dark western sky.

Towering clouds churned, twisting and rising with incredible power.

The wind howled, stinging his face, and Ted squinted against the bite of something cold in the air. Ice or sleet. He held his hand out, feeling the sharp, frozen points prickle his palm before the gusts snatched them away.

His boots slapped against the pavement as he trotted through the crowd, fear buzzing in his veins. The storm was closing in fast. He ran up the stage steps, heading to Rolo at the mixing table. The guy was still working, oblivious to the storm behind them. His fingers danced over the controls as the band played on, ignorant of the madness unfolding around them.

Vic saw Ted reach the stage, but he barely acknowledged the venue owner, dismissing him as he turned back to the crowd, whooping his way into the next song. The lights pulsed, the music thumped, but the sky behind them had gone so black it felt unreal—like a painted canvas, a backdrop in some twisted theater. Lightning crackled, the bolts too close now, lighting up the sky in flashes of icy fire.

Ted scanned the crowd, his chest tightening. What the hell were they doing? Why wasn't anyone running? The storm was coming in fast. The wind whipped dust and ice across the lot, making it difficult to see. Yet people kept dancing and cheering like the storm was another part of the show. A bizarre thought hit him—do they think this is pyrotechnics? Were they too drunk or too caught up in the music to notice what was coming?

"Rolo!" Ted shouted, his voice barely carrying over the storm and the singing crowd. "We need to stop this! There's a storm. We need to get people to safety!"

Not understanding a word, Rolo grinned and nodded, his head bobbing to the beat.

A bolt of lightning cracked across the sky, blinding in its brilliance, searing through the dark clouds like a jagged knife. For a split second, everything was bathed in white fire—every face, every movement captured in the intense flash. The thunder that followed roared, a sound so deep and violent it felt like the earth itself was being torn apart. The crowd exclaimed and recoiled, thunder ripping into their bones. A booming crack rattled Vic's teeth, making his skull hum with the force of it.

When he looked up, his stomach dropped. The sky had become a swirling maelstrom, like something from a Nordic painting. The storm descended on the concert arena with a violence that took his breath away. Black clouds twisted and churned. A dark, swirling vortex formed above them like a portal to hell.

The wind increased then, howling across the Mississippi River with a fury. It tore through the venue like a war in motion, shredding the temporary stalls set up along the perimeter. Flags crackled and twisted violently, their colors fading into a blur as they ripped from their poles. The cables strung across the venue—those that held lights and sound equipment—snapped like thread, whipping through the air like lashings from a giant's hand.

Vic's heart pounded as the wind screeched through the concession stand, raking the entire structure from its foundation. Walls buckled and groaned under the pressure before collapsing inward, the roof crumpling like paper as it fell.

He couldn't see Ted anymore. The man had either run off or been blown from the stage. A cascade of trash flew past him, and Vic ducked, covering his face. The wind tore through the crowd, pushing people to the ground as the arena fell apart at the seams.

The storm was deafening. A screaming, relentless power drowning out everything.

Another jagged bolt of light shot from the sky, a brilliant, incandescent streak of pure energy. With a deafening crack, it slammed into the drum kit, lighting Ase in a blinding halo of electric fire. The explosion sent a shockwave rippling through the stage. The air crackled around them. Ase's lanky body jerked as the blast of millions of volts held him in place, his hands twitching, sparks flying. Dead in an instant, he never knew what hit him.

Neil, his long hair wild and standing straight up, was flung through the air and impaled on top of one of the stall poles, the aluminum driven clear through him before he crashed to the ground in a tangled heap. His body hit the dirt with a thud, leaving a trail of dust swirling around him, his blood running over the hardpan in a wet pool.

Vic's eyes widened in disbelief as the blast threw him sideways off the stage. His narrow face etched with surprise, comical amid the mayhem. He hit the ground hard, the air knocked out of him, and his mind scrambled to make sense of what had happened.

The world spun for a second. Then, instinct took over. Terrified and disoriented, Vic scrambled to his feet, eyes wild as the chaos unfolded around him. The storm still howled, a downpour sweeping through, but his feet were already moving. His legs carried him, as if on their own, toward the nearest safe haven—a port-a-potty.

He flung himself inside, banging the door behind him, the tiny restroom rattling with the violence of the storm outside. His heart was pounding in his ears, and his breath came in ragged gasps, but for a moment, everything was muffled.

Then, the door yanked open, and Vic jerked back, startled. A blond woman stood there, panic in her eyes, clutching a small blond child to her chest. The wind tore at them. Her face twisted with fear, her eyes begging for shelter. Time slowed for a heartbeat, and then something cold and primal took over. Blindly, Vic jerked the door back shut without feeling a damn thing, the lock clicking into place.

He didn't look at the door. He stayed still, pressing his back against the thin plastic wall, squatting over the hole in the board. The screams and horror outside were muffled, but not enough to drown out the deafening pounding in his chest.

The world shifted in an instant. One moment, Vic huddled in the dark, trembling inside the cramped walls of the port-a-potty; the next, the storm's furious grip tore the ground from beneath him, and the flimsy plastic walls were weightless. The wind howled, shrieking like a living thing as it yanked the structure from its base.

Up he shot, higher and higher, the wind screaming around him, rattling the box like a toy in a child's hands. Each second was a brutal blow, battering his body. His ears rang with the howling wind, and he exhaled in short, shallow gulps as the air grew thinner and colder with every passing moment.

His clothes froze against his skin, a thin layer of ice creeping over every surface, making it feel as though he were locked in a tomb. The wind had no mercy. The storm played with him, hauling him thousands of feet into the atmosphere, where time and space blurred into a dizzying spiral.

He didn't know how high he'd been carried, or sense how long he had flown. His mind struggled to keep up, but the pain and cold were all-consuming.

And then, without warning, everything shifted again. Once so powerful, the wind released him. The port-a-potty plummeted, free-falling through the sky with terrifying speed. Vic's stomach lurched, the fall endless.

His heart pounded. The echoing twang of a discordant note rang in his ears as the world became a blur of motion, too fast and too jumbled to process. His mind screamed for anything to stop the fall, but there was nothing. No ground to grip, no air to hold.

For the Broken Heads, the concert was over forever.

St. Louis, MO, Friday, August 15, 7:30 p.m.

Tau Wang pressed his forehead against the cold glass of the hotel window, black, silky hair falling in neat waves as his dark eyes watched the thunderstorm tear through St. Louis. The wind howled, hurling the rain sideways in sheets. Streetlights flickered, barely visible through the blur of water that obscured everything. He strained, but even the towering Arch had disappeared into the gray.

"This is a supercell thunderstorm?" Tau directed his question to the man who flopped on the sofa before the television, his eyes glued to the weather report flashing on the TV. Walter Simmons looked like someone who'd wandered out of a grad seminar and into the real world by accident. Tall and lanky, with a slouch that spoke more to years hunched over keyboards than any lack of confidence, he moved with the awkward grace of someone constantly lost in thought. His hair was a tousled mess—like he'd meant to fix it, got distracted by a data model, and never got back to it.

A junior analyst at the USGS in Reston, Walter was more of an observer than a participant. He watched the disheveled and soaking-wet reporter broadcasting from Columbus, Kentucky, describing the immense supercell storm that had just swept through a concert venue, killing dozens and injuring hundreds. Shocked and wide-eyed, she kept stuttering as she tried to speak and failed. The first thought to cross his mind was that he was glad *he* wasn't at the concert in Columbus, Kentucky.

To Tau, who crossed oceans and continents chasing a life filled with knowledge and excitement, the Midwest felt less like a stop on his journey and more like it was drowning in rain. He flinched as something dark hit the window, and thunder boomed again. Walter didn't even turn.

"Walter!" he said, cutting through the tail end of the thunder. "Come and see this!"

"I can see it," Walter said without lifting his eyes, his voice flat. His eyes jumped between the giant TV and his phone. "Radar's going nuts. I prefer my chaos on a screen."

Tau's gaze slid back to the gale outside, his lips in a tight line. He knew Walter still had nightmares about their narrow escape from the Portland disaster in May. Tau didn't push. He never did. He wasn't built the same—he carried the memories, but they didn't chase him through sleep.

His fingers traced the scar on his arm—a reminder of the vicious Komodo Dragons they'd escaped from at the Infinite BioLab. It should've haunted him. But his nights stayed quiet. He didn't dream at all, and that left him wondering what his father would've said. Be brave, the old man used to tell him. Maybe this was what bravery looked like—feeling everything and showing nothing.

Outside, the wind shrieked, bending trees like matchsticks. Inside, something uneasy shifted in Tau. They were here in St. Louis for the symposium, presenting the model that had predicted the spring's cataclysmic events: the quakes, the eruptions, the continent reshaping itself in days. But no one was listening.

Tau's laptop hummed on the table, half-buried under printouts and seismic maps. He'd been up half of last night rerunning simulations, tweaking parameters, reading the earth like a language only he and Walter were fluent in. As a senior data scientist at the USGS, Tau lived inside the numbers, finding patterns the algorithms hadn't caught yet. Walter, meticulous and relentless, matched him beat for beat. They were a good team.

Miguel Santiago, their boss, had sent them ahead to prepare the ground—sell the model, plant the seed. He was flying in tomorrow, hoping the key meeting got people listening. Tau wasn't so sure anymore. The data was solid. It *should* have turned heads. Instead, it met with polite nods, veiled skepticism, and closed doors.

All three of them believed the model could be the key to understanding what had been happening beneath their feet over the last several months. More importantly, was it all connected?

The storm outside showed no sign of breaking, and neither did the silence from the scientific community. But Tau knew what the data said. They brought concrete evidence that the model predicted the catastrophic quakes and volcanic eruptions in Oregon. But it didn't matter. No one indulged them long enough to hear the facts.

And then there was this storm. The concierge recommended a downtown bistro for dinner, but neither of them had the energy to fight through the rain. They would have dinner in the hotel dining room instead.

Walter sat back and continued scrolling through his phone. Suddenly, a familiar name caught his eye. He sat up and drew out his wallet, searching through the folds for a white card that had been given to him by a pseudoscientist back in May.

When he found it, Emmet Shale's name peeked between his fingers, and he looked at the picture of the self-proclaimed fringe geologist on the podcast list. He wore the same green jersey and cap, looking as odd as ever. His white hair was still wild and uncontainable, more Einstein than elegance, but his face was clean-shaven, angular, and alert. The most recent episodes of his new audiocast started a few months ago.

Walter sat up straight and motioned to Tau. "Look at this," he said, surprise changing the tone of his voice.

Tau moved around the couch and sat down, looking at the phone screen. "Whose Emmet Shale?" he asked. "And what's 'The Storm You Don't See Coming'?"

"It's a podcast. I guess Emmet Shale found his way out of Oregon and he has a new podcast going. He was the guy who owned the pet store where we radioed for help when we were fleeing Corvallis. You know, the guy with the earthquake-attuned animals. He had a boat and said he would ride the river out of Corvallis, right down the streets. The guy I told you about that predicted the Big One," Walter chuckled uneasily. He knew he sounded just as condescending as the scientists they had met with this afternoon.

"The Storm You Don't See Coming. What is he? A conspiracy theorist?"

"Exactly. Except, when we ran into him in Oregon, he was the only one who knew the earthquakes, tsunamis, and volcanoes were imminent besides my model. He was ready for it."

"You sure he's not just a quack who got lucky?" Tau rolled his eyes.

"I looked up some of what he told me. You know how I've been feeding animal behavior data into the model lately and the positive results we've seen? That was his idea. That's how he knew the West Coast would be devastated. He watched the animals." Walter held up his hand. "I know how it sounds. But I want to listen to this podcast."

"Whatever," Tau said. He thought they had bigger problems, but didn't want to argue. He hoped tomorrow would be better weather-wise and at the conference.

Walter's model had remained inactive for weeks, its lines flat, its projections quiet. Then, a week ago, it blinked on—an unexpected stream of activity, a red line crawling up the edge of the graph. Seventy percent. Not a siren, not yet. But Tau had learned to stop waiting for screaming alarms. Oregon had taught him that.

With rain rattling the hotel windows and the storm echoing the tension in his chest, Tau double-checked the data he'd just finished pulling. Every tremor, every underground shift, fed into the model. They'd booked time with the USGS supercomputers tonight—crucial minutes carved out to rerun the numbers. He and Walter hadn't said much, but the edge in their movements gave away their nerves.

On the couch, back deliberately to the window, Walter slipped on his earbuds and started the first episode. He recognized Emmet Shale's style right off the bat.

"Welcome, my fellow storm watchers, to another shocking episode of *The Storm You Don't See Coming*. I'm Emmet Shale, your guide into the ever-darkening skies, where science and madness collide, and the influences of nature are growing ever more destructive! In today's episode, we dive into an idea that will seem improbable at first glance, but the more you think about it, the more it makes sense. What if the violent supercell thunderstorms ravaging the American Midwest this year are actually contributing to something even more catastrophic: earthquakes?"

"I know it sounds crazy! But new evidence I've uncovered suggests that atmospheric pressure fluctuations, particularly during storms, play a role in triggering the many landslides and minor earthquakes we've seen this summer. Today, we will explore this theory, its research, and why experts are raising their eyebrows at the thought that supercells are the hidden spark behind seismic events."

Walter listened for several more minutes and then hit pause, his thoughts racing. It was so far-fetched he wasn't even sure any science applied to this theory, but he was reluctant to dismiss the old guy. It wasn't like anyone was taking them seriously, anymore than he was willing to take Emmet. He weighed the pros and cons while he watched the storm sweep across the television radar.

Outside, the wind howled louder, the rain slashing against the glass like a thousand tiny needles. Tau stared into the storm, hoping they could get someone to listen tomorrow.

7 Island Conservation Area, MO: Friday, August 15, 9 p.m.

"Listen boyo, this isn't your typical weather forecast. No, no! This is a warning—a *desperate* warning. In a matter of days, the storms of a lifetime are coming to the central United States. And here's the thing—*they*—the animals, the ones we so often dismiss, *they know* what's coming. Today, I'll tell you how, through their heightened senses, these creatures are offering the only real warning we have left."

Matthias Walker, formerly known as Matthias Clark, adjusted his behind on the log, wishing his glossy, gray Weimador, Shadow, could have accompanied him on this Boy Scout Retreat. Not that he was scared, but listening to Emmet Shale's podcast with the other scouts brought up bad memories. Shadow could tell when he was sad, and she was always there with a nudge to make him feel better. He shoved his glasses up his nose with a sigh.

"Let me take you deep into the heart of what I call the *supercell crisis*. For decades, scientists have been watching these storms grow in intensity. Supercells, once rare and localized, are now becoming more frequent, more violent, and… more intelligent. I know, I know… You're thinking, 'Emmet, what are you talking about? Supercells can't get *smarter*.' But bear with me, because the truth is we don't understand these storms as much as we think we do. They're shifting, evolving, adapting. You know who's been ahead of the curve? *The animals*."

The boys snickered, a few of them rolling their eyes. They weren't supposed to have brought the radio on the retreat, but since one scout had broken the rule, the others joined him to listen to the crazy podcaster. The Scout leaders were in a meeting, so the risk was low, and too entertaining to pass up.

"Birds, especially—these sky-bound creatures with their unparalleled sensitivity to the changes in atmospheric pressure. I've seen it with my own eyes. They know something we don't. *Before* the storm hits, they gather in enormous flocks, clustering together like they're preparing for a battle. They seek shelter in strange places, avoiding the wide open skies as if they sense that the air itself is turning violent.

Some say it's instinct. But I say it's something more. They're *detecting* the storm before it even forms, hearing the low rumbles of thunder miles away, sensing the change in electrical energy in the atmosphere that humans can't even fathom."

"He's the birdbrain," one boy tossed out.

"Shh," said a different boy. "This guy is sick!"

"My mom listens to him every day," offered another.

"…the dogs and cats. Have you ever noticed how your dog behaves before a storm? Or your cat? They pace, whine, act anxious, and get clingy, as though they *know* the danger is imminent. *They do.* It's those heightened senses of hearing and smell. They hear the faintest rumble of thunder before you do, and their keen senses of smell pick up the wetness in the air that precedes rain. They detect the faintest change in the air— ozone, moisture, the storm's very breath."

"The storm has bad breath. It'll kill us with halitosis!" Everyone laughed as the boy holding the radio ridiculed the podcaster, and the next words were lost. Even Matthias chuckled, a little weakly.

"My cat just slides under the bed," a boy with bangs falling in his eyes told Matthias. "I don't think she cares about storms."

"My dog stays close." Matthias pictured Shadow's loyal face. He missed his friend.

"…not just pets, no… Even livestock—the cows, the horses, the cattle. They know. I've watched cattle huddle together, trembling, their feeding patterns changing before a storm hits. They feel it. Something primal stirs inside them, urging them to prepare for the onslaught of the supercell. It's not a coincidence. It's *science*. These creatures can read the signals, the air vibrations, and the earth's changes. And we, as humans, have become so disconnected from these signals that we don't see the storm approaching until it's too late."

"So why does this matter, you ask? Why should we care about what animals are doing? Well, it's simple. These storms are growing in intensity, fueled by the changes in our climate, our atmosphere, and the energies swirling in the sky." He paused, and white static hissed. When he spoke again, his voice was solemn and profound.

"This is no ordinary season of thunderstorms."

The boys looked at each other, enjoying the scare. As Midwesterners, they had seen dozens of thunderstorms throughout their brief lives but Emmet Shale's warnings generated a new level of excitement.

"The supercells heading our way will be unlike anything we've ever witnessed. Their power is unprecedented. And it's coming *soon*. The first signs will hit in the next *few days*. But will we listen in time? Millions of lives are at stake. The storm will be so catastrophic that it will cause widespread damage, potentially reshaping entire cities. Some parts of the Midwest and Central U.S. will face complete devastation. Entire communities will be wiped out. Those who stay behind will catch the storm's fury, while those who heed the warnings—who get east, away from the epicenter—*might* stand a chance…"

The boy with the radio turned it off hastily as one of the Scout leaders called out to them. He shoved it in his pocket, and everyone assumed an air of innocence. Matthias jumped up, a little guilty, and went to help get ready for the evening flag ceremony.

Emmet Shale's words buzzed in his head. He remembered hearing the man broadcast when they were on the road outside Sweet Home last May, as they fled the lava lake and made it to Bend. The rhetoric was the same. Earthquakes, millions will die, run. He dropped his head. The guy needed a new subject. He didn't find it as funny as the other scouts, but then, he didn't know if he could ever find humor in earthquakes after fleeing from them as they had.

The evening storm had passed, but its lingering presence clung to the air. The damp frontage ground along the Mississippi River produced a faint smell of wet earth, mixed with the musty scent of rain-soaked tents. Matthias drank in the night, hoping the worst was behind them. He listened for any more rumbles of thunder, but all he heard was the soft rustling of the trees between the camp and the Mississippi River, the wind a mere whisper compared to the fury it had unleashed a few hours earlier.

Gale-force winds ripped loose a few tent stakes, but Matthias and some older boys fixed the damage by hammering the stakes back into the soft ground. Some younger scouts remained shaken, their eyes wide with fear, but Matthias was not among them. After the terrifying days they spent escaping the West Coast, a thunderstorm did not bother him much. He had been through worse. The thunder and lightning were just noise compared to their experience during the devastation of the West Coast.

Unzipping his sleeping bag, the fabric rustling as he settled back against the cold ground, he turned to tuck his glasses in his bag. He ran over tomorrow's agenda in his head. He planned to knock out a few more badges over the weekend.

Even though they were gone, he itched to make his mom and uncle proud.

The crackle of a nearby campfire starting up filled the silence, and the occasional pop of the burning wood caught his attention. He was happy he had helped cover the fire pits before the storm; having them going after the rain was nice. But even the flames didn't drive away the ache in his chest, the space his mother and uncle once filled.

He let his thoughts drift to them. The smell of his mom's lavender soap was still vivid in his memory, along with how she smiled at him before leaving for work. His uncle with a joke ready to lift his spirits. They had been his constants before everything fell apart. The loss still stung, a weight on his chest, but he kept moving forward, just as they would have expected.

His new guardians, Reed Walker and Chloe Cooper, had made this Boy Scout Retreat possible. They had found him a new pack, and a chance to join the close-knit troop marked a new beginning for him. They'd ensured he joined in everything—from the muddy hikes to the hands-on skill lessons and community service projects. All summer, they put in the effort to help him move on, to help his brother and sisters find their place in a world turned upside down.

Life was different now. But it wasn't bad different—it was just different. He thought about Shadow again, but knew the energetic dog was better off at the farm with his family than at camp. He didn't think he could have kept her from exploring, and the camp had a schedule he was eager to follow. The scent of pine and smoke from the campfire, the warmth of his sleeping bag, and the quiet hum of routine settled around him like a blanket, a new normal.

Before he fell asleep, he practiced rope knots in his head. Albert Frost, the old man they'd met on their frantic escape, and Stella, the mop-haired pooch that had adopted him, now lived with them at the Walker farm. He had taught Matthias every knot, every trick of the rope he had learned over the last fifty years. They both understood that the once-trivial skills now felt like survival tools. Always be prepared.

The adults were doing everything possible to normalize life for the four Clark kids. Walker kids, he amended, remembering Reed's generosity with his last name. With his mom gone and his dad in the wind, assuming the Walker last name had cut through reams of red tape as they resettled.

Somehow, in escaping the earthquakes and volcanoes, they had bonded into a new family. As sleep claimed him, Matthias knew how lucky he was.

***

Dan Clark swatted at a mosquito, muttering a curse as it buzzed away. Stuck in the swamp with no way around it, he hiked back to the road, his boots sinking into the damp earth with each step. His truck was half a mile away, and he was ready to sleep in it tonight. Tomorrow, he'd corner Matthias and confront the kid—he just needed to figure out how to shake him loose from the Scout Leaders and get him alone.

Finding his kids had been more luck than strategy. After months of searching the survivor lists in vain, he'd given up and focused on rebuilding his weed business in Montana. The $5 million they had socked away was gone, incinerated by a volcanic eruption. Bitterly, he accepted the loss.

But Nadia... His partner Nadia wasn't the giving-up type. Her Russian stubbornness had seen her through weeks of recovery after inhaling volcanic ash. While convalescing, she'd scoured the internet, piecing together fragments from the most unexpected sources. When she found Matthias's face in *Scout Times*—a story about a scout who lost everything in Oregon but was rebuilding in Kentucky—Nadia had hit the jackpot.

Dan didn't understand why his son was listed as *Matthias Walker*, not *Matthias Clark*, but it explained why he never appeared on any survivor lists. Their only lead was a camping retreat mentioned in the article as Matthias's first big step back into scouting. Dan had tracked down the Boy Scout troop's campsite in the Seven Island Conservation Area and left Montana three days ago. Nadia wanted to come with him, but her health was still unstable, and he needed to move quickly. As much as it irritated her, he'd gone alone.

Still, he couldn't return to Montana without the jewelry. That's what kept them searching for the kids. Nadia's collection—left to her by her late husband—was valued at several million dollars at its last appraisal. The kids had found the jewels in the go-bags in the back of his truck that Nadia had left behind by accident. They'd taken the gems with them but left the cash behind to burn when the volcano erupted— stupid kids.

He'd find Matthias, make the brat cough up the jewelry, and then get out of there. If those kids knew what was good for them, they'd hand over the gems, and he'd leave all four of them in the Midwest. He would not lose everything again.

Dan reached the GMC rental and climbed inside, slamming the door. Nothing was going to stop him this time.

Chapter Two

Walker Farm, Harrowood, KY: Friday, August 15, 9 p.m.

Reed Walker leaned against the wooden porch rail, the cool, damp evening air a welcome contrast to the unrelenting heat of the last several days. Tall and strong, Reed had a steady, grounded presence that put people at ease. His brown eyes were sharp yet kind, reflecting a calm focus that had become second nature in his role as an EMT. Lately, he missed the job, not the adrenaline, but the sense of making things right when they go wrong.

Watson, his Golden Labrador, sat at his feet, ears flicking at the soft patter of rain still dripping from the eaves, watching the other dogs in the yard. The last glimmer of lightning stretched across the horizon, its brief light flickering high above the trees in the distance. Off to the right one hundred yards, the green lawn dropped into a wild, brush-covered levee as the Mississippi River flowed past, its wide, dark current pushing south with hardly a splash.

Coco's curly chocolate ears bounced with each step near the front steps as he zigzagged through the grass, snuffling low to the ground. Across the yard, Bella moved with a careful intensity, her creamy coat rippling over lean muscle as she pressed her black-marked snout into the earth, tail flicking with every fresh scent. They moved through the scattered, storm-stripped leaves, sniffing the unfamiliar debris with suspicion. Neither had patience for anything out of place.

Reed's thoughts drifted back to that chaotic day when the quakes had torn everything apart. He had been at the Animal Rescue, where he'd volunteered for over a year. He had lost two people he respected for their kindness and humanity, and his Bronco had been flattened under a massive pine that had fallen when the tremors hit. The shelter was destroyed, too. The scent of pine and smoke still lingered in his memory.

After he freed the dogs trapped in the wreckage, he was surprised when some of them—Bella and Coco among them—followed Watson and him down the highway, sticking close as if they were leading the pack. He hadn't known it then, but they weren't just following him to safety—they would stick with him for good.

From inside, the muffled sound of laughter and chatter drifted out through the screen door. Chloe's voice rose above the rest, warm and light as she bantered with fifteen-year-old Piper and her ten-year-old sister, Winnie.

Caught up in a back-to-school debate—clothes, styles, the normal little things, their voices filled with excitement and joy. It felt good, starkly contrasting the weight they'd carried not too long ago. He knew the girls missed their mom, another victim of the disaster.

Since May, when the West Coast quakes dropped Albany High School into a massive sinkhole, Chloe Cooper had traded lesson plans for late-night talks and hugs, listening more than she spoke. The girls leaned into her presence the way roots search for water, drawn not by grand gestures, but by the reassurance that someone was there.

A scrape of the door behind him broke the peaceful lull, and his dad appeared, a cookie in hand. Royce was an older version of his son. His once-dark hair streaked with white, and lines carved deep at the corners of his eyes. Age had started its inevitable drag. Still, he was strong and steady, and the person Reed trusted most when the West Coast failed.

Royce said nothing at first, just leaned against the railing beside Reed, the soft crunch of the confection filling the space between them. The two of them stood there for a moment, side by side, listening to the wind and the sounds of life inside the house. Reed was a man of few words, and tonight, the comfort of their shared silence said all he needed it to.

Royce broke the silence with a contented sigh as he finished the last bite of his cookie. "These are great," he said, chewing with satisfaction. "That Chloe may be a biology teacher by trade, but she sure can bake."

Reed chuckled, nodding in agreement. His dad's voice carried a bit of awe, and Reed couldn't help but feel the same way. Chloe's knack had amazed them for creating delicious meals out of thin air—no recipe books, no formal training, just pure instinct. It was as though she had a secret kitchen wizardry.

She'd just laughed when they asked how she did it, shrugging and saying, 'The internet still works.' But Reed wasn't sure it was as simple as following online recipes. There was something more to it. Chloe's dishes didn't taste like they came from a screen—they were richer, somehow. Full of heart.

Watson scratched an ear, then lay down between them. Reed glanced over at his dad, who was licking the last crumbs from his fingers. After a beat, Reed cleared his throat, breaking the silence. "So... how do you like being mayor of Harrowood?"

Royce looked up from his fingers, eyebrows lifting slightly before a smile covered his face. Reed was taken aback when he heard his dad had accepted the position. Harrowood wasn't much—only 283 people calling it home—but the thought of his father, content with the quiet of his own company, stepping into a role like that was hard to reconcile. Reed had always imagined a small-town mayor would be someone loud and outgoing. Not his dad, who, like Reed, kept his words few and to whom social interactions often felt like a chore.

Mom navigated the gatherings, conversations, and greetings when she was alive. Dad had been content to stand quietly by her side, smiling in the background. But now... something had changed in his dad, even if Reed couldn't pinpoint exactly what it was.

Royce sat on the bench, the slight creak of the wood drawing Reed from his thoughts. "After your mom passed away, I guess I needed something more," he said, his voice quieter than usual. He didn't seem eager to keep going, but he continued.

"The town needed someone. Two years ago, Greg Tilman disappeared. Packed up and moved to St. Louis without a word. Didn't even bother to quit officially. Just gone. The whole town was in turmoil. They asked me to fill in for a few weeks. It sort of... snowballed from there." He shrugged, a self-deprecating grin brightening his face. "So, now I'm the mayor."

Reed raised an eyebrow, glancing at his dad with a mix of surprise and understanding. "You never know which way life will go," he said.

His dad chuckled, shaking his head. "That's for sure. If someone had told me that my forty-three-year-old, workaholic, bachelor son, living alone in Oregon, would show up here with a woman, four kids, and six dogs… I would've thought they were off their rocker."

"Well, it took an earthquake the size of the West Coast and multiple eruptions to make that happen," Reed said with a smile.

"That it did," his dad leaned back. "I was so damn scared when it all started. I prayed to your mom every chance I got, begging her to watch out for you. The day you called, said you were okay… that was the happiest day of my life."

Without a word, Reed placed a hand on his father's shoulder, grounding him with the unspoken bond between them. The smell of wet earth and fresh grass filled the air. A soft growling sound drew Reed's attention as Coco, all scruffy forty pounds of him, took issue with a branch lying across the path. With a delicate grip on the twig, Coco gingerly plucked it off the path and dropped it farther away, into the wet grass, his tail wagging. Coco liked everything just so.

"So, I wanted to talk to you about something," his dad said a few minutes later.

"What's going on?" Reed asked, sitting beside his father on the worn bench, as the distant hum of insects started back up now that the rain had stopped.

"Albert made the town an offer, and it impacts you. I wanted to see what you thought."

Albert Frost was another refugee from May. While Reed and his group were escaping the devastating earthquakes, they encountered an old farmer injured in the initial tremors. One of Reed's canine followers, Stella, found an unconscious Albert and alerted the others. Stubborn to a fault, the Schnoodle also jumped in to drag the old man to safety. She was both smart and resourceful.

Once the threat was over, Stella followed Albert, ignoring his attempts to shoo her away. They had been together ever since, and when they ran into Albert and Stella a few weeks later at the evacuation center, Reed invited them to join him in Kentucky at his dad's place. If Stella had adopted him, Reed knew Albert had to be okay.

"What kind of offer?" Reed asked, his curiosity piqued.

His dad hesitated for a moment before answering. "He offered to fund a clinic for the town. A part-time doctor, too. If he's not out on another call, the nearest one is an hour away. Albert's idea was that with your EMT skills, you could run the clinic for basic checkups and injuries. The doctor could come in once or twice weekly, whatever we can swing."

Reed blinked, startled. "Albert has enough money to fund a clinic?" he asked, the doubt clear in his voice.

Royce shrugged. "Well, he offered. We didn't get into the details, though. The bigger question is whether you want to stick around here or if you're thinking about leaving again."

"I wouldn't leave you here alone to take care of the kids," he protested, the response slipping out before he could second-guess it.

"I know you wouldn't, Reed and those kids look up to you. But that's not the same as settling down here in Harrowood."

"There's a lot to keep me here," he said slowly, "But I haven't made any decisions yet. Can I think about your offer?"

"Of course," Royce stood and called the dogs over. Bella and Coco bounded up the steps, swirling around his legs. Royce didn't see the faint shadow slip away from the doorway, tiptoeing through the house.

Inside, Chloe moved away, her blue eyes dark, biting her lip. She knew eavesdropping was rude, but she couldn't help herself. Reed Walker was the most unusual man she had ever met, and she still hadn't figured out what made him tick. She guessed he'd say, "No way, I'm out of here," but that wasn't what he said. The men she had dated over the years had been self-indulgent, looking for the easiest way forward. Reed, though, seemed different—but was that even possible?

Chloe sighed, pushing the thoughts aside as she climbed the stairs. Her blond ponytail swung across her neck as she moved. Heading to Piper and Winnie's room, she found ten-year-old Winnie sitting on her twin bed, with Charlie, her black and white Borgi curled beside her, impatiently waiting to cuddle. Fifteen years of teaching biology had prepared her for everything—except starting over in Harrowood, KY, co-parenting four kids, and navigating a complex relationship with a man she didn't understand.

She looked forward to teaching in the tiny school in Harrowood next week, but the question lingered: Would Reed still be here, or had he decided to leave?

New Madrid County, MO: Friday, August 15, 10 p.m.

A deafening bang cracked the air, followed by a heavy rumble that vibrated the ground. For a split second, the earth trembled, enough to send foxes and mice darting from their burrows. The insects fell silent, and a flurry of birds burst from the trees in a panic.

Only a hint of moon peeked out from behind the shredded storm clouds that lingered from the tempest that had passed over New Madrid County just hours before. Most people were in bed by now, the promise of a calmer day ahead lulling them to sleep.

Mark Mellor parked his Jeep on the side of the State Highway, a lonely spot along the Mississippi River, and stepped out into the dark. The moon barely made a dent in the blackness, but his flashlight cut through the shadows. The air was humid, a remnant of the storm's aftermath. Groadstone Cemetery was five hundred feet beyond the wild brush, and he drew his windbreaker tighter to shield himself from the dampness.

Usually, he'd be here in daylight, with the sun to guide him. However, the local history manuscript he was working on had reached a point that required a visit to check the engravings on a few gravestones. Being more of a night owl, he figured he could finish his research and then write into the early morning if he felt like it.

Some found an old cemetery eerie, especially after a storm, but Mark didn't believe in superstitions. Still, he was startled when he reached the graveyard and stopped to get his bearings. In the distance, flickering blue lights danced against the dark.

A quarter mile away, the Associated Pellet and Barge Co. docked at the Mississippi River, where two massive grain silos loomed above the levee. The blue light was faint, but enough to outline the silos and warehouses.

Mark knew the APG facility well—it was one of a hundred terminals and export sites, typically bathed in the steady glow of yellow security lights. But tonight, the familiar golden beams were gone. Instead, blue flames flickered, casting a ghostly glow over the area. He squinted to make sense of it, but the distance and the darkness kept the scene out of focus.

Then, the ground beneath his feet rippled, as though he were standing on water. He missed a step, eyes snapping downward, but the tremor had already stopped. A series of popping sounds from his right broke the silence. He swung his flashlight in that direction and froze. A gravestone, bathed in the beam, wobbled like it was caught in a breeze—then it dropped, disappearing into the earth as though the ground had swallowed it whole. His mouth fell open, and he rubbed his eyes, thinking he was seeing things.

Heart racing, he stepped forward, the beam of his flashlight tracing the hole that had replaced the stone. The rim was uneven, its edges sloping downward, far beyond the reach of his light. The darkness below was impenetrable. Another pop sounded, louder this time, from behind him.

He spun around just as the ground around another section of graves dimpled and sank, dragging more gravestones into the earth. Trembling, Mark backed away, careful not to lose footing in the growing network of holes. Now that he was looking, he could see cavities peppered throughout the graveyard. The pops vibrated around him, more soil falling away, with blue lights flickering in and out like something alive.

Mark had spent the sixty years of his life in the country, and nothing had ever prepared him for what he was seeing now. His heart pounded as he stumbled out of the clearing, back through the brush, his legs unsteady as he made for his Jeep. He needed to get to town. He needed to get the sheriff out here.

Then the ground jerked beneath him.

Before he could react, the earth lurched violently, lifting him off his feet and thumping him down with a brutal blow. He hit the ground hard, the air knocked from his lungs. Beneath him, the earth groaned. He had no way of knowing that after over 200 years, the localized fault deep beneath his feet had torn loose with a savage thrust.

The cemetery collapsed. Soil and stone gave way, disappearing into a widening crevice that ran to the river. The levee buckled with a sickening crack, and in an instant, the Mississippi River shot through the gap, surging with a deafening roar. Water dug its way beneath the damaged levee, tearing at the foundations. The earth shifted, and the walls that had held the river back for decades crumbled, disintegrating in the rushing tide.

The roar of water drowned everything else, a relentless, thunderous wave that filled Mark's ears. He pushed himself up, but before he planted his knees, the roar turned into something much worse—a deafening, wet sound. A wall of dark water, fifteen feet high, surged forward, sweeping through the brush. The strength of it hurtled into him, tumbling him into a whirl of limbs and twisted vegetation.

And just like that, he was gone.

Marston, MO: August 15, 11 p.m.

Frank Howell leaned over the edge of his well, his flashlight cutting through the darkness, but it couldn't reach the bottom. He peered into the blackness, straining for a sound—nothing. No trickling, no gentle splash of water. Only silence. He sighed and glanced at the empty bucket dangling from the rope, its metal clinking faintly against the stone.

The rumors had been swirling all day. Farmers in town talked about their wells going dry, one after another, in the past day or so. Now it was his turn. When he lowered the bucket, there was a sharp, hollow *bang* as it hit the bottom, but no satisfying splash or gurgle.

It wasn't a lack of rainfall. This year, spring and summer saw exceptionally heavy rains throughout the Tennessee and Lower Mississippi Valley, saturating the soil and raising the level of the Mississippi River to Major Flood. The last two years had produced prodigious spring rains, hitting the Missouri and Upper Mississippi watersheds and causing flood concerns. Yet, no water in the wells.

The minor earthquakes rattling Marston since yesterday morning hadn't appeared to cause much of a problem. Frank rubbed his chin, wondering if the tremors were messing with the water table.

He turned and loped toward the barn, his thoughts already on the next task. Tomorrow would be a lot of work—carrying water from the community supply for the animals was a must. There weren't any other options. Distracted, he didn't notice the absence of insect activity in the night. Even the mournful howl of a wild coyote was lost on him.

Inside the barn, the horses paced nervously in their stalls. Frank stopped by the mare's pen, his hand instinctively reaching out to her.

"What's wrong, Melly?" he whispered, gently rubbing her nose as she nuzzled his palm, the horse uneasy in a way he couldn't quite place.

He wondered if the heavy storm this evening had upset her. Sunset had been a grey, shadowy flicker, from dark storm clouds to the night sky covering the farm. Melly gave no answers. With a last pat, he headed toward the door. Sarah, his wife, was waiting for him. Turning off the lights, he shut the big barn door, latched it, and crossed the yard.

Tomorrow he was going to call the University. Maybe one of those professors had some suggestions that would help. As he climbed the steps to the porch, the ground beneath him bulged with a faint, restless tremor. Deep in thought, he didn't notice.

Tomorrow would be a better day.

Chapter Three
St. Louis, MO: Saturday, August 16, 8 a.m.

Walter poked at his eggs, watching the steam rise from his plate as he glanced at the time on his phone. Director Santiago's plane was landing soon. Dulles Airport delayed the flight for over an hour, but Miguel promised to reach the hotel as soon as possible when they spoke to him before dawn this morning. Everyone understood the urgency after running the most current data overnight. There was no question in Walter's mind that something big was happening.

The clock ticked closer to 10 a.m., the start of their presentation.

Sitting across from him, Tau was already halfway through his breakfast—three scrambled eggs, six strips of bacon, four pancakes, toast, and orange juice. Walter couldn't fathom where the slender man put it, but this wasn't the first time he'd witnessed Tau devouring a massive meal.

You'd think apocalyptic seismic forecasts would be enough to kill a man's appetite. Not Tau's. His partner knew the value of getting breakfast in before something interrupted the meal.

The sound of a familiar voice cut through his musings. Walter's head snapped around. Sure enough, Emmet Shale stood in the corner, animatedly gesturing to the waitress. Tall and broad-shouldered, he carried himself with the confidence of someone who'd spent decades solving problems.

"Not by the window, Holy Cow, we're twelve stories up! Anything could happen over there. And not by the serving line. What if the propane tanks keeping the food warm explode? Not under those chandeliers, either. How about that corner table by the doors? That looks safe."

39

Emmet had ditched the green ball cap, but he still wore a green jersey with a cartoon duck dressed as a hockey player, the duck gripping a stick. A pair of pressed jeans covered his legs. Old but polished boots matched his belt, and his white hair was sticking out in every direction. One arm held a stack of folders and rolled-up maps. The last time Walter had seen Emmet, the podcaster was practically buzzing with excitement over the earthquakes in Oregon. Today, his energy was more subdued.

He watched as Emmet settled into the corner booth, ordered his breakfast, and took a long sip of coffee.

"That's Emmet Shale," Walter said to Tau, his voice thoughtful with surprise.

"The podcast guy? *The Storm You Don't See Coming…* 'Is It the End?'" Tau's voice deepened, mimicking a doomsday announcer.

"I want to talk to him," Walter said, ignoring Tau as he reached for his phone.

"Fine, let's talk to him." Tau didn't get Walter's fascination with the fringe elements of their work, but he respected the analyst's insight into earthquake predictions. They had become close partners and good friends over the last few months. While he didn't expect they'd learn anything from Emmet, he was willing to follow Walter down the rabbit hole again.

When the moment felt right, Walter pushed his chair back and stood up, his gaze already fixed on Emmet's booth. Tau followed, a skeptical crease forming between his brows.

"Uh, Hi, Mr. Shale."

Emmet's expression brightened as he recognized the young man dressed in a casual charcoal-colored suit standing in front of his table. A wide grin spread across his face. "Walter, right? Walter Simmons! I wondered if I'd see you here at the symposium. I'm glad to see you made it safely out of Oregon!"

Walter shrugged, offering a wry smile. "Sometimes it felt like it was barely, but Miguel and I made it. We're on the East Coast now, working with the USGS in Reston."

"Glad to hear Director Santiago made it, too. You guys left just as things got interesting. By dawn, I was floating down the streets of Corvallis, drifting toward the Willamette River. Surreal, man! I heard Corvallis is gone now—underwater, the whole place. They're calling it Willamette Lake!"

"I saw that, too," Walter said, shaking his head. "I'm glad your boat got you out in time."

Emmet chuckled, a deep, hearty laugh. "I was ready to sail out days before the end came. I knew exactly what was going on."

Walter nodded, his bangs falling over his forehead as he adjusted his weight. "That's actually why I wanted to talk to you. I listened to your new podcast last night—most of it, anyway. I wanted to ask you a few questions."

Emmet raised an eyebrow, his grin widening. "You're the only one, boyo. Been trying to get these scientists to listen, but all I get are eye rolls and excuses to move on. Doesn't seem like these guys are too open-minded."

"We're getting the same resistance with my model," Walter said. He tapped the pile of Emmet's work with one finger. "Would you mind explaining your data? Honestly, I never would've linked supercell storms with earthquakes."

With ideas like this, Emmet had long since drifted from the mainstream. Officially, he studied "alternative geological energy vectors." Unofficially, he chased seismic anomalies the government "didn't want you to know about."

Alternate geological science was his fuel—using animal behavior, changes in water levels, solar activity, or specific weather patterns—he wove them into terrifyingly plausible explanations with a little too much ease. People rolled their eyes—until they realized half of what he said was disturbingly close to the truth.

He wasn't reckless, just fearless in his own eccentric way. You could call him fringe. You could call him crazy. But you couldn't call him wrong because too many of his theories had enough truth laced through to make you wonder.

"Sure," Emmet said, already grabbing his empty dishes, moving them to the table next to them. His movements were fast and purposeful. Light blue eyes sparked with a mixture of mischief and razor intelligence, constantly scanning, analyzing, and guessing at connections others couldn't—or refused—to see. Hesitantly, Tau joined them, adjusting his suit jacket as Emmet began spreading out his documents, papers crinkling as they unfolded.

"This is Tau Wang," Walter introduced the slim scientist. "We're working together to test my model's accuracy."

Tau shook Emmet's hand, surprised by the old man's firm grip. Emmet's strength was unexpected. Still, as a senior data scientist at the USGS, Tau worried others would see them talking to the podcaster. Their credibility was already on an uphill climb.

"Nice to meet ya," Emmet said with a nod before diving straight into the conversation. "So, I'm sure you both know the strongest recorded earthquakes east of the Rockies happened just down the river in New Madrid, right? Yeah?" He glanced between them, waiting for their acknowledgment.

Walter and Tau assented in unison as they sat down.

Emmet spread out the old documents in front of them, the yellowed pages curling at the edges. He pointed to the delicate script; the words written in a spidery hand that took an effort to decipher.

"Here's something interesting," he said, tapping the first page. "Johan Daviston's diary. He lived in what was then the remote western frontier, sparsely settled by European settlers. His entries from 1811 describe a year plagued by intense thunderstorms. Not just any storms, though. These were what we now call supercells. That year was brutal for anyone on the prairie—destroying crops and wiping out small settlements."

Walter raised an eyebrow; his fingers drummed restlessly on the table. "Okay," he murmured, trying to keep an open mind. He waited for Emmet to get to the point.

Emmet leaned forward, eyes gleaming with intensity. "Now, bear with me. This is a theory, but let's break it down. When a supercell forms, it's a powerful low-pressure system. That means the air pressure at the surface drops significantly. You see, atmospheric pressure constantly pushes down on everything, but when it drops, it can have huge effects on the ground beneath."

He gestured to the diagrams in the stack of papers— sketches of swirling clouds, maps of transformed ground. "That sudden drop causes what's called a *'low tide'*—not in

43

the ocean, but in the soil and rock underneath us. Think of it like releasing a cork from a bottle. When pressure drops, underground air and water that were previously compressed shoot up to the surface."

Tau leaned in, his curiosity piqued. The images gave weight to Emmet's words. "This drop in pressure is key," Emmet continued, pointing to the illustrations showing the modifications to the terrain. "It reduces the friction holding rocks, soil, and tectonic plates in place. Friction—it's the force that keeps these elements from sliding around. But when pressure drops, that friction weakens. The plates or rocks that were once stuck suddenly move, triggering an earthquake or even a landslide."

Tau furrowed his brow, struggling to connect the dots. "That's… a pretty big leap."

Emmet didn't flinch. "I get it. But let's say it's a possibility. Think of a breaking slab of ground that's held its position for weeks. It stays in place due to the friction between the dirt and rocks. But if the air pressure suddenly drops, it's like releasing the brake on a bulldozer. The entire mass of dirt and rocks can shift catastrophically."

Emmet ran an insistent hand over one of the diagrams—a landslide barreling down a hillside, its force captured in chaotic motion. "It's a lot easier to accept on paper, but the connection to supercells makes it really compelling."

He leaned back, emphasizing the point. "This past summer, we saw an unprecedented number of storms between St. Louis and New Orleans. With their intense low-pressure systems, these storms created the perfect conditions for triggering seismic activity or landslides. During a supercell, plummeting air pressure causes sudden ground shifts beneath it—ideal conditions for an earthquake."

Walter nodded, rubbing his chin thoughtfully. "I mean, anything is possible, but this is going to need a lot of research to prove."

Tau crossed his arms, his coat drawing across his shoulders, unconvinced. "Yeah, a lot."

Walter turned to him, his tone constant. "But do we need to prove the entire theory to test the elements? Think about the animal behavior data we've been tracking. That alone helped strengthen the model. If we added this theory into the mix, we might be able to see how it plays out."

Emmet leaned forward, his expression confident. "You'll see the patterns. The timing of these storms and seismic events is too frequent to be a coincidence. I believe these storms are contributing to a rise in earthquake risks."

Tau didn't answer right away, but the weight of Emmet's conviction encouraged a seed of possibility in his mind. "Are you going to the symposium?" he asked, eyeing Emmet with a mix of curiosity and skepticism.

"Of course," Emmet replied with a grin. "I even got an invite. Someone on the committee listens to my podcast. The thing is, none of the so-called experts have cracked this weird seismic behavior, and people are panicking. Maybe my fringe theories aren't so fringe after all."

Walter twisted uncomfortably, pressing his fingers on the table. "Emmet, here's the deal. My model's showing a sharp increase in risk," he said, frustration clear in his voice.

Emmet paused, his eyes narrowing. "You think the earthquakes will start again in Oregon?"

Walter tilted his head, expression tightening. "No, not Oregon." He glanced at Tau, then back to Emmet, lowering his voice. "It's the Midwest. The model predicts a massive earthquake along the New Madrid fault line within the next thirty days. We saw what happened on the West Coast when the Cascadia Subduction Zone slipped—hundreds of faults, including the San Andreas, woke up. Now we're worried it could happen again, here. The problem is that science knows even less about what's beneath the Midwest than we do about the West Coast. There's no telling how bad it could be."

Emmet's lips parted in a low whistle, and he scratched the duck on his chest. "You told any of these experts about your findings?"

Tau grimaced, rubbing the back of his neck. "More times than I can count. We mostly get patted on the back and told to play with the younger crowd. Director Santiago hoped we could get some support for the model, but it's been crickets. And we definitely can't take it to the administration. The West Coast's mess will cost trillions and take years to clean up. The last thing they want is more bad news about earthquakes. We'd need solid, irrefutable proof before they'll listen."

Emmet's face lit up, and he sprang to his feet, gathering his papers and rolling up his maps with swift precision. "Well, boys, let's hit the symposium. Let's see who we shake up today. The American people are counting on us!"

Walker Farm, Harrowood, KY: Saturday, August 16, 8 a.m.

"...expect plenty of sunshine throughout the morning, with clear skies and warm temperatures. It will be a hot one,

reaching a high of 94°F by midday, and winds will pick up, making it feel even hotter. Be prepared for gusty conditions throughout the day, as winds will be strong, especially in the afternoon."

Brett Walker could hear the forecast through the screened door as he passed the porch. Royce must have left the television on again. The man took his job as mayor seriously and kept a close watch on the weather as part of his responsibility, or maybe that was the farmer in him.

"This afternoon, a line of thunderstorms is expected to move up the country's middle. These storms are expected to be severe, with the potential for dangerous weather, including high winds, large hail, and even tornado activity. Radar indicates the possibility of tornadoes forming. Tornado warnings may be issued in affected areas, so stay alert and monitor local weather updates."

Brett sighed. More storms. Unlike the steady rains in Oregon, these superstorms produced a full load of thunder and lightning. And the winds!

"Stay prepared and keep an eye on the skies for any rapidly changing conditions. Stay indoors when storms hit and have a plan in place for severe weather."

When he went back inside for lunch, he better check out the weather report again. He didn't know how long the adults would be out, but these days, he always wanted to be prepared.

Seventeen with an athletic build, Brett was tall and muscular from years of physical activity and hands-on work. He rubbed a hand over his head, his hair a medium shade of brown, kept short and out of his face, a no-nonsense style that suited someone who spent hours bent over engines and mechanical projects.

Kicking at the damp leaves, he ran across the driveway, Bella trailing behind. The Alaskan Shepherd joined him every morning, nose twitching, eyes scanning ahead, ready to check every inch of the barn and ensure no felines had breached the perimeter. Bella hated cats. Once satisfied, she'd go on to whatever else she did during the day, but not until the barn was clear. He had given up distracting her and let her have her routine.

Bits of vegetation lay everywhere, scattered remnants from the storm that had raged through last night. The wind had shredded the trees. Now the yard was a mess. Brett shook his head, kicking another leaf aside.

"You'd never see a storm like that in Oregon," he muttered. Not that it mattered anymore. He'd traded the West Coast for Kentucky. Frankly, he was just grateful there weren't any volcanoes nearby.

He glanced at the Mississippi River, deep waters flowing south, never failing to appreciate the view. Reed's dad had positioned the house to take advantage of the scenery. He couldn't see over the levee's slope from here, but it dropped a good twenty feet to the river's edge, limiting any chance of floods to his soybeans and wheat crops. The white farmhouse perched above the levee, a graceful, Southern structure.

As he approached the barn, he punted a few more leaves aside, the scent of wet earth and damp wood thick in the air. His thoughts drifted from the storm and the old life in Oregon to the task ahead: the combine waiting inside. Royce Walker had told him it hadn't run in thirty years—a forgotten relic of rust and dust. Most people saw it as junk, but not Brett. He was a sucker for mechanical puzzles.

Since June, he'd spent every free moment cleaning out the engine, replacing spark plugs, fuel lines, and filters. He'd tracked down a new battery, swapped out the bearings, rebored the cylinders, and installed fresh rings. Each step had been slow and deliberate, the work of a teenager with more patience than most. He could almost feel the machine coming to life.

Today just might be the day. He could almost hear the old engine humming. He wanted to get it working now because his days were about to be occupied elsewhere.

School was creeping up, and Chloe Cooper, a high school teacher and one of the two adults who had rescued him and his siblings from the destruction in Oregon, was insistent. She wanted him to finish his senior year at the one-room schoolhouse in Harrowood. Brett had resisted. He preferred to skip it, take his GED, and move on from the whole high school routine. But then, his sister Piper had spoken up, reminding him—quietly yet with certainty—that their mom would have wanted him to finish in person and reap the benefits of an in-school senior year.

It had been a rough few months since they lost her in the aftermath of Albany's collapse, but Piper was right. Mom had always said, *Do things the right way, even when it's hard.* He felt it was the least he could do to honor her.

Matthias, Winnie, and Piper would also be at the same school. That was a small comfort. Despite that, the idea of being boxed into a one-room schoolhouse with all the grades wasn't his idea of fun. His old high school in Albany had hundreds of students, a football and baseball team, and lots of girls. He was sure the Harrowood school would be different.

Harrowood had a population of 283—tiny, by anyone's standards—and Royce had made it clear that the town had difficulty affording the school. Still, Brett had no choice. His last year set, he'd have to finish, whether he liked it or not.

Brett passed a twenty-one-foot side-console fishing boat parked on cement blocks just before the barn. The fiberglass-hulled craft was another of Royce's free pickups. After he got the combine working, Brett intended to see what he could do with the engine on the open fishing boat. Royce claimed the boat was seaworthy, but the Yamaha motor was as dead as a zombie in a late-night movie.

Years of wear and tear had marked the hull, but the name was still legible. *Seismic Wave.* He supposed that was a riff on the New Madrid Fault somewhere around here, but Brett found nothing about earthquakes funny. He would paint the hull and change the name if he got the motor running.

Swinging the barn door open, Bella was off like a shot, her paws skittering on the dusty floor as she darted into the shadows. Her nose twitched, already hunting for something to investigate. He smirked, knowing the fracas she'd cause if she found a cat. He didn't think she had the guts actually to kill one, but she'd sure chase it until it was long gone.

The combine sat discarded in the corner, still parked against the front barn wall where it had been since Royce had hauled it out of some friend's field, one more free-for-the-taking endeavor. Royce had planned to fix it, he'd told Brett, but the old machine had become another project that slipped through the cracks between the farm and his mayoral duties.

After the chaos in the spring, Brett was grateful for something like this to keep him busy. And he liked Royce. Reed's dad was good people.

He grabbed a socket wrench and got to work.

Inside her bedroom, Piper, a poised and graceful 15-year-old with a tall, slender frame that matched the stature of her siblings, stood behind Winnie. She twisted the young girl's brown curls into place. Winnie had developed a fascination with elegant hairstyles and now insisted on intricate twists every morning. It was a ritual that had grown in meaning over the past few months, one that Piper knew helped Winnie feel some semblance of normalcy.

Piper didn't mind. She had inherited her mother's patience, which allowed her to sit still and focus on the small tasks when everything else was too overwhelming. A smile turned Piper's lips, but it didn't quite reach her eyes.

She wished for something to make herself feel better. She was a quiet girl, never one to share the storm brewing inside her. Lately, her thoughts spun and tangled together, making it difficult to think straight. Only her mother had ever known when something was wrong before she said a word.

Now there was no one.

Her emotions spiraled between deep sorrow at the loss of her mother and terror at what was to become of them.

She liked Chloe and Reed. She liked Albert and Royce, but the more she allowed herself to relax and believe they could stay, the more that little voice in her head whispered that it was temporary. That they'd never belong, that one day, maybe soon, they'd be told to leave. After all, who wanted four kids that belonged to someone else? Not even their dad had wanted them.

She knew there was no reason to feel this way. Chloe and Reed hadn't given her any sign that they were looking for somewhere else for her and her siblings to go. No one had said anything, nor had anyone done anything. But the fear was there, gnawing at the edges of her mind, louder than any of her grief. If they were pushed out, she had no confidence that she could take care of herself, let alone Matthias or Winnie.

She hadn't cried since that morning at the dealership—the moment everything changed, when she realized her mom wasn't coming back. It felt impossible, even now, to let herself feel that kind of sadness. How could she? There was too much fear in her chest, too much uncertainty for her to feel anything else.

With a deep inhalation, Piper shoved the feeling down, far away to where she couldn't reach it. She glimpsed herself in the mirror. Her hair—a waterfall of straight, silky brown—fell to her waist, forever neatly kept, symbolizing the control she maintained in her life. She focused on the task at hand, finishing Winnie's elaborate updo. Another day to get through. Another day to pretend everything was okay.

As she worked, she distracted herself by teaching Winnie a bit more Spanish. A high school junior this year, Piper had been drawn to languages, a gift she'd nurtured as she grew. The small school in Harrowood didn't have a dedicated language teacher, but Chloe had been exploring online courses to incorporate into Piper's curriculum. Piper had confided in her about her dream of someday becoming a translator at the United Nations, and Chloe was happy to encourage her in this goal.

"*Charlie es mi perro*," she said, while she pinned the brown curls.

Winnie grinned, her eyes bright with excitement. "That's easy!" she giggled, scooping up their small black-and-white dog from the floor. "*Charlie es mi perro*. Charlie is my dog."

Piper patted her sister's head, smiling as she stood up. "*No olvides tu mochila*." She told her little sister not to forget her knapsack, knowing Winnie would never forget the go-bag.

Winnie carried the knapsack she escaped with out of Oregon everywhere. Piper assumed it was a security blanket of sorts and left her to it. God knew they all needed something to hold on to after last spring.

Winnie started giggling again. "Si, hermana," yes, sister, she said, grabbing the bag and pulling it across her shoulders. She felt the familiar heaviness settle at the bottom, reassured that her special baubles were safe. Happily, she followed Piper to the kitchen.

It was a little quieter around the house today. Chloe, Reed, and Watson had left for the bi-monthly trip to Boxco, the big superstore in Cairo, Illinois. Royce, Albert, Stella, and Shadow had driven into Harrowood to inspect a building they were considering for a project.

That left her with Winnie, Brett, and the rest of the dogs at home.

Everyone except Matthias would be back by lunchtime, and she wanted to surprise Chloe by making po' boys for the meal. The Southern sandwich had become a new favorite, especially among the Clarks. No—the Walkers, she corrected herself firmly. Chloe had taught her how to make them fresh and delicious.

With Winnie's help, she laid out the ingredients. Charlie, and Duke, a nosy puggle she had a special fondness for, were underfoot no matter how much she shooed them away. Coco stretched out on the porch, a silent sentinel. The cocker spaniel/poodle mix had claimed the yard as his territory and liked to monitor things.

She glanced out the screen door at the sunshine-dappled yard. It was a nice morning, and this place was starting to feel like home.

Which only made her more desperate not to lose what they had.

Chapter Four
New Madrid, MO: Saturday, August 16, 8:58 a.m.

Now that was just downright weird.

Murry Hunneycutt stopped his tractor along the rocky outcrop, running between his property and the next, squinting at the sight before him. Timber rattlers—so many he couldn't count—slithered from the mounds in a frenzied mass. Some were small, no bigger than a hand, but others were thick-bodied, pushing five feet, coiling and hissing as they scrambled over the rocks and into his soybean field. Their movement was frantic, a writhing, twisting frenzy, as if the earth had suddenly opened up beneath them.

He blinked, watching the first several scatter, and then his gaze flicked back to the dark, shifting ground. The snakes spilled onto the field, vanishing into the tall green rows of soybeans like a flood of scales and venom. His mind struggled to grasp it. What the hell was going on?

His eyes darted from one snake to the next, but the sight didn't change. There must have been hundreds of them. He'd never seen anything like it. A chill slid down his spine. What made a five-foot rattlesnake run like that?

He searched the horizon. Nothing out of the ordinary— a clear blue sky, nearly ripe soybeans, and the sun beating down on the moist soil after last night's thunderstorms. The usual quiet of mid-August.

Then the ground shuddered.

It wasn't like anything he'd ever felt. It started as a low, deep rumble, like the growl of a truck beneath the earth. He whipped his head around, searching for the source. The soil trembled, and the soybeans swayed, their tender stalks jerking violently. A mysterious energy shook the tractor beneath him, causing it to buck and groan under the pressure.

The New Madrid Seismic Zone!

He gritted his teeth, struggling to keep his grip as the tractor steering wheel thrust up, smacking him in the chest. His insides compressed, organs rattling, and sharp pain erupted from his torso. Far off in the distance, thunder rumbled, a warning of destruction, but he saw only snapshots of the quaking land beneath him.

Grimly, he held on as the Missouri landscape broke apart around him.

For all his years of tending to the land and coaxing green sprouts from the earth, Murry had never spared much thought about what lay beneath. He knew the topsoil, every inch. He knew how the Mississippi River had carried its nutrients here, how the silt, clay, and sand blended right for the crops he tended. Murry knew how to work it, how to balance it. But the deeper layers—those hidden beneath the earth's surface—were an afterthought.

Murry was familiar with the stories about the great quakes that had shaken the land in the early 1800s when rivers reversed course and entire towns disappeared beneath the earth. Far from any plate boundary, earthquakes in the middle of the continent had seemed like ancient history to Murry. Sure, he had felt the occasional tremor, but the land had been still for so long that he had dismissed it, like most farmers here, too busy with the next harvest to worry about the crust beneath their feet.

Now, the fault was awake.

The epicenter of a massive 8+ earthquake cracked open deep in the crust below his farm, sending ripples through the soil. The weak zone—the 150-mile scar in the earth where the continent had once tried to break apart—was shifting again. Small, east-west compressive forces from the continental drift had reactivated ancient faults, and now Murry's farm was caught in the middle of it.

New Madrid, population 2,724, was disintegrating. The streets he'd walked a thousand times, the buildings that had stood for decades, were vanishing. The sturdy brick walls and old wooden houses reduced to rubble as the earth oscillated. Floodwaters came next, tearing down the levees that had once held back the Mississippi River. Water poured over the banks, sweeping through downtown with relentless strength. In moments, the little city had vanished under the combined wrath of the quake and the flood. Then the earth began to crumble and fall away.

A few miles away, here on his farm, Murry's mouth went dry, the band across his chest constricting as his heart thudded. He wanted to scream, to warn someone, but the words wouldn't come. All he could do was hold on, wheezing.

The stink of sulfur swept over him, burning his nostrils. He gagged; air caught in his throat. His heart pounded harder, and he couldn't think, only hang on, jerking with the tractor as the ground beneath him heaved and cracked. His thoughts flashed to his family, his house, and his livestock. Terror rocked him as hard as the earthquake.

The ground rolled, vast waves of earth fanning out, and the earth wrenched again, fissures splitting the soil. He felt the tractor tilt as its wheels slipped through the loose soil. Before he could react, a new wave of judders hit—one side of the land collapsing in on itself. He had no time to brace before the earth split wide open. The rocky outcrop shattered, sending boulders tumbling into the air, and the ground beneath him dropped away.

The tractor slid, its metal frame scraping against stone as it pitched downward into the newly formed fissure. He couldn't see the river, but the sound of levees ripping apart rang through the air, deafening, bone-shaking booms. The Mississippi River rushed free, walls of water bursting through the broken barricades, flooding the fields below in a rush.

He fell farther than he thought possible. When his tractor finally landed with a crunch, the yards of loose soil underneath him cushioned the blow. But it was a momentary blessing as the tractor sank into the quicksand-like earth. Terrified of being buried alive, he frantically tried to find a way up the crumbling sides of the sinkhole.

But a minute later, it didn't matter. Water from the breached levee poured over the rim, a waterfall of brown foam, liquid, and vegetation filling the pit in seconds as it swept inland. Murry never had a chance. The sheer power of the cascade hit him like a tidal wave falling from the sky, driving him and his tractor deep into the muck.

Still, the earthquake roared.

7 Island Conservation Area, MO: Saturday, August 15, 8:59 a.m.

Matthias ran his fingers over the patch on his tan sleeve. Earning the Tenderfoot rank felt like a lifetime ago. It had been in March, a few months before everything happened. Before the earthquakes turned western Oregon into a fractured memory, and his hometown of Albany into nothing but a huge pit. The helicopter news clips depicted the city as a half-filled sinkhole with horrible lumps and dark water. The badge achievement now felt distant, as if it belonged to someone else.

He remembered those fun afternoons with Uncle Jess, the sun warming their backs as they sat on the rear porch, studying charts and compasses. Jess's patient voice still played in his mind, teaching him how to orient a map, use a sextant, and follow the compass.

Now, every time Matthias pulled out the compass or thought about the next rank he was working toward, the ache in his chest swelled. His uncle was dead. He missed the relationship with the man who had been more of a father to him than his own.

With a sigh, he pushed his glasses back up his nose and focused on the task at hand. Most of the boys and the Scout leaders, except Pete Deller, the leader of Matthias's troop, had hiked inland early this morning. They wouldn't be back until tonight. In the meantime, the wood and vine ladder the boys had been working on this morning was nearly complete. Carefully, he tied the last of the knots, paying close attention to the work. The project looked good; it was ten feet long and tied with old woody, dark green creepers.

Pete, Matthias, and a few boys in his troop, Jamie and Pedro, had built the ladder to complete the requirements for the Woodworking Merit Badge. His knife, saw, and ax sat under a river birch, where he had demonstrated the differences among the tools —a crucial step toward Second Class Rank. Working a few hundred yards from the river, in the shade of the birches, the morning was pleasant, though humid. He picked up the knife and saw. He then grabbed for the ax from a fallen log.

As he reached for it, something made the implement hop. It wasn't the subtle movement of wind or a twist in his grip; the ax *jumped* as if a ghostly influence had nudged it. Matthias's heart skipped a beat. His hand jerked back, instinctively pulling away, eyes wide, staring at the ax.

Before he could steady his pulse, the ground beneath him rumbled, a deep, powerful thump that vibrated through his sneakers. His legs wobbled, and the ground pitched beneath him, throwing him off balance. He stumbled, his knees buckling, catching himself against the log. Adrenalin shots focused him, and his mind clicked into action.

A split second later, he was sure. The ground moved again, and his body instinctively braced itself as the telltale signs of an earthquake swept over him. He knew what this was. He had just gone through this a few months ago. It was happening again. He clenched his teeth, eyes scanning the sparse trees, waiting for the next vibration.

It hit hard and fast. The river birch and cypresses shuddered, their trunks quivering. Sycamores, cottonwoods, and maples rattled, their crowns a riot of flying leaves. The air thickened, vibrating with a low hum, and before the scouts processed what was happening, the ground lurched upward, tossing dirt, rocks, and bodies into the air.

The mighty Mississippi River came alive with terrifying ferocity. Regaining his feet, Matthias saw the river's surface rippling unnaturally across the wetlands. The river hesitated briefly, its steady flow faltering. Then, from one second to the next, dark water gushed upward. Matthias's heart banged against his chest.

It wasn't simply a flood. The river exploded out of its banks, a massive wall of water crashing over the cattails, swamp roses, grasses, and sedges in an unrelenting rush. A heavy, hollow rush of noise blew ahead of the surge, with a churning, frothing mass of brown currents racing toward the boys and their leader. The ground quaked beneath him again, each blow as fierce as the one before, knocking him to the ground.

Matthias's eyes darted toward the others. Panic flooded his veins. They only had seconds to react. The ground stilled, enough that Matthias could reach Pete. Back on his feet and grabbing the ladder with one hand, he pulled up the sprawled scout leader with the other.

"Up the trees!" Matthias shouted, barely able to get the words out. His chest squeezed, and his breathing faltered. Pete didn't hesitate. He grabbed the other side of the ladder, and they took off up the hill. He knew they had to climb and climb fast.

"Run!" he shouted, forcing his eyes off the river and pointing to a stand of oaks halfway up the mound. The boys ran, feet sinking in the soft ground. The earthquake juddered again, as if to knock the boys over so the sweeping river could catch them. Matthias didn't dare look back, barely keeping his balance as the quake knocked him forward.

The ground trembled violently beneath his feet. Each step sent shockwaves through his frame, rattling his teeth together. He reached the nearest tall tree, braced the ladder with Pete's help, and climbed.

The old overcup oak was thick and gnarled, standing at a height of sixty or seventy feet. The closest branches were nine feet over his head. His hands were slick with sweat and fear, but Matthias gripped the rough bark with his fingers, using every ounce of strength to pull himself upward. He intended to go as high as possible.

Jamie scrambled up behind him. Pedro, a few years younger than Matthias, struggled. At the end of the line, Pete boosted the youngster, almost lifting him into the branches, where Matthias and Jamie grabbed his arms and hauled him up.

But it was too late for Pete. The flood arrived, a ten-foot-high rolling wave instantly picking up their leader and the ladder, sweeping them both into the maelstrom and carrying them away. Matthias, laboring hard and terrified, urged Pedro to keep climbing, refusing to look down at the raging waters underneath him even as they rose around the sides of the tree. Spray coated his glasses, blurring his vision. He rubbed his face against his shoulder to clear the speckles.

The oak shuddered violently against the quake as the boys scrambled up, the tremors making the branches sway dangerously. They kept climbing, their panicked exclamations filling the air, leaves rustling as they shoved their way into the crown.

Floodwaters surged around the tree trunks, drowning the ground and sweeping everything before them. As Matthias scrabbled higher, his stomach twisted. The water rose, a relentless river driving over the swamp floor. The noise was deafening, with the roar of the flood and the shouts of Jamie and Pedro as they fought to escape.

Matthias reached up, his heart pounding in his ears. When he couldn't go any further, he stopped, clinging to the thick branches. He dared a glance down. As far as he could see, the wetlands had disappeared, consumed by the river.

The mighty Mississippi had burst its banks, leaving nothing in its wake but destruction.

***

Dan Clark climbed fast and high. His limbs burned with the stress, but he pushed on, ignoring the ache in his muscles. He knew how to climb a tree for all of his affected refinement. Five minutes ago, he was moving into position to confront the boy, less than a few hundred yards from where Matthias was busy doing some freaking nature thing when the earthquake hit.

Now he was trapped in this damned shaking tree.

He wanted to scream in frustration, but needed his energy to climb. Dan's stomach lurched, and panic spilled through him, but he fought to stay calm, forcing his body to keep scaling. His grip tightened on the branch, his fingers white against the rough texture, and his splutters coming in uneven whistles. When he finally reached a sturdy branch, high enough to give him some semblance of safety, he stopped, chest heaving, legs shaking.

The water below churned and boiled, thick with brown silt, barely a few feet beneath him. This water was deep. He scanned the area, his eyes skimming the tree line, and it hit him. His truck, parked on Levee Road, was in the direct path of this deluge. His rental would probably be swept away without a trace.

It felt like his luck had run out. The thought of losing everything, yet again, made his blood boil. Then he remembered Matthias, his only link to finding Nadia's jewels. The boys had been closer to the river than Dan, but before he started up the tree, he saw the scouts running this way. Perhaps they made it to the thicket?

His pulse thundered in his ears as the reality of the situation settled in. The quake had trapped him here, high in the tree, with no obvious way down.

Calming himself, Dan gritted his teeth as he surveyed the mass of moving water. Chaos stretched before him. He had to get out of this damn tree, find the kid, and make this whole mess right. He needed to figure out how to make that happen.

Harrowood, KY: Saturday, August 16, 9 a.m.

Royce Walker and Albert Frost, with their two canine companions, were inside the building they wanted to convert into a medical clinic when the quake struck. Through luck or serendipity, all four were inside an old walk-in refrigerator in the back room as the first spasms tore through town.

The ground roiled beneath them. The walls groaned as the building swayed, and the door to the old walk-in slammed shut with a deafening clang, cutting off the light. Boxes tumbled from shelves, and the world around them was a blur of frantic motion, bodies tangled in appendages and cardboard. A terrific crashing noise, like the sound of the building collapsing, scared them both.

Royce hit the cold concrete floor with a grunt, his hand instinctively reaching for Albert as they rolled over the cement. The tremors continued, one after another, but the thick walls of the fridge provided a shield, leaving them shaken but unharmed. Multiple wallops and thumps later, the tremors faded, and the ground stilled.

Stella, first on her feet with her deep bark cutting through the havoc, prodded them back to reality. She scrambled up, snarling low in her throat. Shadow followed, paws sliding against the slick floor, also growling. The two dogs stood, their bodies trembling as they scanned the room, the shock still vibrating the air.

Royce struggled to his feet, his heart pounding, and yanked Albert by the arm. Puffing heavily, they waited to see if anything else would happen.

Albert grabbed the nearest shelf, steadying himself. His gray hair was mussed, and a streak of dust crossed one cheek. "What in the hell just happened? I'd swear we were back in Oregon if I didn't know any better. Since when does Kentucky have earthquakes?"

Royce's eyes darted to the cracked cement floor beneath them, where faint lines webbed out. "We get tremors every so often, but nothing like that. Not in the years I've lived here. Maybe the New Madrid fault let go."

"The what?" Albert frowned, pushing past Royce to the door, his hand trembling on the handle.

Royce started moving boxes out of the way. "The New Madrid fault. It's a system that caused those massive quakes in 1811 and 1812. Back then, nobody lived here, but it was supposed to be huge—some people said they felt it even in Boston."

Most of the boxes were filled with old junk, so he wasn't too worried about anything breaking. He waited for his heart to settle down.

Albert didn't respond at first, eyes fixed on the door as if waiting for another shock. Stella's low snarl echoed again. Albert looked over at Royce. "Huh? Never heard of it. So… What, we're in for something worse?"

As if in answer, the floor trembled again, a violent shake that rattled the room. Dust fell from the shelves that were still standing. Both men froze. The dogs growled louder now, instinctively backing toward the corner. Royce's eyes met Albert's, a silent understanding passing between them. They weren't safe here—whatever was happening was far from over.

The door rasped open, and Albert gave a sigh of relief when he saw the floor clear in front of the walk-in fridge. It was a small blessing, given the mayhem that had unraveled inside the building. Packed with forgotten junk—decades-old equipment, boxes, and rubbish heaped in every corner—it was Harrowood's dumping ground, a town storage unit for anything nobody wanted.

It was the last building on the right side of Main Street, and the one farthest from the river. Main Street was a bit of a misnomer—a narrow stretch of pavement snaking through the small town, with dirt trails branching off into nowhere beyond the few houses that lined them. Main Street connected to State Road 94, the only way in or out by car, but even that felt distant.

Twelve buildings lined the road—five on the right side, seven on the left. The grocer's, a diner, the Mayor's office, the schoolhouse, a farm store, and a couple of other small businesses. Two stood vacant, including the one Royce and Albert had chosen to convert into a clinic.

They pushed through the mess of the hall, the shattered windows from small rooms letting in little light. Dirty glass shards crunched underfoot, scattered fragile bits across the floor. Equipment lay in haphazard piles, a chaotic jumble of discarded tools, boxes, and papers. Shadow and Stella darted ahead, eager to make it outside, their paws picking over the trash.

Albert moved faster, anxious to get out too, but before they could catch up, the dogs howled, a mournful sound echoing down the hall. Both men halted, eyes meeting in sudden alarm.

"Stella! What's wrong?" Albert called. Another cry lifted into the air.

They hurried toward the sound, the light growing brighter with every step. The hallway opened into the large front room, and they both stopped in their tracks, staring in disbelief.

The front wall of the building had vanished—not collapsed, not crumbled—just gone. Jagged edges of the ruined structure hung suspended in midair, with fragments spiraling downward into a void below. Thick particulates of dust coated old webs suspended in the air.

Royce stepped forward, eyes scanning the edge of the gaping hole where Main Street used to be. He leaned over the crumbled remains of the floor, but the ground dropped away so steeply that he couldn't see the bottom. He could only make out the sheer cliffs of the rift, falling into black nothingness.

Across the chasm, the other buildings on Main Street still stood, and despite the choking dust, he could see through the gap in the diner's wall where there had been a glass window before the quake. A group of people huddled together. Mel, the grill cook, Pat, the morning waitress, and Jake Worth, whose farm was about eight miles out. Two of his farmhands were beside him. They stood, frozen in place, powdered in grit.

It was as if someone had taken a big knife and sliced Harrowood clean in half. The pavement, the cars and trucks, the sidewalks, and the fronts of buildings were all gone, engulfed in an enormous rift that stretched as far as he could see in both directions.

It was like someone carved a deep canyon right along Main Street in Harrowood in just minutes.

Chapter Five

Walker Farm, Harrowood, KY: Saturday, August 16, 9:01 a.m.

A low rumble vibrated through the floorboards. Piper's fingers froze. The flour bag slipped from her hands.

Her pulse raced, the hairs on the back of her neck standing on end. A gasp caught in her chest, and before she could react, the flour bag hit the floor with a thud and exploded on impact. White powder billowed out, a cloud that filled the kitchen, choking the air with its sudden, blinding haze.

For a split second, a fog of white dust obscured everything. But then, the earth throbbed. The floor beneath Piper's feet trembled, then thrust upward, throwing her off balance. She stumbled forward, her hands instinctively reaching for something to steady herself, but nothing could hold her upright as the house swayed.

She turned, just in time to see Winnie's face pale, her brown eyes widening in terror as she bolted toward Piper. No words were needed; neither mistook the sound of a heavy truck or distant thunder. They both knew what it was, the unmistakable roar of an earthquake beneath them.

Duke and Charlie scrambled around her in panic, their fur cloaked in the same white powder. Duke's deep growl turned into a high-pitched whine as he shook the flour from his short coat, only to be knocked off balance with more tremors. Charlie leapt and spun in circles, his tail stiff with fear, then bolted for the door, then ran back to Winnie, his little paws slipping across the floor.

The kitchen was in motion. Dishes rattled in the cabinets, glasses clinking together like fragile chimes, threatening to shatter at any moment. The walls groaned as the house itself seemed to creak and bend, as if it were holding on, the foundation beneath it cracking. Another slam sent the table rattling violently, and Piper's hand finally found the counter, clutching the edge to keep from falling. Her other arm wrapped around Winnie. The floor buckled, and the tremors continued, relentless.

Piper's inhale caught in her throat as the ground pulsated, sending another vicious wave through the kitchen. She watched in horror as the flour from the bag, still suspended in the air, whipped around like smoke in a storm, a thick fog choking out everything. Terror making up her mind, Piper yanked Winnie toward the door. They bolted outside.

Duke scrambled around her legs, whining and barking, desperate to follow. Charlie had stopped running to nudge Winnie's knapsack, left behind in the chaos. Biting onto the strap, he dragged the bag toward the door. Barely twenty-five pounds, the heavy blows tripped the Borgi with their intensity. Still, the little dog struggled; he knew the bag's importance to Winnie. She rarely left it behind.

He shot through the screen door just as the kitchen wall collapsed inward, burying the table in smashed timber, plaster, and part of the second floor. The ground shook again, a brutal shake that nearly knocked them off their feet.

Coco's deep bark rang from the porch, calling them. Piper's heart raced, her feet barely able to keep up with the growing rollers beneath them. The dogs were frantic behind them as they tripped, slid, and regained their feet.

Around the corner of the house, Piper's chest hitched as her eyes landed on the barn. It was swaying—no, *dancing*—in time with the tremors. The heavy structure, built to withstand the seasons, now looked fragile, as though it might crumble under its own weight. The barn's foundation shifted with a mighty shrug, the base no longer connected to the footers, like a building disjointed, struggling to stay standing.

Running around the outside, barking madly, was Bella. The barn door had banged shut in the quake, and she couldn't find her way back in.

Inside, a frantic shout from Brett tore through the noise, a desperate cry for help, and then—another blow. The impact slammed them onto the grass, and Piper's knees smashed into the earth, scraping her skin raw. The world around them twisted and cracked like glass shattering under pressure. She heard a sickening, deep screech from the barn, the beams and timbers protesting as the ground pounded harder, this time in the opposite direction.

The barn's massive frame lurched sideways with a deafening crack, the force too much for the structure to handle. The ground beneath it gave way, and in a horrifying instant, the barn collapsed—wood splintering, nails snapping, and splinters flying everywhere. Dust billowed up, choking the air. Piper's ears rang from the deafening crash, but there was no time to process the horror.

"Brett!" Piper screamed, her voice raw, the terror flooding her chest as she pushed herself up from the ground, but the earth beneath her wouldn't stop knocking her down. The dogs howled in confusion and fear, their barking lost to the roar of the earth, the rumbling coming from every direction.

There was no sign of Brett. Only the collapsed barn splintered into a heap of wood and dust. Another massive strike, and the earthquake stopped.

Deafening silence followed the blast of destruction.

Piper's throat closed. Covered in dust, tears running down her cheeks, she clambered to her feet. Her scraped knees and hands stung. There was no air to breathe, only terror that lodged itself deep in her chest.

"Brett!" she cried again. Winnie sobbed next to her.

Without warning, a devastating crack split the air like a gunshot, and then another. They whirled, clinging to each other, to stare at the green and brown wall of the levee to the northeast. The massive embankment, a wall of earth and rock that had stood for decades, shuddered as its structure groaned under immense pressure.

Piper could see a dark line of destruction spreading across the riverbank. The split drove forward, and then, in an instant, the levee cracked wide open. The earth beneath it ripped apart as if it were paper, splintering under the quake's effects.

Then, with an ear-splitting explosion, the levee burst. The earth itself imploded, and in an instant, water shot skyward in a massive geyser, the strength of the eruption sending a roar through the air. The water cascaded outward, a dark, churning liquid wall, as the earth beneath the embankment crumbled inward.

Mud, rocks, and chunks of concrete flew into the air, hurtling toward the sky as the river's bank gave way, helpless to contain the tidal wave now racing toward them. No longer constrained by the levee, the Mississippi surged savagely, its current faster and more furious than ever. The roar of water crashing against the shattered earth was deafening, like the sound of thunder and the collision of waves combined as the water poured across the land.

Inside the barn, under the mess, Brett heard his sisters' frantic cries. Brett's body wedged under the combine, it was protected from the weight of crushed beams and fallen roof tiles. The air was thick with particles, and every draw felt like it scraped his lungs raw, but the frenzied screams of the girls outside sent a burst of adrenaline through him.

Groaning in pain, he pulled himself from under the combine, his muscles screaming in protest, but his mind focused only on shifting the wreckage pinning him in. He was grateful the massive machine had shielded him from the worst of the collapse, but he could see the remains of the barn trapping him in. The walls were now a mess of smashed boards, and the air was muffled.

Panic clawed at his chest, but he fought it down. *No time to panic, gotta move.* His hands grabbed for anything solid. Desperately, he crawled up the combine's side, his body aching with every movement. Sunlight penetrated the gaps in the ruins, piercing through the haze. Each lungful hitched.

He used every ounce of his strength to crawl over and under the busted pieces of the barn. His hands slipped on the slick hay, but he kept inching his way to the seat. With a grunt, he wiped off bits of boards, finally settling himself on the worn cushion. He drew in a shallow mouthful of air, his chest tightening as he heard water splashing against the remains of the outer walls of the barn. Piper, Winnie, and the dogs had gone silent.

Cold, dark water ran in from every crack. Where was the water coming from? He couldn't figure it out, but could see the liquid rising and knew he had to do something.

His heart hammered as he gripped the combine's levers, praying, *Come on, come on, I know you were almost ready.*

He twisted the key, and the engine sputtered and coughed, but died again.

No, he thought, *you have to work.*

Desperation clawed at him, but he tried again, his hands shaking as he turned the key. A loud bang followed by a deafening clanking sound, and a cloud of black smoke erupted from the exhaust, choking him with the acrid fumes. He coughed, the smoke stinging his eyes and throat, but he refused to give up.

And then, miraculously, the machine *roared* to life. The engine dropped to a rumble, a sound so loud it vibrated through the entire pile of lumber. Brett's heart raced in time with the engine, the sound almost ear-piercing. He yanked on the levers, praying for movement, but the weight of the collapsed barn was too much. He couldn't go forward. The machine was wedged too tightly in the debris.

The water was rising faster now, higher, and panic swelled again. He mashed the gearshift into reverse, praying the combine could move backward. The engine choked again, but then it heaved, and the machine lurched backward with an unexpected burst of power.

Brett felt the wall behind him give way with a crack. The entire side of the barn, already bent and shattered by the earthquake's brutal energy, exploded outward in a shower of boards. The wood splintered, the metal snapped, and the barn wall flew apart like toothpicks, tumbling through the air in pieces.

The combine and Brett sloshed backward, bursting free into the yard, the remains of the wall collapsing behind them in a heap of scrap. The water gushed in waves, pouring around the machine, but Brett didn't stop. He forced the combine's throttle wide open, rolling over the broken timber on the ground as the floodwaters rose. Spinning around, he got a good view of what was happening in the yard and beyond.

Terror washed over him, and his mouth fell open. Piper, Winnie, and the dogs had somehow managed to get into Royce's old fishing boat, which was perched on cement supports several feet from the collapsed barn. Water lapped at the blocks, already knee-high. They were calling and waving to him while the dogs barked madly, as if they, too, comprehended the danger. He understood their fear when he looked past them.

The long, shrub-covered hill holding back the Mississippi River had been breached dead center from where Brett sat. Water jetted through the opening like a massive fire hose of brown water. A grating noise filled the air, and to his horror, another huge piece of the levee tore away, increasing the flow a hundred times over. The river shifted twenty tons of mud and stone aside like Styrofoam packing, and the flood widened, forming a wall of water twenty feet high, topped with five-foot wave crests.

He didn't have time to think. He jumped from the combine with a desperate cry, landing hard in the cold water. Now up to his waist, the current was strong enough to knock him off his feet with each swell. The momentum of the water threatened to tear him away, to drown him before he could even get close to his siblings, but Brett didn't stop. The more he struggled, the stronger the current became, and the river pushed him back.

Then the boat moved, lifted off the three-foot cement blocks, and headed straight toward him. He timed his movement, bracing himself as the boat rushed toward him. With a last burst of energy, he leapt.

His hands grabbed hold of the side of the boat, the torrent dragging him. But the moment he caught hold, a floating piece of timber clipped him, nearly knocking him free. He barely kept his grip, his fingers slipping, but Piper and Winnie were there, clutching his arms, pulling with all their strength. Coco, frantic, leapt forward, sinking his teeth into Brett's shirt, twisting the fabric in his mouth as he yanked the boy back.

It was just enough leverage, and Brett half climbed and half fell onto the floor of the spinning boat, nausea cramping his stomach, causing him to retch uncontrollably. Shivering, the girls fell next to him and held his body until the spasms stopped. His thoughts were a blur.

A shadow fell over them, and the world stopped. The sky had darkened suddenly, the sun of the August day consumed by a thick, dark smog that rolled in like a storm. A damp gust of air swept past, making the day even colder, and the boat creaked under the pressure of the winds.

A brilliant flash of lightning streaked across the sky, so close and so bright it nearly blinded them. Brett's heart skipped a beat as the boat slammed into something massive— the crown of an old oak tree. The boat was caught in its twisted branches, trapped in the canopy.

The water ran around them, but for a moment, they were suspended, the terror of the flooded Mississippi rushing past, leaving them caught between an angry sky and the rising flood. Charlie howled as the boat rocked, a long mournful sound, and Winnie wrapped her arms around him, trying to comfort the little dog.

Cairo, IL: Saturday, August 16, 9:03 a.m.

Like every other Saturday, Boxco was packed with shoppers. Reed found a parking space overlooking the Ohio River, with floodwalls and levees blocking most of the view. He and Chloe chatted about the kids on the way in, just as they did every other time they were alone together. Though neither one would admit it, they were both trying to find a way to turn the subject into something more personal. Today was not the day they found the right words.

"Why do you suppose they built Boxco on the east side of the Ohio River, instead of downtown Cairo?" Chloe asked instead, looking for a neutral subject.

"Land is at a premium in Cairo. Locked on all sides by the rivers. I heard they were able to work out a deal with the state. Give up a small piece of the Wildlife Area by the Cairo Ohio River Bridge for easy access, and Boxco diverts a chunk of change to the state for wildlife management." Reed switched off the engine and climbed out, grinning. "Win, win for everyone. And it makes it easier for us to get to Boxco."

With a quick rub on the head, Reed told Watson to stay in the pickup's bed, where he rested on an old blanket. The golden dog was used to the drill, and he stretched out, closed his eyes, and prepared to wait for Reed and Chloe to return.

Grabbing a cart, they scanned their card and headed toward the back. They used the same strategy every time: arrive at the opening, start in the back where pallets of water, paper towels, and sealed boxes were stacked in front of the huge metal racks lining the back wall, then move forward through the store toward the registers. They worked together like a well-oiled machine. Chloe wasn't thinking about earthquakes as she reached for a case of water.

At 9:02, the first shudder gently rocked the building. It wasn't much, but Chloe's heart lurched in her chest, and Reed's muscles tensed, every nerve suddenly aware. The weight of the moment pressed on them. A silence stretched between the two as they instinctively halted in front of the stacks of goods and the sturdy floor-to-ceiling racks, their hands still clutching boxes of water and tissues.

Out in the pickup, Watson's eyes popped open. A low growl rumbled in his throat. Without hesitation, the big Labrador launched from the truck bed, hit the asphalt running, and tore across the lot. He moved like a golden comet, cutting between bumpers and dodging carts with purpose. Barreling inside, he was through the open double doors of the big box store, startling the guards with his sheer speed and size.

Inside, shoppers glanced around, unsettled. The air changed—an invisible tension seeped into the fluorescent-lit aisles. Some laughed it off, others hesitated mid-reach, hands hovering near the high stacks of summer and fall goods. No one quite knew what to make of the tremor, but awareness was there—in the twitch of shoulders, the darting glances.

Watson didn't pause. Nose to the floor, he followed their scent, ducking past piled-high carts, sliding around the short refrigerator aisles full of restaurant-named main courses and sides. He shot past confused customers and startled employees, zeroing in. Around the next corner, he caught their scent stronger now; a flash later, he was there. His bark startled those closest, but Reed turned instantly, his brown eyes locking with Watson's.

"It's nothing, just a tremor," someone called out. But the laughter was thin.

The floor groaned beneath their feet just as Watson slid to a stop between Reed and Chloe. She bent and hugged his neck, quickly glancing at Reed. They were both on edge, waiting.

In one terrifying second, the big box store lurched aggressively, twisting as if caught in a vise. Amid flexing walls and shrieks of steel, Reed acted.

"Go!" Reed shouted, yanking Chloe up by the arm and pointing. They sprinted for the massive refrigeration unit, with its roll-up door open, it was the only structure in sight big enough to offer protection. Watson stayed tight on their heels.

They dove into the opening just as the store ripped apart—metal, concrete, and screams of terror blending into a single, deafening sound. Watson pressed between them, tail low, head high. Reed wrapped one arm around Chloe, the other braced against the frame. They held on as the quake hit full blast, shaking the world apart around them.

The building lifted. Walls shuddered, and the shelves above clanged as if the entire structure were being pushed and pulled by a storm they couldn't see. Bottles of cleaning supplies, cases of diapers, and bags of frozen food hurtled past like missiles. The sound of glass shattering was drowned out by the chaotic crash of objects flung to the floor.

Then came the thunderous roar of the building bucking against itself. Carts careened down the aisles, their wheels screeching as they smashed into displays, scattering goods like confetti in a storm. Shoppers cried out, some tripping over fallen items, others scrambling for cover, their feet slipping on the slick floors. It was madness, and it seemed to last forever.

Chloe's body was stiff as she grabbed Reed's sleeve, pulling him tight into the corner of the refrigerator's doorway. The aluminum barrier now jammed in an open position against the fallen crates and cases.

They couldn't believe their eyes. Shelves were left bare, burying people beneath tons of canned goods and boxes. The bakery and delicatessen areas were a jumble of pastry and meat. Bodies lay around them, mowed down by shopping carts and bulk boxes, cut and bleeding from thousands of shattered bottles.

The building settled with a thump as if it had been dropped and then shuddered again. A ferocious racket, louder than the crashing piles of stock, split the air, followed by the overwhelming sound of rushing water. The dim light revealed a massive breach in the entranceway, with torrents of water surging through. Shock crashed over Reed. The levees must have broken. There was too much water to be anything else.

The tide crashed against everything in its path. Long, towering rows of merchandise slowed the flow before everything, including screaming people, was picked up and squeezed together in a massive dam that slid toward the back, growing with every aisle.

Reed pulled Chloe out of the refrigerator and pushed her up onto the nearest stack of bulk tissues. "Up!" he yelled at both the woman and the dog. With his long legs, Watson jumped from package to package until he was at the top of the stack.

Chloe and Reed climbed behind him, tumbling over and onto the heavy steel bolted to the wall, most of its contents now on the floor. She didn't stop, but climbed frantically ahead, glimpsing others on the last aisle following their lead up the metal shelving. Reaching the top shelf, she spun, helping Reed pull up the big dog. Watson used his hind legs to boost himself, scrabbling and fighting to the top to stand on an empty pallet.

With Watson safe, Reed threw himself over the top shelf. Chloe jerked his arm, and they both fell backward, landing onto a wooden pallet with a thick layer of twenty-four-pack paper towels still elastic-wrapped. Watson jumped beside him, licking Reed's face, his relief clear. They had landed on their backs across the packages, gasping for breath and hanging on to each other when suddenly…

Forty feet away, the concrete-encased transformer vault exploded, blowing the door off. Sparks flew, crackling, the light stunning. The noise shocked Chloe, and in the sudden light, they saw a fifteen-foot wall of muddy water, its face pocked with goods, rushing toward the back. The stench of burnt plastic permeated the air as the torrent of water slammed into the vault, sparking against the exposed wires.

Thousands of volts slammed through the water, electrocuting everyone in the water and on the steel shelves. People in the water went rigid, their eyes bulging as the electric force overpowered them in a flash. They collapsed, dead, in seconds. Only Reed, Chloe, and Watson, sitting on the paper towels on a wooden pallet at the top of the building, were unaffected.

The lights flickered out. Reed and Chloe hung on to each other, Watson whimpering between them. Then, seconds later, a generator from somewhere kicked on, and an even dimmer light illuminated the tragedy. Everywhere they looked, corpses bobbed on the surface, caught in the flow. Shocked and horrified, Chloe clung to Reed.

A massive current at least fifteen feet high flowed through the vast room. The powerful tide pulled everything in its wake except the main racks in the store, one of which Chloe and Reed sat on.

"These shelves... are we safe here?" Chloe asked, fighting to get the words out.

"Yes, I think so." He got to his knees and peered around.

"But... all these people. They're dead!"

"I think the wooden pallet and the paper towels saved our lives. Dry wood is a poor conductor of electricity. Everyone else was in the water or touching the metal."

The entire building shuddered, the racks quivering in place as the floor rocked.

"Don't worry," he said, seeing her face. "These racks will hold. When they build these big box stores, the framework of the main racks is usually set into the foundation. We'll be okay here for a few minutes. But let's stay on the paper towels for now."

His face was wet. He wasn't sure if it was water or sweat as he wiped his forehead. The air was cool and heavy, like a tomb. Reed shuddered at the thought.

Reed was relieved to see that the water wasn't rising much more. The current running through the store must be escaping out the truck-sized garage doors along the back. Otherwise, this place would fill up like a bucket under a faucet.

A massive pile of product choked most of the back, blocking the doors. He didn't look too closely, but knew bodies were mixed in the tangle. They peered through the twilight to see if anyone else made it. It was too quiet, with only the rushing water and bumping stock making noise.

He called out several times, but no one answered. They looked at each other, solemn and scared.

"Are we going to do this again?" Chloe asked him, letting go of his arm, but fear darkened the blue of her eyes into a storm color.

"I don't think we have a choice." With the doors flooded and blocked, he knew they wouldn't be leaving that way. He couldn't believe they were caught in another life-and-death situation. Thoughts of his father, Albert, and the kids flickered in his mind. As if reading his thoughts, Watson growled, his anxiety clear.

They needed to figure out how to escape and check on the others.

St. Louis, MO: Saturday, August 16, 9:06 a.m.

The conference room buzzed with murmurs as the speaker stepped away from the podium. The symposium wasn't just another conference; it was the aftermath of the disaster that had changed the West Coast forever. As such, Walter and Tau felt supremely qualified to share their experiences, but they had gained little traction so far.

Walter hunched over the table, elbows planted on a scatter of coffee-stained notes, his eyes locked on the simulation dancing across his screen. Irregular red pulses flickered against a black background—waves of seismic energy blooming across the map like a slow-motion detonation.

A precise web of data and algorithms—the model had shown its true power months ago. The first quake hadn't been an isolated event—it was a domino. And the model had predicted every falling tile: the Cascadia rupture, the San Andreas fault triggering, and the swarm of tremors, and then Oregon's volcanoes—six eruptions in five days. There was no time to react, no data to explain it, and no discernible pattern in the geologic record. It challenged everything they believed to be true.

Now, the model had stirred again, throwing out a new number this morning that chilled them both more than any ground shaking ever could: eighty-nine percent. An eighty-nine percent chance of another seismic catastrophe, not on the coast, but deep in the country's midsection. And it wasn't years away. It was coming within the next few weeks.

They had the data, but the answers were proving tougher to find.

Out of the hotel windows, Tau could see the St. Louis riverfront. The mighty arch soared skyward, its stainless-steel façade sparkling in the morning sunshine. Barges and riverboats cruised up and down the Mississippi River, crossing under bridges as automobiles came from both sides. Even this early, the city was a hub of activity. It was a beautiful morning.

Suddenly, the window and the view shattered in one massive jolt. The room was ripped apart, and again, Tau found himself in the fight of his life.

***

Miguel Santiago felt unsettled. Something had rattled his usually steady nerves, and he looked out the plane's window again to calm himself. The symposium weighed heavily on his mind—the need to convince his colleagues of Walter's model and its potential was gnawing at him. But no matter how often he shuffled the papers before him, the right words didn't come.

He dropped the last of his papers in his briefcase, snapped it shut, and pushed it under the seat in front of him. Adjusting his suit coat, he heard the pilot's voice crackle over the intercom, announcing their descent. Flight attendants moved up and down the aisle, collecting trash and checking seatbelts.

Every moment that passed only heightened Miguel's unease. His hands clenched the armrest, willing the plane to land faster. A deep, instinctive pull told him that once his feet hit the ground, he could get to that hotel, to the meeting, and make a difference.

Then, an abrupt exclaim from several seats behind him shattered his uneasy calm. Voices grew louder, a mix of confusion and fear. A flight attendant hurried toward the disturbance but stopped short, leaning over the rows to peer out the window. Miguel's stomach lurched, fear crawling up his spine.

His eyes followed theirs, dreading what he might see. St. Louis sprawled below, but it was unrecognizable, consumed by chaos. The Gateway Arch swayed violently, a slender reed in the wind. Skyscrapers collapsed inward, their concrete facades buckling under seismic impact. Windows exploded outward in storms of glass. Entire buildings crumpled into twisted metal and dust piles, leaving pointed remnants where thriving office blocks once stood.

More horrifying still, the city's southwest side began to darken and fold, collapsing into a massive sinkhole. The sight was too familiar—like Corvallis, a nightmare he couldn't outrun. The dread caught in his throat, and the words tumbled out before he even realized it: "No, no, no…" The voice was his own, distant and disbelieving.

While he watched, the Mississippi River surged in the wrong direction, the massive waters pouring north. The flow, churned by the seismic tremors, writhed like a living thing, a turbulent black mass reversing its natural course. Ships and barges were crushed and submerged, some half-sunken in the water, others tossed onto the riverbanks, steel bodies mangled and twisted in the mud and water. Scattered cargo spilled into the murky waters and onto the shore, adding to the junk that now littered the riverfront.

The levees that had long stood as a barrier against the river were no match for this earthquake's power. Cracks appeared in the protective walls, wide and jagged, snaking along the tops of the earthen fortifications. Water burst through in explosive torrents, surging into the city's streets with the momentum of a dam breaking. It crashed over the smaller buildings, rolling down the avenues and flooding everything in its path—the river reclaimed cars, people, and entire blocks. Streets became rivers, and rivers became rapids. The floodwaters rose quickly, consuming everything—storefronts, streetlights, anything not anchored to the ground.

From above, the scene was devastating, like watching a disaster unfold in slow motion. The catastrophe was impossible to grasp in its full magnitude. Just as the burning St. Louis Lambert International sank, the plane banked north. The turn pulled them away from the wreckage. Below was a patchwork of ruin, rutted edges cutting through the remnants of what had been. A hollow ache settled in Miguel's chest.

It was happening again. Only this time, the middle of the country was being slaughtered. He watched St. Louis collapse as the earthquake tore the city apart. The death toll would be tragic, and there was no telling how far the destruction would go. Then, as if hit, he fell back on the seat, one thought piercing his mind.

Walter and Tau were down there…

Chapter Six
The Midwest: August 16, 9:10 a.m.

It began deep in the heart of New Madrid County—an eruption of violent energy, a magnitude 8.6 earthquake that shattered the earth's crust with a deafening roar. Shockwaves radiated outward in every direction as the ground around the epicenter convulsed and fractured in a split second. The Midwest buckled beneath an unstoppable tidal wave of destruction.

In a repetition of the activity on the West Coast, hundreds of mapped and unmapped faults triggered, hopscotching across the Midwest, destroying cities and towns on the surface. Uncharted cracks split open, and a relentless series of jolts pitched across the landscape like a hellish storm.

The New Madrid triggered the long-dismissed Wabash Valley Seismic Zone—one immense shock after another, each one a punch to the gut of the region. Magnitude 8+ tremors rippled from Illinois to Indiana, reducing everything in their path to rubble.

In northern Illinois, the Sandwich Fault Zone awoke with stunning suddenness, having been building for millennia. DeKalb to Dixon, rocked by magnitude 8.5 quakes, was gone in minutes. The ancient, cracked earth, silent for 400 million years, now split the land into fragments, throwing buildings, streets, and lives into the churning chaos of enormous sinkholes and fractures. A history of dormancy didn't diminish the impact one bit.

But another terror lay deeper. Long hidden from geologists' tools, a massive scar —a weakened area extending north from the Illinois Basin, buried far beneath the surface where the crust and mantle met —ignited with catastrophic brutality. Lying dormant since the land was young, it tore through the crust beneath Chicago. For hundreds of millions of years, it had remained silent—until now.

Built on soggy lakebed soil, geologists believed Chicago impervious to earthquakes. Engineers had filled the land, stacking debris and rubble from past disasters, ensuring the city's foundation was solid. But nothing could protect it from this—nothing could withstand the energy of the earth as it buckled and cracked beneath the Windy City. Streets warped, skyscrapers sank, and the city collapsed. Foundations shattered, its skyline became a pile of skewed metal and stone. Millions perished as their world tumbled down.

Across the Midwest, no one was spared. Farmland fractured and fell, torn apart by earthquakes so powerful and inexorable that nothing remained untouched. The Mississippi River heaved wildly, levees shuddered to pieces, and brown water crashed over banks that could no longer hold. From Canada to the Gulf Coast, the devastation spread like wildfire. North, south, east, west—the Earth's pulse was unstoppable. The entire region became a shattered puzzle in a heartbeat, the pieces scattered far and wide.

Much like the West Coast, this land would never be the same.

***

South of New Madrid, in Caruthersville, Missouri, the tremors hit with brutal impact, ripping through the ground like an unexpected uppercut. As his bait shop shook fiercely, Tom Prescott, an avid fan of Dante Alighieri's Inferno and who had been leaning against his counter reading a dog-eared version of the paperback, ducked below the scratched oak top, covering his bald head with his arms. The book flew into a corner as a showcase of hooks slid over and shattered over it. For several long minutes, the world crashed around him, the thrusts nauseating his stomach as he crouched tightly in the corner. Splintered walls walked off their foundation, leaking in a hazy light and an acrid, bitter odor.

Whitecaps spun on the trembling Mississippi. Solid bangs struck the rattling roof above him. It felt like a storm hitting—heavy patters laced with a series of thuds, spaced apart, shaking the aluminum in a deafening rhythm. He spent a few terrified seconds wondering if it was raining and how that would impact the quake.

The ground shivered again, and then slowly, mercifully, the shaking and tapping faded. Hardly able to draw air, he stood, his thin legs vibrating with the effort. Carefully, he picked his way across the buckled floor—every shelf, showcase, and jar of bait tossed to the ground, the shop a wreck. He reached the door with a bony hand, kicked it open, and stilled.

The porch—his porch—was gone. Shattered wood lay in the front, twisted and scattered. A misty blanket clung to the yard, drifting toward the riverbank. But that wasn't the most shocking sight. Spit caught in his narrow throat as his eyes nearly popped from his head.

Boils and fissures peppered the land around his store, some wide enough to drop a car into. And everywhere were small pellets up to golf ball-sized tar balls, like a black blizzard that had passed through in minutes. Solidified petroleum scattered across the yard in a thick layer. It stunk like new asphalt being laid. He knelt to touch one of the round globules, but pulled his hand back instantly with a sharp hiss. The tar ball was scorching hot.

It clicked then. What he thought was fog wasn't fog at all. Steam billowed up from the land, rising in the cool morning as if the earth was hyperventilating—hot, seething, alive. Tom stepped back into the shop, the reality of what was happening sinking in. He knew where he was. Numbness held his feet while he struggled against his fear.

He was in Hell.

When the low rumble of an aftershock started, he grabbed the door frame and held on as the steam boils erupted again. Now, he was sure he had somehow fallen into the Underworld. The Mississippi was gone, and he was staring at the River Styx—a dark, wild, demon-ridden place of death and misery.

He sank to his knees and prayed for redemption.

***

All the way south to the Gulf, the land shook and fractured. Big cities like Little Rock, Memphis, and Jonesboro were devastated, with older structures decimated and newer ones suffering severe damage. Infrastructure failed, including bridges, overpasses, and roads, ceasing to exist, cutting off critical supply routes.

Power, water, and gas lines ruptured, and tens of thousands were injured or killed in the first minutes. Fires broke out, and the roads became impassable. Extensive landslides of the bluffs north of Memphis caused the river to fill with rubble as the tree-covered slopes caved into the river. The river didn't stop—it carved a new path, drowning towns and businesses in its rush to reach the Gulf.

The quakes rushed southward, racing down the Mississippi River, splintering the land and demolishing civilization. Forty-five miles upstream from Baton Rouge, where the mighty Mississippi met the Atchafalaya River, the pulse of destruction hit full strength.

The Old River Control Structure—America's so-called Achilles' Heel—had stood firm for decades, a two-billion-dollar monument to humanity's hubris. Designed to control the flow of the Mississippi, it kept the river from cutting a new path into the Atchafalaya Basin. Levees, locks, and floodgates kept the river's power in check, an iron fist holding back a wild, unstoppable force. For over fifty years, it had worked.

But not today.

Deep shockwaves rattled the massive concrete and steel structures, severely battering the infrastructure. The ground beneath heaved again, then throbbed—surface waves, both vertical and horizontal clout, slamming into the huge floodgates. The shock was unbearable. Metal disintegrated, and concrete cracked. The quake tore through the Old River Control Structure like it was cardboard.

In minutes, it was gone. The locks and levees shattered, the floodgates ripped apart, and the Mississippi exploded as if it had been waiting. The river diverted its course, roaring into the Atchafalaya Basin, unstoppable in its power. Thousands of cubic meters of water per second poured into the natural channel.

The Atchafalaya River surged to life, swelling, a monstrous wall of water heading straight for the Gulf. Small towns vanished beneath the tide. Levees crumbled like sandcastles, powerless against the flow. Morgan City, already weakened by the tremors, was the last to fall. On the verge of collapse, the levees were no match for the surging water. The flood swept through, drowning everything in its path. The city's 12,000 residents caught in the maelstrom—no time to run, no way to escape.

In a matter of minutes, the landscape had changed forever. The river's course altered forever as it carved a different path to the sea. What had once been the Mississippi River's tributary was now part of the whole. The ripple effects of this change would devastate the environment, the economy, and everything in its wake.

***

North of St. Louis, the central United States fared no better. Kansas City, located 150 miles west of the New Madrid Seismic Zone, experienced violent shaking. Even far from the epicenter of the quakes, unreinforced buildings were doomed. Tall buildings were vulnerable, especially older structures not designed to withstand such massive seismic activity. The entire city rocked as the ground broke and failed.

Assi Bhargava gunned it west on I-70, speeding toward Kansas City. His mind buzzed with the upcoming interview—this was his chance, the job he'd been working toward for months. He checked himself in the rearview mirror again, a quick flash of satisfaction at the sharp cut of his jawline and the confident gleam in his eye. He threw his head back, letting his wavy black hair fall into place, giving him that perfect, effortless look. *Looking good, Assi,* he thought, flashing a grin.

His foot pressed harder on the pedal, the car humming beneath him, the road stretching out ahead, empty and open.

Then the earth exploded beneath him. The car jerked hard, throwing Assi against the seatbelt, his hands gripping the steering wheel instinctively. Everything shuddered briefly, but his bright blue Chevy Trax suddenly went airborne. Stomach lurching, panic pummeled his chest.

Did I hit something? The thought was barely a whisper in his head, drowned out by the furor unfolding in front of him.

The tires slammed back down onto the asphalt, and the car jolted, skidding wildly as Assi's hands flailed for control. He went for the brakes, but ended up flooring the gas by mistake. He wanted to correct it, but the Earth had other plans. The violent shaking of the car battered his whole body. His mind went numb, and his panic escalated.

The ground tore open ahead of him—a massive crack that split the highway, ripping the earth apart. It was too wide. Too deep. As the car sped forward, Assi's curse caught in his throat.

The tires hit the canyon's edge, lifting along with Assi's heart. For an agonizing moment, he *thought* he could make it across. He watched, petrified, as the gap stretched wider in his windshield, the disintegrating walls almost hesitating…

The Chevy plummeted.

For that brief single second, the world went silent. Then the car's nose dropped below the lip of the gorge and bashed into the crumbling wall. The impact was violent, bone-rattling, as the fenders and hood crumpled on contact. The crushing weight of the engine, shoved against his legs, pinned his body to the seat, driving into his lap with brutal savagery. Pain exploded through his hips, legs, and spine. He screamed, a raw, guttural sound that tore from his chest, as the world caved in around him.

The car slid deeper down the steep slope, sinking into the widening chasm, mud and clay pouring over him like water, trapping him. Assi's mind shrieked in denial as the world darkened, his last thought a desperate, helpless hope that he might somehow wake up. But it was too late. The earth swallowed him whole.

***

Soft, water-filled clays and loose alluvial soils overlay the ground beneath the central strip of the United States, deposited by the Mississippi, Missouri, and Ohio Rivers. Extensive liquefaction tremendously amplified the shaking. The earth undulated fiercely in wave-like patterns, knocking down immense forests and surging up through Indianapolis to the east and Cedar Rapids to the west.

In downtown Indianapolis, high-rise buildings fell one after another, like dominoes, killing thousands. Ruptured gas lines started fires and severed water pipes, limiting access to water and allowing the raging infernos to sweep across the city.

Cedar Rapids had its own set of problems. Before they could even assess the damage caused by the earthquake to the infrastructure, a bigger problem overwhelmed the population. Entire city sections were burning and impassable. Key bridges failed, isolating thousands more. Transportation was at a standstill. Flooding from the Cedar River aggravated the damage caused by the quake. Water levels rose because of the destruction of the levees and flood control systems, exacerbating the already dire situation.

In downtown Chicago, Violet McPherson, a twenty-six-year-old middle manager, stood in her office in the Trace Tower on the 41st floor, typing on her iPad. She was among the few people still unaware of the disaster unfolding in the Midwest.

Suddenly, the building shivered, startling her. She looked up, uneasy as her assistant ran through the door. Della's hazel eyes were wide, and her words spilled in a jumble.

"Earthquake…city's shaking! The building…we need to get out!"

Violet moved fast, dropping the tablet on her desk and grabbing her purse. She didn't ask questions. Since 911, everyone knew the escape protocol in a big skyscraper. Wait for the shaking to stop, then get out. Ask questions later.

She wasn't waiting for the shaking to stop.

They rushed to the stairs, dodging coworkers, chairs, and plants. Della ducked as ceiling tiles fell and snapping wires whipped toward her. They were on the stairs in seconds, even as the jolts grew stronger and a weird shivering clutched the building.

Violet didn't stop. She assumed the shivers were the slowing end of the earthquake, but she still wanted out. The staircase was vibrating under their feet. Glad she wore flats to work and not dress shoes, she watched Della tear off her red-heeled sandals. Together, they hurried down the steps, gripping the railing and balancing against the jarring motion of the quake.

Others pushed past, some mumbling apologies, others wide-eyed and desperate, not a word spoken. They helped each other. Della grabbed her arm when one man pushed hard, and Violet slipped. All the while, the building jerked, pieces tearing loose and filling the stairwell.

It was only minutes, but it felt like hours. The air was heavy with dust, and shrieks and groans echoed up the shaft. A weird feeling slid over her skin, and she stopped, resisting Della's efforts to tug her along.

"Do you feel that?" she hissed to her friend. "It feels like we're sinking!"

Della glanced around, but there was nothing to see in the windowless well. "Come on!" She grabbed Violet; this time, the young woman pulled herself along. Numbers on the wall announced they were on the 20th-floor landing.

It felt like they were descending in a funhouse, the steps permanently sloped and uneven. It was hard to stay upright. Security doors on each floor were sticking in place, hinges warped, and they heard glass shattering down the halls.

The stairwell ahead sagged, and the next landing felt unstable. Cracked tiles bounced under their feet. Della winced, avoiding the sharp bits, but her feet still bled, leaving crimson footprints as they continued down.

On the 10th-floor landing, Violet was horrified to see gaps appearing on the interior walls and the outer walls bowed outwards in an unnatural blister. The artwork crashed to the floor, and suddenly, the shivering intensified, laced with heavy earthquake thumps. Violet blinked in shock. There was a horrendous screech. She looked up just in time to see the above staircase come loose from the wall and fall toward them.

Grabbing Della, she jerked them both through the half-hung security doors and fell hard on the floor behind them as the staircase exploded into the foyer. A cloud of sharp specks blasted over them. Wind whipped through the hall, sending dusty pieces of plaster and metal flying; the blinds rattled in their damaged frames.

Covered in grit, she pulled herself up, her chinos and blouse ripped. Her long brown hair hung in strings, and scratches covered her face and hands. She limped over to the window, and shock froze her to the jamb.

They were on the 10th floor. She was sure she had read the painted letters on the wall correctly before the staircase fell. But, looking out, the ground was only a dozen feet below. As she watched, the particles trembled, and the earth resembled quicksand as it ebbed and flowed around the concrete.

The building was sinking! Multiple floors beneath it were now buried in the earth, and the structure above was tilted at a dangerous right angle. She looked over the city, dismayed at what she beheld.

Suddenly, a dark shadow dropped over her, and the 60-story Arber building across the street came down, crashing on top of Trace Tower. Both buildings crumbled into a huge heap of cement, rebar, and glass. Violet and Della never had a chance. They were buried at the bottom of a small mountain of rubble.

The Earth finally stilled, and the fault stopped moving for another one hundred million years.

By 9:10, the Midwest was a gutted, burning ruin of what had been thirty minutes before.

Chapter Seven

7 Island Conservation Area, MO: Saturday, August 15, 10 a.m.

"Matthias," the call ricocheted again, sharp and urgent.

In the process of cutting, cleaning, and braiding old kudzu vines with his scout knife so they'd have some type of rope, Matthias stopped, scanning the water below. For a moment, hope flickered—did Pete swim back? But one glance at the swollen current dashed that thought. There was no way Pete could have fought his way back against it. The tree shivered again, causing him to clutch at a hanging mass of brown kudzu for balance.

"Who is that?" Jamie's voice broke through his thoughts. He sat beside Matthias on a sturdy branch, winding the vine as they perched across from Pedro, crouching low in the crook of another limb. The younger boy was shivering. Their uniforms were wet and dirty, but Matthias thought it was more fear than cold. He was wondering how to reassure the young scout, as it was obvious, between the raging river and the quivering tree, that they were in trouble.

"You heard that too?" Matthias asked, surprised by the question.

"Yeah, I did." Jamie shifted, craning his neck, peering through the dense layers of leaves and branches. The noise was everywhere, but the trees and vines hid whatever was making it.

"Matthias," the voice called again, louder this time, and, weirdly, it sounded like his dad. Matthias' heart skipped a beat, uncertainty gnawing at him. Was he imagining this?

He crawled over to the trunk and shimmied up the side to where the leaves thinned, the higher branches offering a better view. He had rubbed most of the grit off his glasses and could see better now.

"Here, Matthias!" There, across a gap, another oak tree stood. Thirty feet away was his father, waving one arm desperately. Matthias blinked, stunned.

He hadn't seen his dad since the man escaped in a small cargo plane as a lava lake erupted around them in May. Dan had left them behind, flying out with his girlfriend and business partner, Nadia. If it weren't for Reed and Chloe, Matthias wouldn't have made it out of Oregon. Now his father was here?

His dad balanced on the branch of another oak, a few dozen feet south of where they sat stranded. Dan looked worse for wear. His stylish haircut was short, and he had a discolored area across one cheek, like a healing burn, while his clothes were far from the clean, well-kept image Matthias remembered. Today, he was wearing scruffy old jeans and a ripped T-shirt.

"Dad!" Matthias called back. He clutched at the trunk uneasily as the tree shuddered again. "What are you doing here?"

Dan shifted to find a better angle through the thick tangle of branches between them. "I saw your picture in a scout magazine," he said, voice tense with an edge Matthias couldn't place. "Wanted to talk to you. Got here just before... whatever this is, that's happening."

"I think we went through another earthquake," Matthias shouted. He knew it was an earthquake before his friend Jamie said so. He just couldn't figure out how this was happening to them again. Sure, everyone around here was aware of the faults underneath them and the history of the

New Madrid Seismic Zone, but no one really expected a sizable earthquake.

"All this water—it's the Mississippi River." Matthias called over. "Do you have any ideas on how to get over here or help us get out of this mess?"

"Matthias," Dan's tone sharpened, impatience slipping through. He moved again, as if the branch beneath him was as unstable as his tolerance. "I'm here for a reason. Back in May, when you kids took my truck, there were bags in the back."

Matthias stopped moving and stared across the gap. "You're here about the money?"

Jamie, his hair wild and sticking up in clumps, had crawled up the trunk and was now perched next to Matthias on the branch. He rubbed his hands against his tan shirt, scrubbing off sticky sap. "What money?" he asked, confused.

"No," Dan's voice tightened further. They could hear frustration creeping in even from this distance. "I saw what happened to the cash."

Matthias glanced at Jamie. "He lost some money. I think he's looking for it."

"Can he help us down?" Jamie's voice was hopeful, the desperation clear in his eyes. The ground shuddered beneath them, sending a tremor up through their feet.

Matthias let out a disgusted sigh, his eyes flicking back toward his father. "He's not really much help." Then he called out, his words sharp. "We left the bags behind when we had to walk. The money probably got burned up when the Sisters erupted again."

"I saw the bags of money," Dan retorted, his voice bitter. "And no thanks to you kids, the money did get burned up."

"Well, what do you want, then?" Matthias heard the sharpness in his voice, but he was frustrated, too.

Dan struggled to keep from snapping. "I want the jewels out of Nadia's bag. The ones you kids stole."

Matthias reared back as if slapped. "We didn't steal anything," he almost yelled, then sat down on the branch. The tree shuddered again, this time leaning a little with the current.

"Hey Matthias, what's with the tree? Why is it shaking like that?" Both boys looked down to see Pedro only a few feet below them, his dirty hands clinging to the trunk, and his black hair sticking up. He looked as if he was about to cry.

"I think the roots are pulling out," Matthias told him. Pedro turned pale.

"Are you listening to me?" Dan yelled, his patience wearing thin.

"Our tree is leaning and keeps shaking," Matthias shouted back. "Is your tree doing that?"

"Boy, are you listening to me? I asked you about Nadia's jewelry." Dan's voice was full of anger.

"Your dad's a jerk," Jamie told him.

"Yeah, I know." Matthias gripped the rough bark tightly as the tree quivered beneath him. Slowly, it tilted toward the water, its roots wrenching as the current pulled harder.

Pedro let out a frightened yelp, his small body trembling as he clawed at the branch, climbing higher. His dark brown eyes were wide with terror. Jamie reached down and yanked him up with a grunt, pulling him onto the same branch. "What are we gonna do?" he asked, panic under his words.

"I don't know," Matthias cast about for an answer, looking for something they could use. Chunks of wood, splintered rooftops, twisted metal scraps, and garbage sped past in the river's furious current, but nothing that looked remotely safe. The water rushed beneath them. His chest tightened, helplessness gnawing at him. "I don't know," he repeated as the tree groaned again, its roots bending dangerously.

"Can we use that?" Pedro asked, pointing toward the river.

A bright red shape sliced through the water, moving fast—a personal watercraft, still floating, its sleek form bobbing in the current. It was coming straight for them.

"It's close," Jamie said, his tone hopeful. He scrambled to his feet, gripping a branch to steady himself, eyes locked on the approaching PWC. "I bet I can lasso it."

"Matthias, what are you doing? Answer my question?" Exasperated, Dan moved further out. Like a kaleidoscope, the wind blew the leaves around, filtering his view. He found a better position. Peering over a large branch, he was startled to see a vine rope fly out of the trees and snag something red bobbing in the water. He struggled to see what the boys had caught. It looked like a jet ski.

"Wow," Matthias blinked, awe shooting through him. "You're pretty good."

Jamie's grin was modest but triumphant. "Cattle, man. My dad taught me how to rope 'em."

The dried vine tightened. Jamie pulled, his muscles exerting as he hauled the water scooter closer. *'SEA-DOO'* was printed along the side.

The tree groaned under the pressure. The current washed more soil from its roots, and the branches dropped lower, tipping perilously toward the water, startling Pedro into another yelp.

Not wasting any time, as soon as he could reach the watercraft, Matthias dropped onto the bench, reaching up for Pedro as the boy slid down to land alongside him on the wide seat. The old oak dropped with a jerk again, causing Jamie to lose his balance. The branch he'd been standing on dipped beneath the water, and for a heartbeat, it looked like he was going down with it.

"Jamie!" Matthias yelled. He kicked the nearest branch, his wet tennis shoes sliding on the bark. It was a struggle to keep the craft from getting pinned by branches.

Jamie didn't hesitate. His hands were already on the vine, looping it around a thick branch, his movements fast. The rope-like creeper soared through the air, and Matthias caught it, yanking it.

"Hold tight," Jamie barked, releasing his end. The aquabike jerked forward, a few feet, but Matthias held firm.

"Wrap your arms around me," Matthias snapped at Pedro as the boy wobbled in the seat. The scout obeyed, his small hands locking around Matthias' waist like a vise.

Jamie was already moving, stepping quickly across the branch, his sneakers treading the bark with practiced ease. The branches swayed alarmingly, but he didn't slow. As soon as he was near, Matthias leaned forward, his arm outstretched. Jamie's hand gripped his wrist in a flash, and without a second thought, he launched himself across the gap, soaring over the water.

Jamie hit the footwell with a heavy splash, sending a wall of water slapping against them. With Pedro acting as a counterweight, Matthias caught his balance as Jamie scrambled aboard, rocking the runner and shoving himself onto the seat behind Pedro.

The vine slid out of his grip, unraveling like a snake, as the tide seized them. The current swept them along, straightening the wave runner in its flow. Unfortunately, they were riding backward.

Cursing erupted from the tree where Dan stood, still trapped on a branch.

Matthias pressed the ignition, but nothing happened. The watercraft was missing its key, its powerful motor useless in their hands. They were nothing more than drifting flotsam, at the mercy of the raging current. But at least they weren't in the water.

While they watched, their tree lost its grip on the earth, and a final, thunderous splash boomed behind them.

"Get over here!" Dan's voice was a distant shout, the water carrying it farther away with every second. Matthias clenched his teeth, the river's tow insurmountable, no matter how much his dad yelled.

Relieved, he didn't know why his dad accused them of stealing Nadia's jewels, but when the time came to answer his allegations, he wanted his brother and sisters with him. His dad had a bad temper.

"Where are we going?" Pedro asked, twisting his head around Jamie's bulk to see what was in front of them.

"As long as we're out of the water," Jamie said, nodding to the left for Matthias's attention. The boy looked over and was horrified to see a body floating with the current, tangled in netting and mud.

For now, they were out of the water but still subject to its mercy.

Harrowood, KY: Saturday, August 15, 10 a.m.

"Like the damn Grand Canyon," Albert groused. Stella growled as if to agree, her paws restless on the cracked ground as she prowled around Albert, her eyes scanning the shifting earth.

Royce didn't argue. The rift split down Main Street like a rugged moat, nowhere near as wide as the spectacular gorges in Arizona, but it was wide enough to trap them here. No way across.

The front of their building had been sheared off clean, like a knife through butter. What used to be the entrance was now splintered edges, the ground dropping away into the black abyss where the earth had buckled. The other side of the street was marginally better. The fronts of the buildings still stood, but the sidewalks were gone, having been engulfed by the same earthquake that had torn through Main Street, leaving nothing but chaos in its wake.

Only the back parking lot, where Royce's truck still sat hanging on the edge of the ravine that circled them, wasn't completely gone. But even that was barely standing. The rift had crept up to the lot's edge, gnawing away at it, leaving nothing but a thin strip of land to balance on. The drop on the far side was deep, and it was only a matter of time before the ground beneath them gave way completely.

Cracks spread like a spider's web, reducing their strip of land to an island with no way off on any side. Royce's eyes tracked the fractures as they paced the perimeter, but it was useless. Deep rifts sliced under the building, their depths hidden in darkness. He couldn't even guess how far down they went. What he knew was that there was no jumping over these. Not for them. Even the dogs couldn't jump over the shorter ten- or twelve-foot voids. The rims were too crumbly to trust. Shadow prowled the edges, careful where she put her paws. The cracks were too broad, too unstable.

"Are these sinkholes?" Royce asked, bewildered.

"Sinkholes, subsidence, fractures, call it what you want," Albert spat, "But it's the same thing that happened back in Oregon. The land just… dropped. Like it wasn't even there anymore."

Royce rocked his head back and forth, his eyes tracing the zigzag edges. "Never heard of anything like this before— what happened to you in May, sure, but not this. This town's sitting on some of the highest ground for miles. Flooding wasn't even on my radar, even if the levees went. Hell, I never thought the earth would just split open like a damn zipper." He paused, his gaze shifting toward the back of the building. "I need the PA system. We have to call out. Find out where the hell everyone is."

Royce's truck sat in the back parking lot, battered but intact. Part of the roof that had slid off crushed the bed, but the cab remained intact, including the PA System that he had installed for the 4th of July fireworks. Without wasting a second, he flicked the switch, and the system hummed to life, crackling with his voice.

"Hey, anyone who hears this message. This is Royce Walker. If you are able, make your way to the diner."

A deep, guttural tremor rolled up through the ground beneath him as if answering the call out. The sound, like the hiccup of thunder, resonated in the air. Both men froze, eyes darting toward the sloped edge.

From the Feed Store, a hundred yards away on the right, the owner, Stu Welter, stuck his head out the door, scanning the gap between the buildings. He hesitated, then trotted across, careful not to get too close to the crumbling edge.

"Holy sweet Carolina!" His voice rang out in disbelief. He leaned over to peer at the rift, but the ground sheared with a sickening crack beneath his boots. He jerked back just in time.

"Stu, are you by yourself?" Royce called out, his voice tight with urgency.

"No, got the Hocker boys inside," Stu called back, stepping closer, but still wary of the edges. "The north wall caved in, and Joe Hocker may have broken his leg."

"Shit," Royce's heart skipped. He shoved the worry aside. "We need to clear the town. Can you make it to the diner?"

Stu pointed towards the gaping chasm. "That thing runs straight to the river but hasn't torn through the levee. At least, not yet. But the bridge failed, and most of it fell into the river and was swept away. The buildings on this side lost their fronts, like the one you got there. My store too. The land seems solid between my store and the river. Dave Hocker and I made it that far. The levee's still holding, but that canyon is eating its way north. It's gonna tear through the levee soon."

Royce's eyes locked onto the rift, the cracks running deep, splitting the town apart. He wiped his hand across his face, trying to think fast. "Did you check the school, the community center, the old bait shop?"

"Mrs. Milligan and her two kids are in the Community Center. They're fine—some bumps and bangs. Nobody in the school. The bait shop collapsed, but it's been empty for years. Didn't see anyone else around."

"Good. You need to move Joe. Splint his leg, round up the Milligans, and use the levee to get to the other side. The school bus is at Hank's garage—he was tuning it up for the kids, for next week. The garage is still standing, so pull it out back. Grab anyone you see on that side, load them up, and head south on 94. I don't know how long that levee's gonna hold, but the quake might not be over. The rest of the town could collapse into these fractures at any second.

Stu hesitated, shifting his weight uneasily. "What about you and Albert?"

"We're working on that. Get the others to safety. We'll meet you at the diner." Royce tried to make it an order, but he knew no one in this damn town was any good at taking orders.

Stu shuffled his feet, mouth open as if he wanted to say more, but he quickly turned and rushed back into the Feed Store.

Royce looked at Albert, who was scowling at the chasm cutting the town in half. The dogs circled both men, anxious, feeling the tension in the air. Royce felt it, too—the urgency building in his chest. The clock was ticking.

Albert's mind raced as he surveyed the gap. Sixty feet of nothing but empty air. The diner on the other side loomed like an oasis, its smashed windows framing the frightened faces inside. It wasn't just getting himself and Royce across—he had to bring the dogs too.

"Got any ideas?" Royce finally asked.

"Too far to jump, truck's wrecked, can't fly over that," Albert waved a hand at the moat circling them. "Got to get the dogs over, too."

"Well, we'd better think of something. I don't think this piece of land will hold up much longer, and we need to get back to my farm and check on the kids."

As if to agree, the island rocked, slabs shearing off and dropping away.

"I have an idea," Albert said, heading back inside when he could walk. Royce followed, hoping it would be a great idea because he didn't think they had much time left.

Walker Farm, Harrowood: August 15, 10 a.m.

Another deafening boom sent ripples across the surface of the water. Brett flinched, unable to tell if it was the sound of another levee shattering or an aftershock splitting the earth beneath them. Either way, the sound made him sick with fear.

Dark clouds menaced, swallowing the sky and casting the world in shades of gray. The green leaves of the oak were the only color in the monochrome landscape. Brett recalled the weather report from earlier that morning, but this wasn't some passing storm. This felt different.

The water kept rolling in, a massive wall of brown churned liquid. Snagged in the crown of a tremendous oak, the *Seismic Wave* swayed wildly. Winnie sat on the console floor, clinging to Charlie, her eyes wide with fear, her breath shallow. Brett and Piper worked quickly, using an old rope from the locker to secure the boat to the tree.

Bella paced nervously over the casting deck, stepping back and forth over the worn, thin cushions in an anxious rhythm. Duke and Coco sat still, their eyes fixed on her. Whimpers and growls stretched tight between the dogs, interrupted only by the ever-growing roar of the rising tide.

Brett scanned the rushing water, heart pounding. His light brown eyes glowed a rare, almost golden hue, especially when he was stressed. The intense glint hinted at his fear today. The soybean field had vanished under a murky sheet of floodwater. He considered moving everyone to the oak's sturdier branches but quickly dismissed the idea. The dogs wouldn't be able to keep their balance. If any of them slipped… He hissed, unwilling to let that thought take root.

Pushing aside a few low branches, he peered at the river. The levee had crumbled to nothing, consumed by the onslaught. Brett's chest tightened as he watched the water roll past, engulfing everything in its path. The road was submerged, and the fields vanished.

Worse still, the Walker house and barn were underwater. The surges were tearing at the house and washing pieces away in the deluge. The Clarks had lost another home. Besides Winnie's knapsack, they had nothing but the clothes on their backs. They didn't even have time to grab the new go-bags that Matthias had carefully packed. Everything was going to be carried off or sunk.

"I can't believe this is happening again," Piper's voice cracked, her hands gripping the edge of the seat.

"Did that earthquake follow us from Albany?" Winnie hiccupped from the floor, close to tears.

"No," Brett knelt, running his hand over Charlie's black and white fur to calm them both. "There is a fault under the ground here—the New Madrid Fault. I can't believe the timing, but it must be that."

Winnie's eyes filled with tears, her voice small. "What about the others? Is Chloe coming back?" The question hung in the air like a weighted stone. Brett could see the fear in her eyes—the same fear from the last time when their mother and uncle hadn't come home.

Brett tried to sound confident. "Chloe's with Reed and Watson. They were in Cairo. I'm sure they're fine." The words felt hollow. His chest tightened. This was too familiar, like watching a nightmare unfold again.

Piper, ever the rock, wrapped an arm around Winnie. "Chloe and Reed can take care of themselves, you know that. We have to be big girls now, okay?" Her voice was steady, but she couldn't fully mask the worry behind her words.

Winnie scowled but stayed silent. She sort of believed it, even if she didn't want to hear it.

Piper rubbed Duke's head with her free hand, her fingers slipping through his thick fur. The dog licked her cheek to comfort her, but Piper didn't smile. "Brett, what about Matthias?"

Brett's stomach tightened. "I was just thinking about him," he said, standing up and scanning the flooded field beyond the tree. "He's about six or seven miles downriver. We could head after him in the boat, but with no motor, steering's impossible. They were camping off the wetlands. If the river floods the campground—" He cut off, glancing down at Winnie, who was listening intently, her small hands twisting in her lap. "I'm worried."

Piper's jawline clenched. Without a second thought, she yanked a hair tie from her pocket and drew her long brown hair into a tight ponytail. "We should go after him," she said, her voice sharp, her light brown eyes gleaming with fierceness. "But how do we steer?"

Brett's eyes narrowed as he studied the surrounding trees, his mind turning. "First, we need to get to the river and catch the current," he said slowly, almost to himself. He looked up at the tree towering above them, a plan forming. With one hand gripping a branch above his head, he hauled himself over the gunwale, advancing with quick, practiced movements as he crawled along the wooden limbs, searching for any way to gain an advantage.

The boat bobbed, and Winnie squeaked in fear. Coco, ever a protector, lifted his curly brown head. Without hesitation, he nudged his way past Duke and Bella, his heavy body settling beside Winnie. He gently poked her hand with his nose, then lay his head in her lap, his warm weight a comforting anchor. Winnie's lips quivered before a small, shaky smile tipped the corners of her mouth.

"Thank you, Coco," she whispered, her fingers brushing the soft fur of his ears the way she knew he liked.

Piper, one hand hanging onto a branch above them, craned her neck, eyes fixed on Brett. Her grip tightened around the bark, keeping her balance as the boat swayed beneath her. "What do you see?" she called, her voice edging impatiently.

Brett dropped back down to the boat, his face set in a look of concentration. "I think I've got an idea," he said, brushing leaf bits from his forehead. "This tree—it's right on the edge. You can't see it from here, but it's just before the ground drops off. If we use the natural channel, the current will draw us back toward the river."

Piper nodded and held up a long, weather-worn paddle.

"Found this," she said, tossing it to him. "There are two of them. We can use them to push off rocks or whatever."

Brett caught the paddle easily, but his expression didn't change. "We're going to be moving fast," he warned, eyeing the swirling water around them.

Piper agreed, her voice firm. "No life jackets on this boat," she said, her chin jerking toward Winnie, who was still nestled against Coco. "We need to make sure the dogs are secure, too." Her eyes met his, knowing time was running out.

"I wish Matthias were here," Brett griped, eyes scanning the churning water. He leaned as far over the boat's edge as possible, judging the current's strength. "I want to stay tethered to the tree until the last second. Let the rope guide us, then jerk it free with a slip knot."

Piper's fingers twisted the rope nervously in her hands. "I don't know how to make a slip knot," she admitted.

"I do," a small voice piped up from the floor.

Brett looked skeptical. "How do you know how to make a slip knot?"

Winnie's face lit up with pride. "I watched Albert and Matthias work on knots. I know how to make a slip knot."

Piper caught his eye, shaking her head in amusement. She held the rope up, her voice steady. "Show us, Winnie."

Winnie set Charlie down, the little dog's paws silent on the stained outdoor carpeting as he trotted over to the side, out of the way. The other dogs, always nosy, crowded in, pushing against the helm. Piper and Brett prodded them back, giving Winnie space. The little girl took the rope and deliberately spread it out across the floor.

She hesitated momentarily, her small fingers adjusting the fibers before she began. First, she made a loop, carefully laying it over the paddle's handle. Then she fed the end of the rope behind the paddle, forming a second loop on top of the first. The dogs' quiet panting filled the space as she twisted the rope around, her small hands moving with surprising precision. She made a third loop and pushed it through the first, tightening it with a steady tug.

"Pull that end to release," Winnie said, pointing, her voice confident. She leaned back and crossed her arms, her round face expectant.

Doubtfully, Brett tugged on the free end of the rope. The knot was good and tight. Then, he yanked the first end, and with a swift pop, the knot loosened easily. His eyes widened.

"Wow!" he exclaimed, impressed. "That's a great job, Winnie."

She smiled, but her eyes were still worried. "Can we go get Matthias now?" she asked.

"You bet." Brett's voice was determined. He and Piper moved quickly to retie the rope and settle the dogs into place. The boat rocked as they secured the last knot, and in minutes, they were ready to go. Each grabbed a paddle, positioning themselves on either side of the boat. The dim light hadn't changed. The world was still wrapped in heavy shadows, and the current had only grown stronger.

Brett glanced at Piper over his shoulder. "Fingers crossed," he murmured, his voice barely audible over the rush of the water.

She gave him a thumbs up, but he saw the tightness around her eyes, the way her fingers gripped her paddle. She was scared, too.

He made quick work of the branches holding the boat in place. The current immediately grabbed them, dragging hard. Brett's muscles strained as he steadied himself, feeding the line out as the boat drifted away from the tree. The flow twisted them sharply, the boat swinging like a leaf caught in a storm.

His eyes flicked to the water ahead, trying to time the maneuver just right. The boat pitched again, sending a beat of adrenaline through him. He seized the quick-release end of the knot, yanking it free with a sharp jerk.

With a whip-crack, the rope snapped back toward the tree, and the boat lurched forward. Piper barely stayed upright, her hands gripping the paddle, and Brett stumbled, nearly thrown to his knees as the shock of the current slammed into them. Bella let out a frantic howl, and Coco joined in, barking madly as the boat careened.

Brett's heart pounded harder as he fought to maintain control.

But his aim was true, and they shot past the trees, the boat plunging over the edge, the water roaring as they dropped into the wild, churning rapids. The world spun in a blur of spray and crashing waves. Brett and Piper worked together, paddling furiously as they steered the boat between rocks and submerged branches, their paddles smacking against the debris in the river.

Although the wild ride felt like an eternity, it lasted only a few minutes. The boat pitched forward, dropping into the heavy current of the river channel. The flow took hold of them, pulling them swiftly down the Mississippi. A foul odor rose around them. Winnie wrinkled her nose in dismay.

Panting, their clothes soaked with spray, Brett and Piper exchanged a glance, voices caught. They had the same thought. Maybe the rest would be easy.

Chapter Eight
Cairo, IL: Saturday, August 16, 10 a.m.

"We need to get out of here," Chloe's voice wavered as she glanced down at the floating bodies, their twisted forms drifting in the dark water below. The sight of them made her stomach churn. The narrow escape still fresh, she was shell-shocked at how close they came to dying this time. Watson peered over the side with her, huffing with worry.

Reed hesitated, his eyes scanning the metal racks, assessing their danger. "I'll go first," he said, but Chloe raised a hand quickly, stopping him.

"Can we test it with something besides us?" she suggested, her oval face pale in the dim light, her gaze never leaving the water. With her blond hair pulled back, she looked like a ghost.

He sat back and looked around, not sure what to use. The plastic-wrapped towels they sat on were damp from the heavy splashes. He pried loose a strip of wet wood from the pallet's front, holding it carefully as he leaned over the edge of the paper towels to tap the metal rack. Nothing happened. Dropping the wood onto the rack, he waited. Still nothing.

"Kick my arm with your shoes if this goes bad," Reed said, a faint trace of humor masking his nerves.

Chloe's feet slid into position, her eyes fixed on him. She was ready to react—just in case. Reed extended one finger, then tapped the rack sharply. He waited, listening for any crackle of electricity. When none came, he pushed himself up, sliding his feet over the paper towels until he stood. He exhaled, the tension easing from his shoulders.

"Come on," he told her.

Chloe stared at the water below, feeling the weight of uncertainty freezing her feet. "Where are we going?" she asked, glancing up at the tangled pipes and steel beams above. The water roared beneath them, and the thought of swimming through that murk twisted her stomach. Watson didn't move either, doubt etching his furry face.

"Up." Reed pointed to a steel ladder bolted to the wall. "See that wheel on the ceiling? With any luck, it will unlock a hatch to the roof. Let's go up and see what's out there."

He made it sound simple, and to Chloe's surprise, it was not that tough. Reed went first, and when he reached the wheel, it spun with a few hard pulls; the hatch lifting. He climbed up and out onto the roof.

A minute later, he climbed back down. He urged Chloe up the ladder, knowing she was eager to escape the crypt full of death around them. It was harder to get Watson up. The dog weighed around sixty-five pounds, but Reed could lift him most of the way, with Chloe hanging down to help shift the Labrador up through the hole and onto the roof.

Her heart fell when she finally reached the top, scrambling over the flat surface to the side of the roof and gazing out at the surrounding view. The wind hit her first, a damp, stinking, sour odor. Her eyes streamed from the breeze, but she wiped her face and leaned over the edge.

The parking lot, the roads, the bridge, and the buildings in the distance—everything was under the flood, and turbid water was everywhere. No matter which way she looked, there wasn't any land. Clouds covered the sky. A dirty smog slid over the surface of the water, dark whips of wind blowing her hair.

She leaned over the roof's edge, dismayed to see the deluge lapping the sides of the building only twelve feet below her.

"I think our truck's gone," she told Reed.

"Yeah, I think you're right," he agreed sourly.

Suddenly, the building trembled. She grabbed the ledge and hung on. Watson whimpered again. "Is that another earthquake?" she asked fearfully.

"I hope so," Reed answered. Greasy muck had smeared his cheek and his clothes. They were both a mess.

She looked at him in amazement until he finished the thought. "The alternative is that the building is falling, which would be a bigger problem."

The wind blew from the west, forcing her to look into the gusts. She stared at the river. "That's an understatement," she muttered.

The high banks holding back the Ohio River had caved and collapsed. They were surrounded by floating uprooted trees and overturned vessels. Parts and pieces of structures, carcasses covered in muddy water, human and animal remains, billboards, street signs, and unidentifiable junk rolled by. It smelled awful. Chemicals, pollution, and death stewed into a cascade that just kept coming. She couldn't imagine staying afloat in that mess.

She choked and covered her mouth and nose with her shirt.

"This is going to be harder than I thought," Reed said behind her. The roar of rushing water filled Reed's ears as he stared west, watching the swollen river surge through the shattered levees. A sheet of gloomy mist clung to the landscape, but something—long, dark, and ominous—moved through it, skimming low over the water.

"Reed." Chloe's voice wavered, laced with fear. "What's that?"

He squinted, tracking the shadow as it glided toward them. A shape emerged—massive, rectangular. Recognition rolled over him like cold spray.

"It's a flat-deck barge," he sounded worried. "Those are cargo containers."

For a moment, they just stared, watching as the barge barreled forward, its speed unsettling. Then the realization hit them both at once.

"It's going to hit Boxco!" Chloe took a shaky step back, wind whipping her hair loose from the ponytail.

As if answering her, the rooftop beneath them shuddered. A web of fresh cracks splintered through the tar and gravel, spitting fragments into the air. Watson ran forward, barking angrily at the fissures.

"What are we going to do?" She spun, scanning the barren rooftop. No cover, no supplies—just them, stranded.

Reed didn't hesitate. He strode to the parapet wall, gripping the edge as he leaned over. "We're going to catch a ride." Determination hardened his voice.

Chloe's rib cage hitched. "You have got to be kidding me."

"Not kidding, and we don't have time to argue." He turned to her, eyes sharp with urgency. "Come on, Chloe. You outran an erupting volcano and survived. You can do this too."

She muttered something he didn't catch, but he was already moving, sprinting to the corner of the building, whistling for Watson to follow him. He reached for the ladder bolted to the side and rattled it. It held.

"Over here!" he called. Watson was already beside him, paws on the parapet.

Glancing up, he felt a tightness in his stomach. The barge had already covered half the distance. Time was running out.

Reed swung onto the ladder, gripping the rails as he stepped down a few rungs. He stretched a hand toward Chloe, eyes locked onto hers as he pulled her up.

"Timing is everything," he said, guiding her into position between him and the wall. "When I say jump, we go together. Aim for the containers—low jump, just a few feet."

"This is crazy," Chloe panted, her forehead creased in fear.

"No, crazy was hauling an unconscious man while you were running away from a pyroclastic flow. You did that and saved me. We got this."

She didn't argue. She didn't have the breath to spare. The barge loomed larger, a hulking shadow cutting through the churning current. Reed's calculations were playing out— the massive vessel would strike the big box store on the right, and if luck held, the current would tow it around to them. Assuming, of course, the building didn't crumble first.

A dozen questions burned in her mind—what if they missed? What if they hit the water? But she choked them down. If Reed had an answer, he didn't have the seconds to share it.

Then time ran out.

The barge smashed into Boxco with a bone-rattling boom, concrete exploding into the air. The entire structure buckled beneath the impact. Cement panels on the building's front disintegrated as the barge scraped and slid along. Chloe's feet slipped from the ladder. She let out a sharp cry, clutching for a hold, but Reed's arm locked around her waist, keeping her from plummeting.

"Jump!" he roared. "Watson, jump now!"

She wasn't ready—wasn't sure she'd ever be ready—but Reed didn't wait. With a hard yank, he tore her free, and suddenly they were falling. A flash of golden fur passed her, and she knew Watson was with them.

The scream died in her throat. The wind rushed past her ears, and the barge was there to meet them in a blur of rust-red steel. Three seconds and...

Impact.

She slammed into a corrugated surface, pain thumping through her spine. Her head cracked against the metal, and for a moment, stars burst in her vision.

The barge rocked beneath them, rolling with the surge of the current. She gasped, blinking fast, forcing her senses to catch up.

Reed sat up beside her, chest heaving, eyes gleaming with adrenaline. He let out a wild whoop.

"We did it!"

Chloe acknowledged him with a wave of her fingers, swallowing against the nausea twisting in her gut in time with the wallowing craft. Watson struggled to his feet also, but he didn't look any happier than Chloe felt. She reached over to hug him, and he whined into her neck.

"Good boy," she whispered, rubbing his neck firmly.

They turned back to see Boxco, fatally damaged by the earthquake and the barge, surrender to the water. As the churning flow drew them away, nothing remained to mark where the structure stood.

7 Island Conservation Area, MO: Saturday, August 16, 10:30 a.m.

The three boys drifted swiftly with the current, their soaked clothes clinging to them as they hung on to the wave runner and each other. For fifteen long minutes, they said nothing, their exhalations coming in hiccupping gasps until their pulses settled. Then, as if struck by the thought, Matthias yanked open a storage compartment near the steering handles.

He wasn't sure what he expected—maybe a flare, maybe nothing—but when his eyes landed on the bright red plastic lanyard lying at the bottom, his heart leapt. With a triumphant whoop, he snatched it up and held it high for the others to see.

Jamie's eyes widened. "Is that—"

"The key," Matthias confirmed, grinning as he jammed it into the ignition.

For a split second, the three boys held their breath. With a turn of Matthias's wrist, the engine grated—then roared to life.

Their cheers rang out over the churning water, their exhaustion momentarily forgotten.

"Anything else in there?" Jamie leaned over Pedro, eyes scanning the compartments.

Matthias kept the machine idling as they checked every storage space, even lifting the seat in a last-ditch effort. Nothing.

"So…" Jamie shot Matthias a look. "Are we going back for your dad?"

Matthias hesitated only briefly before twisting the steering handles and turning the water scooter into the current. "We'd better."

"I want to go home," Pedro called over the engine's whine, his small hands clutching tightly around Matthias's waist.

"We all do," Jamie said loudly, his voice carrying over the rush of water. "But Matthias's dad is the closest. We make sure he's okay first, then figure out what's next."

Pedro frowned. "We don't have room for him on here."

"No, but we can at least check if his tree is still standing," Matthias reasoned.

He twisted around to look at Pedro, his emotions conflicted. "Don't worry. I'm not giving him our ride. He's a jerk, but… I don't want him to die. Let's see if we can help first, then we'll get you home."

Pedro chewed his lip, then bobbed his dark head, tightening his grip on Matthias.

A silence settled over them until Pedro asked in a small voice, "What about the other scouts? The guys who went hiking this morning? And Pete?"

Matthias glanced at Jamie. The other boy shrugged.

"They were headed inland," Matthias said, more to convince himself than Pedro. "And the elevation rises the further you go. They're fine. Pete…"

Jamie tried to be optimistic, though doubt flickered across his face. "Pete's a strong swimmer," he suggested weakly.

None of them voiced the worry curling in their stomachs. Each boy silently hoped Pete made it somewhere safe. They held tight as the watercraft surged forward, cutting through the floodwaters toward the river.

The engine hummed over the eerie silence of the drowned wetlands. Uprooted trees jutted from the water at odd angles, their tangled roots grasping at nothing. Torn branches and shattered planks bobbed past—remnants of homes, fences, and signs torn apart by the quake.

With every fragment of debris he spotted, Matthias's worry increased. Soaked paper spread like hundreds of lily pads, swathes of fabric, furniture, and fencing drifted past aimlessly. The wetlands weren't the only thing the quake shook. Towns were also affected. He wondered about Harrowood. He knew too well how far an earthquake could reach.

Brett, Piper, and Winnie. Had the shockwaves reached his brother and sisters? Did Royce's old house stand against the tremors, or did it crumble like everything else in the river?

Shadow. The thought ripped his stomach. His best friend, the sleek, dark gray Weimador, was back at the Walker farm. He hated leaving her, but the retreat was important and only for a few days. He told himself she'd be fine, that she needed time to roam the property, chase rabbits through the trees, and lose herself in the thrill of the hunt. Her name was Shadow for a reason.

Forcing down his apprehension, he vowed never to leave her behind again if he got out of this. They'd check on his dad, but he had to get home afterward. He knew Jamie and Pedro felt the same way.

A sharp cry rang through the air. Matthias tensed. More calls followed, a chaotic chorus of caws and screeches. He scanned the trees ahead and spotted a scrub oak, its branches overcrowded with displaced birds—wet herons, mallards, grackles, red-winged blackbirds, and lots of others, their feathers slick and ruffled. They shifted restlessly, calling out in frantic confusion.

At least they could fly.

A bloated deer drifted past, its lifeless body bumping into another corpse, a swollen fox. Further on, the stiff legs of a cow poked from the current, and flies already swarmed the carcass.

He refocused on the water ahead, gripping the handles tighter. The wind bit against his face, drying the cold sweat on his skin.

The closer they got, the heavier his chest felt.

What was he supposed to say to his dad?

***

Dan sagged on the bough, his thoughts spinning in discouragement. He hated this tree. Hated all these trees. The swamp, the suffocating humidity, the whole damn state. He wasn't supposed to be here—perched like some fool waiting for rescue, dealing with yet another mess his reckless kids dragged him into.

A sharp sting bit into the back of his arm. He hissed, rubbing the spot until the pain dulled.

He had the boy in his grip. A few more minutes, and he would have had the information he'd come all this way for. He cursed his earlier hesitation. When he arrived last night, he should have approached the kid and demanded the information he wanted.

He thought about what Matthias said about an earthquake. Since when did Missouri shake like Oregon? Sure, he'd felt the tremors—everyone had—but he'd figured it had something to do with a failing dam upriver, not the ground splitting open. The river surged past its banks, swallowing everything in its path. That didn't happen from a little rumbling.

Another sting, then another.

Dan swore and slapped his arm. The bites burned, a sharp, fiery pain spreading across his skin. Frowning, he twisted to look behind him.

His breath caught.

The trunk of the oak was alive.

A writhing, red mass of ants swarmed over the bark, spilling in long, moving fingers along his branch. Their tiny bodies marched straight for him. A few scouts had already reached him, their venomous bites setting his skin ablaze.

Dan jerked, nearly losing his grip as a fresh wave of stings shot up his leg. They were relentless.

Dan slapped furiously at the crawling fire on his skin, his eyes darting wildly for an escape. Up. That was his only option.

A thick and mercifully ant-free branch hovered just inches above his head. He didn't hesitate. Bunching his legs, he leapt, hands clamping onto the rough bark. His body swung as the horde of red surged onto the spot where he'd stood just seconds before. With a grunt, he hauled himself up, kicking his legs to gain momentum, then threw his weight over the limb, stomach scraping against the bark as he gasped. But it wasn't over.

The ants kept coming, undeterred, a ruthless red river climbing the trunk. He had seconds—maybe less—before they reached him again.

A sudden snarl ripped through the leaves behind him.

Dan whipped his head around, his pulse hammering. Something was crouched in the foliage in the tree crook, barely a foot away. Glowing eyes locked onto the ants, not him. A raccoon—fat, almost the size of a beaver—clung to the branches, its sharp claws gripping the wood as it peered down at the seething mass below. Its fur bristled, lips curling, but its fury wasn't for Dan.

It was for the ants.

Without warning, the raccoon decided. With one massive bound, it launched itself from the tree, landing with a dull *thud* on a strip of floating planks. The makeshift raft rocked violently, and for a split second, Dan thought the creature would plunge straight into the river. But the wood steadied, and the raccoon, ringed tail twitching in the wind, was swept away by the current.

Dan choked back his spit.

The ants kept coming.

They were closing in fast, a creeping tide of red that left no room for second thoughts. He scrambled to his feet, eyes darting through the dense canopy. Leaves blocked his view in every direction, but he knew this tree was part of a larger stand. He passed several others before choosing this one to hide behind.

That meant there had to be another tree nearby. But he couldn't see it.

His heart pounded. He'd have one chance.

This was going to be a risky move.

A sharp sting jolted him. Dan slapped at the burning spot on his neck, then dropped, swinging from branch to branch as fast as his aching limbs allowed. The ants weren't giving up. Whether they fell by accident or chased him down with mindless determination, he didn't know, but twice he stopped to claw at his arms and hair, flinging the unrelenting little bastards away.

Two feet above the water, he hesitated. No watercraft appeared beneath him. No convenient escape. Just the river— dark, churning, and filled with who knew what.

His lips curled in a frustrated snarl, mirroring the raccoon's just moments before. With no choice, Dan stepped off the branch.

The current seized him instantly, yanking him under as if the river were waiting for him. Cold, filthy water surged over his head, filling his ears and nose. He kicked, breaking the surface with a desperate gasp and spitting out the foul taste of mud and decay. Wiping at his stinging eyes, he barely caught a second to look around before the river hurled him forward.

A massive trunk loomed at the last second, and with no time to react before he slammed into it, the jarring collision snapped his head back. White-hot pain exploded in his skull. Stars burst into his vision.

The river didn't care.

It drew him under, to spin him away and carry him downstream like another scrap on the watercourse. But luck, instinct, or sheer stubbornness threw him a lifeline—his arm hooked onto a half-submerged branch. Water rushed over his face, choking him as he clung to the rough bark, fighting for air, for consciousness.

A knot the size of an egg was already rising on his forehead.

Summoning the last of his strength, Dan swung his leg over the branch and hauled himself up, muscles protesting. He flopped against the trunk, chest heaving, the river lapping at his legs.

He barely hauled himself one branch higher, collapsing into the elbow of the tree, out of the water, but battered, exhausted, and seething.

Rage burned hotter than pain, hotter than fear.

He would find Matthias.

And when he did, everyone would pay.

"Hey, fella!"

The voice cut through Dan's haze of exhaustion and pain. He flinched, almost losing his grip again. He was so lost in his thoughts that he hadn't noticed the puttering aluminum rowboat as it drew up beneath his branch.

A grizzled man, soaked to the bone but solid-looking, stood in the boat, one hand gripping the branch with an ease that suggested hidden strength. His eyes swept over Dan, assessing.

"You okay? Need a hand?"

Dan opened his mouth, but his throat felt like sandpaper. He coughed out a hoarse, "Help," and let himself slide downward.

Two other men were in the boat. They caught him and eased him onto the damp metal bench as he tumbled in. One of them wore a soaked Boy Scout uniform. His brown face and arms were covered in scratches, and his eyes were sharp with concern.

"You'll be okay, sir," the scout leader steadied him.

"We're looking for survivors," the older man said, finally letting go of the tree as the boat drifted with the current. "You see anyone out here?"

Dan coughed, his mind racing as he tried to give himself time to think.

"There were three boys," the scout leader cut in, his voice tight. "Scouts. They made it up a tree, but when the river jumped the banks, we got separated. I lost track of them." He exhaled heavily. "Lucky for me, Rube here was out overnight frog hunting. He fished me out."

"Got swept overland during the quake," Rube chuckled, shaking his head. "But I caught the biggest damn toads last night."

Dan barely heard him. His brain worked furiously, piecing together a story that might keep him ahead of the game. He looked up, affecting just the right amount of weariness.

"I saw those boys," he spoke haltingly. "They floated off on some kind of jet ski. A big, wide one."

The scout leader exhaled loudly, almost crumpling in relief. He rubbed a dark hand through his tight curls. "Then they're safe. Did they get the engine running? Maybe they're already on dry land."

"Yeah, sure," Dan said, nodding. "They drove it right off." He paused. "Name's Dan. I'll help you look for them. We should check their homes—make sure they made it back."

Rube grunted and scratched his whiskered cheek. "I need to get back to my truck and refuel. I'll get you boys to dry land first, then you can find your scouts. By now, they might already be home."

Good plan," the scout leader said, giving Dan a grateful nod. "Thanks, Dan. I'm Pete Deller. Hopefully, we'll find the boys safe."

Dan barely heard him. His gaze was locked on the dark, twisting waters ahead.

Finding Matthias's home was priority one.

***

Brett shoved off another hunk—a jagged slab of wall or part of a roof. It hardly mattered. The current claimed it all. With no engine and no real control, the river had plenty of strength to push them forward.

He and Piper worked out a rough method to steer, using paddles to push off floating wreckage and adjust their course. They stayed close to the bank, where the current was sluggish compared to the raging center, which tore past like a tsunami in the making.

Brett wasn't much of a sailor. In fact, this was his first time on a boat—if a half-floating fishing skiff even counted. The river was thick with trash, shifting logs, and the occasional bloated corpse of an animal, all threats that could flip them instantly. He gritted his teeth, gripping his paddle so tightly his fingers ached.

The dogs weren't convinced of his skills, either. Coco stood stiff, hackles raised, eyes locked straight ahead. Bella barked at every bit of debris that knocked against the hull. Charlie curled up in Winnie's lap, shivering.

"Duke! Knock it off!" Brett yelled as the dog lunged over the side, snapping at floating branches.

Then Piper screamed.

Brett barely processed the raw terror in her voice before the boat pitched forward. His stomach lurched as the river dropped out beneath them. The skiff nosedived over a jagged precipice—a ten-foot waterfall born from the earthquake's anarchy.

The impact hit like a car crash. Water exploded around them, slamming them into the churning pool below. The boat spun wildly, nearly capsizing as Duke tumbled across the floor, scrabbling for footing. Only luck kept them inside.

Spray shot skyward, drenching them. Coco crouched low, soaked and trembling. Piper clung to Bella, her fingers buried in the Alaskan Shepherd's thick fur.

Brett hit the deck, his breath vanishing in a painful gasp. His face smacked against the wet floor, and pain flared in his nose. A fresh warmth dripped down his lip—blood.

Dazed, he rolled onto his back, gasping for air. Above him, Winnie and Charlie huddled together in the cockpit, wide-eyed but still there.

Somehow, they survived the drop. But the river wasn't done with them yet.

Spray exploded around them, drenching everything in an icy sheet of water. His chest still heaving, Brett shook his head like a wet dog, just as a deep, rough roar rumbled through the air. It grew louder, inescapable.

He sat up and turned.

The river ahead was seething.

White water churned over jagged rocks, waves surging like walls. The earth's violent heave split the riverbed open, forcing stone spires through the current like blades. The river transformed into madness, a gauntlet of rapids ready to tear them apart.

Blood ran down Brett's face, mingling with river water. He wiped his sleeve across his nose, wincing at the pain. Heavy droplets flew through the air, smacking him in the face. The sound of rushing water pounded in his skull, drowning out everything else. He barely braced before the boat careened to the right.

Something massive hammered against them with a crunch—a thick, waterlogged sycamore, its sodden green leaves tangled in shards of thin branches. The impact sent them spinning.

Brett lunged for his paddle. A wave crashed into him, stealing what little vision he'd regained, stinging his eyes. Blindly, he shoved against a chunk of cement that loomed up in their path. The boat scraped past, the stone grating along the hull with a terrifying shriek. Was that a piece of a levee? No time to wonder.

A rusted iron girder shot alongside them, barely missing their stern. Brett jabbed it with the paddle, his heartbeat hammering.

More remains surged past, twisted beams, shattered timber, serrated planks riding the current like deadly spears. Another wave thrashed the side, drenching Piper and Bella. The girl drew herself up against the dog, both shivering. Bella whined unhappily as Piper found her paddle. Grimly, she hung on as another tree caught the bow. The boat jerked sideways, spinning wildly in the raging current.

Brett's legs buckled as the boat lurched again, tossed like a puppet in the churning rapids. With no control, they were just passengers in a nightmare ride.

The hull pounded into unseen masses, thrusting them airborne before crashing back down, walls of water drenching everything. The dogs scrambled for footing, claws skidding uselessly across the slick floor. Only Charlie stayed put, wedged under the steering wheel with Winnie, his nose buried deep in her shirt. She clutched him tight, eyes squeezed shut against the onslaught.

Another surge hit, nearly knocking them over. Brett coughed, his chest burning—was it blood or river water choking him? No time to care. He wiped a wet sleeve across his face and forced himself to focus.

Piper's arms trembled as she shoved against whatever she could reach—split rafters, half-submerged trees, fragments hurtling past too fast to recognize. Every second was a fight, a desperate struggle to keep them upright and moving.

Then, a jarring, bone-rattling impact. Something solid crunched beneath them, the boat filing against it with a sickening scrape. The vibration shot through the hull, up through Brett's feet, into his bones.

And then—release.

The rapids spat them out.

Chaos subsided as the river smoothed into a swift, full flow.

Brett sucked in a gulp, chest heaving, heart pounding. Piper sagged forward, leaning on her paddle. The dogs stilled, except for Coco, who shook vigorously, flinging water everywhere. Duke lay flat on his stomach, covering his nose with oversized paws. Clearly, he was done.

They were still alive and moving down the river. The bank was curving off to the right, and a half-bent sign leaned against a tree on shore. It said, "Seven Island Conservation Area—1 Mile."

-Brett slumped in relief. They found the campground. Now they just needed to find Matthias.

Chapter Nine
Harrowood, KY, Saturday, August 16, 11 a.m.

The inside of the old storage building was a mess. Boxes were toppled, and shelves bowed from the quake's strike. But the parts Albert needed were there—coils of thick wire, heavy-duty rope, and pallets leaning haphazardly against a cracked wall. Together, they cleared debris from the crooked steps and muscled the pallet, rope, and wire to the second floor. The air was sharper up here, and the damage worse.

"Stay back, Stella," Albert warned as he stepped onto the warped wood. Royce watched as he crossed the room.

The floor was uneven, and walking on it was like stepping on an old pillow. It sagged and creaked with each stride. The far edge crumbled into open air, and vertigo clawed at him as he gripped the wall to steady himself. Stella ignored him and followed. Sinking her teeth into his jacket, she tugged him back with a sharp yank.

"I *said* stay back," he growled, but didn't push her away. Truth was, the dog made him feel steadier than the floor did.

Back inside, Albert's hands worked fast. He knotted and twisted the wire into a braid, drawing the improvised cable taut, strong enough, if they were lucky.

Now to get it across the gap. When they first arrived, he noticed archery gear stacked on a shelf. Back downstairs, they dug through the rubble, shoving aside shelves and boxes until they found it. Perfect. He grabbed a compound bow and flexed the string. It was not great, but serviceable.

Royce watched him skeptically. "You even know how to shoot?"

"It's been a few years," Albert admitted, not taking his eyes off the target. He stood at the gaping second-floor edge, scanning the diner across the street—more intact, its heavy wooden beams still standing firm. "I'm aiming for those support braces. Keep your fingers crossed."

Royce glanced at the sky. "It's pretty breezy, the wind is blowing back at us."

"Figures," Albert grumbled. He tied the braided cable and rope to a thick bolt, lashing them to the arrow's shaft. He planted his feet. The bow creaked as he drew back, aiming high to offset the drag. One breath in. One out. He let go.

The arrow soared, trailing cable like a tail, arcing over the cracked street below. A solid *thwack* rang out as it embedded in the diner's frame.

He held his breath. For a moment, nothing—then two men scrambled from cover, reaching up, grabbing the line. Working fast, they separated the rope from the cable, securing the silver line around the wooden beam, wrapping it repeatedly, and twisting it tight. Hanging on to the rope, they stood ready to pull the pallet when Albert launched. They gave a thumbs up.

Albert grabbed his end of the line and looped it tight around the corner beam, the cable biting into the wood with each turn. He gave it a final yank and signaled Royce. Together, they leaned back and pulled, muscles exerting, boots digging into the boards. It held firm, solid enough to trust with actual weight.

Albert turned back to Royce, face grim. "Step one."

Royce dipped his chin, eyes on Albert's pile of spare parts. "This looks mighty dangerous."

Ignoring him, Albert hauled a pallet over and flipped it onto its side. He cobbled together a rough pulley system from a tangled pile of salvaged gear—broken wheels, rusted carabiners, a fraying tow strap.

He got started by looping the thickest ropes around both sides of the pallet, weaving them through the slats, and securing them with tight knots. The loops weren't just for stability but for anchoring the men and providing a dog harness. He clipped the carabiners through reinforced tie points, connecting the ropes to a separate guideline that would let someone on the far side haul the platform across.

"You've got to be kidding," Royce muttered, eyes scrutinizing the tangle of wires and ropes Albert had strung across the wooden pallet.

Stella, her wiry coat even more tousled than usual, gave a low woof of agreement. She sniffed the rig like it might bite, then took a cautious step back. Shadow, tail low, crept after her with a whine.

Albert didn't even look up. "Got a better plan?" he grunted, tightening a knot with quick, practiced fingers.

Royce didn't answer. He didn't have a better plan—but that didn't mean he liked this one.

Two more ropes were slung over the highline, each looped through carabiners attached to opposite ends of the pallet—front and back. These would keep the raft steady on its descent, preventing it from spinning or flipping under its own weight. He grabbed the rope end held by the diner crew, cinching it tight with a practiced knot. Then he hustled to the other side and twined another rope around the wood. This one was his to pull, guide, and keep the load from swinging wildly once it dropped into the open space below. Stella watched him, huffing a little with nerves.

"You trust me, right?" he murmured, scratching behind Stella's ears. She leaned against him, but he knew she wasn't happy.

Albert stood and grabbed two lengths of rope, coiling them over his shoulder. He moved to the edge and slung both over the high line stretched across the gap, watching them drop back. Gripping the ends, he returned and tied them—two to the front, two to the back of the pallet—securing the knots with his stiff fingers, trying to make them as tight as possible.

He tugged, testing the tension. The ropes held.

When it was ready, the pallet hung a foot above the edge, tethered by the twin ropes. It wasn't elegant—but it was a working zipline ferry rig: half raft, half pulley cart, ready to slide above the abyss on little more than rope, gravity, and nerve.

"You and Shadow go first," Albert told Royce. When the older man protested, Albert overrode his objections with facts.

"If this thing gets tangled up or there's a problem on this side, I can fix it. Besides, you and Shadow weigh less, so you get to go first." Albert's reasoning might not have convinced Royce, but then, the ground beneath them shuddered. A series of crashes sent them hurrying back down the steps. To their dismay, they found that the rear of the building, along with the truck and parking lot, had vanished.

Exchanging anxious glances, they both knew the time for arguing was done. They half-ran back upstairs, the dogs barking as if to hurry them along.

One at a time, Albert hoisted the mayor and the dog onto the pallet, securing them with rope loops before he pushed their life raft off the edge. He stopped to wrap his palms with old clothes, knotting them with his teeth.

With a grunt, he pulled, guiding them over the chasm, the rig grating under the weight. The diner crew yelled for them to hurry, hauling from their end, steadying the load.

It went more smoothly than he expected. After a slight skid on the cable, the pallet arrived at the diner. Working together, three men held it tight as Royce untied himself and slid off. One of the younger men climbed onto the frame. He freed Shadow, who sprang off the wooden ramp with a bark. She dashed through the diner, sliding over the linoleum floors, through the chips of dishes and food, and then back to the front, leaning on the empty window frame and barking at Stella.

Moving fast, Albert pulled the pallet back, jerking the rope with deep tugs until it landed back on the edge.

Securing first Stella and then himself with the harnesses, Albert grabbed onto the pallet and pushed off with his feet. The wooden raft slid forward, the whole rig swaying under their weight. Wind rushed past, the drop yawning below. The men pulled the heavier load with no help from Albert this time. It took longer than anyone wanted. Royce helped tow, anxiety giving him strength.

Halfway across, the rope creaked loudly. A sharp *snap* came from the corner—a knot ripped out, and the pallet jerked, tilting awkwardly. Stella swung her heavy head, her dark eyes wide with alarm.

The jolt sent a violent shudder through the rest of the ropes, snapping fibers with sharp, whip-like cracks. The men hauling from the diner shouted in alarm, yanking frantically to regain control, but the weight shift was too sudden, too much.

Royce lunged backward, drawing the line with him, but another knot tore loose before he could reinforce the hold. The pallet lurched, tipping wildly until it swung perpendicular to the diner's crumbling wall.

Then—*snap*.

The beam anchoring the temporary bridge on the second floor wrenched free with a splintering *crack*. For a split second, everything hung in a dreadful silence as the entire rig dropped.

Out of sight, the pallet slammed into the sheer clay embankment far beneath the diner.

With a second to brace before the impact drove the air from his lungs, instinct took over. Albert threw himself around Stella, curling his body over hers just before his skull struck the slatted wood with brutal force. A sickening thud rang out as wood met earth. A white-hot explosion of pain ripped through his head, his vision going black at the edges.

Stella yelped, twisting against his hold. The pallet swung in a slow, gut-wrenching arc, scraping against the crumbling clay wall as debris showered down from above. Only the rope held by the crew of the diner kept them from falling.

Desperate voices called his name. The rope strained. The rig dangled precariously, the last remaining knots dragging under the weight.

Dizzy, stars bursting in his vision, Albert willed his eyes to open. His grip on Stella weakened, and the rope above them frayed with every second.

Stella's teeth sank into his fingers, sharp pain slicing through the haze clouding his mind. Albert gasped, the sting jarring him back to reality. The dog twisted in his grip, barking wildly, her body a writhing mass of muscle and panic. He fought to keep hold, but the pallet beneath them gave another sickening lurch, sliding downward in small bounces. The ropes twanged. Any second now, they'd both plummet.

Stella clamped onto his jacket sleeve and pulled hard to the right. Albert gritted his teeth, barely holding on, but something about her frantic tug made him look.

A dark hole the size of a doorway gaped in the clay wall beside them, two feet away. His breath caught. A shaft. Some shallow crevice exposed by the quake.

The pallet groaned again, tilting. He didn't have time to weigh options. Digging his fingers into the coarse rope and wire binding them, he ripped Stella free, ignoring the burn in his muscles and her squeal of pain. With a grunt, he heaved her sideways toward the opening. She yelped as she hit the dirt, skidding deeper into the darkness.

The moment he released her, the pallet shifted beneath him.

Albert didn't hesitate. He tore at his own bindings, his fingers fumbling as the ropes dropped the pallet another inch. He freed one arm, then the other, hanging on. Using every ounce of strength left in his battered body, he lunged toward the dark hole.

The world tilted. He hit the dirt, slamming face-first into the tunnel floor. Dust exploded around him, filling his mouth with grit.

Behind him, the rope gave a final splintering snap as it parted. With the air knocked out of him, Albert rolled onto his back. His heart hammered. Stella whined, her cold nose nudging his face, her warm snort puffing against his cheek.

They were alive.

Albert's back twisted with a painful pull as he sat up, wiping dirt from his face with the clothes tied around his hands. His pulse thundered in his ears, a mix of exertion and sheer disbelief. That had been too close.

Stella whined again and pawed at his chest. He reached up, scratching behind her ears with shaking fingers. She scrambled next to him, tail low but safe.

"Yeah, yeah, I know," he groused, though his voice was hoarse. "Next time, we'll take the long way around."

A gust of wind funneled into the tunnel, carrying the distant shouts of the men in the diner. Climbing painfully to his feet, he turned toward the opening and peered out. The ropes hung limp, snapped strands swaying against the rock wall. The pallet was gone, consumed by the abyss below. He and Stella would have plummeted with it if he'd hesitated a second longer. While he watched, the ropes slid up the side of the wall.

The ground shifted beneath his boots as Albert inched closer to the edge. The floor of the tunnel crumbled under his feet. As dirt fell away, clods tumbling, he knew the opening was disintegrating. He took several steps back.

Cracks appeared around the mouth, growing wider and separating the rocks and clay. While he watched, the tunnel's face collapsed, exposing a new, irregular hole.

Like a mini landslide, the dirt slid away, cascading into the abyss below. Stones plunged, clattering into unseen depths. His stomach clutched as the tunnel's mouth shrank before his eyes, devoured by the expanding rift.

He didn't wait to see how much farther it would reach. Heart pounding, he staggered backward, gulping in sharp bursts. Dust swirled around him, thick and choking. Stella growled low in her throat, ears pinned back, sensing the danger.

Another tremor. More dirt sloughed off, widening the gap.

Albert took another step back. Then another.

They needed to move—now.

When he was far enough back that he felt comfortable, he stopped. He pressed his back against the tunnel wall, forcing himself to think. They weren't out of danger yet. With no idea how far this tunnel cut through, he knew it was still better than clinging to the crumbling wall.

Stella let out a low growl and turned toward the darkness behind them. Albert followed her gaze, squinting into the shadows. It looked like the remains of a natural cavern, one of the hundreds purported to exist in this area. The shaft stretched further than he'd thought, the hard-packed floor inclining upward. It wasn't just a shallow cave—it led somewhere.

He clenched his jaw. They could either sit here and wait for rescue, and he wasn't even sure how Royce's people could attempt that on the crumbling wall, or they could move forward and find their way out. He slid out his cell phone and activated the flashlight function. It didn't help much, but it was better than the solid darkness.

A fresh wave of adrenaline surged through him. Wiping the sweat from his brow, he pushed himself to his feet, his legs still shaky from the jump. "Alright, girl. Let's see where this thing goes."

With Stella at his side, he turned away from the abyss and stepped into the black throat of the passage.

Mississippi River, Kentucky/Missouri: Saturday, August 16, 11 a.m.

The sound hit them first—a high-pitched whine cutting through the river's steady flow, like an angry mosquito hovering just out of reach. Brett whipped his head around, scanning the churning surface. Then, slicing through the weird brown fog hanging over the floodway, a red wave runner burst into view. It bounced over the swollen current, its engine howling as it fought against the upstream tide.

Three figures clung to the aquabike, their soaked uniforms catching the wind. As they drew closer, Brett's eyes locked onto the familiar tan fabric—Scouts.

Heart pounding, he gripped the gunwale, Piper pressed in beside him, and the dogs erupted into a frenzy. Coco's deep-throated barks boomed over the river, while Bella's frantic yowls carried through the air.

Matthias hunched over the handlebars on the watercraft, his face set in fierce determination as he cut through the roiling water. He saw the battered fishing boat ahead, another hulk bobbing in the current, but unlike the wreckage they'd passed so far, this one rode high, skimming the waves instead of drowning in them.

Matthias squinted, scanning the figures in the boat. His pulse kicked up. Then he heard Coco's unmistakable bark and Bella's frantic cries. His grip tightened.

"It's my family!" he shouted over the engine's roar, twisting the throttle.

Jamie and Pedro reacted excitedly, talking over each other as he veered toward the crumbling riverbank, fighting the surging current.

"Matthias!" Piper's voice rang out, raw with relief.

Winnie popped up beside her, waving wildly. Duke and Coco joined the excitement, their barking rising to a deafening chorus that drowned out even the turbulent river.

Ten minutes later, the watercraft bobbed alongside the fishing boat, secured to a cleat with a hastily knotted rope. The flow was weaker near the trash-strewn banks, allowing them a moment to rest.

As soon as Matthias stepped onto the deck, the siblings crashed into each other, their arms locking in fierce hugs, while the dogs exploded in a frenzy, jumping, barking, and their tails whipping wildly. Piper threw her arms around Jamie and Pedro, squeezing them tight despite their startled protests.

"We were coming to get you at the campsite," Brett said, pounding Matthias on the shoulder.

"It's gone," Matthias said, his voice raw. "Flooded. Everything got washed away. We barely made it up a tree before the water ripped through. Then that tree got uprooted." He pushed up his glasses, exhaling sharply. "If this wave runner hadn't drifted by, we'd be swimming right now."

"The same thing happened at the house," Brett admitted, his jawline tight. "The levee broke—took everything with it."

Matthias's gaze darted around, his expression changing, panic rising in his throat. His voice cracked. "Shadow…"

"No!" The word shot from all of his siblings, quick and urgent.

"Shadow's safe," Piper said. "She went to Harrowood with Albert and Royce. She was pacing and missing you, so they took her along to distract her."

"And Chloe, Reed, and Watson went to Boxco," Brett added. "No one else was at home when it happened."

Matthias swallowed hard, nodding as relief welled up in his chest.

"We didn't lose anyone," Brett said firmly, gripping his brother's shoulder, pushing back the lingering fear in his eyes.

Winnie tugged on Matthias's sleeve, determined to add her report. "We got in the boat just before the water came!" she said, puffing out her chest. "Duke needed a little push, but the others jumped right in!"

The scout let out a shaky huff. For the first time since the floodwaters came, fear wasn't so consuming.

"Why are you bleeding?" he asked Brett. Blood and muck streaked the teen's face and T-shirt.

"Fell and banged my nose," Brett admitted, wiping the worst off his face with the bottom of his shirt. "But I'm okay. Just sore."

Running a hand through his wet hair, his glasses smeared with dirt, Matthias cleaned them against his filthy uniform. His voice was edged with disbelief. "I can't believe we got caught in another earthquake." His gaze darted between his siblings. "I thought we were safe here in Kentucky."

Brett let out a dry laugh, shaking his head. "Freaking crazy, I know. But now that we have you guys, we need to figure out how to get to solid ground and check on everyone else. I don't know how far this quake reached, but I guarantee they're struggling to get back to the house and find out what happened to us." He tilted his head toward Jamie and Pedro. "And you two need to get home, too."

Pedro gulped. "I want to go home. My mom is worried about me." His brown eyes were solemn, his voice a little scared.

"This is Pedro, I'm Jamie," the taller boy said, rubbing at the flaking mud streaking his arms. His scout uniform was a mess—wrinkled, stained, and torn. "I'd like to get home too. But…" He hesitated, glancing at Matthias. "You better tell them about your dad first."

"What?" Piper and Brett said simultaneously, their heads snapping toward Matthias.

Matthias exhaled, shoving his glasses on. "Get this," he started. "After the river jumped the banks, and we climbed that tree, Dad was there. Thirty feet away, up in another tree."

Piper's mouth fell open. "Dad?"

"What was he even doing at your retreat?" Brett asked, frowning.

Before Matthias could answer, a gust of wind whipped through. Piper shivered. It felt like it was getting colder. She brushed the chills away, her eyes locking on her brother. "Well?"

Matthias sighed. "I have no idea. But he saw us. And he was angry, as usual. He didn't even try to help when our tree was uprooted."

Brett's stomach twisted. "Where is he now?"

Matthias ran a hand through his damp hair, his expression tight. "It took us a while to find the key to the runner. Once we finally started the engine, we went back to where we last saw him. But…" He hesitated, his throat working. "The tree was empty."

Piper stiffened, her lungs catching. "You mean he fell in?"

"I don't know." Matthias tipped his head, frustration flashing in his eyes. "It didn't look like it. There weren't any signs of a struggle, no damaged branches. He was just… gone. We searched, did a grid search, and checked both sides of the river, but didn't see him. Pete, our Scout Leader, was washed away when the earthquake's first waves hit. We looked for both of them, but no luck. So, we figured the best thing to do was to get home."

Brett frowned, his mind racing. "What was Dad even doing here? How did he find us? I never put our names on the survivor lists, and I know I didn't see his name when I looked for Mom and Uncle Jess."

Matthias let out a slow puff. "Okay, this is going to sound insane—it sounded crazy to me—but Dad thinks we stole Nadia's jewelry. He wanted me to tell him where it was."

Piper's eyes went wide. "What?"

Brett's confusion deepened. "Wait—you mean the cash we found in those bags?"

"No." Matthias' gaze darkened. "Dad said the money burned up. He's looking for Nadia's jewels."

The river pulled at the boat as the current picked up again. Water lapped against the hull, but no one spoke. Matthias's words settled over them like a storm cloud.

Then Piper turned, her gaze locking onto Winnie. "Why would Dad think we took Nadia's jewels?"

Winnie's face flushed, but she lifted her chin defiantly. "Nadia let me play with her dress-up stuff."

Brett rubbed a hand through his short cut. "Winnie never even went into the house. None of us did. We followed them to the quarry, then the lake exploded. When would she have had the chance?"

Piper crouched in front of her sister, her voice gentler now. She emulated their mother. "Winnie, what would Mom say?"

That single sentence knocked the defiance out of Winnie like a gust of wind. Her shoulders slumped, and her lower lip trembled, but she held her ground. "I didn't steal them," she muttered. "I was keeping them safe for her."

Piper exhaled sharply. "Where are they, Winnie? Were they in our bedroom?"

Brett scrubbed a hand through his hair. "If you hid them in the house, they're long gone. The house is washed away."

Winnie bit her lip, slowly sliding off her knapsack, and shoved it toward Piper. "I wasn't gonna keep them," she insisted. "I just didn't want them to get lost. All the clothes Nadia packed were ruined. I knew she'd be upset if her pretty jewelry got burned up, too."

Piper hesitated, then reached into the bag. Near the bottom, covered in clothes, her fingers brushed a pile of something cool and smooth. She wrapped her hand around a few pieces and drew them out. Red colored her cheeks.

"Oh, Winnie," she gasped.

A handful of glittering jewels, diamonds and reds, blues, and greens, gleamed in the dim light reflecting off the water.

Even Pedro and Jamie gawked, eyes wide.

"Great," Brett muttered, running a hand down his face. "Well, Dad and Nadia's jewelry is the least of our problems right now. Stick them back in there, Piper. We'll figure this out later. First, we need to decide what we're doing next. Matthias, what happened to the rest of your troop?"

"I think they're okay," the boy said, the weariness plucking at him, marking his face. "They left early for an inland hike. I hope they were far enough away to be safe from the floods. When the earthquake started, only Pete, Jamie, Pedro, and I were at camp."

Brett looked relieved. "So we just need to get out of the river and head back home."

"Uh oh, look." Jamie's voice was high, his arm shooting out as they approached another bend in the Mississippi.

Brett followed his pointing finger and felt his stomach drop. Ahead, the river choked to a narrow passage before curving south and doubling in width again, but now, just before the river made the sharp left turn, a massive wall of wreckage bottlenecked the channel.

Twisted tree spears, crushed boats, and barges jutted from the tangle of remains, their shattered hulls barely visible under a mountain of splintered timber. Cargo containers sat wedged between the fragments of buildings. So many barrels tossed everywhere, some bright yellow and stenciled with chemical hazard symbols. Mattresses, chairs, and entire sections of houses clogged the neck of the river, forcing it to churn violently as the water sought a way through.

Brett lunged forward, gripping his paddle and stabbing into the water, searching for the muddy bottom. Nothing. It was too deep. The current towed them straight toward the barricade of wreckage.

"We need to get out of here!" His voice was sharp with urgency. "If we hit that dam, we'll be pinned, and that's it—we're done."

Piper scanned the river, eyes darting to the collapsing shoreline. "Where? The banks are nothing but crumbling mud. We can't climb that."

Brett's gaze locked onto a sandbar poking out of the water up ahead, a narrow strip barely holding against the rushing current. It stretched about twenty feet long, five feet wide—enough to beach the boat. Several feet beyond it, the remnants of the levees loomed, their edges sloughing off in thick, wet chunks.

"There!" He pointed. "We ground ourselves on the sandbar, buy some time, figure out our next move."

Piper's hands tightened on the side of the boat. "We have to get over there."

Brett didn't answer. He paddled deep, muscles stressing as he fought the current. They didn't turn at all. The river wasn't going to give them anything without a fight.

Matthias's gaze darted across the boat. "This is that old fishing boat from the yard, right?"

Brett didn't look up. He pushed harder, sweat beading on his forehead. "Yeah, and we're floating. Barely. But it doesn't have an engine."

"The sea-doo," Matthias and Jamie said in unison.

The two scrambled to the side, fumbling with the knot securing the small craft. Matthias grabbed the handlebars, eyes locked on the swirling current.

"I'll take the wave runner and push," Matthias decided.

Jamie gave a quick nod, already working the ropes loose. "Good. Push us from the stern—it's the widest part. You'll have better control. I'll steer this boat toward shore while you push."

Years of scout training kicked in. There was no hesitation, no wasted movement. They worked fast, the sound of water hammering in their ears. The wreckage dam loomed closer, the river surging toward it, with them caught in its grip.

Brett and Piper stayed busy with the paddles, keeping the boat from floundering or getting holed by some random piece of trash. Winnie grabbed Pedro's hand and drew him out of the way to crouch on the aft cushions. The dogs milled back and forth, unbalanced as they swung unsteadily in the current.

The *Seismic Wave* lurched and sputtered over submerged trash, the hull shuddering beneath them. But Matthias had already fired up the watercraft's engine, the machine growling hot and ready. He whipped it in a tight circle, then gunned it toward the boat, carefully avoiding the rusted engine block bolted in the up position, mid-deck.

Bracing against the surge of water, he wedged himself between the old motor and the boat's stern. "Get ready!" he shouted over the roar of the current.

Jamie clenched his fist in a signal.

They worked the angle together, nudging the battered boat toward the sandbar. Even with the water scooter's power, it was a struggle—each correction nearly sent them veering off course. At the last second, Matthias pulled away, throttling back to gain some distance.

"Brett—catch!" He hurled the rope they used to tie up the runner.

Brett reached—missed. The rope whipped past him.

Then Coco lunged. The cockapoo clamped down on the line, his powerful chops holding tight. Brett dove, snatched it from the dog's mouth, and looped it fast around a cleat. "Got it!" he shouted. "Good boy, Coco!"

Matthias didn't hesitate. He spun the watercraft wide, yanking the rope taut. The sudden momentum caused the boat to lurch sideways. Everyone standing fell in a heap as the bow swung around, skidding onto the sandbar with a teeth-rattling bump.

For a moment, there was only the sound of panting and the river's relentless roar. Then, a cheer went up.

Matthias drew alongside, idling the machine and grinning. "Now *that's* how you park a boat."

Their jubilation was short-lived. A blast of sound ripped through the air, deep, shrill, and bone-rattling—the unmistakable wail of a steam whistle.

Brett spun toward the noise just as the *Magnolia Lady* loomed into view, rounding the bend like a ghost of the past. The massive 600-foot riverboat surged forward, its once-pristine white railings packed with passengers, their faces twisted in terror. Their screams and shouts collided with the eerie steam calliope, its desperate, high-pitched notes echoing across the river.

She was a beauty—or had been. Her grand, curving hull, lined with intricate Victorian ornamentation, was now smeared with mud and scratches. The giant red paddlewheel, splintered in places, hung useless at her stern. One of her twin smokestacks leaned at a dangerous angle, swaying with every lurch.

Brett's fists caught. High above the decks, he locked eyes on the pilothouse—figures inside, moving frantically.

Then it hit him. They weren't simply sounding the whistle—they were warning them.

The *Magnolia Lady* was out of control.

The river had her now, an unrelenting grip dragging the ferry like a helpless log toward the looming big island. With no power, no control, she was at the mercy of the waterway. As the current pushed her left, the northern channel disappeared, sending her towards the rocky headland of Cort Evans Island.

The crash was brutal.

First, the bow struck, the jarring collision shuddering through the entire vessel like a hammer blow. Passengers and crew hit the deck, some barely catching the railings to keep from being pitched overboard. Metal clanged, wood splintered, and the ferry clung to the land for a long, agonizing moment, held fast against the protruding rocks.

Then the river took her again.

Water surged beneath her, wrenching her free. There was no time to right her or even a way to point her bow into the river. The massive boat floated sideways, helpless in the torrent, and rushed straight toward the dam, choking the stream ahead.

And Matthias had floated out into her path.

Brett's stomach clenched. The water scooter bobbed in the current, Matthias frozen in awe as the massive steamboat bore down on him.

"Matthias! MOVE!" Brett bellowed, scrambling to yank the rope tied between them. There was no resistance, and he realized his brother had dropped the end.

Matthias didn't hear. He didn't even look at him, eyes locked on the massive ship. Because now, even over the roar of the river and the shrieks from the deck, they could hear something worse—the *Magnolia Lady* grinding as she picked up speed, her battered hull heading straight for Matthias and the debris dam.

Chapter Ten
St. Louis, MO: Saturday, August 16, 12 p.m.

It took hours to clear a route down the only stairwell that wasn't completely blocked or collapsed. Tremors rocked the building repeatedly, adding to their caution.

As soon as the first knock twisted the room, Emmet was moving, yanking the two men with him out of the conference room, into the hall against an inside wall under one of the enormous support beams. At the last second, Walter snagged his laptop with his fingertips, pushing it shut with his hip and clutching it close. He had barely registered the first massive blows of the quake when pieces of ceiling tiles, plaster, and light fixtures started falling on them. He wished for his desk in Corvallis, where he had hidden the last time a mega-earthquake cut loose.

In the 10th-floor lobby, the elevator doors suddenly twisted and bowed as they struggled to open; the next jolt ripped them free and threw the polished steel sheets sliding over the carpet. The three men turned in shock in time to see the gawking faces of the half a dozen well-dressed people caught in the metal box, hanging on to each other and the side rails. There was a high-pitched screeching noise, followed by a series of loud pops. One man realized what was coming and tried to throw himself out, but it happened too fast. The elevator dropped like a rock, taking its unfortunate passengers and disappearing into the gaping black hole.

With a roar, the shaking intensified, and the building swayed in rhythm with the earth. Emmet reacted swiftly, yanking the closest round table over and shoving the others under the tablecloth just as a hail of glass rained down from the shattering windows. Glass shards embedded themselves into the wall behind them like ninja throwing stars. The floor cracked, the gap widened, and the wall at the end of the hall peeled off with a crash, sunlight catching the floating bits in the air.

Then, the last of the quakes hit like a pile driver. The three men were tumbled together in a shocking series of blows. Emmet belly-crawled against the wall and covered his face. Tau thought he was going to vomit, his fear filling his throat with bile. Walter held his laptop to his chest, inside his suit coat, with his knees up and his head down. Making the smallest target possible, he grimly waited for it to stop. A loud, rending noise filled the air, the sound of a building tearing itself in half, and Tau wondered if this was the end.

When it ceased, the only sound was a high note of wind blowing through the corridor. Nothing moved, except for a few particles falling. Twisting his neck to clear the weird humming noise vibrating in his head, Tau worried his eardrums had ruptured.

He scrambled to his feet, covered in chalky gray powder, and darted back to the conference room. The doors were shut. He grabbed one and jerked it open, falling back with a shout of surprise.

The conference room, podium, speakers, and attendees were gone. He was looking through a doorway that led outside, 10 stories over the city. The entire conference room had been torn off and flung away, taking all the geological experts with it. Only Walter, Tau, and Emmet survived, thanks to Emmet's quick thinking.

Emmet rolled over and groaned. "I'm too old for this."

Tau hurried over and helped the fringe scientist to his feet. He pulled Walter up as well, and they went back to the doorway, staring out at the city.

Downtown St. Louis was unrecognizable.

The city was razed, buildings reduced to piles of shattered concrete and twisted steel. What hadn't pancaked under the quake's assault now leaned at precarious angles. Some were split in half, where massive fractures in the earth absorbed their foundations. Cracks ran so deep that the bottoms were lost in darkness, swallowing what remained of streets and structures.

The Mississippi reclaimed its territory, surging past its banks and drowning busy streets. The Poplar Street deck-girder bridge and MacArthur railroad bridge beyond it lay twisted and partially submerged, their beams bent like paper clips. A massive riverboat lay capsized in the muddy floodwaters, with its smokestacks snapped off and floating downstream. Water lapped at its hull, and several survivors huddled on its listing underside, stranded above the torrent. Around them, other barges, tugboats, fishing vessels, and private cruisers were sunk at their moorings, cables and garbage tangling in the swirling brown water.

The devastation stretched far and wide.

Only the silver Gateway Arch stood, a lone sentinel against the destruction. But even it bore scars. Multiple brilliant stainless-steel panels had peeled away, exposing the cracked concrete underlayer. Beneath it, the museum and concourse had caved in, leaving a gaping wound in the earth.

Tau's gaze swept further—Busch Stadium's rooftop area and the ring of buildings around the field had collapsed, skeletal remains sticking out. City Hall's walls were split open, like something enormous had beaten it to rubble with giant fists.

Not a single tree stood.

Smoke corkscrewed into the sky from multiple fires, black columns twisting upward, marking new disasters burning in the ruins of the old.

The ground had barely stopped shaking.

Walter's exhale was choppy, his hands still gripping the edge of the shredded doorway. "That was an earthquake," he muttered, his voice unsteady.

Tau turned toward him, his dark eyes wide in his powder-dusted face. "Your model was right again," he said, swallowing. "But there were no warning signs. It just… started. Like in Oregon."

Walter's stomach twisted. "You think it's happening again?"

"I don't know." Tau's gaze flicked to the jagged fissures splitting the walls around them, the fragments of ceiling tiles littering the carpet. "We need to check the model." He exhaled sharply. "Thank God you grabbed your laptop."

Walter started to open the top, but Emmet stayed his hand. He swiped at the sweat trickling down his temple, leaving tracks in the dust on his skin. His usual calm was fraying. "Boys, we need to get downstairs. Now. This building isn't stable."

Walter and Tau shared a glance. Both longed to bury themselves in data, but they didn't argue.

Together, they made a fast pass, looking for survivors. There wasn't a lot to check. They slipped through the remains of doorways, sidestepping spears of glass and twisted metal.

The rooms were gutted—walls sheared away, leaving spikey edges framing space. Most of the building's outer shell had peeled off, exposing its insides to the ruined city below. No one answered their calls.

What was left of the structure swayed again, and the floor felt loose beneath their feet—a reminder that this wasn't over.

They reached the only functional stairwell. Two others were gone; the third was impassable, filled from the steps to the ceiling with the shattered floors.

The last one, next to the wrecked elevator shaft, still held. Barely.

Walter looked at Tau. No choice. They slid out their cell phones and tapped on the flashlight apps. The gloom lightened measurably, but it still wasn't bright.

Bracing themselves, they started down.

The stairwell was a treacherous mess—posts twisted, complete sections of stairs and railings missing, darkness swallowing the lower floors. Walter kept one hand on the crumbling wall, fear tight in his chest. Sometimes they climbed down over fractured cement, sometimes they were compelled to jump or free solo, hanging onto broken rebar. It was terrifying. They wound down, listening to the shattered building falling apart and the sound of their footsteps.

Eight steps below the fifth-floor landing, leaning against the wall, a figure stirred. A young man, his ebony skin stark against his dust-coated white uniform, sat hunched on the steps, cradling his arm. His black eyes, wide with pain, locked onto them as they rounded the turn.

"Help me, please." His voice wavered. "I think my shoulder's broken."

Emmet crouched beside him. "What's your name, sir?" he asked, assessing the injury.

"Jabo," the man gritted out. "I'm a waiter here. Just finished delivering room service when the whole damn building dropped."

Tau and Walter positioned their lights as Emmet's hands moved, tracing from Jabo's neck across his shoulder. Jabo flinched, wrinkles creasing on his brow.

"Fracture," Emmet confirmed grimly.

Jabo let out a shaky huff. "I hit the wall when everything started shaking. The steps broke away and took the railing with it. Thought I was going over too."

Tau directed his light down. Below him, the rest of the steps in this section were gone. Their next challenge would be a ten-foot gap between them and the next landing.

Jabo's other hand ran through his dust-matted curls. "What the hell happened? Do you guys know?"

"Earthquake," Tau said.

Jabo's eyes went wide. "I thought it might be a bomb. A terror attack or something. You're saying it hit the whole city?"

"Maybe further." Walter traced what was left of the surrounding stairwell, trying to devise a plan. The floor beneath them shivered once, then stilled. "We need to get out of here. Can you move if we help you?"

Jabo bent his head, coughing. "I'll move. I'm not staying here."

"Hold on," Emmet unbuckled his belt with quick movements, looping it around the tall man's chest, steadying him. "This is going to hurt."

163

Jabo hesitated, then braced himself. Emmet lined up his arm against his body, securing it within the belt. He pulled as tight as he dared. Jabo flinched, sweat beading his high forehead.

"It'll hurt less if your arm is pinned to your body, less moving around," he told the young waiter. Jabo gasped out a thanks, his hands shaking.

In the meantime, Tau scanned the gap, his hands tightening. "It's about ten feet. Walter and I will drop first. Then you lower Jabo... slowly. We'll catch him." His dark eyes touched Emmet. "Once he's down, you come next."

Jabo choked back his fear. He wasn't thrilled to move, but the screeching steel and crumbling walls left no room for debate.

Walter and Tau dangled from the uneven edge, their muscles tensed, then dropped the remaining few feet, landing in a crouch. Dust stirred beneath their boots.

Emmet turned to Jabo. "Alright, boyo. Nice and easy." He gripped the young man's good shoulder, giving a reassuring squeeze.

Jabo exhaled sharply, then swung his legs over the edge. His chest hitched as he gripped the rim with one trembling hand, steadying himself.

"Got you," Emmet said, locking his hands under Jabo's belt.

The moment Jabo felt his weight swing, panic surged, but before he could flail, firm hands gripped his legs from below. Walter and Tau braced, taking his weight, guiding him down. His feet hit solid ground.

He was so relieved he almost collapsed.

Emmet didn't hesitate. He swung over the side, legs kicking to find balance. Walter reached up, caught his boot, and with Tau's help, they hauled him onto the landing.

They were all breathing hard, but there was no time to celebrate.

"Move," Tau ordered, already taking point. Walter covered the rear as Emmet hooked an arm under Jabo's uninjured shoulder.

They descended fast. The air thickened, heavy with dust and the scent of scorched metal. Walls shuddered, sending tremors through the ruined stairwell.

The air grew thicker and heavier as they neared the ground floor. It was getting darker as they descended lower. Dirt swirled in the beam of their lights, making the stairwell look like a place consumed by night.

They reached the main lobby, and Tau's gut clenched. It was worse than he imagined.

The small vestibule before the stairwell and the elevators was swallowed in darkness. Dust hung in the air, clogging his throat and swirling in the weak beam of his phone light. Rubble covered the floor—shattered marble, twisted metal, and ruined furniture. The entire wing, ancillary to the main lobby and reception area, was buried beneath tons of hotel. Every hallway leading out was choked off.

They were trapped.

"Why is it so dark?" Walter asked, sweeping his phone flashlight through the blackness.

Tau exhaled sharply. "I think the sides of the hotel collapsed around us. We're buried in here in the core."

Walter cursed softly. "Can we go back up? Find one of the open sections and climb down?"

Emmet whipped his head in a negative, his gaze jumping upward to the quivering chandeliers. "That's suicide. With every tremor, that crap could shift and crush us." He clapped Jabo lightly on the back. "And with his shoulder busted, it's not even an option."

"Then what?" Walter's voice wavered, frustration edging into fear.

Jabo took a step forward. "Wait." He turned toward the deeper shadows, his cell light catching on something. "Over here."

He led them toward a set of "Staff Only" double doors and shoved at one with his uninjured arm. It squealed but swung open, revealing a dim passageway. A grin broke across his face.

"The kitchen," he said. "I've got a buddy, Edgar Smalls—he's been a cook here for thirty years. If anyone knows a way out, it's him."

Tau didn't hesitate. "Let's move." He ducked through the door, phone light leading the way.

Walter shot Emmet a skeptical look, but followed.

Emmet took one last glance at the trembling ceiling. The chandeliers swayed, glass tinkling like distant wind chimes. Another tremor shook the building, dislodging dust from the rafters.

Not waiting for an invitation, he stepped through the doorway, letting the door swing shut behind him.

They pressed forward, navigating the narrow corridor and making two sharp turns. Then, suddenly, they burst into an open space—stainless steel counters, industrial ovens, a maze of overturned carts, and scattered cookware.

The hotel kitchen.

Two figures, a man and a woman unconscious or too weak to move, sprawled on the cold tile, their black and white uniforms stained with blood. Make-do bandages—ripped table linens, maybe—were tied hastily around wounds.

A snowy-haired black man, dressed in cook's whites, knelt between them. Clutched awkwardly under his arm was a powerful flashlight. He pressed a bloodstained towel against the man's leg. At the sound of the door banging open, he spun around, shoulders tense. His eyes grew wide when he saw the four men, disheveled, covered in powder and bits of rubble.

"Jabo! You're alive!" Relief flashed across his face, then his sharp eyes zeroed in on the awkward angle of Jabo's arm. His brow furrowed. "What'd you do, break your arm?"

"Broke my shoulder, I think," Jabo downplaying it. "Edgar, these people helped me get down here. We need to get out—the lobby's crushed, and the halls are blocked. You got any ideas?"

Edgar released a sigh, glancing at the injured on the floor. "I sent the kitchen crew, waitstaff, and a few guests out about an hour ago. Anyone who could walk, I told 'em to go. I stayed with Eric and Cindy. Eric's ankle is busted—big gash too, but I wrapped it. Cindy got knocked out and still hasn't come around. Bleeding's stopped, but…" He rubbed the wrinkles around his chin. "I figured someone would send help, but if you're here instead of a rescue crew…" He let the sentence die.

Jabo's expression tightened. "It's bad out there, isn't it?"

"We need to move them," Emmet said, scanning the trembling ceiling. "What's left of this place isn't gonna hold."

Eric groaned, attempting to sit up. "I can walk."

167

Edgar hesitated. "I don't know, man. Moving them without medics could make things worse."

"If this building collapses, there won't be any medics," Emmet countered.

Edgar ran a hand over his face, stress lining his features.

"Emmet's right," Tau said grimly. "It's chaos out there. If we don't get out on our own, we don't get out at all."

Edgar blew out a shallow snort, then assented. "Alright. You help me with Eric and Cindy, and I'll get you out of here."

Tau adjusted his grip on his phone. "How?"

Edgar jerked his thumb toward a narrow door at the back of the kitchen. "We need to get down to the basement. Past the dry storage, there is an old service exit. They sealed it off twenty years ago—it leads into one of the tunnels that runs under this city."

"Tunnels?" Walter frowned.

"Yeah. Back in the day, you could take the service door, head up a staircase, and come out inside the old Seward House—still on the property."

Jabo's brows shot up. "You mean the Underground Railroad house?"

"That's the one. Developers wanted it gone, but the city wouldn't budge. So, they built the hotel right up against it and turned it into a small museum. St. Louis ambiance, y'know."

Emmet took a step forward. "Then what are we waiting for? Let's move."

Edgar held up a hand. "Not that simple. When I took those folks through this morning, we hit a problem." He blew out a puff, rubbing the white bristles on his cheek. "Some of the hotel collapsed on the Seward House. Crushed it flat. The trapdoor to the surface is buried."

"Well, that just sucks," Walter exclaimed, his voice louder this time.

"The tunnel's still open, far as I know," Edgar continued. "I sent them northwest. A bunch of blocks further, there's another exit—a ladder leading up to the Brevis Museum of Black History. Another Underground Railroad stop. The family turned it into a museum for a tax write-off, but hopefully, it still stands. If the tunnel held, they should've gotten out there."

"We don't have a choice," Walter said, weighing Cindy's limp form in his head. "She's small—I'll carry her. Tau, Emmet, you help Eric." He clutched his laptop for a minute, then shoved it toward Edgar. "This has critical data. Keep it safe."

Edgar accepted the notebook, then opened a closet and dug out a battered brown knapsack. He stuffed the PC inside, then yanked out a handful of flashlights and passed them around.

Tau pocketed his nearly dead phone in his pants, relieved for a fresh beam of light.

Then the floor trembled. A deep, vibrating shudder rolled through the building, followed by a deafening crash when something collapsed somewhere above.

"Move!" Emmet barked.

Edgar spun and, for a man of his age, crossed the space fast, jerking open the basement door and heading down. Walter hefted Cindy onto his shoulder, careful of her head, while Tau and Emmet hauled Eric between them.

169

Jabo took up the rear, pain streaking across his side. Nobody stopped to shut the door behind them.

Minutes after they left, the kitchen ceiling buckled. Dust exploded into the air.

The building was coming down.

Cairo, IL: Saturday, August 16, 12 p.m.

A rogue current had them now. Reed knew there was no fighting it, no steering. The barge creaked, popped, and pinged as it was hauled inland, helpless in the overflow of the swollen, angry Mississippi. Its bow was crumpled on one side, a deep dent punching inward like a giant had taken a swing. Somewhere during the quake, it must've struck something, perhaps a bridge pier or a jut of rock. Or it resulted from demolishing Boxco.

Still, it floated.

The deck rolled under their feet with each wave, sluggish and heavy. Ravaged objects and tangled vegetation scraped along the hull, stressing metal against wood and plastic. Each collision reverberated through the hold, reminding them that the barge could only take so much.

The air was thick with the stench of chemicals—sharp, acrid fumes seeping from ruptured tanks upstream. It mingled with the rank smell of mud and river rot, the sour bite of decay, and something more industrial. They passed through clouds of the stuff resting on the surface, forcing Reed and Chloe to cover their noses with the crooks of their arms, eyes stinging. Watson growled, hiding his head in Chloe's lap when it got too bad.

It had only been a short while since they escaped onto the barge. After checking from one end to the other, a frustrated Reed conceded they were the only people onboard.

"I looked for help, but there's no one here. This barge is a ghost vessel." He frowned, working out their next move as he studied the doors on the last cargo container. "These barges are typically used for transporting dry cargo. They move goods like harvested corn and soybeans down the river."

"Anything edible?" she asked wistfully. Watson woofed beside her, ears perked at hearing food mentioned.

"I don't think so, but I bet they have some tools stored somewhere." Walking around the corner of the last steel box at the back end, he yanked open a busted toolbox bolted to the deck, tossing rusted chains and frayed rope aside. "We need to find something to pry these containers open."

Chloe paced the width of a steel box, Watson trailing behind her. She watched the phone in her hand like it might suddenly work if she stared long enough. "Still nothing," she said, jamming it back into the pocket of her jeans. "The kids... They've got to be so scared."

Reed didn't offer false comfort. The silence between them said enough—if the New Madrid fault was tearing apart the land, the house, the children, everything was at risk. The irony amazed him. Not quite recovered from the most devastating earthquake in history, they were now amidst another massive disaster.

The barge grumbled beneath them, its warped deck sloshing with puddles of oily water. Holding rusted bolt cutters, Reed leaned over the edge as far as he dared, squinting past the tangled trees and floating scrap. "The land past Boxco is part of the Boatwright Wildlife Area. The Kentucky

Department of Fish and Wildlife Resources owns and manages this area. It's nothing but water and woods out here. I don't think there's anything or anyone around. Hard to tell how far we've drifted in."

Chloe joined him, careful to stay a few steps back, her arms crossed tight. "Too bad we didn't drift across the Ohio River and land in Cairo. We might've been halfway home by now."

Reed shrugged. "Cairo's a bowl—low ground. Those levees were the only thing holding the rivers back. If they gave way…" He trailed off.

Her eyes brushed his face. "Your dad's place—it's protected by levees, too. If they broke…"

"I know." His voice was flat. Then he snapped a crowbar free from a chipped case. "We can't guess from here. We need solid ground under us."

He strode toward the nearest container, the crowbar in one hand and bolt cutters in the other. Chloe followed, eyes scanning the murky horizon. The sky to the west looked darker. She wondered if it was earthquake dust or if clouds were gathering. Another storm was the last thing they needed.

Then the first big aftershock hit—sudden, ferocious, a gut-strike from beneath the river. The barge heaved sideways. Sickening *cracks* rang out as heavy lashing rods and turnbuckles snapped, metal whips slicing through the air. A deep *clunk* rolled through the vessel, followed by a screech like nails across a blackboard—but amplified a thousand times by rust and rivets.

Reed's heart jumped to his throat. He ran toward the lashings, checking the damage, his boots thudding over the vibrating steel. Another strap was fraying, and one container sat tilted at an angle at which it had no business leaning.

Then a second strong aftershock rolled through, worse than the first. The barge lurched like it had hit a wall. More high-pitched pops as straps vibrated and snapped. Reed dropped to one knee, arms braced to stay upright, eyes darting from one container to the next. The closest containers hadn't busted loose. Yet.

But it was close. The water settled uneasily around them.

Chloe crouched beside Watson, one hand on his thick ruff, the other trembling slightly. "How deep do you think it is?"

Reed didn't answer right away. He glanced back at the trees—half-submerged, their trunks vanishing beneath the murky flood. "Deep enough," he said at last, forehead creased. "This barge rides five or six feet tall without cargo. Add another five for the weight of the cargo containers. That water's got to be fifteen to twenty feet, at least."

Chloe's eyes widened.

"And that's not even the real danger." Reed's voice dropped. "Think about what's in there—fuel leaks, busted septic lines, animals drowned by the quake… this is a toxic soup. We swim in that, we don't make it far."

Watson barked. His ears shot up, hackles rising as he leaned over the edge, growling low and deep. Fragments floated past—warped lumber, shattered plastic, a child's shoe.

Reed stepped beside him, staring at the dark current—a knot twisted in his gut.

Chloe stood quickly and joined him. "What is it?"

"We're not drifting with the current anymore." Reed pointed. "See that sycamore? That big one - top's still ten feet out of the water? We aren't passing it."

Chloe blinked, watching. "We're stuck?"

"Yeah," Reed released a heavy sigh. "We hit something solid. Could be a hilltop or a rockpile. Whatever it is, we're lodged on it."

Chloe spun slowly, taking in their flooded prison. "So now we're stranded, surrounded by water. Again."

Reed turned toward the nearest container. "Then it's back to the plan. Let's get one of these open. See what's inside."

Chloe wiped her hands on her jeans, her frame set. "Fine. Let's crack one."

Reed hammered the crowbar into the rusted lock of the nearest container. Metal shrieked. She handed him the bolt cutters, and several long minutes later, he lifted the latches on the door handles, pulled the handle up, and rotated the lock rods out of their brackets. He pulled hard, and the door swung open.

Disappointed, they both stared at the wall of pallets, their contents stacked to the ceiling and filling every inch of the container.

"What is it?" Chloe asked?

"Looks like grains of some type. Let's check another one."

They opened the next five containers. Reed had the feel of it now, and they hurried down the line. Each container was packed tightly with more grain, liquid bulk barrels, limestone, and other aggregates, but nothing of use to save themselves.

Chloe whooshed out a hiss, hands on her knees, as Reed swung the sixth door open. Quick glances at the river confirmed that the amount of junk passing them was increasing. There was so much stuff that entire cities must have been affected by the quake. Unrecognizable lumps swept in by the current thudded against the barge, the sound hollow and weird over the surface. But it was the recognizable flotsam that broke her heart. She looked away.

"We need to move faster," she said, voice tight. "I don't trust this thing to hold together during those aftershocks."

Reed ducked into the container, boots thudding on the metal floor. It wasn't jammed like the others—room to move, pallets spaced with purpose. He weaved between them, his eyes scanning labels and peeling back plastic.

"Roofing gear," he muttered, mostly to himself. "This wasn't random. This was prepped for a job site."

Behind him, Chloe stepped inside, her silhouette framed in the open doorway. Watson stayed behind, stationed like a sentry, eyes on the shifting river.

Reed's voice echoed against the steel walls. "Tar paper, vinyl rolls... two-by-fours stacked in the back." He disappeared around a pallet, then reappeared, holding a square of bright blue foam. "Styrofoam sheets—three inches thick. A dozen of them. Glue buckets. Boxes of spray foam—pressurized, ready to go."

Chloe's brow furrowed. "Okay, but... how does that help us?"

Reed turned, eyes lit with a spark she hadn't seen since the quake hit. "We make a raft. Plug these foam sheets underneath a pallet base—seal it with spray foam. We'll keep it light, wide, and stable. Float our way off this barge."

"And steer how?"

"We'll figure it out—use boards or pipe, anything flat. Once we hit solid ground, we can start moving again. Find the house and the kids."

Chloe glanced up out the door. Clouds covered the sky, and a brown fog had rolled in, wrapping itself around them. It was eerie. "There's more light outside, but let's build it in here," she said. "Out of the wind."

Reed agreed, already moving. He plucked a pry bar from the wall, unloaded a pallet of boxes, and hauled it towards the front. Together, they cleared a space to work.

Using the crowbar, Reed struck the edge of the pallet and leaned his weight into it. With a sharp *crack*, the slats gave way, nails screeching as they tore free. Chloe was already stacking the blue Styrofoam sheets in a clean spot near the center, each nearly weightless but thick and rigid.

"Start laying them flat," Reed said, exhaling loudly. "We'll glue them in rows."

She cracked open a five-gallon bucket of adhesive with a screwdriver, the thick chemical scent curling into the air. The glue oozed like molasses as she slathered it across the wood surface using a flattened packaging strip. "This stuff's nasty," she muttered, wiping her hand on her jeans.

"Good," Reed said. "Means it'll hold."

Outside, the wind kicked up, spitting through the gap in the container doors. Watson barked once, pacing, agitated.

Reed grabbed one of the foam sheets, slapped it into the glue, and pressed it down. "Get the spray foam," he called. Chloe grabbed a can, shaking it, and tested the nozzle—thick yellow foam hissed out with a sharp *chfftt*, expanding fast along the edges.

"Seal every seam," Reed said, wiping sweat from his forehead. "We need this thing watertight."

They moved fast, snapping together a second layer and then a third. Reed found a roll of industrial shrink wrap and wound it tightly around the outside. Then he wrenched a couple more boards from the pallet and formed a brace along one edge.

"Grab that metal conduit pipe," he said, pointing. "We'll lash it to this. Give us a way to push or steer."

Chloe hauled the pipe over, and they tied it down with nylon strapping, pulling it taut. Waiting for Reed, she glanced out at the river.

It churned slowly, bloated, clogged with splintered wood, twisted metal, and half-submerged wreckage that spun like forgotten relics. A ghostly mist slithered over the water, curling around the debris like fingers claiming the dead. The barge floated in a pocket of silence so deep it pressed against her ears—no birds, no breeze, not even the creak of metal.

The cold slithered up her spine, unshakable.

It didn't feel like a river anymore. It felt like a drowned graveyard, filled with ghouls and terrible things.

Chapter Eleven
Atlanta, GA: Saturday, August 15, 1 p.m.

Miguel Santiago hadn't been invited to the meeting with the President. But that didn't matter. He knew what was at stake as the USGS Director of West Coast Dynamics.

The 737-9 MAX hit the runway in Atlanta hard, brakes screaming, fuel tanks nearly empty. As soon as the wheels screeched to a stop, Miguel was already unbuckled, phone in hand, fingers flying across the screen. There was no time to wait—not when the Midwest was tearing itself apart.

Within minutes, laptop up in some little shoebox of an office at Hartsfield-Jackson, he was patched into the secure video feed—courtesy of Deputy Director David Vancris, who was also in the meeting. Vancris had learned enough about the model to value its input, and more importantly, he trusted Miguel and his men still on the ground in Missouri.

The briefing room on screen was a war zone of tension: President Avery Wallace sat at the head of the long table, lips pressed into a grim line. FEMA Administrator Nancy Arnold carried a tablet in her hand, but her eyes were distant, as if she were still processing the numbers.

Across from her, Chairman Willard Q. Brown of the Joint Chiefs sat in stony silence, flanked by brass and Homeland Security. It had only been three months since the disaster on the West Coast, but the man looked to have aged years.

David didn't waste time.

"The Midwest quake—it's not just bad. It's catastrophic," he said, activating a live feed of seismic overlays. "Chicago's taken a beating. But the worst is further south. From St. Louis down to Memphis, Tennessee… we're seeing devastation across five states. Fissures. Sinkholes. Whole towns gone."

Nancy spoke up, "We've confirmed widespread land displacement. Raised ridges, sudden sinkholes, massive sand blows. Parts of the Ohio Valley are virtually unrecognizable."

"St. Francis River is gone," David added, flipping through fresh satellite captures. "One of the lakes formed there—its water was displaced by sand. It's like the land turned inside out. Fish are dead on the lakebed. The whole ecosystem... inverted."

President Wallace leaned forward, eyes locked on the screen. "And casualties?"

Nancy answered, voice low. "We're estimating in the millions. No reliable count yet. Chicago's on fire. Memphis is underwater. Major earthquakes, including the New Madrid Seismic Zone, have devastated the central Mississippi Valley. Riverbanks collapsed, and islands are gone. Tremors were felt as far as Boston. Entire regions are in darkness, and it's the middle of the day."

David acknowledged grimly. "A sulfurous smell was reported across several epicentral zones. Locals described a roaring noise, like a thousand freight trains. In some areas, the uplift is over three meters. Roads are gone, and vehicles can't cross some of the larger fissures. People are falling in."

Chairman Brown finally spoke. "We're deploying Task Force Bravo, redirecting National Guard units from Florida and Texas. But it will take days to stabilize anything—highways are destroyed, rivers have shifted. There's evidence of new channels forming off the Mississippi. Whole towns were washed away when the river reversed course for an hour."

David flipped to one last screen—satellite topography warped with red fault lines. "We think the Rome Through Fault System and the Cambridge Cross-Strike are currently active. This isn't just the New Madrid Seismic Zone waking up. It's a full-system failure. A cascading continental event. Like the West Coast quake in May—but spreading inland."

Heavy silence followed.

Then the President broke it. "We've declared a national emergency. FEMA's mobilized. We need to secure fuel and food corridors. And get eyes on every damn river between here and Denver."

On the screen, Deputy Director David Vancris leaned into the camera, his face pale and tight. The chatter in the war room flickered, quieting as he raised a single hand.

"There's more," he said, voice like ice chips. "When the mega-quakes struck the West Coast in May, something unexpected happened—one of our men was tracking an experimental seismic model. One he hadn't wanted to test in public."

Brows furrowed around the table. A ripple of murmurs spread through the room, skepticism visible in narrowed eyes and sideways glances. Vancris raised both hands now.

"I know what you're thinking. But listen to me—it *predicted* everything. Fault lines, sequence, and volcanoes. All of it. Then... silence. Flatline. No activity. For weeks."

He paused, then leaned closer.

"A week ago, the model came back online. Started lighting up again. But this time, the alerts were clustered in the Midwest."

An icy wave moved through the room. On the screen, Vancris hesitated only for a beat before adding, "If this model holds—like it did in May—we haven't seen the last quake."

He turned his head. "Miguel?"

Miguel Santiago looked up. He stared into the camera, his pulse thudding in his ears. He spoke quietly but firmly.

"There was supposed to be a symposium today in St. Louis. A discussion about aftershock patterns and energy displacement on the West Coast. My team was right there. Dead center."

His breath stuttered.

"I haven't reached them since the first shockwave hit. But before dawn, we had one last video call. They were spooked. The data was surging. Unstable. We ran it through the Reston servers... and what they found scared the hell out of us."

The image behind Miguel changed—data visuals rippling across the screen: jagged graphs, deep red epicenters, numbers no one wanted to see.

"This morning's quake? Preliminary magnitude 8.6. Multiple secondary faults triggered at 8.0 or higher. Catastrophic damage zone stretches across five states."

Miguel looked directly at President Wallace.

"But that's not the end. According to the model... a magnitude 9, possibly 9.5 is still to come."

Sputters hit the room like small explosions. One aide dropped his pen. A general swore.

"That's over thirty-two times more energy than this morning's quake," Miguel continued. "A rupture of that magnitude in the New Madrid Seismic Zone will do far more than flatten cities. It'll rewrite the map.

The President sat frozen, knuckles taut as she clenched the armrests of her chair. "When?" she asked.

Miguel waved his hands nervously. "We don't know. Hours. Days. But the model's accelerating. And if we're right..." He let the sentence hang there like a funeral bell.

Vancris stepped in again. "Madam President, this isn't just disaster response anymore. This is continental survival. We've entered a new era. The aftershocks of this will echo for generations."

No one said a word.

The screen changed again. New data. More red.

And somewhere under the silence, the Earth was still moving.

Mississippi River, KY: Saturday, August 15, 1 p.m.

From Matthias's perspective, the *Magnolia Lady* was no longer drifting—it was charging, her cracked calliope whistle screeching louder than the river's roar. Metal shrieked against the current. Cries echoed from her deck. The flood had turned her into a juggernaut, and now she was bearing down on Matthias and the wave runner.

A blink, a breath—and she was on him.

The river shuddering beneath her momentum, the ferry grew enormous in an instant. As the port-side shadow swallowed him whole, Matthias snapped out of his trance. His hand shot to the right lever. The idling engine screamed as he twisted it, jetting the small watercraft forward. The nose dipped, skipping the current.

For a split second, it looked like he might not make it.

Then he veered hard left toward Cort Evans Island, and the world blurred.

He blasted beneath the bow railings of the *Magnolia Lady*, water spraying up like a curtain as she surged over him. The belly of the ferry passed so close he heard steel flex and passengers yelling. Daring to look up, he saw people slumped on the decks and others clutching the rails, hanging on in terror. Still others ran around frantically.

The kids shouted at him from the *Seismic Wave*, ducking as the ferry's surge flung water over them. They couldn't see Matthias—only the wall of the ferry roaring past like a steel tsunami. One moment, they gawked at the hull, watching faces flash by like ghosts. The next, it was gone, racing downriver toward the huge debris dam like an iron battering ram.

Brett shuddered, clutching the gunwale, scanning the wake behind her.

"Matthias…" he whispered. He couldn't see the watercraft or his brother.

Piper sobbed beside him. The dogs were barking madly while Winnie's voice sliced through the noise, screaming from the stern. She had one arm around Charlie, the other raised, as if calling Matthias back. Pedro hung onto Jamie, his eyes huge.

The Magnolia Lady hit the dam like a warhead.

The first impact was a bone-rattling crunch, metal shearing against splintered tree trunks, crushed boats, and the twisted remains of bridges and buildings caught in the flood. Then the port side of the massive ferry slammed into the dam, not head-on but at an angle, scooping wreckage as it went. Steel split. Trees exploded. The battered hull dragged house parts, flipped cars, broken barges—anything caught in the flood—into a nightmarish heap.

The barrier shattered.

Logs snapped like toothpicks. A shipping trailer burst like a kicked can, its contents erupting into the heavens: crates, insulation, plastic—shrapnel in the storm. A semi-trailer embedded in the wreckage burst open, sending crates and torn plastic sailing skyward. One of the ferry's smokestacks cracked loose and fell, slamming into the river in a geyser of foam and spray that briefly engulfed the deck.

The impact wrenched the vessel, lifting the stern from the water and exposing its rusted underbelly before slamming it back down again. Screams rose, muffled by the steel crashing. The windows that were left blew out. Sections of railing tore free and vanished into the churning foam.

The river surged, pouring into the ruptured hull. The *Magnolia Lady* ground deeper into the wreckage, ripping the dam apart as it passed.

Everything—trees, steel, concrete, corpses—was towed in her wake. The ferry broke through, splitting the barricade wide, shoving tons of waste into the open channel. The river boiled where the dam had stood moments ago, frothing with wreckage and timbers.

Then the current took hold.

The ship, ruins, and bodies were swept downriver. They whipped around the bend and disappeared.

Where the remains of civilization had once been blocked and dammed, the flow now thundered south, faster, deeper, unchained.

Brett stood stunned, lips parted. The gunwale still gripped tight, like it might anchor him in reality. His chest ached. There were no words.

Then—a sound. At first, faint, almost lost in the roar of water and wind.

BzzzzzzRAAAAAAAAWWWWW—

A scream of machinery, climbing fast. A pitch only one thing made.

"Do you hear that?" Piper jerked upright, turning toward the noise, eyes wide. "Is that—?"

A red blur broke from the curtain of mist across the river, a spray trail cutting the water like a blade—the wave runner.

Matthias.

He was standing, hunched forward over the handlebars, every muscle locked in as the craft tore across the choppy current. Water kicked high behind him, catching the light as he weaved around floating garbage, accelerating even more.

"IT'S HIM!" Piper screamed, stumbling to her feet.

Brett staggered to the rail, shouting, "MATTHIAS!"

Coco and Duke barked wildly, tails thrashing, and Bella jumped, nearly falling overboard in her excitement. Charlie let out a high-pitched squeal of joy, his excitement compounded by the rapid beating of Winnie's heart.

The wave runner sped closer, bucking over a submerged tree limb before spinning hard with a slap of water. Matthias swerved, cutting a tight arc and bringing the craft alongside the *Seismic Wave*, the engine sputtering as he let it idle.

His face was soaked, his glasses covered in spray, and his hair slicked to his forehead, but his grin was unmistakable.

"Miss me?" he called, voice cracking with adrenaline.

Brett didn't hesitate—he hauled him onto the deck in a wet, sputtering heap, pounded his shoulder, and wrapped him in a crushing hug. Jamie tied off the watercraft; his face split into a big smile.

"I thought you were dead, you lunatic!"

Matthias wheezed out a laugh. "Almost was. But now I can claim to be the King of Wreckage River!"

Everyone laughed, even Jamie and Pedro, though they didn't understand the analogy.

"Legos," Matthias told them, laughing at the confusion on their faces. "My brother is the King of Wreckage Road, from when we escaped Albany. But I claim King of Wreckage River."

"It's yours," Piper said, hugging him hard again.

"That ferryboat was massive!" Matthias said in disbelief. "Did you see all those people trapped on it?"

"It must have been damaged in the earthquake," Brett said. He didn't say anymore, not wanting to scare the others. But the ferryboat changed things. Piper caught his eye and signaled her understanding. This quake must have stretched pretty far north, possibly to St. Louis. That's where the ferry boats started from, if he remembered right. He thought about Reed and Chloe, then Royce and Albert. They needed to get back to Harrowood and check on everyone.

He stared at the water. As he watched, he realized the river was morphing, fuller and faster.

Swells rolled past the *Seismic Wave*, deep and loaded with scrap—roof shingles, twisted metal, pieces of trees, and entire chunks of homes. Downstream, the dam was gone. The current was no longer held back.

And it was rising. Fast.

The sandbar they were stranded on had shrunk to half its size. Some bigger swells slapped the hull, sending cold spray over the deck. The *Wave* rocked a little, catching everyone off guard. The excitement died down.

"What now?" Matthias asked, still breathless and vibrating with adrenaline.

Pedro's voice cracked. "Can we go home?" His eyes scanned the endless water. "I need to check on my mom."

"Yeah. Me too," Jamie added, clutching the edge of a rail. "Our families need us. My dad's gonna need help with the farm for sure."

Brett didn't answer right away. Instead, he grabbed the rope from the handlebars of the water scooter and guided it carefully around the sandbar and alongside the boat's port side, looping it to a cleat. He wanted to get it clear of the junk in the water.

"Everyone won't fit," he finally said. "But the wave runner is strong enough to tow us."

Matthias and Jamie crouched beside him, inspecting the engine and fuel tank. The watercraft purred at idle, steady—for now.

"It's got gas," Matthias affirmed. "But it's not full. Let's see how much is left."

They worked quickly, checking gas levels and damage, tightening the towline, and looping it double. Behind them, Bella paced the deck, tail stiff, nose twitching at the passing flood. She put her paws on the side and leaned over, ears back, growling low.

"Bella—no. We're not chasing cats today." Piper hauled her away, but the dog slipped free and tried again, anxious. Coco and Duke watched her. Piper worried they'd take off given the chance. She knew they didn't like the boat.

Pedro sat beside Winnie at the stern, his fingers brushing Charlie's big ears as the little dog sat in her lap.

"What's his name?" he asked, eyes still darting toward the water.

"Charlie," Winnie said with a big smile. "He's brave and everything. Doesn't bark unless it matters."

Pedro scratched behind Charlie's ear, watching it twitch. "I like his ears. I bet he hears everything before we do."

"You can bet that's true," she exclaimed. "There's this one time…"

Pedro leaned against the marine upholstery, grinning, as Winnie stood, cradling Charlie on her shoulder. She recounted how he once stole a taco off the kitchen table and then barked at the ceiling for hours, as if it had betrayed him to the others. Both kids laughed out loud.

Piper crouched near Bella, putting both hands around the big dog's collar. Bella's eyes were locked on the muddy shore, tail twitching. Piper whispered reassurances, but her grip stayed firm. One cat and the dog launched like a torpedo.

She watched the older boys huddled at the PWC, testing tension on the tow rope, tapping the gas tank, and arguing over how much fuel was enough to risk a pull.

No one looked upriver. No one saw it coming. Then it appeared.

A peaked barn roof broke around the bend, silent and monstrous. Like a drifting iceberg, it slid through the channel, barely breaching the surface. Beneath the waterline, the rest of the structure—walls, beams, insulation—dragged it low, making the entire thing list to one side. The tallest gable dipped like a scythe as the current shoved it forward.

The first hint was a ripple—a deep swell that splashed over the sandbar, rocking the *Seismic Wave* oddly sideways. Different from the rest of the rubbish in the river. This piece had weight.

It was huge.

It bore down on them, the only warning was the wake that rushed ahead of it.

Winnie stood on the seat cushion now, holding Charlie out so a smiling Pedro could rub his black ears, unaware of the shadow trolling toward them.

The ridge clipped the hull with a sudden blow. The gabled peak banged along the starboard side, tipping the *Seismic Wave* at a sickening angle toward the roof.

Winnie shrieked as her feet flew out from under her. Charlie soared out of her arms mid-fall, legs pinwheeling, flying over her head.

"Winnie!" Pedro lunged, barely grabbing the front of her shirt as she pitched toward the gunwale. His feet skidded on the wet fiberglass deck, but he held on, yanking her back from the edge just as a jagged rafter raked across the boat's side, splintering on impact.

But Charlie—the little Borgi spun through the air like a kicked football, ears flapping, yelping once before he landed with a soft thump on the drifting rooftop.

"Charlie!" Winnie screamed.

The boat wobbled, nearly rolling off as the wake from the collision shoved it half off the sandbar. Water sloshed over the deck.

Brett and Matthias grabbed the gunwales to steady themselves. Jamie hit the deck, tangling with Bella and Piper as they were soaked in dirty water. Coco barked angrily as he slid hard against the wall, and Duke howled mournfully, paws back over his nose.

"Hold on!" someone shouted.

Then the roof broke free.

Still tilted and massive, the barn top slid off the side of the boat and back into the main channel, carried by the river's unleashed frenzy. Charlie scrambled upright, claws slipping on wet shingles. He barked as if confused about being separated from the others, and then the current towed the floating raft past the boat and down the bend.

"Charlie!" Winnie's voice cracked, high and panicked. She struggled to her feet, but Pedro held her tight.

"It's too fast," he said, puffing, wide-eyed.

They watched, helpless, as the slanted hulk drifted into the bend, caught the speeding current, and vanished downstream. Charlie was still aboard, a tiny figure perched on a runaway ruin.

Harrowood, KY: Saturday, August 15, 1 p.m.

Albert and Stella climbed in silence, his boots scraping against stone, her paws padding lightly. The narrow tunnel sloped upward with each step. His cell light flickered across rough rock walls and rubble scattered along the path.

After what felt like ten minutes, the passage abruptly widened. The beam from Albert's phone spilled into a chamber—square, about ten by ten, with a ceiling high enough for him to stand.

He slowed, eyes locking on the far wall. Unlike the rest of the cavern, this was no accident of nature. Stones had been stacked by hand, uneven and ancient, perhaps sealed once but now exposed by a jagged gap scarcely big enough to crawl through.

"Look at this…" Albert murmured, rejuvenated by the discovery.

A faint glow filtered through the hole. Daylight.

Ignoring the rusted tools and crates piled to either side, he dropped to his knees on the rim, pressing forward. Cool stone scraped his palms as he leaned through the gap.

A well.

He blinked, stunned.

Above him, weathered wooden beams arched into a ruined roof; the slate was long worn, and shafts of gray light pierced through. Moss clung to the inside walls. Below him, dark water shimmered a foot or two down, black and still.

191

"We're at the bottom of a well," he called back, voice echoing against the stone. "I think we're close to the surface."

Behind him, Stella woofed an answer. Her nose twitched as she sniffed the dusty air, her shaggy mop of fur bouncing with each wary step. She padded away from Albert, curiosity drawing her toward a forgotten pile of crates and rusted tools. Her tail froze mid-wag, and she let out a low whine.

Albert turned at the sound. "What is it, girl?"

He followed the Schnoodle to where she stood, ears low, nose pressed to a splintered wooden box. Beside the crate sat a figure slumped against the wall, skeletal hands curled over a rotted canvas satchel. Kneeling next to the case, Albert brushed aside the cobwebs and pried open the lid. The sharp scent of old alcohol hit him like a punch—moonshine. Dusty glass bottles clinked softly inside. Counting, he found at least a dozen cartons.

The man had died sitting upright, back against the stones, one leg twisted at an unnatural angle. A fractured hip? Scattered bottles surrounded him, several of which were cracked and empty. The stench of age clung to the air.

Albert frowned. "Guess you couldn't make it out."

The bag disintegrated at his touch, fabric crumbling like dry leaves. But inside—still protected—gold glinted in the beam of his flashlight. Coins. Dozens of them. Nestled beside a brittle, water-damaged journal with frayed edges and ink faded by time.

Albert gently flipped it open. Scrawled handwriting and dated entries. The last page was stained, and the words were shaky and final.

"Been down here a long time," he murmured. "Since Prohibition, probably. Damn."

He bowed his head briefly, then tucked the coins and book into his coat. "Thanks for the history lesson, old-timer. Hope you're at peace now."

Stella circled back, tail wagging as if sensing his mood.

"Okay, girl. Let's get out of here."

He turned toward the hole in the stone wall. Warily, not wanting to slip, he stepped through, easing into the water. It reached his knees. Looking up, he saw horizontal iron bars hammered into the well's side—old, but still solid. One by one, he tested the ones he could reach and then said a little prayer that the rest would hold.

Unzipping his coat most of the way, he reached back into the hole and lifted Stella into his arms, sliding her inside. Her front legs hung over his shoulders, and her back legs snugged against his stomach as he adjusted her rump. Her warm body pressed close as he pulled the zipper higher, holding her tight. She was heavy, but he wasn't leaving her behind.

With one hand gripping the cold metal, he climbed, boots searching for footholds. Water dripped around them, and the air grew cooler. Above, pale daylight flickered through missing roof slats like distant stars.

Albert scaled the side, each rung of the iron ladder biting into his palms. Light-headed, with short, burning gasps bursting from his trembling lips, he had sweat mixing with dust and grit on his face before he got far. Stella squirmed slightly in the front of his jacket, her body a comforting weight—but a weight, nonetheless.

Halfway up, his arms trembled. He wedged his shoulder against the wall, chest heaving, forehead pressed to the cold stone. Stella whimpered, encouraging him. His legs quivered. One more minute.

Then—something.

He paused.

Voices.

Distant, scattered on the wind. Not echoes, not tricks of the underground—real voices. A woman calling. A kid answering. Footsteps on gravel.

Albert's heart kicked hard in his chest.

They hadn't left.

He tipped his head toward the shaft above and shouted with everything he had left. "HEY! DOWN HERE! HELP!"

His voice scraped raw, echoing the well and vanishing into light.

"ROYCE!" he screamed again, clutching Stella tighter with one arm, the other wrapped around the iron bar like a lifeline. "WE'RE ALIVE!"

He kept shouting, his voice cracking, hoping, begging for someone to answer. For someone to hear.

***

Royce leaned as far over the edge of the fissure as he dared, arms stretched, boots skidding on loose grit. Big Mike Evans, one of his best friends and owner of the now destroyed diner, had a death grip on his belt, anchoring him to solid ground. But it didn't matter how far Royce reached—only blackness was below. No movement. No sound. Albert and Stella were gone.

Despair choked him. He drew back unsteadily, fists clenched, eyes burning. For over thirty minutes, they had tried to find some way down the sides of the chasm, but the steep, crumbling sides allowed no purchase. The air reeked of shattered stone and ozone, and somewhere deep in the earth, something shifted—as if the tearing of the earth was getting worse.

He staggered back, lungs burning as he dragged in a cough thick with dust. He swayed, caught his balance, and locked his eyes on the town—what was left of it. The bus waited behind the diner. Beside it, Big Mike's pickup stood, paint dusted gray from the quake.

The rest of the vehicles were gone. Parked on the street, they were lost somewhere at the bottom of the rift gaping across Main Street, black, deep, and final.

Mike's face was carved with soot and tension. He gripped Royce's arm, voice low. "I'm sorry, Royce. I think we lost them."

Royce didn't answer at first. He stared past Mike, into that pitted wound in the earth, his hands curling. "That rift… It's eating the town." He tipped his head, snapping himself out of the shock. "We've got to move."

"Yeah," Mike said, stepping back, scanning the scruffy group near the diner. "We can't help the ones down there. But we've got these folks. How do you want to run it?"

Royce's throat was raw, voice cracked. "I left the kids at my place. I've got to get to them." He forced the words out. "You need to get any survivors you can find to Union City."

Mike didn't hesitate. "Take my truck."

Royce accepted with thanks, already on the move. Mike stepped beside him, laying out the plan as they went. "We'll swing by the Milligans. Get the rest of them if they want to go. Then I'll head up 125, stop along the way, and see who needs help. Joe Hocker needs a doctor bad."

Dust swirled around them as they clasped hands, firm and fast—no time for goodbyes.

Dark clouds massed on the western horizon, thick and threatening a storm. Thunder rolled in the distance, a slow-building growl chasing them east. Great. Just what they needed.

He scrubbed a hand down his face, wiping away sweat, dust, and grief.

Seventeen people and two dogs had been in town when the earth buckled beneath them. Now, only sixteen souls, one dog, and a widening canyon right through the middle of town.

He didn't look back at the rift.

Raising his voice and barking orders, he pointed people toward the faded yellow school bus parked crookedly in the dirt lot, its windshield dirty. "Go! Load up! Let's move!"

Dave Hocker carried his brother Joe over his shoulder, the splinted leg dragging as they staggered out of the crumbling diner. Joe winced with every step, but he didn't complain. Sally Milligan was right behind them, her arms wrapped around her two kids, Ted and Sandy, as she pushed them toward the bus, where Stu and a few others were loading supplies. Big Mike had filled two duffels with whatever food and water they had left in the diner, tossing them to folks as they climbed aboard.

"No point leaving it behind," he said, puffing.

But just as Royce thought the exodus might happen cleanly, a voice cut through the bustle—a child's voice, high and wild.

"The ghost! The Haunted Well! It's awake!"

It was Ted, seven years old and full-on panicking. He thrashed against his mom's grip, pointing frantically toward the rear of the garage. "Don't you hear it? It's howling! It's howling!"

People froze. Even Big Mike stopped in his tracks, half a crate of bottled water in his arms.

Royce turned, heart jumping as he scanned the spot the kid was pointing at.

The old water well.

Tucked behind the garage, choked in weeds and forgotten, the old stone-ringed mouth was barely visible. A few old slats still hung onto the roof boards. A relic. Locals said it dried up back in the Depression. Some said it was haunted. Royce had never believed the stories, but he hadn't exactly gone leaning over it at night either.

Now, sounds were coming out of it. Voices?

It was not exactly a voice. More like the noise scraped out of lungs, too exhausted to scream—a cry, ragged and desperate, echoing up from the dark.

Royce's pulse kicked.

"What the hell…" he murmured, moving.

Big Mike was already beside him, his thick boots kicking sand as he advanced cautiously.

The moaning grew louder, not supernatural now, but *human*—injured, raw, and real.

Royce broke into a run. He and Big Mike simultaneously reached the edge of the old well, skidding to a stop, sand and burrs around their boots. Royce leaned over the mossy rim just as Big Mike did the same, their heads nearly colliding.

Something shifted in the dark below.

Royce's breath caught as a hunched figure clung to the interior wall—*two heads* turned upward, the light glinting off four wide eyes.

"What in the—" Big Mike started.

"Bout time you showed up," Albert wheezed from the wall, one arm wrapped around the rusted iron bar, the other holding a squirming bundle zipped into his coat. "I don't think I can climb any higher. Stella weighs a bit more than she'd admit."

Royce let out a bark of relief, the knot in his chest unravelling. "You stubborn old mule," he chortled, grinning.

"Don't stand there! Pull me up!"

"Hang on, we've got you!"

Voices shouted behind them as others rushed over. In moments, a chain of arms formed, reaching into the well. Hands grabbed fabric, arms, and fur until Albert was dragged over the lip and onto solid ground, mud-caked and shaking, Stella still wrapped in his coat. Unzipping, he allowed her down.

Cheers erupted, and none louder than Ted Milligan's. The boy dropped to his knees, hugging Stella like a long-lost friend, the schnoodle licking his face between excited yips.

"I didn't know it was a dog haunting the well!" Ted laughed. "If I knew that, I wouldn't have been scared!"

Albert let himself slump to the ground, chest heaving, face pale. "I could use a—"

The ground bucked violently beneath them.

A deep groan came from the earth itself, followed by a sharp *crack* as a nearby telephone pole wobbled and snapped.

Walls creaked. Chunks rattled down. An aftershock was building—louder and stronger.

"No time," Albert shouted, staggering upright. "This place is coming apart!"

Royce was already turning. "Move! Get to the bus—NOW!"

The group flew into motion; the rumble chasing their feet. Royce was halfway to the bus when the ground bucked again, harder than any shock so far from the initial quake.

A deep *CRACK* split the air as another aftershock pummeled through the town like a hammer blow. The grocers leaned sideways and pancaked. The garage collapsed. Across the street, what was left of the storage building and Stu's feed store dropped, and the ground underneath them fell away. The fissure widened—its craggy edges stretching toward the river, poised to tear through the levee.

"We don't have time," he shouted, running back to urge the stragglers forward. "Move, move, move! If that rift hits the riverbank, this whole place goes under!"

Tires spun on gravel. The bus door banged shut. Royce slid into the truck's front seat as Big Mike swerved the school bus onto the shattered highway.

He needed to find the kids.

Chapter Twelve
Granite City, MO: August 15, 1 p.m.

Tony Abson, Dam and Lock Operator at Dam No. 27 in St. Louis, gripped the railing. The massive earthquake four hours ago had completely upended his world, but unbelievably, it now looked as though things would get worse.

The metal was trembling beneath his gloves, not from the wind. From something deeper. Something wrong.

The aftershock had shaken the station enough to knock the few wrenches still on their hooks to the floor and send his coffee mug skittering across the console. But that was fifteen minutes ago.

Now the vibration was back, low and mean, humming through the soles of his boots like a warning growl from the earth itself.

"Not good," Tony muttered. It was going to be spectacularly bad, he thought grimly. Dam and Locks 27, a crucial navigation structure in the Chain of Rocks Canal, was not built to withstand extreme overtopping or seismic activity. Seventy years ago, no one had thought to earthquake-proof the structure. After riding out the quake this morning, he wasn't sure if that was possible, anyway.

His eyes darted over the monitors. The readings were off. Pressure building. Flow rates spiking. The Mississippi, bloated from weeks of rain and now swollen with seismic upheaval from the latest aftershock, crested against the aging infrastructure. Sirens wailed—internal alarms first, then the ones wired to the city grid.

Cracks raced across the spillway like veins under glass, unnoticed beneath the turbulent surface.

Another aftershock hit—harder than before. A deafening *boom* ripped across the river valley. The entire structure lurched. Concrete split, and on the far side of the facility, a section of the saturated earthen berm collapsed, disappearing in a rush of brown water and flying trash.

Water poured through the breach like a living thing, snapping steel and wrenching rebar like brittle twigs. One of the massive tainter gates—designed to regulate flow—buckled under the pressure, twisting sideways with a metallic scream.

Tony staggered backward as a shockwave of spray splashed up into the air. He watched in horror as Gate 5 screeched, twisted sideways, then ripped free, flipping like a dying fish as the river gushed through the gap. Steel bent like plastic. Rebar tore loose with a sound like machine-gun fire.

Downstream, three miles away, the lock chambers flooded in seconds, drowning the machinery, while chunks of concrete crumbled into the frothing water.

And then the Mississippi roared.

A freed monster, unchained and unmerciful. It charged south, with no more gates or barriers, just raw velocity. Trees, trucks, dock pieces—gone, caught in the spill and spun like leaves in a storm gutter.

At St. Louis, the river rose with terrifying speed.

Tony bolted for the radio room to raise downtown, but the lines were dead. He stood there, chest heaving, as the surge built momentum and St. Louis braced for the second of the one-two punches today.

The floodwall system protecting downtown, designed for historic highs, was never meant to withstand a dam collapse just miles upstream. The wave overtook low-lying areas first.

The Chain of Rocks Bridge vanished under churning brown water. Riverview Boulevard was flooded, drowning crushed buildings, street signs, and vehicles in minutes. Emergency workers and first responders attempting to dig out survivors were battered and swept away in the flow. Laclede's Landing was swallowed first, still standing despite the earthquake damage to the old cobblestone riverfront. What was left of businesses, museums, and restaurants disappeared as the waves smashed over the first floors.

Water gushed from storm drains and sewer grates, turning roads into rivers. The MetroLink tunnels flooded, and what little power was regained then shorted, leaving trains as dark islands along the tracks. The commuters who escaped the tunnel collapses were evacuated, but many MetroLink engineers were still underground when the flood crashed through.

Deserted, the Gateway Arch still stood, but the base of each leg flooded. The lower plaza vanished beneath swirling foam. Cars were trapped on the Eads Bridge, unable to escape as the Missouri and Illinois shorelines disappeared under water.

The river had breached containment.

Floodwalls disintegrated. Manhole covers burst skyward, geysers of water spraying into the air. Storm drains reversed course. Roads vanished. The Arch grounds became a churning lake, and the low-lying neighborhoods of Carondelet and South Broadway found themselves submerged within hours.

The river, no longer held in check, had reclaimed its floodplain, reminding the city that it had never been tamed, only paused. By nightfall, the crushed remains of Busch Stadium held a murky lake. Union Station's lower levels flooded, and water lapped at the doors of City Hall. Refugees from the quake poured into high ground—Lafayette Square, Central West End, Forest Park.

For the first time in over a century, the Mississippi reclaimed parts of downtown St. Louis, not with a slow, creeping flood, but with a sudden, violent swell unleashed by the failure of Locks and Dam 27 and others upstream.

St. Louis, MO: Saturday, August 15, 1 p.m.

The tunnel swallowed light whole, smothering it in thick, velvet blackness. Only the narrow beams from the flashlights Edgar shared cut through, jittering across the slick stone as the group moved at a downward angle, their shoes splashing in the stagnant puddles.

Walter hunched his shoulders, ducking beneath the too-close ceiling, heart thudding in his ears. The air hung heavy with mildew and rot; every breath felt like inhaling a wet sponge. The walls closed in, greasy with grime and streaked with graffiti—ghost tags left by those who'd wandered down here before. Some names, some curses, some desperate prayers.

Moss clung to the stone like old scars. Patches of mold bloomed between cracks, fed by the damp darkness. The passage tightened only wide enough for two to squeeze side by side, shoulders brushing the rough walls.

Emmet grunted, locking arms with Eric to steady him as Walter hauled Cindy forward, her limp form trailing against his side. Ahead, Edgar kept the pace steady, flashlight swinging like a beacon. Jabo followed close behind, cradling his busted shoulder, teeth gritted. Tau brought up the rear, his light scanning the ancient stone with a mix of awe and disbelief.

The data scientist touched the stone as they passed, fingertips brushing history. Underground Railroad. He'd read about it, sure—but walking it? Feeling the weight of the earth above, the frigid air of escape tunnels trod by trembling feet, and desperation? That was different.

Tau's vivid imagination pictured them, barefoot, hunted, bleeding, and in fear of being caught and returned, slipping through these same tight corridors in the dead of night, chasing freedom with every step. They held burning torches, the flickering light the only illumination in this passage, their fearful faces in the glow, determined to escape slavery and find a better life.

Now, a hundred and fifty years later, they were escaping too. Shivering, he tried to distract himself. Then he realized it wasn't him shivering, it was the walls.

The tunnel convulsed.

A deep moan resonated through the stone, the ground underfoot rippling like something alive. Dust rained from above, sifting into hair, mouths, eyes. The walls vibrated—tight, suffocating, pulsing with a low, ominous hum.

Walter froze, bracing himself against the coarse rock. Jabo gulped, clutching his arm tighter across his chest as he stumbled. For a heartbeat, no one moved. A palpable tension filled the air, heavy with the scent of ozone and the impending sense of ruin. The tunnel squeezed inward; the ceiling pressing down, and the shadows creeping closer.

Then—stillness. Like the earth had exhaled and quieted again.

Emmet understood their panic. He didn't waste a second. His voice cut through the silence, loud and fast, bouncing off the stone, even as he urged Jabo and Edgar forward. "That was just an aftershock. This tunnel stood through the big one. It can stand a few aftershocks. Let's talk about Midwest earthquakes—two big theories on why they happen."

He spoke like a man throwing a rope to drowning friends, keeping anxiety at bay with cold facts. "First: glacier pressure release. During the Ice Ages, glaciers a mile thick pushed down on the land, crushing it flat. When they melted, the earth started springing back, like a mattress slowly rising after you get up. That rebound messes with fault lines, even old ones."

He waved his flashlight like a professor pacing a lecture hall—if the lecture hall were buried underground and shaking itself to pieces.

"Second: far-field stress. Imagine whacking your elbow and feeling it in your hand. Same deal here—stress from distant tectonic shifts ripples across the plate, builds up over time, and—boom. Quake."

Still scanning the ceiling warily, Tau asked, "You're thinking the New Madrid Zone gave way? That's one thing, but Walter, what if this is a repeat of the West Coast event? Your model…"

Emmet interrupted, not missing a beat. "New Madrid's different. It's smack in the middle of the North American Plate. The crust here? Cold, old, dry, brittle like bone. When it breaks, the shockwaves travel far. A quake here hits twenty times the area of a similar quake out west."

He ducked under a low arch, the flashlight flicking across a spray of moss. "And yeah, this place has a history. 1811's the big one, but we've found traces of monster quakes from 900 A.D., 1450 A.D., and even earlier. One hit near Marked Tree in 1843, another pulverized Charleston in 1895."

Walter glanced back, the fear easing a little as Emmet's voice carried them forward. The facts were terrifying—but they were solid. Concrete. Something to hold on to when the ground itself couldn't be trusted. Walter needed facts to steady himself. He started thinking about Tau's question and his model.

The model predicted this activity. There had been no opportunity to run the latest data, and he didn't know how much ground this disaster had covered, but his model had predicted a mega-quake within this time frame. He needed to review the data.

They kept moving deeper into the dark, flashlight beams piercing the black.

Above, outside the crumbling shell of the hotel, a roar ricocheted as the surge from the failed dam thundered over what was left of the levees and riverbank. It hit the hotel grounds, finishing the work of the quake, sweeping across split asphalt and lawn, flattening the few sections of fence still standing, washing away uprooted trees. The parking lot vanished beneath a churning wall of water, cars bobbing like toys before colliding and spinning out of control.

The river, no longer confined, consumed everything in its path.

What was left of the second floor collapsed into the first. The front entrance, once grand, was now a waterfall, torrents pouring through and down, the flow thick with mud.

The river rushed through the shattered hotel. First, it devoured the crushed lobby, sweeping past flattened chairs and shattered chandeliers. Water poured through crumbling hallways and burst through the kitchen doors in a foaming wave before crashing down the basement steps. Shelves, crates, sacks of food—everything vanished beneath the flood. Then the flow spilled through the old door, the forgotten entrance to the historic tunnel—and the river lunged through.

Blocks ahead, Edgar's flashlight caught the glint of rusted rungs—an old ladder anchored into stone, stretching up to the Brevis Museum. His heart leapt. No one was there. That meant the others had made it out.

We can too.

He bolted forward, feet splashing through the dark muck—then something brushed past his leg.

A shrill squeal pierced the darkness.

Tau shouted from the rear, "What the—!"

A wave of rats—hundreds of them—exploded through the tunnel from behind. Fur brushed against legs, claws scrabbled over shoes, beady eyes glinted in the flickering light. They came in a tide of shrieks and squeaks, leaping, darting, clambering over one another in sheer panic.

"Move! MOVE!" Edgar barked, voice rising over the din.

Emmet spun, nearly losing his footing as Eric sagged against him. He braced himself against the tunnel wall, shielding the injured man with his body. Rats swarmed around his feet, a living carpet of filth.

"Go, go!" he shouted, shoving Walter forward, Cindy clutched in his grip. Tau grabbed Eric as Emmet passed him off.

Emmet raised his flashlight, sweeping it behind them—then stiffened.

A dull thunder was rising. Low. Relentless. Getting louder.

Water.

He saw it then—dark, churning, unstoppable— charging down the tunnel like a beast.

"RUN!" he hollered. "It's flooding! The tunnel's flooding!"

No one needed more convincing. They sprinted, splashing through filth and rodents, lungs burning, shoes slipping on stone.

Behind them, the river came roaring.

Edgar slid to a stop at the base of the ladder, sneakers skidding in the rising flood. Water poured around his knees, rats swimming in panicked circles, squealing as they clawed at the slick stone. He didn't flinch. No time.

He grabbed Walter's arm as the big man lumbered up beside him, soaked and wheezing, Cindy slumped over his shoulder like a cloth doll.

"I got her—*go!*" Edgar shouted, yanking Cindy free. Her short legs buckled, splashing into the water, and her blond head lolled against Edgar's broad chest.

Walter didn't hesitate. He seized the ladder, fingers slipping on the wet metal, and climbed, each rung grumbling under his weight. The top of the tunnel narrowed into a vertical shaft—old brickwork and rusted iron giving way to a round access pipe that slanted up toward a faint glimmer of light.

There was a steel hatch at the top. Walter twisted the latch—it stuck—and then, with a grunt and a shoulder slam, it flew open. Musky air flooded the shaft.

"Send her up!" he called down.

Tau was already behind him, laboring as he passed Cindy's limp form upward. Walter hauled her through the hatch, laid her on the floor above, then turned, hand outstretched.

Eric came next, grimacing in agony but moving. His face was ashen, jaw clenched, but he hopped, one foot useless. Tau got underneath and gave him the last shove he needed. Walter hauled him out, dropping him beside Cindy.

"Next!" he shouted, looking back down the chute. The water topped Emmet and Edgar's waists now, the current nearly undercutting their feet.

Jabo was already climbing, clutching his arm against his chest, teeth gritted against the pain. Tau boosted him further, then Walter grabbed hold from above, straining as he lifted. Jabo tumbled through, huffing in pain on the floor next to the others.

Tau scrambled up next, his boots slipping, fingers clawing at the wet rungs. Edgar was close behind, white hair matted with grime, face streaked with tunnel filth.

Only Emmet remained below—neck-deep now, clinging to the bottom rung like it was his lifeline. The current seized him, slamming his back against the wall, rats riding the wave beside him. He swatted them off, choking on the fetid water.

"GO!" he shouted as Edgar's rear disappeared into the shaft.

Edgar didn't argue. He heaved through the hatch, dripping and breathless, rolling aside. Tau and Walter dropped to their bellies, arms plunging back into the shaft.

"Grab him!" Walter shouted.

Emmet's head was in the shaft, but the current was too strong now. One hand slipped and went underwater. Walter slid in further, Tau holding him, and grabbed the hand still clutching a rung. The other hand broke the surface, flailing. Walter jerked him up into the access pipe. Tau caught his free hand—and together they hauled him up against the sucking pull of the flood.

With one last heave, they yanked him clear of the rising water.

Tau slammed the hatch shut behind them, trapping the water below. The sound echoed like a gunshot in the dark room's silence.

They collapsed together on the floor of the museum's basement, coughing, drawing in air, shivering—but alive.

Tau staggered away from the hatch, tore off his dripping suit coat, dropping it on the floor. He inhaled and looked up, voice cracking under the weight of adrenaline. "Where in the *hell* did that water come from?"

Edgar wiped muck from his face, chest still heaving. "That was the Mississippi," he said grimly. "I'd know that stench anywhere. Something shoved it out of its banks. Maybe a dam broke... hell, maybe all of them. This day's a full-blown disaster."

Emmet let out a coarse laugh and pushed himself upright. He scrubbed a hand over the duck on his chest, wiping at the faded green fabric.

"Boys," he said, clapping a hand on Walter's back and then Tau's shoulder. "You pulled my sorry hide out of the river. I was one wave away from being fish food."

Walter waved it off, brushing mud from his coat. "Just evened the score. If you hadn't hauled us out of that death trap of a conference room, we'd be buried with the rest of the science team."

Tau cracked a grin through the grime. "Like the Three Musketeers," he said. "All for one, one for all—even when we're half-drowned."

"The three what…?" Walter asked in confusion.

Emmet barked a laugh as Tau explained what a musketeer was, and stood fully, his body stiff and sore but still moving. He turned to Edgar and extended a hand. "Appreciate the exit strategy. Just in time."

Edgar shook it, flashing a tired smile. "Didn't plan on swimming, but it worked. Let's get moving—see what's left of the city."

Tau drifted toward the door. He paused, nose twitching, then looked back. "Wait… do you guys smell that?"

Everyone stilled.

Tau sniffed again, face tightening. "Smoke. That's smoke."

Edgar's smile vanished.

"Oh, hell. Now what?"

Chapter Thirteen
Atlanta, GA: Saturday, August 15, 2 p.m.

Miguel snatched the phone on the first ring, his other hand still flying across the keyboard.

"Santiago," he said, eyes glued to the live satellite feed.

"It's David," came the answer, low and urgent. "Are you sitting down?"

That tone cut through the noise in Miguel's brain. He stopped typing mid-keystroke.

"You sound rattled. What's going on?"

"Have you been watching the weather in the Midwest?" David asked.

Miguel blinked. The last five hours had been a whirlwind—one fault after another activating, levees along the Mississippi and other rivers breaking, communication lines down, damage and death everywhere. The weather barely registered on his radar.

"No. I've been focused on the Mississippi corridor. Why?"

"Open the NOAA feed," David said. "Now. I'll hold."

Miguel's stomach tightened. His fingers hovered over the keyboard, then flew. A few clicks brought up the NOAA stream. The screen loaded—an anxious meteorologist before a glowing storm map—a long, thick line of yellows and reds cutting from Arkansas to Illinois, angry and alive.

"...massive, fast-moving supercell system sweeping east..." the announcer said, his voice taut. "Impact zone includes southeastern Missouri—St. Louis, Cairo, Paducah— arrival time approximately 3:15 PM Central..."

Miguel's eyes locked on the screen as the forecast turned grim: hook echoes in multiple cells. Tornado signatures popping up like flares. Hail the size of baseballs. Wind gusts strong enough to peel a roof off a shelter. Flash floods. Power outages.

"…already devastated by this morning's seismic activity," the announcer continued. "Rescue efforts are likely to be delayed or halted. Mobile shelters at risk. Underground spaces are potentially unstable…"

Miguel's pulse thudded in his ears.

"David," he said slowly, "this storm's a monster. It's going to sweep right through the quake zone. First, St. Louis and southern Illinois will be affected, followed a few hours later by the tail end, which will sweep through eastern Missouri and western Kentucky. They're going to get clobbered!"

"Exactly," David snapped. "The military and FEMA have first responders heading into the field, search teams combing debris piles. We're setting up evacuees to camp in open lots—and this thing will hit them dead-on."

Miguel's hands moved before his brain could keep up, launching emergency weather protocols across the system.

"How long do we have?" he asked.

"For St. Louis? Seventy minutes. Maybe less."

The words stole the air from Miguel's lungs. "I can't reach Walter and Tau."

There was silence on David's end. Then he said, "God help them," before he hung up.

St. Louis, MO: 2 p.m.

They burst out of the fractured museum entrance, coughing and blinking through the haze. Tau and Emmet hauled Eric between them, his foot lagging and dirty. Walter staggered behind, Cindy draped across his shoulders like a sack of grain, her arms dangling, eyes closed, face ghost-pale and slick with soot.

Behind them, the Brevis Museum leaned under the weight of fire and falling stone. Flames spat through shattered windows, and stone crumbled as the fire consumed everything inside. A black column of smoke twisted into the sky, thick enough to cover the accumulating clouds. Just minutes before, they'd been dashing through that tomb. A few minutes longer underground, and they would have been trapped inside.

Outside, the street was a war zone.

Flames guttered from shattered storefronts. Sparks danced through the air like fireflies from hell. People flowed past—faces streaked with soot, some crying, others silent and wild-eyed. Bloodied, limping, wrapped in torn blankets or rough bandages. The street was an escape route carved through a disaster zone.

Car alarms screamed, distant sirens howled, and the heat from the nearby fires shimmered on the asphalt, warping the horizon.

Edgar spun in a tight circle, scanning the crowd. Then he snapped his fingers and pointed. "They're headed for the NGB site! National Geology Bureau's new build is a huge area, one hundred acres easy. Half-finished, but it's open space—parking lots, staging zones. If there's a rescue setup, that's where it'll be."

Emmet's eyes scrunched, a plan already forming behind them. "Perfect. That'll work." He met Walter's tired gaze. "I've got an idea when we get there."

"We're on Cass," Edgar said, jogging a few paces ahead. "Stay on it. It'll take us straight in."

Walter didn't waste time asking questions. He adjusted Cindy's weight and pushed forward, gritting his teeth against the ache in his shoulders. "Let's go. She needs help now."

They crossed the parking lot and plunged into the human tide, boots crunching on glass and ash, weaving between collapsed power lines and half-buried cars. The wind altered directions, and with it came a low rumble from the west—the sky darkening fast. Something massive was moving in. A storm was coming.

"Great, just what they needed," Tau thought dourly, forcing his feet forward.

The National Geology Bureau site loomed up faster than they'd imagined. They followed the stream of desperate survivors, surging like a flood, onto the sprawling, half-constructed complex. Concrete foundations, skeletal steel beams, and wide-open parking lots stretched across the site— an unfinished city built just in time to save one.

As they reached the triage zone, chaos finally met order.

Hundreds of cots lined the walls inside huge Army tents, medics in neon vests barking for IVs, calling for splints, and waving in gurneys. Walter lowered Cindy gently onto a stretcher; within seconds, she was engulfed by the crowd of responders and wheeled toward a white tent with a red cross painted across the canvas.

Eric and Jabo were settled onto crates, both pale but conscious, their eyes darting at the whirl of organized commotion around them. There was structure for the first time that day—people who knew what to do and weren't panicking. That alone felt like breathing after almost drowning.

Edgar pressed Walter's laptop into his hands. "Didn't drop it. Didn't get it wet."

Walter blinked. The laptop looked untouched, a clean slate in the disorder. He clutched it tight, a lifeline of data and purpose.

Heads together, Emmet and Edgar melted into the commotion, and Tau reappeared with a nod. "Found something," he whispered, already in motion. "Come on."

He guided Walter toward the edge of a command tent, the flap fluttering in the wind. It was pitched against the remains of a partially collapsed wall, brick dust clinging to the canvas. They crawled between. Tau knelt, a slender shadow, Walter less graceful. Tau used his pocketknife to slice a slit in the fabric and pulled it apart.

Crouching behind the tent wall, they breathed shallowly as they peered through.
Inside, the tent buzzed like a hive struck with a stick. Folding tables sagged under the weight of servers and laptops. People shouted over each other, phones to their ears, hands flying across keyboards. The whine of portable generators outside added a low mechanical growl beneath the human frenzy.

In the center, a man in military camo drummed a clipboard onto a table, barking orders to young men and women, who presumably rushed away to carry them out. The screens displayed radar feeds, seismic overlays, and maps of streets in Missouri and Illinois.

Tau signaled toward the glow of a nearby Wi-Fi router. "Generators are keeping it up. They've got internet."

Walter didn't need further convincing. He slid back behind the wall, opened his laptop, and booted up.

"What's the password?" he asked, fingers flying.

"There isn't one," Tau said. "They're too busy to lock anything down."

He was right—Walter connected in seconds. Bypassing the local network firewalls with a few taps, he opened his seismic prediction model. He accessed the USGS site, logged in using his credentials, and fed his model the latest quake data.

The model drank the information like a man in the desert. Code streams cascaded across the screen, and algorithms, stress fields, and fault simulations adjusted in real-time.

Walter's eyes focused. He wasn't watching a replay of today's activity now. That was for later. He was hunting for the next hit.

"Let's find out if the Earth's going to crack again," he said.

Tau leaned in over Walter's shoulder, finger tracing jagged anomalies on the screen. "That spike doesn't match the morning's aftershock pattern."

"I know." Walter's voice was tight, eyes flicking across columns of data. "Tau, this data is moving too fast. Way too fast. Someone already ran this model—Reston's signature is all over it. They already have this prediction."

Tau's brow furrowed. "What did they find?"

"Give me a second." Walter's fingers danced across the keys, inputting additional seismic readings, filtering through the system's assumptions. The model recalculated, spitting out numbers that made the blood drain from his face. He adjusted twice, outpacing what he hoped was a glitch.

But the screen didn't lie.

Inside the tent, voices spiked from a dull hum to a buzz of tension—commands sharpened, voices blurred. Something was happening on their side of the canvas.

Walter tuned it out. The next disaster was still buried in his code.

Tau peeked through the slit again, eyes scanning the turmoil inside. His eyes locked on the central monitors just as the cluster of bodies shifted. Angry, thick red lines webbed across a digital map, reaching from the New Madrid fault to the Wabash Valley and the Ohio River fracture zones. Alarms flashed across the screen like a heartbeat gone wrong.

"Tau…" Walter's voice cracked. "It's predicting another event. Huge. Right along the same lines as this morning. A magnitude in the nines. This thing isn't done—it's got more juice."

"I think they know," Tau whispered. His eyes locked on the glowing fault overlays. "It's lit up. Everything. Anna Fault. Rome Through fault. Wabash Valley fault. Red and pulsing, as if it's about to bleed. When?" Tau's voice trembled despite himself.

Walter stared at the forecast line. "Ninety-one percent probability… within the next twenty-four hours."

Tau reeled back. "That'll tear the Midwest in half. We need to get to Reston. Now. You'll need the full system there to track this."

Walter shook his head, dread snaking up his spine. "We're on foot. No Miguel, evac team or spare helicopter this time."

"And we're screwed," Tau finished for him.

Then—like a ghost from the rubble—Emmet's white head popped around the side of the tent. He was grinning, his wild eyebrows twitching over tired eyes.
"Hey, boys. I got us a way out."

Walter and Tau exchanged a look—anticipation lit like a flare.

"I need a minute," Walter said, snapping back to his screen. "Let me send this to Miguel. The data's already being downloaded back to Reston, but I want to make sure they see what's coming. The timeline, the probability—everything is here."

"Yeah, and tell him we're alive," Tau added. "For now."

As Walter typed, Tau stepped away to fill Emmet in, ready to run the second they had a direction—any direction—that didn't end with the ground cracking open beneath their feet.

Tau leaned close to Emmet as they stood between abandoned vehicles and concrete slabs, keeping his voice low. "Another quake's coming. Bigger than this morning—off-the-charts big. Walter's model is reading something worse than today, possibly in the 9s."

Emmet rolled his shoulders, one foot crunching glass beneath his boot. His brow furrowed, and he blew a long, low whistle through his teeth. "Damn. You sure?"

Tau gave a tight nod, eyes scanning the blackening sky. "The data's stacking up too fast to be a fluke. If we can get back to Reston, we can get confirmation. But we need to move fast. We've got to get out of the Midwest before the ground turns to soup."

Emmet glanced over his shoulder at Walter, who was chasing a stray black plastic bag in the increasing gusts of wind. He turned back to Tau, arms folded. "I got an idea."

Tau's face brightened. At least one of them found a solution. Emmet laid it out fast, his voice low and steady.

"Edgar's gone to find his family," he said. "Told me to thank you boys—said you saved their lives. He's grateful. Eric and Jabo are getting patched up in the med tents. Word is, they'll be airlifted out by the end of the hour. Cindy, too— she's stable, and they think she'll make it. I'll get a message to Edgar to get his family out of St. Louis tonight."

"Tell him to go west as far as he can," advised Tau.

Emmet glanced over at Walter, who, having caught his prize, was fumbling with the plastic. "That leaves us. And I've got a way out."

Tau leaned in, already intrigued.

"Before Edgar left, he helped me grab a city map. Traced a route to a buddy of mine—Stitch Stavo. Lives right across from the old fairgrounds. He flies hot air balloons."

Tau blinked. "He flies *what*?"

Emmet grinned and held up a hand. "Hold on, hold on. Let me finish. The fairgrounds are a big open space. Stitch uses it to launch. If we get to him, he can move us *up* and *out*."

Tau's eyes lit up as understanding bloomed. "A balloon? That's genius. Above fires, the jammed up streets, even avoid blocked roads…"

He shot a look at Walter, who was walking toward them, then looked at Emmet. "Don't mention the balloon part yet. Walter's not the most... sky-friendly type."

"Noted," Emmet agreed. "It's about two miles from here. Not far if we move fast."

Walter rejoined them in time to hear Emmet's last comment. He wrapped his laptop in a black trash bag and bound it tightly across his back as he shared his opinion about moving on.

"Two miles through hell," he muttered. "Fires, dead bodies, toxic air, and let's not forget—aftershocks."

Emmet pointed northeast. "There's a golf course between here and the fairgrounds. Wide open, no buildings to collapse on us. If we cut through it, we avoid the worst of the fires and save time. Half the journey or more will be on open ground."

"Best-case scenario: an hour or two," Tau added.

Walter looked westward at the storm clouds building into big thunderheads along the horizon. "That's if we don't run into any 'anomalies.'"

"When *don't* we run into anomalies?" Tau shot back.

"You got a better plan?" Emmet asked.

Walter sighed and shouldered the laptop like a soldier hoisting gear. "Nope. But if I get eaten by a bear or swept away by a surprise flash flood, I blame you both."

"Come on," Emmet said, already walking. "We can make it before the skies open up. I need to make one stop before we go, and send a message to Edgar."

Walter and Tau followed, boots crunching over ripped asphalt, smoke stinging their eyes, a storm on their heels, and two miles of bedlam ahead.

Mississippi River, KY: Saturday, August 15, 2 p.m.

There really was no question about what would happen next.

The second Charlie disappeared downriver, the Clark kids were in motion. They only had one choice. Brett saw the loss in Winnie's eyes—wild, rimmed with tears, jaw clenched like iron.

"It's my fault," Winnie cried. "I didn't hold him tight enough."

"It's not your fault. We're going after him," Brett told her firmly. "Don't worry."

Piper kept her arm around Winnie, but she caught Brett's eyes. "Can we do this?" she asked, the fear she hated asking the question.

"We got this, Piper." Brett glanced at the water. "We'll follow Charlie downriver, and when we catch up to that roof, we'll figure out how to get him off."

Jamie and Pedro shifted next to Matthias, uncertainty flickering across their boyish faces. They wanted to help, but they had homes to get back to, families waiting, wondering about their fate.

"Not you two," Brett said, understanding their hesitation. "You need to let your families know you are okay. Take the wave runner. You'll need it to fight the current heading upstream. The river's moving fast. It'll carry us down after Charlie."

Jamie hesitated even as his fingers found the handlebars. "But what if you need help?"

Matthias stepped over, ready to lug the *Seismic Wave* off the sandbar. "It's okay. We've got this. Charlie's our family, and we're sort of experienced in saving each other."

Jamie looked like he wanted to argue, but then he conceded. "Be careful."

"You too. Get Pedro home." Brett said, clapping him on the shoulder.

The boys fired up the watercraft, its engine coughing before growling to life. With one last look back, they cut through the current, carving a wake as they angled upstream toward safety.

Matthias and Brett didn't wait. They shoved the *Seismic Wave* into the churning river, thigh-deep in water, sand yanking at their sneakers. The craft rocked, ropes creaked, and then they were off, paddles flashing as they fought to catch up with the faster current.

The water grabbed them immediately—cold, swift, relentless—towing the *Seismic Wave* forward and chasing Charlie down the river.

Brett expected the water to be rough. It was so much worse.

Over and over, the *Seismic Wave* bucked beneath them as tremors pulsed through the earth. Each aftershock came with its own brand of terror—sudden veils of fog rolling in like ghosts, the sky darkening without warning, a low sulfurous stink curling through the air like a warning from the pit. From the woods came bangs and crashes as weakened banks gave way and entire shelves of land slumped into the churning water.

More than once, Brett stiffened as deep, rumbling booms echoed across the river, shaking the wheel from his hands. Blowholes erupted without warning, spewing geysers of sand that exploded into the sky and settled into strange, yellow stains along the banks. A sick mist clung to the air, thick with dust and grit that coated their skin and burned their throats.

Uplifted banks pierced high above the normal shoreline, over ten feet in some places. Where water once ran clear, it now flowed over new ridges of cracked mud and sand. The kids stared, silent, at the ghastly sight of hundreds of fish lying dead in shallow pools, bellies up and eyes glassy.

In the distance, they saw new offshoots—tributaries that hadn't existed yesterday—carved by giant fissures that split the alluvial ground like lightning bolts frozen in the earth. Fertile farmland had drowned beneath thick, sucking muck; sand blows left the fields looking like alien deserts.

This wasn't just a disaster—it was a transformation. The Mississippi wasn't a river anymore.

It was a battlefield.

The waterway twisted like a shredded ribbon as the *Seismic Wave* skimmed past the wreckage along the banks. Each mile brought worse devastation—collapsed trees and ruined vegetation, animal and fish carcasses, and land reshaped into something raw. They had not yet passed any civilization, just Mother Nature torn apart.

Then, weathered signs stuck out from the shoreline, their lettering barely legible through layers of mud and river silt. But the name still stood out, bold and unmistakable: *New Madrid*. After miles of empty banks and broken silence, it would be the first glimpse of a city they'd seen since launching downriver.

Only—the shore was bereft. Where a city stood… was nothing.

"Where's New Madrid?" Matthias asked, dumbfounded.

No one answered.

The boat slowed as it started the curve, gliding downriver past a wide, unnatural pit where the city had stood this morning, now an open cavity in the earth. Walls of pale sand loomed as high as six feet around it, a crater carved by a giant hand—yellow and white grains piled under the murky sky, a monstrous sand boil that had consumed everything. Where there were buildings, streets, and life, there was only silence and sand.

The docks were gone. Boat ramps crumbled into the water, half-sunk. Waves had shattered what little stood near the shore—splintered structures, half-drowned rooftops, trees stripped bare.

Piper didn't say a word; she let the tears fall, her eyes locked on the gaping hole of what used to be a town. Winnie didn't want to look. She clung to Coco, face buried deep in the dog's fur, her shoulders shaking.

Brett turned away, his eyes hooded. Matthias reached for a paddle, anxious to get away from the pit.

"Let's get out of here," he said, pushing off the wreckage in the river to head south.

Mist curled in low ribbons across the surface of the water. Thick, gray clouds pressed down from above, muting the world in a heavy, suffocating gloom.

It wasn't just a city lost.

It was as if the earth had erased it entirely.

As the river swept them away, Brett thought about the people who died on the West Coast and then the people who were lost today. If there was a reason for these deaths, he couldn't understand it. So, he pushed the sadness aside and set himself on finding the small black-and-white Borgi, the only thing within his control.

Walker Farm, KY: Saturday, August 15, 2 p.m.

Royce could make it home from Harrowood on a normal day in thirty minutes. Today, crawling across the wrecked countryside took more than an hour.

The truck bucked over the fissured asphalt, weaving past bent trees that were intertwined and uprooted. Hills had crumbled into themselves—mud and boulders spilling over the road. Gashes split the land, some so wide they had to build speed to jump the smaller ones. The uplifted earth bulged skyward like tombstones, while nearby fields sank into wide basins, the soil drowned by sudden lakes.

The land was wrecked everywhere they looked. Water burst from craterlets and clefts, turning roads into rivers and farmland into marsh. The levees were obliterated, and Sutton Road was gone beneath a brown tide coated with fuel and garbage. They abandoned the roads, cutting through fields, the truck bouncing over crushed soybeans as its tires sank into the soaked earth.

But it wasn't until they crested the final ridge that Royce's stomach truly overturned.

He killed the engine.

The two men and their dogs stood stunned, eyes locked on the muddy expanse below. Where his house once stood— barn, porch, windmill—was nothing but brown water. A vast lake, still streaming inland, had engulfed it whole. Not a rooftop, not a fence post in sight.

Just endless, merciless floodwater.

A profound silence hung in the air, heavier than any words.

"The kids?" Royce finally managed.

"No," Albert tilted his head sharply, refusing the question. "Those kids are smart and resourceful. They figured out something. Maybe they floated downriver on a piece of the house or barn?"

"I guess that's possible…" Royce stared at the inundated field below, willing something to show itself.

Then came the loud rumble of an engine, cutting through the stillness. Stella bristled, barking once as a battered pickup rolled to a stop behind them. Shadow, true to her name, slipped behind the bed of their truck.

Pete Deller climbed out, limping slightly, a smear of dried blood crusted near his temple. His scout uniform was ripped, with mud streaks across skin and cloth, and his eyes were bloodshot.

Albert swayed. "Matthias?" he rasped, voice cracking.

Pete threw up a hand. "Wait—no. He's alive." He turned and motioned to the truck. Another fellow climbed out, dirty and with red bumps marring his face, wearing the remnants of a torn shirt. Pete had lent him a jacket to cover up, but it fit tightly. "This is Dan…"

Dan didn't offer a last name, so Pete continued. "…he saw Matthias. Said he was with two other scouts after the flood hit. Soaked but alive."

Royce's heart stumbled. "Flood?" he said, paling. "You're saying the river flooded at Seven Islands, too?"

"Just like here." Pete's arm swept out toward what had once been Royce's home, lost beneath the murky water. "We climbed a tree, but the current towed me off. By the time I got back, the kids were gone."

Dan pushed forward impatiently. "I saw them take off on some kind of watercraft. Saw them drifting—looked like they were trying to get it started."

"We already checked with Jamie and Pedro's families," Pete added. "They took some hits in the quake, everybody is okay, but the boys haven't made it back yet."

Dan cut in again, this time sharper. "Where's your house?"

Royce turned slowly to him, masking his pain. "Gone. River took it."

Dan's face drained of color. "Gone? Completely? Everything in it?"

"Yeah," Royce said, frowning. "You alright?"

Dan's fists clenched, jaw ticking. "Pete said Matthias has siblings. A brother and sisters. Where are they now?"

Royce exchanged a look with Albert. Something about this guy's urgency wasn't sitting right.

"We don't know. Maybe the kids were on the roof or something and rode out," Royce said carefully. "We're looking for them now."

Dan's frustration leaked through, but he choked it back, teeth grinding. "Pete and I can help," he said.

Royce turned back to Pete, filing Dan's reaction away for later. "How's your family?"

Pete gave a tired chuckle. "Josie's already building an outdoor kitchen. She says earthquakes are another ding-dong day for her. The house took a hit, but it's standing. We'll rebuild. But I want to find those boys first."

Royce agreed grimly, eyes scanning the submerged fields. "Then let's move."

"Where do we start?" Albert asked, turning toward the shattered landscape behind them.

Royce didn't hesitate. "Patterman's Airfield."

Albert blinked. "That old airstrip? It's far enough from the river to still be dry, but what if the quake tore the runway apart?"

"Then we fix it." Royce headed toward their truck. "One of those crop dusters is still the fastest way to cover ground. We fly low, we might catch sight of the kids."

It took some wrangling to get the dogs in the truck. Stella resisted, hackles up, and Shadow circled the vehicle twice, ears pinned and tail low. They stared as the two strangers walked back to their old pickup. As soon as Dan opened his door, Stella growled deep in her chest, as if she were urging him to leave.

"Your dogs are in a bad mood," Dan called back to them. He climbed in fast and swung the door hard.

"Tough day?" Albert offered in return, a scowl on his face.

"Shadow thinks something is wrong," Royce murmured, watching the Weimador tense and pace the grass, circling their borrowed truck like she was guarding something.

"Me too," Albert growled.

When the two men finally climbed in, Shadow bolted over Royce to the middle, whining.

Royce squinted. "What do you think is going on with the dogs?"

Albert buckled up, moving his legs as Stella pushed in, climbing up onto the seat with Shadow. "I don't know. But Stella's got a nose for trouble."

Royce tapped the wheel, uneasy. "I've known Pete Deller for twenty years. He's solid."

Albert shrugged. "Okay. But the guy riding shotgun with him? Dan? Something's off. Dogs feel what we don't."

Stella snapped a sharp bark toward the other truck as if to punctuate the point. Shadow whimpered, sliding to the floor and curling tight on the floorboard.

Royce exchanged a look with Albert. Neither said anything more, but both kept one eye on the road and the other on the mirror.

The quake left its mark on Patterman's Airfield—chunks of asphalt split like smashed dinner plates, hangar doors buckled, and tools, barrels, and boxes scattered in a chaotic sprawl across the floor of the old building. But two crop dusters still sat on the asphalt lot, wings intact.

Ty Patterman looked up from beneath the hood of one of them as Royce's truck rolled in, dust kicking up behind it. Tall, lean, and grease-streaked, Ty wiped his hands on a rag and dipped his head in greeting.

"Glad to see you in one piece, Royce," he said, eyes flicking to the others, then to the dogs. "Heard it got real bad out your way with the river and all. Pretty bad here too, but there wasn't much to wreck before the quake, so we came through okay."

"We need your help," Royce said, cutting straight to it. "Kids are missing—the kids that came home with Reed a few months back after what happened in Oregon. We think they might've been carried west in the floodwaters."

Ty's face tightened. "Damn. I've got two birds still flight-worthy. Runway's rough, but it'll hold for takeoff."

"'Preciate the help," Albert said, holding out a hand.

Dan stepped out of the truck, and his eyes lit up at the sight of the planes. "You fly?" he asked, voice casual but urgent.

Royce, Pete, and Albert all said no.

"Well, I do," Dan said smoothly. "Commercial and private. I can help search. Two planes are better than one, right?"

Ty hesitated, eyes glaring slightly. Something in Dan's tone, the eagerness in his step, didn't sit right. But he looked at Royce, then at the distant clouds building on the horizon, and gave a curt nod. "Alright. But you stick to the river paths and report back. Watch the weather, something's gathering. We don't need cowboys up there."

Ten minutes later, fueled up, engines screamed to life. Ty climbed into one plane, and Dan into the other. The crop dusters rushed forward, bounced once, and lifted into the air with a roar. They banked west, skimming low over the twisted landscape.

Royce half-closed his eyes, watching Dan fly away from Ty as they each took a grid. "Where'd you dig up that guy?"

Pete scratched the back of his neck, dirt flaking from his cracked nails. "Rube Taylor and I found him… literally up a tree. After Rube fished me out, we went looking for the kids. The boys were gone, but this guy was perched on a limb like a buzzard. Said the kids found one of those personal watercrafts and floated out with the current."

Albert crossed his arms, gaze piercing. "And you believed him?"

Pete shrugged, weariness clinging to his posture. "I want to. Those kids—Matthias especially—they're sharp and tough. If anyone could ride out a disaster like this, it's them."

Royce exhaled, slow and heavy. "Yeah... I want to believe it, too. But something's off about him. He talks too smooth, watches everything like he's collecting secrets."

"You might be right," Pete shrugged. "Still, his story fits what little I saw."

Royce gave a tight nod. "Go check on your family. They need you more than we do right now. Albert and I'll hold the line here and let you know once they come back."

Pete hesitated and looked at Royce. "Communication is going to be crap, but if you can, swing by and let me know. Anything."

They shook hands, dirt and sweat sealing the pact, then Pete climbed into his truck and drove away, taillights blinking into the dust.

Royce watched him disappear down the buckled road, then turned to Albert. "Let's keep an eye on Dan. Something tells me we don't have the whole story."

With the dogs pacing the airstrip like sentries, Royce and Albert rolled up their sleeves and waded into the mess in the hangar—stacking scattered crates, hauling overturned tool cabinets upright, shoveling out glass fragments and trash. It was the least they could do for Ty.

He looked at his phone, but there were no bars. No word from Reed. No word from Chloe.

But Royce knew his son.

He wasn't the kind to go down without a fight. They'd be back. One way or another.

Chapter Fourteen
St. Louis, MO: Saturday, August 15, 3:15 p.m.

It was like crawling through the wreckage of a fallen world.

Emmet, Tau and Walter walked what was left of the streets. Cracked asphalt, geysers from split water mains, and long power lines sagging like dead vines. Houses had collapsed into heaps of lumber and glass, crushed cars half-buried beneath them. Fires flickered everywhere—orange tongues consuming anything flammable, smoke curling like serpents into the darkening sky.

The western horizon churned with an oncoming storm, discolored by heavy clouds rolling in low and fast, towing a cold, damp wind reeking of gas.

Tau tilted his face to the breeze and cursed softly. "Rain will help the fires," he said aloud, "but not if it brings another storm like last night."

Lightning flickered on the sky's edge, and thunder rolled in the distance. The others they passed, faces etched with fatigue, hurried back the way they came, desperate to reach the safety of NGB. Above, several helicopters sped ahead of the approaching storm.

As they crested a rise, Briarwood Golf Course came into view. Behind high wrought-iron fencing, the quake marked its open lawns, furrowed with fissures and overturned old trees. Still, it was passable. The three men cheered up a little. Just a bit farther. Past the golf course and then a few more blocks to the fairground.

If they escaped the city before the next quake hit, they'd outrun the worst of it.

The wind picked up, shoving at them now in angry gusts. They leaned into it, hunched and labored, fighting to stay upright. The road curved, torn apart by sinkholes and stalled-out vehicles, but they pushed forward, their eyes scanning the fence for a gate.

They found something better.

A stretch of the wrought-iron barrier had collapsed, a twisted mess of bars flattened against the turf like someone kicked the fence down. They slipped through the gap and onto the edge of the golf course.

A sudden, sharp sting hit Tau's cheek. Then another on his neck. He flinched.

"Hail!" Emmet barked, shielding his face with one arm. "Keep moving!"

The sky opened, hurling down ice with a vengeance. Shards of frozen rain smacked their clothes and cracked against their skulls. Walter let out a grunt as a chunk nailed his shoulder, then another skipped over his head. It was a glancing blow, but it still hurt.

They sprinted across the open green, ducking their heads, dodging a golf cart flipped on its side, the riders long gone.

Up ahead—a pavilion. Weather-beaten but standing despite the earthquake. A metal shelter over a concrete pad where players could fill water bottles and check their scores.

They dashed beneath it as the hail fell faster, bullets of ice hammering the roof in a deafening barrage. Crouching, breath steaming, muscles trembling, they waited for the storm to ease. The air was chilly now, the wet gusts wrapping around them.

Then, as if the clouds unzipped, the rain came—sheets of silver flying down with the strength of a hurricane wind driving each drop.

Tau kept glancing east, toward the ground, imagining the ticking fault lines beneath their feet.

The rain finally eased, and the wind lapsed, but eerily the sky remained dark. Emmet urged the men out from under the pavilion, anxious to get across the golf course. They ran, dodging furrows and fallen trees, and climbed or circled sand traps until they were at the center of the course. The wind gusts suddenly intensified again, stronger than before, and Tau slid to a stop, forcing his companions to stop too.

"What's wrong?" asked Walter.

"Do you hear that?" Tau asked. The wind and far-off sirens were the only sounds Emmet and Walter heard. Smoke surrounded the green fields, and it looked as if the rain had doused the worst of the fires. The air stank of wet burn as the wind carried the smoke.

Suddenly, the wind died with a strange abruptness, as if the earth sucked in a breath and held it. Trees that had bent and thrashed moments ago now stood like statues. The air grew dense—charged. The hair on Tau's arms stood up.

Then came the sound.

Low at first. A distant hum that sounded like a train. But there were no tracks here.

It grew louder—a churning roar, deep and grinding, like metal tearing through stone. The ground beneath their feet vibrated, but it wasn't the earthquake they feared. Leaves swirled upward in strange spirals. The sky turned a sickly green-gray, heavy with rotating clouds that moved with impossible speed.

Lightning forked over them, crackling and white-hot, and then the clouds dipped—a funnel twisting out of the sky.

"Run!" Emmet shouted, but the sound was nearly lost to the roar.

The tornado touched down behind them with a sickening boom, the pressure in the air assaulting their eardrums. Trees snapped like toothpicks. Power lines danced and sparked. The funnel widened, its sides spinning with flying debris—timber, vegetation, and shreds of civilization it picked up.

The air was alive now, howling with a sound so deep it rattled the bones. Walter staggered, clutching the laptop strapped to his back. Tau grabbed his arm, jerking him toward the shelter of a wide cement bridge near the fairway.

Behind them, the funnel surged forward, chewing through the landscape. Flags and abandoned golf clubs vanished into its gut, devoured in seconds. A riding lawnmower—300 pounds of steel—lifted off the ground and spun into the air like a leaf.

Rain and trash lashed at them as they dove under the concrete overpass, their feet splashing in the small stream. A roaring crescendo—felt as much as heard in their ribs, teeth, and the very ground—threatened to rip them apart. The world whirled around them, caught in a tornado's path. They clung to each other, tucked at the top of the conduit, holding on to exposed rebar with all their strength.

"Don't let go!" Emmet shouted.

"The refugees and the Med Center," Tau gasped.

"It's going east. It'll miss NGB," Emmet screamed the words out as the tornado swept past them, twenty feet away.

Then, as quickly as it came, the rumble faded, crawling eastward across the shattered land, sucking up the earthquake's remains and spreading it far and wide.

Everything went still again.

Tau was the first to move. Coughing, he lifted his head from the cold, unyielding dirt under the bridge. His hands scraped against grit as he pushed himself up. "You okay?" he rasped.

Emmet groaned behind him. "Still here. Mostly."

Walter sat hunched on the incline, blood smeared down one temple where a flying stone clipped him. His eyes were wide, fixed on nothing. "It sounded like the world was ending," he said, his voice surprised.

"Maybe it is," Tau mumbled, standing. His legs trembled from adrenaline. He staggered toward the bridge's side to look around the concrete barrier.

The sky lightened, but it was the wrong-colored light, filtered through a yellowed sky. He climbed up first, stepping into a world unrecognizable.

The path of the tornado was obvious.

The greens, cart paths, and hedges were replaced with churned earth, broken trees, and craters gouged into the landscape where the huge funnel had crossed. It looked like a combat zone. They were beyond lucky the funnel had missed their bridge. A stripped pine tree lay nearby, not one needle on its branches, and its roots torn from the ground. It was half-buried in what was left of a water feature.

Tau turned slowly, scanning the eastern horizon.

Then he saw them.

"Guys..." His voice was barely audible over the fresh wind already rising again.

Walter and Emmet climbed out behind him, squinting. Emmet whistled a mournful sound.

Across the warped course, the sky twisted again—three, no, four funnels dropped from the black belly of the clouds like fingers testing the ground. Dust and debris spiraled around their forming bases. One of them touched down in a distant subdivision just before the Mississippi, the sickening crunch of wood and steel inaudible.

Another annihilated a long industrial warehouse, exploding the roof and blowing out the sides like a matchbox. The third hovered, half-formed but pulsing with menace. The fourth danced toward the river, trailing ribbons of wind behind it.

"They're still forming," Walter said, voice hollow. "First the earth and now the sky. It's like St. Louis is a nexus point."

Wind from the west hit them again, heavy with moisture. The storm wasn't finished. It was evolving.

Emmet turned, his face pale, streaked with muck and scratches. "We've got to move. We need to find shelter. Now."

They ran as the sky above them churned, more rain fell, and the storm gave a deep, thunderous growl.

Boatwright Wildlife Management Area, MO: Saturday, August 15, 3:30 p.m.

The sky to the west turned ugly—clouds boiling in fast, smeared with marked purples and iron gray, trailing dusk with them despite the hour. The wind increased, colder now, laced with the wet sting of rain. Chloe didn't have to say anything. Reed saw it, too.

Another summer storm. A dangerous one.

Thunder cracked like fireworks in the distance, followed by a wall of rain advancing across the river in a solid pewter blur.

"We wait it out," Chloe said, keeping her voice calm as her hands moved faster. "In the container. It'll hold." She hoped.

Reed didn't argue. One look at the sky, and he was already securing gear. "It's going to be a big one."

They hauled what they could inside the steel box—loose ropes and a few tools—and then pulled the heavy door as the first drops turned to hammering sheets. There was no way to lock it, but Reed trusted its weight would keep it closed. Hail followed, slamming into the roof and walls. The container rattled. Chloe grabbed plastic wrap from a roll, tore off lengths, and helped Reed lash buckets to metal braces on the floor so they could sit and not get tossed around.

Wedged near pallet stacks, flashlights from their phones casting pale circles against the creaking walls, they waited. The barge rocked harder now, grinding against whatever held it in place beneath the river. Outside, each lurch sent loose containers around them, grinding and sliding with deep metallic thuds. The blows shook the barge, and Chloe, terrified, caught her breath each time.

Then the wind screeched, a shrill sound that made them both jump. A profound shudder, bigger than any so far, rattled the barge. Chloe grabbed Reed's hand, and, as if it were the most natural thing in the world, he slid his other arm around her.

"It's going to be okay," he yelled over the noise. "It'll pass soon."

The words were hardly out of his mouth when, without warning, the container door blew open with a thunderous bang.

A blinding flash revealed the scene beyond.

Waterspouts. Two of them. Towering funnels of water and wind spun just yards away, ripping into the river and hurling rubbish skyward like confetti from hell. The river surged—foam and wreckage pouring into the container, knocking them back and apart. Chloe went down, soaked and with no air in her lungs. Pain shot through her thigh where she landed.

Watson barked in panic, paws scrambling on the slick floor as the container tilted, water and dog sliding back out the opening. Reed lunged, caught his friend's leg mid-slide, and clung to a bolt brace with the other hand.

The barge jerked violently.

Whatever had anchored it below broke loose. In a heartbeat, they were moving—ripped free and spun by the storm's energy. The world twisted through the open container door—a mad carousel of black sky, lightning-slashed clouds, and spiraling towers of water.

Rain lashed sideways. Debris flew like shrapnel. The frontmost pallet broke free, flying out the door and sliding, spraying water back at them as it shot off the side of the barge.

Chloe braced as their container tilted again, praying the straps tying it down held and the barge wouldn't break apart beneath them.

"We need to get out of here!" she screamed, heart jackhammering in her chest. "If this thing goes overboard—"

241

"No!" Reed's shout cut through the bedlam. "It's suicide out there!"

He lunged through the pitching container, seized her arm, and yanked her back behind one of the remaining secured pallets. Watson scrambled after them, slipping on the wet metal. Reed threw his arms around Chloe, braced his back against the pallet, and caught the Labrador with one leg. The three huddled close, bodies pressed together, clinging to the last semblance of safety.

Outside, a hurricane-like force reigned.

They couldn't see the storm anymore, but they felt it—the roar of wind like jet engines overhead, the barge straining as metal tore loose, the percussive clang of another container breaking free and sliding across the deck. One slammed into the wall inches from their heads, the impact ringing like a gunshot. Metal shrieked, and a deep dent caved inward. The impact shuddered through their bones.

The straps outside were snapping like whiplashes in the air.

Chloe's chest caught with each one, every crack a countdown. She pressed her face into Reed's shoulder, fingers dug into his shirt. Watson whimpered, ears flattened, hiding in their grip.

Then—a moment of impossible silence. For one heartbeat, the chaos paused, the eye of the storm breathing in.

And then it passed.

The waterspouts raged on, but the worst peeled away eastward. The wind shrieked into deep, rhythmic gusts. Next came the rain—a hammering sheet of drops that beat on the container like fists from above—hundreds of fists, thousands, deafening.

They stayed still, soaked and shaking, while the world finally eased.

Chloe's body trembled so hard that it felt like her bones might shatter. Rain coated her skin, and the cold gnawed deep, but Reed's arms stayed locked around her. Watson pressed tight against her other side, his body heat anchoring them both. Wind screamed outside, rattling the container as if to peel it apart.

"It's okay," Reed whispered into her ear, voice almost inaudible over the storm. "I've got you. I'm not letting go."

The words cracked something loose inside her, sharp and sudden. Her chest labored; her heart thundered so hard it hurt. She tilted her head, searching for his eyes in the gloom— only darkness met her. However, that made it easier in some way. The next words poured from her lips before she could stop them.

"What are you saying, Reed? I need to know. I don't want to be in limbo anymore."

He froze. Lightning flashed—long enough to catch the tension in his jaw, the flicker of confusion.

"What do you mean?" he asked, but the storm wasn't done. A crash of thunder rolled over them, making the walls vibrate.

She spoke anyway, her voice steady even as another round of hail pounded off the roof. "We've made a life in your old home. Your father treats us like family. But what about you? When school starts—if it starts—will you disappear? Were you only staying until the kids were stable?"

There was a beat, a silence as heavy as the thunderhead above. Then the barge spun, jolted, and walloped against something unseen. Chloe's pulse spiked, but Reed held her tighter, anchoring them both.

"I don't think there's gonna be school next week," he muttered with a dry edge. "But if you're asking what I think you are…"

Another gust rocked the barge. The wind roared.

"I'm not going anywhere. I was hoping—" raising his voice now, nearly shouting, "—that you'd come to appreciate my better qualities."

Even in the madness, Chloe let out a strangled laugh.

"I have," she said, her voice shaking but sure. "I do. But is this… us… is that something real?"

Reed didn't hesitate.

"Chloe, I didn't want to rush you. But I've been crazy about you since that day in the military truck when I woke up with you on top of me after the Sisters blew. I didn't say anything because I didn't want to scare you off. But the truth is—I love you. I'll stay here. I'll follow you. The kids, too. I want us to be together. One big, messy, wonderful family."

Her throat tightened. She couldn't speak. Couldn't stop the tears from sliding down her cheeks, lost in the river water soaking them both.

She took a deep gulp of air. "Let's survive today first," she said, voice quivering. "Then you and I… we'll have that talk."

Reed lowered his head against her forehead. "Sounds like a plan."

The wind stopped screaming. No more waves thrashed the container. The madness had passed, leaving only the creak of the damaged barge as it rocked gently, snagged on something new—maybe a half-buried tree, maybe an outcrop of stone. Thunder still rumbled in the east, towing the storm away, and Chloe shivered at the sound. Someone else would be caught in that monstrous tail. God help them.

Reed finally loosened his grip. The absence of his warmth left Chloe aching, but there was no time for comfort. Not now. The next wave, the next twister, the next nightmare—it could hit anytime. They needed out of this coffin before it became their tomb.

Their boots hit the deck with a wet thud and came to a standstill.

The barge was intact, but...

...More than half the containers were gone. Just gone. Torn free and absorbed by the flood. Only three remained beyond theirs, metal skins dented and streaked with grime, and beyond that—nothing. A long stretch of slick, empty deck was littered with shredded tarp, flailing tie-downs, and mangled trash. The storm had torn the place apart.

Chloe's chest rose suddenly. If the wind had grown any stronger, if the straps had continued to snap, if one more wave had tossed the barge—they could've been next.

Reed moved first, wading through ankle-deep water as it sloshed around his boots. He reached the edge, peered out, then stabbed a finger toward the churning brown current. "Look!"

Chloe rushed to his side, bracing against the wind, peering through the torn curtain of rain. The flood had turned into a junkyard of destruction. Mattresses, insulation, sections of rooftops, twisted bikes, shattered beams—all of it bobbing in the thick, brown water like some post-apocalyptic stew. Trees—entire trees—floated root-up like corpses. The air still reeked of something sour and chemical, but the storm thinned it out. Her throat didn't burn with every breath anymore.

Reed's teeth clenched. "We could be in that mess."

Chloe rubbed her hands against her sides. "We need to get off this thing."

Reed inclined his head and pointed east again.

Then she saw it.

Poking through the haze, rising like a needle from the flooded trees and low hills, was a steel tower. It looked skeletal in the distance, partially shrouded in mist, but solid.

Chloe's shoulders hitched. "How far?"

"Half a mile, give or take," Reed said. His eyes stayed locked on the tower. "That's a fire lookout. They build them on the highest elevation. If I'm right, there's a ranger station up there—basic supplies, radios. Shelter."

Soaked and chilled to the bone, she shivered in the wind, her wet clothes sticking to her.

"Then what are we waiting for?" she said, wrapping her arms around herself. "Let's get to that tower."

Reed agreed, already moving. "We'll use the raft."

Their rigged craft sat inside the container, still tethered to the floor where they left it before the storm hit. It wasn't much, but it was enough.

Chloe glanced at Watson, who wagged his tail like he knew what came next.

"We ride the wreckage," she said with a grim smile. "Let's hope it holds."

They moved quickly, urgency driving them. The sky was already shifting again, with darker clouds gathering in the southwest. The next storm was coming.

They didn't look up.

Reed gave a quick nod, tightening the last strap. "Let's see if she floats."

They braced their feet, lifted one end of the improvised raft together, and shuffled it toward the edge. Watson growled low as a gust of wind rattled the door of their container.

"One, two—push!" Reed shouted.

With a grunt, they slid the pallet off the edge. It splashed, wobbled… then settled, steady as a dock. Reed's grin cracked wide for the first time in hours.

"Let's load up."

They worked quickly with the few tools they found: an old lantern, half-filled with oil from the bottom of the toolbox, and a thin rope. Reed helped Watson hop down first, the dog scrambling a little before finding his balance. Chloe followed, sitting low on the foam deck. Reed was last, crouching beside the pole lashed to the side.

Behind them, lightning flashed. The sky cracked open. But the flatboat held.

They shoved off, silent and tense, into the dark flow of the flooded wild.

The drops hit like warning shots—fat, cold splashes that struck Reed's neck and dripped down his spine. Chloe hunched, arms wrapped tight around herself, eyes squinting against the wind. Watson lay low on the foam, ears flattened, eyes fixed on the black wall rushing toward them from the southwest.

Rain came down like a falling ocean, blinding and soaking them instantly. The foam raft bucked beneath them, waves slapping against the sides. Water pooled on the surface, sluicing over their supplies. Reed knelt, wedging his body against the conduit pole they'd tied as an impromptu rudder, pushing with everything he had to keep the nose angled into the wind.

Lightning strobed—white, craggy, endless—and for a breathless second, they saw the flooded forest: stripped tree tops jutting like spears, chunks of twisted metal drifting in the torrent, and something else; a shattered mobile home lay half-submerged, spinning like a death trap.

"Left!" Chloe shouted, pointing.

Reed didn't answer. He dug the pipe into the water, grinding it sideways against the current. The pallet craft twisted, sluggish at first, then faster, skipping past the crushed trailer with only inches to spare. The wind screamed, ripping across the water, and the air smelled like spilled gas and river rot.

Thunder boomed directly above them, shaking the sky and the foam beneath their feet. Reed felt the vibration rattle his ribs. Beside him, Watson let out a warning bark. Reed got the message. They needed to find shelter.

A gust hit the raft broadside, tipping them. Chloe scrambled, grabbing the edge as her foot slipped. Reed lunged, caught her wrist, and yanked her back down just before the raft righted itself again.

"I've got you," he yelled over the wind. "Hold on!"

They were past the submerged trees now, open water spreading deeper and more dangerous around them. Reed squinted into the storm to make sense of the indistinct horizon. There—the dark shape of the tall tower.

"We need to head that way!" he shouted.

Chloe gestured agreement, soaked and shaking, her hair plastered to her cheeks. She reached for the spray foam cans—they'd grabbed a few extra—and used one to patch a new seam of bubbling water.

The raft lurched again.

Reed pressed the pipe into the water, shoulders clenched, muscles burning. The storm gusted fiercely around them, and the drowned world wallowed beneath the weight of the flood.

And the improvised platform kept them out of the garbage swamp.

It seemed to take forever, but the tower grew closer and closer. They were watching it, willing the raft to reach the fire lookout.

Until they drew close enough to see the wall of debris stretched across the flooded shoreline—thirty feet thick or more, pressing against the land like a dam made of ruin. The remnants of a wrecked world floated in a swirling stew: broken boards, twisted siding, splintered furniture, pieces of rooftops, tangled wire, fragments of shattered lives. Clothing clung to branches like drowned flags. Tires bobbed like blackened buoys. Plastic bottles, fishing lines, and snarls of netting meshed together in a foul, bloated tangle.

Dead fish floated belly-up in the muck. A waterlogged deer's carcass turned slowly in the current, its glassy eyes staring blankly skyward. An otter's sleek body was caught in nylon netting. Even dozens of birds lay like fallen leaves among the ruins.

Chloe's stomach turned. "How the hell do we cross *that*?"

Reed scanned the trash-choked field, hands tight. That wasn't a question with an easy answer. One wrong step in that sludge and you were gone—sucked down under a suffocating blanket, with no way to claw your way back up. You'd drown in a grave of garbage.

Then he saw an opportunity.

"There," Reed said, pointing. "That boat."

A speedboat, flipped belly-up, hung in the branches of a massive, uprooted tree. The roots of the monster oak still clung to the shoreline, even as the trunk stretched like a fallen bridge across the filth. The boat was tangled in the upper limbs—maybe stable, maybe not. But it was an option.

"We push over to that tree," Reed said, already adjusting their course. "We climb over the boat, cross through the branches to the trunk, and get to the hill. That's our shot."

Chloe suppressed her revulsion at his idea. "You sure it'll hold?" she asked instead.

"Nope," he said. "Although it's better than swimming through that death soup."

The rain faded to a cold drizzle, now more nuisance than threat. A gentler wind stirred their soaked clothes, rather than tearing at them.

Watson whined low in his throat, staying close.

Reed turned to Chloe. "You with me?"

She met his eyes, drew in a shaking inhalation, and responded with a nod. "Let's do it."

Watson whined like they were both crazy and hung his head in resignation.

The pallet boards creaked as they aimed for the boat. Below them, something large swung beneath the surface—another of the unseen traps they needed to avoid. Chloe shivered, cold and scared, but resolute that they had to make this work.

The raft bumped gently against the boat. Barely disturbed, the hull remained still. Reed steadied it with the pole while Chloe reached for the slick fiberglass, hauling herself up onto the bow. Her fingers slipped once, but she found a better hold and scrambled forward, boots slipping on the wet surface. Watson whimpered, pacing, then Reed gave him a lift, boosting the lab up before climbing aboard himself. He let the raft go, watching as it drifted away.

The boat was wedged between thick branches, its fiberglass hull cracked, but mostly intact.

"Go slow," Reed said urgently, peering ahead through the weave of wet branches. "One step at a time."

Chloe shot him a nod, her breath fogging. The overturned speedboat offered a fragile bridge, a hollow shell of escape. They moved across it carefully, crawling low, using the branches overhead for support. Each creak made Chloe flinch. Reed's hand stayed near hers the entire way, anchoring her.

Chloe reached the tree first, crawling up the angled trunk like it was a fallen balance beam. She crouched near the hull and offered Reed a hand as he came up behind her. Watson scrambled between them, nails digging into the wet bark, ears down.

The tree's branches sagged and split beneath their weight, but held.

Leaves slapped at their faces, rain still dripping from every surface. Chloe's shirt snagged on a sharp limb, and for one gut-clenching second, she almost lost her footing—but Reed caught her by the wrist, steadying her again.

They climbed through the branches until they reached the trunk and then walked carefully, arms out for balance, until they reached the shore. Watson made quicker work of the last stretch, landing with a soft grunt. He was happy to jump down and leave the floodwaters behind.

They dropped into ankle-deep mire. Chloe sank, lugging one foot and the other from the muck, and looked up. The slope rose ahead of them, thick with vines and storm-tossed fragments, but climbable. The tower was ahead.

Together, they clawed their way up the slope, using rocks, roots, and anything else they could grab. Grime caked their fingers. Thorns and sharp edges tore at their clothes. The tower loomed closer with each step.

They hit the clearing at the tower's base, wheezing and drenched. The earth finally steadied beneath their boots. Chloe fell to her knees in the wet grass, then rolled onto her back, her breath caught in her throat, mud smeared across her face.

"We made it," she whispered.

Reed dropped beside her. Watson shook himself off, flinging water in every direction.

"Not dead yet," Reed said with a grin. "Good sign."

Chloe stared up at the tower's steel silhouette against the stormy sky. Lightning flickered far to the east. But the west had darkened again, and another line of storms would be marching through.

A tiny room sat under the first flight of stairs. However, she was more interested in the fire outlook. Above them, steps led to shelter. They'd have a minute to plan the next move.

"Come on," she said, starting up. "Let's see what the view looks like from the top."

The steel steps climbed into the sky, each one slick with rain and swaying in the wind. Chloe's legs burned before they were halfway up, and every step was a battle of will over exhaustion. Her lungs heaved against the cold air, muscles cramping in her legs. The last time she'd felt this wrecked, she'd been trudging away from the inferno of the Sisters volcano, ashen, blistered, and half-blind. And now? Another mega-quake. She closed her eyes. How was this even possible?

Above them, the fire tower loomed. By the time they reached the deck, her legs were trembling with every step.

The room at the top was angled and glass, most of it shattered. Shards lay scattered across the floor like dirty ice, the wind whistling through the empty panes, carrying remnants of the storm. Rain had soaked everything. A soggy towel snagged on the frame flapped like a flag of surrender.

Reed ducked through the broken window and unlatched the door from the inside. Chloe stepped in, water squelching in her boots. The room was chaotic—overturned chairs, laminated maps plastered to the floor in wet disarray, paper scattered like soggy tissues. Cabinet doors hung open, their contents spilling in heaps of disuse.

Chloe moved fast despite her fatigue, combing through drawers and shelves. In one drawer, she found a sealed box of energy bars, still dry, and flashlights in another. She grabbed them, then spotted several bottles of water half-hidden beneath an overturned chair. She cracked one open immediately, took a swig, then found a cracked plastic bowl and filled it for Watson. The lab's tail wagged furiously as he lapped it up, his thirst ravenous.

Meanwhile, Reed fought with the equipment. The generator coughed and sputtered to life—flickering dim light over the wet interior—but the radios stayed dead. He cursed softly, slapping a palm against the side panel. Static. Nothing.

"Either the quake fried the lines, the rain shorted the circuits, or there's no one left out there to answer," he told her, gulping the water she offered him.

Chloe looked up from the maps she was spreading across the end of a table. "I struck gold," she said, holding up a handful of laminated sheets and a ring of metal. "Maps of the area—and look, keys."

Reed crossed over, taking the ring from her hand. He studied them, brow furrowed. "These look like UTV keys. Or ATV. There's a maintenance garage under the stairs. We didn't check it yet."

Chloe was already moving, arms full. "Let's hope we can get in there. We need transportation. But anything with a roof and four walls sounds great about now."

Reed grabbed the water bottles and followed her toward the hatch. "If there's a vehicle in there and it runs, we have a shot at getting out of this hellhole."

They pushed the door open, the tower creaking beneath their weight as they descended, hope finally sparking in their blood.

Chapter Fifteen
Tiptonville Cutoff, TN: Saturday, August 15, 5 p.m.

He wasn't the smartest dog, but Charlie had a stubborn streak that didn't quit. The last place he'd seen Winnie was from the slope of this wrecked, drifting barn roof, and he wasn't budging until she came back.

The black-and-white Borgi planted himself like a furry statue, haunches square, eyes fixed upstream. Land flashed by—close enough to have jumped, but he didn't twitch. He held his ground when the roof scraped across one sandbar after another, slowing, almost stopping the wet wood before it broke free and continued its journey downriver.

A pair of Herring gulls dared to land. He barked them off, pacing in tight circles, then flopped back down with a grumble, resting his chin on white-dipped paws. His oversized ears, black with pink centers, drooped forward. Waiting.

Winnie would come. He knew it because she always came. She was part of the pack.

The barn roof glided down the swollen Mississippi, past shattered trees, through Kentucky and into Tennessee, a leaf on the flood's surface. Still, Charlie watched. He perked up when the floating wreckage shuddered to a stop against the angular remains of a shattered levee.

Lifting his ears, he tilted his head. Black button eyes scanned the Tiptonville Chute, an old tributary of the Mississippi that had long been blocked by human intervention. Punching through the weakened levee like a fist through paper, the river welled up through the cataract, carving shortcuts, reclaiming the offshoot. The man-made Tiptonville Cutoff no longer blocked the river. The Mississippi River fed its new channel, and Charlie's raft wedged tight at the remains of the levee.

Deliberately, he turned his back and sat down again, nose pointing upriver. He wiggled, settled, and stared down at the torrent. Winnie would come. He just had to wait.

***

The *Seismic Wave*, the battered 21-foot fishing boat with peeling paint and a dead outboard motor, barreled downriver. The current jerked like a riptide, hauling them through a miles-long watery maze of household remains, structural pieces, machinery, and farm objects. Dead fish floated in the clumps of riverbank mud with dislodged reeds and cattails. When Winnie called it gross, nobody argued.

Eyes sharp, the kids scanned the tumult, dogs watching and whining at every shape that rose from the flood. Somewhere in that endless stew of trash, Charlie was stranded.

Clouds pressed low and heavy, the color of the earth as if the dirt thrown from the earthquakes was suspended in the stratosphere, thought Piper as she stared at the clouds. They sure did not need a storm today. The dim light faded further as the sky thickened to a deep slate. Gray skies and brown water made it depressing.

That was when Piper spotted a tiny hunched shape on a massive roof slab, pinned against the remains of a shattered levee. She strained to make out the lump in the gloom.

But Charlie saw them.

He sprang to his feet, barking, running to the edge and back again. Winnie almost fell overboard in excitement, screaming his name, half sobbing, half shouting. Matthias grabbed her and plucked her back, yelling at Brett. Charlie's bark doubled in pitch and elation.

Everyone moved at once.

"Paddles!" Brett seized his and started pushing against the closest object. Piper followed, teeth clenched, shoving against buoyant lumps, steering them before the flow swept them past. Matthias gripped the wheel and twisted it far to the left, holding it in place.

The river fought the fishing boat, jerking and twisting.

An eddy caught them near the eastern bank, before they had passed the barn roof, spinning the *Seismic Wave* like a carnival ride. The boat jerked, tilted, and righted itself with a slap of water. The dogs skidded into each other. Brett braced himself, and Matthias threw out a leg to steady Piper. Her long hair whipped around as she grimly pushed them closer to the shore. For a second, havoc ruled.

Then the eddy spun them toward the bank—*squelch!*—the boat slammed into mud and held.

Bella launched over the side before Piper could catch her. Coco shot after her, both dogs vanishing into the trees, barking like alarms, strident howling echoing through the flood-scarred forest. Downstream a little, Charlie barked back.

The noise was thunderous—dogs barking, trees creaking, water slapping the shore in angry waves.

Then, a rumble started upriver. It grew noisier, and Brett recognized the sound of a plane's engine. A crop duster banking low enough to rattle leaves and nerves came into view, shooting past them. The kids looked up as it flew over their heads. They couldn't see much but the underbelly of the plane. The pilot buzzed them a few times, as if checking them out, then turned east and left over the treetops.

In the meantime, Charlie leapt from the stranded barn roof, a black-and-white blur hurtling down the muddy shore.

He sprinted, legs churning, barking madly as he closed the distance. Winnie screamed his name, already climbing out of the boat. Brett swept her up mid-charge, slogging through thick, slurping sludge and setting her down on harder ground just as the little Borgi skidded to a stop, leaping into her arms like a missile. She collapsed with him in a flurry of fur, tears, and laughter.

Matthias and Piper tied the boat to a tree while Duke whined miserably at the gunwale. "Come on, Duke," Piper coaxed, but the dog planted his feet, dismayed by the runny muck under the craft. Matthias scooped him up with a sigh, grinning as the dog licked his face in relief.

Bella and Coco burst from the trees moments later, tongues lolling, filthy paws kicking up wet leaves. For a moment, there was only motion—hugging, shouting, barking, relief drawing everyone close. Winnie clung to Charlie like she'd never let go again.

A strong wind swept through the trees, whipping at shirts and hair. The light was dim and gloomy. The river surged higher, creeping closer.

"We've gotta move back," Brett warned, eyes scanning the swollen river. "It's too low here. We need to leave the boat. It will only take us downriver; we don't want that anymore. We ought to get deeper into the woods."

"Do we even know where we are?" Piper asked, glancing around at the unfamiliar trees, the drowned world behind them.

Matthias bent his head, thinking. "After New Madrid, we drifted a long way. I think we're in Tennessee now."

"Tennessee?" Piper's brows knit together. "We need to go *home*."

Winnie's voice cut through the moment like a blade. "Home's gone," she said mournfully. "The river took it. We don't have a home again."

The words hit Piper like a punch. She stared at her little sister's dirt-smudged face; heartbreak was carved into it, and something shifted inside her. Where the earthquakes in May broke her, somehow this disaster patched that wound. No more wishing for courage. No more expecting someone else to step up.

She placed a hand on Winnie's shoulder, steady and sure. "Home isn't a roof or a bed or a kitchen table," she said. "Home is Chloe. Reed. Albert. Royce. It's *us*. We're going to find them, Winnie. Even if we have to walk all the way."

Winnie looked up, wet eyes peeking through the grime, and hair glued to her face. She nodded once and hugged Charlie tighter.

"Okay," she said, mimicking Piper's firmness. "Which way?"

"East," Brett called. He and Matthias were already moving, pushing aside vines and branches as they went. "Matthias found a game trail. If it holds, it might lead us to a highway."

"Do you have your compass?" Piper asked Matthias.

"Yeah, my pocketknife, a small flashlight, my whistle, and some matches. What I usually carry." Matthias looked around. "You want to use the flashlight while I watch the compass?"

Piper agreed, and they didn't wait.

With dogs at their heels, they pushed east, ducking under fallen trees, hopping over waterlogged furrows, and splashing through swollen creeks. The air reeked of torn earth and crushed sap. They circumvented huge rocks and holes, chasing littered patches of trail where loose rubble hadn't yet concealed it. The forest echoed with their movement— branches cracking, dogs panting, sneakers squelching in the wet earth. Thunder rumbled, the sound getting closer. Brett watched for something to use as shelter.

After a while, Matthias paused, eyes scanning the path ahead. In the muck were pressed hoof prints—fresh and deep.

He slid closer to Brett, voice low. "These tracks... they're not deer."

Brett glanced down, squinting. "What are you talking about?"

"Wild boars." Matthias pointed. "See that print? That's a hog's. Big one, too."

Brett crouched beside the impression. "That's gotta be twelve inches," he whispered.

"Exactly. We need to get quiet. Fast."

Brett didn't hesitate. He rounded up the others, herding them in with a stern urgency. "No talking. Dogs heeled. Stay sharp."

Duke and Coco obeyed instantly, falling in step. Bella didn't.

Growling low in her throat, hackles rising as she paced the trees, nose twitching, she wasn't sniffing—she was tracking.

"She's on a cat." Matthias blocked her, but she slid around him. "Cougar or something."

"It's probably somebody's house cat. I wish we had grabbed the rope from the boat," Brett hissed, trying to snag Bella's collar. She slipped out of reach, still circling, unable to pinpoint the odor. She growled at some phantom in the trees.

Whatever it was, the aftershocks continued to stir things up, confusing the big dog with the overlapping scents.

Reluctantly, they moved on—Bella trailing, ears pinned, and body tense.

Up ahead, the trail opened into a clearing, wild grasses waving in the deepening wind. The moment they stepped into it, they paused, staring up. The sky above was an unnatural shade of black, like ink spilled across the clouds.

Lightning flashed—white veins splitting the sky. The first thunderclap cracked so close it rattled their teeth, and fat drops of rain fell.

Brett scanned for cover.

"There, shelter in those rocks," he pointed across the clearing. "Watch your step—there's a drop!"

Off the path, the land fell away—ten, maybe fifteen feet—into a narrow gorge where a swollen stream rushed below. The trail here was little more than a packed groove trod by feral pigs on their way to the water.

On the far side, Brett had spotted an outcropping of rock, low and half-sheltered by overgrown brush. It wasn't perfect, but it would keep them dry. Lightning cracked again, illuminating the clearing in stark white for half a second.

They hurried across, the wind now howling through the trees above them.

"Move!" Brett shouted. "Go, go!"

The dogs broke into a run. The kids followed, slipping and scrambling as the storm roared overhead. Behind them, the forest darkened, thunder chasing them to the shelter of the rocks.

Rain lashed their faces, turning dirt into slick mud. Thunder cracked so close it felt like the sky was breaking apart above them.

Just as they reached the far side of the gorge, Bella froze—ears pricked, body stiff.

She let out a furious bark and bolted, veering off the path toward the drop. Her paws skidded on the wet grass as she charged the edge, barking madly at something across the stream. The kids couldn't see anything.

"Bella!" Brett shouted.

Before she started her descent, a shape exploded from the trees behind them—a blur of muscle, tusk, and rage.

A massive boar, all snout and wet bristles, tore through the underbrush with a shriek that split the storm. It charged across the clearing straight at Bella, foam flying from its mouth, hooves pounding the earth like a drumbeat of doom.

The kids screamed. Duke and Coco barked furiously.

Brett ran. "Bella, NO!"

BANG!

A single, sharp crack boomed through the storm. The boar faltered mid-charge, legs buckling, and collapsed with a heavy thud that shook the ground.

Everyone stopped moving. Even Bella. She stood trembling at the edge, ears twitching, eyes wide as the beast's body slid to a stop a few feet away.

Then, from the trees, a man stepped into view.

He looked to be in his thirties, medium height, with a wiry build. His face was deeply tanned, streaked with water and grime, framed by damp black hair tucked under a battered cap. A soaked jacket clung to his shoulders, his jeans grime-caked to the knees. A knapsack hung from one shoulder, and he carried a carved, weather-worn old hunting rifle in his right hand.

He raised his free hand. "No te haré daño! Amigos!"

The kids stumbled back, dogs bristling, growls ripping from their throats. Brett stepped in front of Winnie and Piper, heart thundering louder than the storm. Bella snarled, crouching low, ready to strike.

Piper's pulse spiked.

"No!" she yelled. She rushed forward, arms out, shoving Coco and Duke back with her legs. "Grab them!" she hissed to Matthias, who caught Coco by the scruff and scrambled for Duke.

Brett lunged for Bella's collar, gripping her tight. "What are you doing?" he threw back to Piper, bewildered.

Piper reached for Brett and Bella, waving her hands. The rain was decreasing, but the wind was picking up. "*Amigos!*" she called across the clearing.

She leaned close to Brett. "He said he won't hurt us. He said 'friends.'" Then, louder, to the stranger: "*Gracias!*"

The man dipped his chin, relief flashing across his face. He lowered the rifle and slung it across his shoulder with a strap.

They spoke quickly, Spanish rolling through the rain as she gestured toward the rock overhang ahead. Whatever Piper said made the man nod again.

He stepped toward them, slow and careful, boots sinking in the mire. As he passed Brett, he tipped his head in greeting and murmured something in Spanish to Bella.

She growled again, deep and low, but stopped fighting and stayed put, ears flicking.

The man gave her a knowing smile and moved on.

"His name's Luis," Piper panted, as she and Brett wrestled Bella back toward the rocky overhang. The dog twisted and growled, still wound tight, ready to chase the cat's odor, which was driving her crazy. Rain slicked her fur, muck streaking her legs as she resisted every step.

Brett gave her a shove toward the shallow, cave-like hollow, shielding his eyes from the wind as thunder cracked overhead. "In," he ordered, pushing the rest of the crew behind her. Luis followed last, his rifle slung tight, water dripping from his soaked cap.

Piper wiped her face with her sleeve, speaking fast. "He heard us crashing through the forest—said we were loud enough to wake the dead. When he realized we were just kids, he got worried. He said the feral pigs had been aggressive all day. He thinks they're spooked since this morning's earthquake tore up the woods."

Brett looked out at the fading trail where the boar had fallen, storm clouds pulsing with lightning above. "He saved her life," he said, voice low. "That hog would've torn Bella apart."

A white-hot flash split the sky, thunder booming behind it, but inside their rocky shelter, they were safe. The wind still reached in with chilly fingers, but they were out of the onslaught of the heavy rain.

Luis spoke up calmly, despite the storm raging around them. Piper tipped her head as she listened, flashlight partially covered with one hand, her brow furrowing, asking him short questions in return. Before she could begin translating for the others, Bella lunged, snarling, toward the narrow opening, nearly pulling away from Brett.

"Whoa—Bella, *stop!*" he grunted, struggling to hold her back.

Matthias dove in to help, grabbing her collar, but there wasn't enough room. The dog thrashed like she meant to bring the walls down.

Then Luis stepped forward, voice sharp and commanding: "Sentada! Quieto! Espera!"

Everything stilled.

Bella stopped mid-bark, her ears shooting forward in surprise. She stared at Luis, then—almost sheepishly—sat down, panting, eyes flicking away.

Luis's voice softened. "Buen perro."

Winnie peeked over Charlie's back, wide-eyed. "He said good dog…"

Brett blinked. "Wait. Bella… speaks Spanish?"

"She must," Piper said, awe creeping into her voice, the flashlight pointed at Bella's coat.

Brett tilted his head, letting out a half-laugh. "Her old owners—maybe they were Mexican. No wonder she never listens. We've been giving commands in English, and she's been listening in Spanish."

Bella snorted, as if insulted, then laid her head on her paws like none of this was her fault. Lying between them, she kept her eyes trained on the wide mouth of the cave's entrance. Now and then, she stared at Luis, as if seeking his approval to tear off into the storm and finish tracking that cat. Her ears twitched at every branch snap, every flurry of the wind.

"She could still take off," Matthias whispered, watching her warily.

"No," Piper said, shaking her head. "She's waiting until he gives her permission to go. She is such a smart dog. I wondered why it was so hard to get her to listen."

The storm grumbled above them. Rain still fell, but not in sheets anymore—just a steady patter on the rocks. Under the outcrop, they pressed close, knees touching, the air thick with the stink of damp clothes, wet fur, and bone-deep exhaustion. Winnie sat on her knapsack, reminding Brett they'd need that conversation soon. There was barely enough space for them to huddle, backs to the cold stone.

Piper sat cross-legged, her hands moving as she spoke, voice barely above the rain. "Luis lives north of Chicago. Waukegan. His wife's there—she's pregnant."

The others leaned in; the shadows deepened around their faces.

"This morning," Piper continued, "he left town with a few men, heading for work somewhere around here. He and the other guys—they're undocumented workers, finding any work they can. After the quake hit—" she looked disgusted, "—the driver ditched them. Dumped them somewhere east of here and took off."

Brett's shoulders clenched. He raked wet hair from his forehead, rainwater dripping down his wrist. "He left them?"

Piper gave a slow nod. "No car. No supplies. They walked and found a campsite abandoned after the quake, with some canned food, bottled water, and an old rifle left behind. They picked up what they could."

Matthias hunched, sneakers scraping on slick stone. "That's where he got the gun?"

"It had one bullet," Piper said. "He used it on that pig."

A gust of wind cut into the shelter, bringing the smell of torn earth and something sour—the swamp, or worse. Winnie held her nose.

"They grabbed what they could and moved on. Found another spot to wait out the storm. But when Luis heard us crashing through here, he left the others to follow us. Thought—" she hesitated, a smile at the corner of her mouth, "—he thought no kids should be alone out here. But he got turned around following us, and he's no longer sure where the other guys are."

Luis turned beside her, rummaging in his battered knapsack, speaking a few words. The zipper rasped, sharp in the hush. Piper flicked her flashlight toward him, and the beam caught inside—bottled water and protein bar wrappers.

"*Gracias*, thank you!" Grinning, she looked at the others. "He's willing to share."

Matthias reached first, tearing into a power bar with a grunt.

"I'm starving," he said, mouth already full.

Winnie, wide-eyed and shivering, peered hopefully into the pack. "Any cherry pastries?"

Piper laughed, shaking her head. "Just power bars. No pastries."

Winnie sighed dramatically but grabbed a bar anyway.

They fed the dogs carefully, cupping water into their palms. Their friends slurped noisily, tails thumping against the stone. Only Bella turned her nose up at the offering, giving the power bars a look of utter contempt before settling, tense and alert, her gaze locked on the dripping trees beyond the outcrop.

Brett glanced toward the cave entrance, then down at Duke and Coco, curled in a damp heap, barely stirring. Winnie and Charlie, huddled, looked smaller and frailer than ever. "We're soaked. I don't know if we can find any dry wood, but we can use Matthias's matches if we do. We'll stay out of the rain tonight and keep each other warm. Does Luis know where the highway is? Tomorrow, we need to head back and find Reed and Chloe."

Piper spoke in quick Spanish, her voice low and steady. Luis answered, his words clipped. She turned to the others. "He says due east. He doesn't have a compass."

Matthias fished a battered silver circle from his pocket, flipping it into his palm like a coin. He turned a slow circle, then pointed into the dark.

"East. That way."

Luis murmured again, tapping his hand to the horizon.

"He says to follow the sun when it rises," Piper translated.

Matthias was already on his feet, brushing needles and clay from his shorts. "I'll find dry wood," he said, scout instincts kicking in. His eyes swept the dripping forest with sharp efficiency.

"I'll help," Brett said, getting up.

"Look under overhangs, hollow trees, lee sides— wherever the rain can't reach," Matthias instructed.

Luis rose too, scanning the trees for trouble. When Piper told him their plan, he shook his head sharply and made a squealing noise in his throat—a pig, unmistakably. He tapped the empty rifle slung across his back.

"No good," he said in terrible English. "Trouble."

"We'll be quiet," Brett promised, but Luis was already handing his pack to Piper and stepping after them. He wasn't letting them go alone.

Bella barked once, sharp and accusing, then paced in tight circles. At a word from Luis—*"¡Quieto!"*—she dropped to her haunches, tail stiff, eyes burning into the forest.

"Boy, she's gonna be easier to deal with now that we know how to talk to her," Matthias chuckled, looking over his shoulder.

The three of them slipped into the woods, bits of swamp sticking to their shoes. Luis took the lead, moving sure-footed through the wreckage. Fallen branches carpeted the ground. Leaves clung wet and heavy to everything, the battered forest steaming under the ragged edge of the storm.

The swollen creek splashed somewhere to their left. The air stank of churned sludge and stripped wood. Their feet squelched, and stray branches sent a cold, slimy shiver down their spines.

They moved single file into the wet bush as the forest closed around them.

In the flickering light of the flashlight, Piper lowered herself onto the cold cave floor. Around her, the dogs squirmed and huffed—Duke curled tight against her leg like a coiled spring, Charlie, a ball of black and white in the little girl's lap. She locked eyes with Winnie, who sat cross-legged on her knapsack, chin lifted in defiance.

"Alright, Winnie," Piper said, steady but firm. "Tell me."

She wasn't angry. The absurdity made her want to laugh. Of course, Winnie would take the jewels if she saw them abandoned in the ash and grit of the volcano. And she'd keep it a secret, too, because secrets and treasure went together when you were ten years old.

Winnie's brows drew together. "I wasn't stealing them," she grumbled. "I found the black bag while you and Chloe were helping Reed. It had necklaces and stuff—just sitting there."

"So, you took it?" Piper asked, crossing her arms.

"I thought we could give them to Nadia when we saw her!" Winnie's voice rose, then fell, like she knew it was a hard sell.

Piper waited.

With a theatrical sigh, Winnie knelt, reaching beneath her. Dislodged from her lap, Charlie whimpered, picking up one little paw and the other from the cold floor. From under her bottom, she dragged out the weathered knapsack she never let out of sight. She opened it slowly, like revealing treasure in a storybook, and pulled out a fistful of glittering stones.

Even in the low cave light, they shimmered—crimsons, deep blues, mysterious greens, flecks of gold. Piper blinked. They looked like something out of a museum case.

"I was going to tell her. Or Daddy. But neither of them came, so… I kept them safe."

Piper ran a fingertip over one of the stones. Smooth, cold, a blue that seemed to go on forever. "Is this why you never put that bag down?"

Winnie bobbed her head, her curls jumping, her lips tight. "I didn't want to lose them."

Piper exhaled slowly. "Well, it's lucky you didn't. If your pack had been left in the house, it would've gone with the flood."

Winnie's face lit up with sudden pride. "Charlie saved it! He grabbed the strap at the last second. He's a *very* good dog."

She threw her arms around the Borgi, who wriggled with delight and licked her cheek like a hero accepting his medal.

Piper bobbed her head, a reluctant smile on her face. "You two are something else."

"Is Daddy mad at me?" Winnie asked after a minute, lashes lowered.

"Probably," Piper sighed. "He's always mad about something."

Winnie looked down, fingers fussing with the edge of the knapsack. Charlie whimpered.

"Don't worry," Piper added, softer now. "We'll sort it out. Chloe and Reed—they'll handle Dad."

As the words left her mouth, she realized how true they were. Chloe's calm strength. Reed's quiet focus. They were there, willing to put things back together, even as everything fell apart around them. Piper had spent so long doubting, thinking it all rested on her shoulders—but she didn't have to carry everything alone.

This morning seemed so far away, her doubts and anxiety eating her up. Tonight, after what they had been through—surviving the failed levee flood, riding the river, finding Matthias, and chasing downriver after Charlie, even using her unique skill of languages to make a friend in the dripping forest in the craziness—she didn't feel helpless or alone. Surprised, she realized she felt strong.

She wasn't the scared girl who woke up doubting herself.

She was the girl who *did* things. Who kept moving when everything else stopped.

She wasn't alone. Not with her brothers, her sister, and the wild pack of dogs curled around them like furry guardians. Together, they could figure out anything.

Winnie smiled and tenderly poured the gems back into the knapsack like she was tucking them into bed. Piper caught the shimmer in her eyes and felt her chest tighten. Winnie didn't cry easily. If she was this close to crying, today cost more than just energy. It carved deep.

Piper reached over and squeezed her hand. No words. Just warmth.

The cave was silent for a long moment, the silence that buzzed in your ears after too much noise. Piper looked up at the clouds, barely visible through the narrow cave mouth.

"We're alive," she whispered, mostly to herself. "And they are too. Chloe. Reed. I can feel it."

Suddenly, she reached back and pulled the tie out of her ponytail. Her long strands slipped free, blowing in the wind. It felt good.

They just had to keep moving. Find each other.

And when they did?

They'd start again, stronger than before.

***

Dan huddled in the borrowed jacket Pete had lent him, drawing it tighter around his shoulders, teeth clenched against the damp chill. The cluster of trees and tangled brush barely kept the wind off, but it was the only cover he'd found since landing the crop duster. He crouched low, back against a mossy trunk, watching the faint outline of the road through the undergrowth.

The pavement stretched empty, absorbed by dusk. A hundred yards away, the crop duster was a shadow.

Somewhere out there, the kids were walking, heading east. He was sure of it. They'd have to hit this highway if they stayed due east long enough. Matthias was a boy scout, for pity's sake. The kid should be able to find the highway. And when they did, he'd be waiting.

His eyes kept flicking down the flat road, scanning both directions. He could see a long way come daylight. He'd find them.

He'd find out what they did with Nadia's jewelry—whatever it took.

No birds. No crickets. Just the wind whispering through hanging limbs and the occasional low grumble from beneath the earth. Now and then, thunder rolled in the distance, as if the storm hadn't decided whether it was coming back.

He thought of Nadia—her voice, her stubborn laugh, their cabin in Montana with its woodstove and thick walls—and a sharp ache bloomed in his chest. He wanted to go home.

Dan hunkered down deeper into the brush, eyes locked on the road.

One way or another, this was coming to an end.

Patterson Airfield, KY, Saturday, August 15, 6 p.m.

Royce and Albert sat on boxes, slumped near the hangar doors, shoulders heavy with exhaustion. It had been a day. Royce still hadn't processed the loss of everything he owned—his house, barn, crops, and the town. His memories were tied up here, and he'd have to deal with it, but all he thought about now was the kids, Reed and Chloe.

Even Stella and Shadow settled, ears twitching in their sleep. Another severe thunderstorm came through, noisy enough, and the cloudburst lit the skies, cooling everything with a wild, wet wind. As it blew through, a sudden growl of tires over drenched gravel snapped them to attention.

The dogs were on their feet instantly, tails wagging like flags in the gale. Royce pulled himself up, muscles resisting, just as Pete Deller's pickup skidded to a halt, mud spraying around the wheels. The engine barely choked off before Pete flung the door open and jumped out, words tumbling from his mouth as he aimed for the hangar entry.

"They're okay!" he shouted, sprinting toward them, breathless. "All of them! My scouts—and Brett, Piper, Winnie—your three. They're safe. Even your dogs! Jamie and Pedro made it home. I just came from Jamie's house."

Albert jumped forward, bright spots on his cheeks. "How? Where are they?" His voice crackled with urgency, fists clenched at his sides.

Pete was practically vibrating, barely able to keep up with his story. He had ditched the grimy Boy Scout uniform for jeans and a sun-faded blue shirt, but the raw scratches across his cheek and arms still stood out. His tightly curled hair was damp, combed hastily with his fingers, but his eyes were lit with relief.

"That's the wild part," Pete said, panting. "Jamie told me—they went downriver in your old fishing boat. The *Seismic Wave*."

Royce's jaw dropped. "That junker? That engine's been dead for a decade."

"They didn't start it," Pete said. "They rode it. Let the current take 'em. Then—get this—they ran into Jamie,

Matthias, and Pedro. Those three had found a brand-new wave runner floating past the tree where I had left them. Damn tree uprooted in the flood, but they caught the runner and climbed aboard. They found the key and got it going. They were heading home when they found Matthias's brother and sisters."

Royce stared at him, wrapping his head around it. "And the kids—?"

"Reunited," Pete said, nodding fast. "They stuck together."

Relief washed over them both. For a heartbeat, everything stopped while he relished this one piece of good news.

Albert let out a long whistle. "So, where the hell are they now?"

Before Pete answered, the sky rumbled with the familiar growl of a low engine. Heads turned as a crop duster buzzed from the horizon, wings dipping, wheels skimming low.

"Ty's back." Royce locked eyes on the descending aircraft. It bounced across the cracked runway, spraying sand as it rolled to a halt. "What happened to the kids?"

Pete shaded his brow, voice still racing. "Your kids gave Jamie and Pedro the wave runner so they could head home and tell us what's happening. But their dog—one of them—got swept onto a floating barn roof. Brett, Matthias, and the girls chased downriver after it."

"Of course they did." Royce kicked a rock, somewhere between exasperated and proud. "Damn kids. The river's a deathtrap after that quake."

Ty had already leapt from the cockpit, pulling off his leather cap as the wind flattened his clothes. Without hesitation, he slid down the fuselage and jogged toward them, his face grim, his eyes sharp. Ty didn't waste a second. He was talking before he got to them.

"It's a disaster out there," he snapped, voice ragged from agitation. "The ground's torn to hell, river's completely out of its banks. And New Madrid—" He stopped, shaking his head. "It's *gone*. There's nothing left but a giant sand ring. It's like the whole town got sucked straight into the earth. Dead center's a pit so deep, I couldn't even see the bottom."

Royce and Albert exchanged stunned glances, the dogs silent behind them, sensing the tension.

"Levees are gone, washed away like driftwood," Ty said, voice rising. "Flooded fields, roads under water for miles. I traced the river's path to find signs of the kids, but nothing. The river is jammed with junk, wrecked houses, boats, containers, and barges. It's a graveyard out there. I can't describe it all. I'd have gotten back sooner, but when that thunderstorm came through, I had to fly southwest around it until the worst passed. But then, on my way back—" he jabbed a finger in the air. "That crazy guy you lugged out here—the one who knew how to fly and took my other plane?"

"Dan?" Royce asked, already dreading the answer.

Ty threw up his hands. "Yes, Dan! I was tracking him in my plane. I *knew* that guy was trouble. The GPS showed it veering toward Tennessee, then it slowed and stopped. That lunatic landed my crop duster on Pea Ridge Road at Darnall Point."

Albert blinked. "Wait—he *landed* it? How do you know?"

"Got scared of the storm, most likely," Ty growled. "I know because the GPS isn't moving anymore. The dot slowed and stopped! I thought he had wrecked in the storm, but when I flew over there, I saw the plane on the ground in one piece, and he was gone. Just up and vanished."

Royce let a curse slip between his teeth. "He must've gone looking for the kids."

"Why would he do that?" Ty asked plaintively. "If he finds them, what will he do, carry them back?"

"Wait," Pete stepped forward, his voice suddenly tense. "Jamie told me something weird. Said that when they were stuck in that tree, a guy was shouting at them from another tree. Matthias said it was his dad."

Albert's brow furrowed. "Dan is Matthias's *father*?"

The scout leader gave a curt nod. "Jamie said the guy accused them of stealing money, jewelry, something. Threatened them. Said he was nasty. Jamie didn't like the way he talked to Matthias. Said the man was... dangerous."

Royce's shoulders clenched. "So he's not just out there—he's *after* them."

"And now they're stranded, somewhere downriver," Albert growled, eyes darting to Stella, whose tail whipped, her nose in the wind. She gave him a plaintive look. He knew that expression. He turned back, chin set. "We need to find them. Before he does."

"Darnall Point's not far," Royce said. "Twenty or thirty miles. Woods out there, bogs close to the river. But if he made it, so can we. We'll have to drive it."

Ty slapped dust from his jeans and slid his cap down low against the sour wind. "Roads are a wreck. Sinkholes, cracks big enough to consume a truck. Traffic's backed up everywhere." He jerked his chin toward the east. "Your best shot's Highway 12. The shortcut is still there—the county barricaded it off when the road fell apart. You'll have to muscle around the barriers, but no traffic. Nothing you can't push through… I think."

"It'll be dark inside two hours," Pete warned, squinting at the churned-up sky. Clouds and smoke blurred the sun into a copper smear. "Less, with this garbage in the air."

Ty wiped his mouth with the back of his hand. "Storm like this, maybe the kids found shelter. Maybe they're holed up somewhere." He hesitated. "That jackass Dan—he had to have seen something if he brought the plane down."

"You're sure it wasn't engine trouble?" Pete asked, skeptical.

Ty shook his head. "Both planes were solid. The hangar got rattled pretty good, but the planes were outside. They're fine."

Albert looked west, where the light already sagged toward dusk. "We leave now. Drive till it's too dark to see. If we have to, we sleep in the truck. Be close when morning hits."

"Agreed," Royce said, reaching out to clasp Ty's hand, then Pete's. "Thanks. Cellphones are dead, so we'll swing back through later."

He climbed behind the wheel and rolled them out of the dusty lot. As the tires hit the broken asphalt, Royce's mouth tightened. No word from Reed or Chloe. Not since the quake.

He gripped the steering wheel harder, his mind reaching into the gathering dark. Keep them safe, he thought, half prayer, half promise. Please hold on.

Chapter Sixteen

Boatwright Wildlife Management Area, MO: Saturday, August 15, 6 p.m.

The garage under the fire lookout wasn't much—four aluminum walls, a bare cement floor, and a corrugated metal roof that pinged with each new spit of rain. No windows. But it was shelter, and that counted for something.

Reed shoved the roll-up door with a grunt, the metal scraping on its tracks before it jerked open. His flashlight beam swept the space—just shadows, gas cans, and the squat, mud-caked shape of a two-seater UTV crouched in the back, as if it were waiting. A winch clung to the front bumper, cable coiled tight.

"Holy crap," he said, stepping forward.

Chloe followed close behind, holding another light steady as he ran his hand along the matte green body. The UTV was battered but solid—paint scratched, tires caked with dried forest grime, and a roll cage nicked from past close calls with trees and rocks. It was a working rig.

He popped the hood and checked the lines. The fuel smelled clean. Gas cans stacked nearby still sloshed with weight. A good sign.

"Think it'll run?" Chloe asked. She spread out the laminated maps, giving them a chance to dry.

Reed gave a tight grin. "We're going to bet our lives on it."

The wind howled outside, rattling the thin walls. There was no way they were driving out in the pitch dark with the storm still throwing tantrums. It was better to wait for morning.

They climbed into the bucket seats, soaked clothes peeling away from skin, boots squelching on the floorboards. Watson flopped down on the floor with a heavy sigh, tail thumping once before he settled.

Harnesses hung beside them—thick, worn straps built to keep you in your seat when the trail tried to throw you. The windshield was streaked, but still intact.
Reed leaned back and eyed the steel canopy overhead.

"This thing," he told her, "will be our ticket out. But let's stay put until dawn."

Chloe leaned into the seat, damp hair clinging to her cheek, eyes still wide, listening to the storm tear at the world outside. Somewhere beyond the walls, trees cracked and distant thunder rolled low across the wetlands.

"I don't know what the magnitude of that earthquake was this morning," she said, voice barely above a whisper, "but to rip open the Mississippi like that... break levees, flood Cairo—" She rubbed her forehead. "It had to be an eight. At least."

Reed didn't speak right away. He sat forward, elbows on the steering wheel, watching the weak beam of the flashlight as it flickered along the UTV's dashboard. Finally, he said, "The quakes in May? Most were magnitude eight plus, but there were a few nines, especially the one that started everything on the Cascadia Subduction Zone. I looked it up afterward—after everything." He glanced at her. "Magnitude eights happen once every year or two. Not common, but not impossible. Sometimes they come close together. Weeks. Months."

"But San Andreas, Cascadia… now this?" Her voice rose slightly. "That's three major fault systems in under six months. You think they're connected?"

He rubbed at his temple, then tipped his head. "No. Too far apart. It doesn't work like… dominoes. At least, normally."

"So what, then?" she asked, a sharp edge creeping into her tone. "Coincidence?"

The silence that followed was thick. Neither of them believed that, but they had nothing to go on. Even if they could have found a signal, the batteries in their phones had died. There was no help there. The wind shrieked again. Something heavy banged against the side of the building, and both flinched, Watson growling low from his place on the floor.

"I don't know," Reed admitted finally. "But guessing won't help us tonight."

Chloe didn't respond. Her arms wrapped tight around herself, and she stared at the dark slit beneath the garage door.

Reed's voice softened. "What we know—what we *can* do—is get home. Check on the kids, my dad, Albert. The dogs. Everything else can wait."

She turned to him slowly. "Your dad's place has a levee holding back the Mississippi."

"I know."

"What if it failed, like the levee in front of Boxco?"

He hesitated for the briefest beat. "Then we'll deal with it. But I don't think it has. The levee in front of Boxco was fairly new. The levee in front of my dad's place has been there a long time, through all kinds of weather, floods, and shakes."

"I hope you're right." Her voice wavered, and she looked away again.

Reed leaned back, exhaling through his nose. "We move at first light. There has to be an old fire road we can use, then cut east."

Watson lay on his side and let out a low, tired huff. The storm was easing, and for a moment, neither spoke. Alone with the rain and wind, their thoughts churned, too nervous to voice.

Neither of them mentioned the quake again—not the kids, nor the silence from home. Fear sat between them like an unnamed shadow.

The wind had died down, but it left behind an eerie stillness. Rain still tapped on the metal walls, slower now, more deliberate. Reed sat beside Chloe in the UTV, the chill of the night soaking through even inside the garage. The weak light from the flashlight barely reached the corners of the space.

Reed broke the silence first. His voice was rough, low. "I'm sorry it took me this long to say anything."

Chloe turned to him, her expression unreadable in the half-light.

"I mean about… us. I wasn't sure how you felt," he said, eyes on the floor. "Didn't want to make a mess of something that could mean everything to me. I was waiting for the right time. Maybe that was stupid."

She didn't answer immediately, just stared at him for a moment, her face softening as he spoke.

"I want to be with you," she said finally, the words simple but solid. "And with the kids. I want to figure this out. Together."

He looked at her, a silent yes in his dark eyes.

Chloe's voice lowered. "Do you think… we could take it slow? Like… date. See where this goes?"

Reed let out a rasp that sounded almost like a laugh. "Yeah. Of course. But… I want you to know something."

He turned to face her fully, his face half-lit and worn. "I'm sure I love you, Chloe. I might not be good at saying it—never really have been—but I know how I feel. These last few years… they were hollow. I stopped connecting. Sure, I was an EMT and dealt with people daily, but it felt like they were on the other side of a wall I couldn't get past. The loneliness grew, fed on itself. Eventually, it was like I went numb. No spark, no interest. Only Watson reached me."

Watson's ear twitched at his name, but he didn't move from his spot.

"But the last three months? With you? With the kids?" Reed's voice thickened, eyes burning. "It was like something woke up. My heart—my whole damn soul—it's overflowing. I wake up eager for the day to begin. And I didn't mind taking it slow, because I loved the journey. Every single moment with you."

Chloe bit her lip, eyes wet. "I almost gave up, Reed. On dating. On men. I kept trying, hoping someone would be different, and every time I did, it … it never lasted. The effort felt like more than anyone was worth." She smiled faintly. "Then you came along. And these past few months, I saw it. You're everything I wanted to find."

Her smile faded as her voice turned soft. "But now I'm wondering… what if this world—what's left of it—won't give us a future? What if we missed our chance?"

Reed reached for her hand and gently wrapped it in his. "Then we make the most of the time we have."

He leaned in, slow and deliberate, until their lips met. The kiss was warm, grounding, and full of everything that had been unsaid.

Watson shot to his feet with a sharp bark.

Reed and Chloe jerked apart, startled. Watson growled deep in his chest, ears forward, body tense.

Reed turned, aiming the flashlight beam at the dog, stiff and alert.

The light slid across the concrete floor and caught it. Not a puddle, but motion—a ribbon of dark water snaking beneath the garage door in short, slithering pulses.

Chloe's throat hitched. "Reed," she pushed herself to a stand in the UTV. "The river. It's here."

Reed didn't answer. He was already out of the UTV and moving.

He tore open the utility tray's bungee net in two sharp yanks. Dropping the full gas cans in the tray, he hauled Watson up with a grunt, the dog's claws skittering against the steel-framed, ridged diamond plate.

"Stay," Reed ordered.

Watson's ears twitched. A low whine bubbled in his throat, but he obeyed, pressing flat into the tray as if he understood the danger.

Reed cinched the fuel cans tight with ratchet straps. Metal bit metal. He grabbed the drying maps, rolled them up, and handed them to Chloe to stuff between the seats. She flicked the LED bars on, and the world flared. Bright light lanced open the gloom, harsh against the slick surface of the garage door.

"You ready?" Reed's voice was tight, his hands braced on the roll-up latch.

In answer, she twisted the ignition. The UTV sputtered, then growled to life, its engine a low, steady thrum. He heaved. The garage door slid upward, and in came the flood.

Shin-deep, cold, and fast.

Reed splashed to the driver's side, vaulted in, and they drove out of the building just as the first misshapen lump bumped against the wheels.

Outside, the river had concealed the base of the fire tower. Water lapped at the support beams, thick with drifting branches and unrecognizable debris. The plateau wasn't safe anymore.

Reed mashed the throttle. The UTV rushed forward, tires hissing through the shallows. Chloe clung to the frame as they barreled toward higher ground.

The tires churned through the murky water, kicking up oily ripples as Reed steered them out into the open. The UTV bucked slightly as it hit uneven terrain hidden beneath the flood, but the suspension held. Chloe gripped the side rail, eyes skimming the rising waterline and the shrouded woods ahead. The storm's remnants hadn't left — wind hissed through the trees like a warning.

A rusted oil drum clanked against a tree trunk, carried on the surface like a toy. Something else floated past — bloated and pale — but neither of them looked too closely.

"Keep your eyes on the slope," Reed shouted over the engine and wind hum. "If this spreads across the ridge, we could get cut off."

The UTV growled as he gunned it up a shallow incline, tires slipping on wet rock and half-submerged roots. Watson barked once from behind, claws scraping at the metal tray as the vehicle sprang upward.

Chloe craned her neck. "There's a break in the trees up ahead—a fire trail?"

"I see it."

Reed angled toward it, the headlights throwing their shadows long and fast across the underbrush. Water slapped the tires of the UTV in angry waves, but finally, they crested the rise. Behind them, the swollen river spread wide, hauling trees and wreckage along its surface.

Chloe looked back. "All this water. I wonder where it's coming from."

Reed tipped his jawline. "Yeah. It's coming in fast."

The trail ahead narrowed, flanked by dense timber and slick, rain-darkened earth. The UTV bounced over a downed limb, metal rattling, and Chloe held tight as they plunged deeper into the woods.

Branches clawed at the roll cage. Muck splattered the windshield. Reed leaned forward, squinting through the smears as he navigated the mess of fallen branches and rubbish.

Watson whined, low and uneasy, but stayed down.

"We need high ground. Let me know if you see anything."

Chloe reached over and placed her hand over his on the gear lever. "We got this. Together."

He looked over, eyes meeting hers.

"Together," he said. Then he pushed forward, deeper into the forest.

St. Louis, MO: Saturday, August 15, 6 p.m.

Tau shoved open the warped door of the Women's Restroom, fear driving his feet. In his mind, the wind behind them roared like a voice from the underworld, deep and predatory.

"In. Now!" he shouted.

They stumbled inside, boots slapping against the cracked tile. Emmet slammed it shut behind them, shoulders heaving. The storm pounded outside—rain like nails, thunder cracking close enough to rattle the mirrors still clinging to the walls.

The Men's restroom across the way was gone. Not collapsed—crushed. A massive bur oak had flattened it, the thick trunk stretching out of the trees like the arm of a giant. Emmet had never seen anything like it. The base alone was wider than a car, leaning against their structure like a fallen shield, absorbing the worst of the wind's strength.

"Looks like we picked the right side," Tau said optimistically, flapping his arms like a dog, shaking water off.

Sitting on the floor a few minutes later, their backs to the cold enamel, they were beaten. But Emmet had one more surprise.

"You guys hungry?" Emmet asked. He rummaged in the bag he'd picked up at the rescue site and pulled out three MREs. He passed around the packets—meatloaf, chili, something that claimed to be lasagna.

Emmet cracked one open, its plastic peeling with a sticky pop. Slow but steady, water trickled from a fractured sink. They filled the pouches with the liquid and mixed the powder to drink, lips chapped and hands shaking from cold and adrenaline.

"This is awesome!" Tau said. "I was starving."

Walter rolled his eyes as Emmet laughed. However, he was appreciative as well. This was the most normal thing that they'd done since the quake. The room was mostly shattered tiles and flattened stalls, but it was dry. That was enough.

While he ate, Walter hunched against the wall, poking at his tablet. No internet, of course, but at least he could review the most recent data he'd downloaded. The screen glowed blue against his drawn face.

"We should stay here," Emmet said around a mouthful of chili. "At least for the night. Safer than being out there with the sky trying to kill us."

"Safer—until the ground tries it too," Walter muttered, not looking up.

Tau looked over. "The model?"

Walter confirmed, lips tight. "It's the same curve as May. Stress values and energy distribution fall into the same pattern. If I'm reading this right, we're staring down a 9.0. or worse."

Emmet stopped chewing. "So, the quake this morning—only a warm-up?"

Walter rubbed his chin. "Statistically? Two shocks like that on the same fault, same forty-eight hours? A five percent chance. But that's what the model is predicting."

Tau folded his empty MRE bag and tucked it into a corner. "Something's off. Are we looking at another chain reaction? Or is there something unique about the pressure waves? None of this fits normal behavior."

Emmet wiped his fingers on his jeans, staring into the shadows. "Super-cell storms didn't trigger these quakes. I get that now. But something *is* triggering them." He looked up, eyes glinting in the dim light. "What if it's not from Earth?"

Tau's eyebrows climbed his forehead. "What do you mean?"

Emmet leaned forward, voice rising over the wind. "What if something out there—an object, planet, whatever—is close enough to tug at us? Not obvious, not visible, but enough mass to wrench the crust like a slingshot?"

Walter looked up, blinking. "You think a space rock is giving us earthquakes?"

"There are more things in heaven and earth, Horatio..." Emmet said quietly, half to himself.

Walter frowned. "Who the hell is Horatio?"

Tau snorted. Then burst out laughing. "Hamlet," he said, pacing now. "Shakespeare." His boots crunched over fallen ceiling tile and shattered porcelain. His hair stood in damp spikes, flecked with bits of leaf and moss from earlier. "It's a line from the play. He's saying you need to keep an open mind. Maybe we go all the way and blame little green aliens."

Emmet chuckled. Even Walter cracked a thin grin.

"We can stick with science for now," Emmet said. "I'm simply saying that astronomical alignment and gravitational forces from other celestial bodies have also been suggested as potential earthquake triggers."

Tau sighed. "It's no worse than the theories some others have postulated. Whatever it is, we won't find answers here. We need to get back to Reston."

For a moment, the storm faded—there was no thunder. Then the next gust slammed into the building, and the walls shivered again.

The restroom fell quiet except for the wind and the distant rumble of thunder. Tau leaned back against the wall and closed his eyes. Then, softly, he sang:

"And if I only could, I'd make a deal with God, and I'd get Him to swap our places…"

Walter exhaled through his nose. "I wish we were back in Reston."

"You survived the last earthquake," Tau said, still singing softly. *"Be runnin' up that road, be runnin' up that hill…"* He opened one eye. "You'll do it again."

"I wish I had your faith," Walter grumbled. "One mega-earthquake was enough for me. I wish we could walk out of here now."

"Better we wait out the storm. It'll be safer at first light." Emmet sat back, hands behind his head. He wondered how much of a hurry Walter would be in when he found out how they were getting out of St. Louis.

Boatwright Wildlife Management Area, MO: Saturday, August 20, 8 p.m.

The UTV idled at the fork in the fire trail, its headlights casting twin beams through the skeletal remains of pine and cedar. Twilight pressed down from the discolored sky, and the storm clouds refused to move on, hovering like they were waiting for another round. The air was thick, still damp from the last burst of rain, and the wind tugged at the treetops.

Chloe hunched over the laminated map on the hood, a flashlight between her teeth. Her finger traced a barely visible trail line. "Okay, if the tower is behind us and we've passed over Gum Cor Road, then we're on this ridge—and that means we could run into this service road—"

Reed leaned over her shoulder, squinting. "Unless we've looped around. The quake could've buried half the markers."

Around them, the forest was in disarray—snapped trunks and root balls torn from the earth. Some trees lay across the trail like barricades. Others leaned like drunks, half-fallen, waiting for one more gust to finish the job.

Reed exhaled. "We need a road—any road—and we can head east, then south from there."

Watson patrolled a wide circle around the UTV, his golden coat mottled and grungy, ears twitching at every rustle. His tail was down, muscles taut. He stayed on alert.

A distant crack echoed—sharp, unnatural.

Watson stopped mid-step, head whipping toward the sound. A low growl rumbled in his throat. Then he bolted into the underbrush, snarling as branches snapped in his wake.

"Watson!" Reed called, already moving around the UTV.

The only answer was silence.

Rain tapped again, slow at first, then harder, a soft percussion against the canopy and the leaves. Chloe followed Reed as he moved toward the brush line.

A sharp yowl split the forest, high, urgent, and unmistakably Watson.

Reed froze mid-stride.

"That's not a warning bark," Chloe drew in a big lungful of wet air, eyes wide.

They pushed forward, flashlights slicing through the trees in jittery cones of white. Twigs cracked underfoot. Chloe fell a few steps behind, ducking low branches and sliding on loose clay.

Reed burst through the last wall of brush into a small clearing, puffing in the chill air. The world narrowed to shapes and shadows, flickering in the beam of his light. Watson struggled across the clearing.

"Watson!" Reed lunged, boots slipping on the wet ground. He splashed through the outer rim of the pit, ignoring the gritty sucking against his shins, and reached for the dog's collar.

The dog writhed, half-submerged in what looked like loose earth, but moved too much and flowed easily. Watson twisted toward him, eyes wide, whimpering, legs kicking in slow motion like he was swimming through syrup. Reed locked one hand under his neck and the other under his bottom and pulled.

The dog didn't rise. Instead, Reed sank.

The ground gave way under his weight, soft and hungry. His knees vanished.

Shocked, his head whipped around.

"Chloe, *stay there!*" he barked, just as she stepped from the trees.

She froze. "What—?"

"Quicksand!" he shouted. "Do *not* move!"

He strained upward to transfer his weight, but the more he fought, the deeper he sank. Watson whimpered again, only his head and front paws still above the surface.

Reed gritted his teeth. "We're both stuck."

Chloe's flashlight jittered as she edged closer to the tree line, scanning frantically. Rain fell harder; the wind stirred the leaves and vines.

"Hang on," she said. "I'll find something. Rope, branch—anything."

Chloe searched the forest floor, hovering at the edge of the clearing. Reed clutched Watson in the middle of the pit, chest-deep in slurping earth.

"Use the winch!" he shouted over the storm. "Front bumper—throw me the line!"

Chloe spun and bolted through the brush. Branches snagged her shirt, rain blinding her as she scrambled back to the UTV. Thunder cracked, close enough to rattle the sky.

She jumped into the driver's seat, twisted the key, and the engine roared. Gunning it, she rolled the UTV forward, bumping over uneven ground until the front bumper kissed a fallen tree at the bog's edge. She yanked the brake and used the flashlight to read the winch controls on the dash.

Her fingers were slick and shaking. She flipped the release and jumped out, metal whining as thick cable spooled out. The winch motor protested but kept feeding the line.

She looped it like a cowboy rope, the weight of the cable dragging behind her like a steel serpent. At the edge of the quicksand, she braced, wound up, and flung it out.

"Got it!" Reed shouted, grabbing the wet line just as it fell within reach. He looped it under his arms with trembling hands and tightened the knot until it bit. Then he wrapped both arms around Watson, locking the dog tight against his chest. "We're ready!"

Chloe raced back, climbed into the UTV—and the ground heaved.

A deep, grinding *crack* rebounded across the woods. Tremors broke the ground underneath, violent enough to knock her sideways out of the UTV and onto the spongy forest base. Around her, branches jerked, rattling their wet leaves, some breaking free and hitting the UTV.

The earth shuddered, a massive heave, as the soil and vegetation shrugged up and over. With a yell, Reed spilled forward, grasping at a sapling as they were both tossed and buried. Sputtering, he dug himself up, freeing his arms, drawing Watson with him. But his waist was trapped, caught by the suction of the loose sand.

Seconds later, the tremor faded. Reed struggled for air, pulling harder on Watson to keep the golden lab's big head clear of the muck.

"Chloe," he hollered. "Are you okay?"

"Okay," she huffed, unsure if he heard her.

Picking herself up, she climbed back into the seat and flicked the rocker switch to rewind the winch. Nothing happened.

Swearing, she flicked it back and forth, fast. The motor grated but didn't pull the line. She hit the plate with her fist, only hurting her fingers.

"Hurry, Chloe!" Reed yelled.

"Freaking piece of…" she grabbed the stick and shifted into reverse.

The UTV coughed, tires sliding a few inches forward—until the bumper jammed against the downed tree she'd pinned it against. It held.

Chloe pressed the accelerator, trying not to jerk the line. She didn't want to injure Reed. The tires spun and caught, and the cable went taut with a sharp *twang.*

Reed jerked forward in the muck. The quicksand hissed, not wanting to give them up. Inch by inch, the winch drew man and dog from its grip.

Reed's boots came free at last with a wet *slurp.* He and Watson tumbled out of the pit, caked in sand, soaked to the bone.

Chloe leapt out and ran to them.

Reed spat, panting, arms still locked around Watson. The dog whimpered but thumped his tail.

"You good?" she asked, dropping to her knees beside them.

Reed looked up, eyes wide, chest heaving. "Remind me never to doubt your driving."

She smiled, her face wet and spattered with leaves, mud, and bits of wood, her hair plastered across her oval face. He thought she was beautiful.

Thunder rolled again overhead—louder this time. The rain came harder, slashing sideways in cold sheets that washed away the sticky sand and sludge. He stood, boots splashing, and looked uphill, where the trail cut a narrow path through tilted pines and boulders split from the quake. Water was already pooling in the low spots, running in muddy rivulets toward the bog behind them.

"We climb," he said, voice hoarse. "We need to be higher before the river finds us again."

No one argued. Watson jumped up to sit at Chloe's feet. Climbing in after the dog, Reed threw the UTV into gear, and they backed up the slope, headlights bouncing wildly.

Darnall Point, TN: Saturday, August 15, 10 p.m.

Royce eased off the gas and let the truck crawl to a stop, tires crunching over chunks of pavement that littered what was left of Pea Ridge Road. The headlights faintly pierced the storm-wrung darkness ahead—leaf clusters and stripped limbs across the asphalt, puddles glinting in the shallow beam. The road had become a scar, carved by quake and weather, slick and uneven beneath them.

Dark clouds churned overhead, thick as smoke. Royce wondered if some of it was smoldering from the big cities, drifting over the landscape. The moon was covered. Rain spat at the windshield in irregular bursts, and the wind rolled over the windows, a cold breeze that caused the windshield to fog.

Albert exhaled and rubbed a hand over his face. In the back, the dogs squirmed restlessly, their nails sliding against the fabric. Stella jumped over the seat, wiggled in between them, and rested her head on his knee, her eyes glinting in the dim light.

"We're not going any farther tonight," Royce said, hands still on the wheel. "Too dark. If the kids are out here, they've already found cover. We push on now, we chance wrecking the truck—or worse."

Albert didn't argue. He stared through the steamed glass, a scowl twisting his face. "I wanted to find that damn plane before we stopped."

"You and me both," Royce let go of the wheel, dropping his hands into his lap. "But out here? I'll hit it before I see it in this haze."

Silence fell between them. No one moved. Even the dogs stilled, ears perked, but not agitated.

297

Eventually, Albert flicked on his phone and leaned forward, casting pale light across the glove box. Opening the little door, he rooted around, grumbling until his fingers closed on a small flashlight. He clicked it on, the beam thin but steady. He grinned.

"Something," he said, holding it up like a prize.

Royce tossed him a bottle of water. They both leaned back, tired and sore. What a day.

Rain dotted the glass in intermittent bursts. A low rumble rolled through the dark. It was impossible to tell whether it came from the distant thunder or another aftershock.

"What do you know about that old well you hauled us out of?" Albert asked, his fingers running through Stella's matted fur.

Royce scratched the back of his neck, eyes on the shadowed tree line. "Not much," he admitted. "Been there forever. Folks mostly pretend it's not. I wasn't even sure it had water."

Albert chuckled, reached inside his jacket, and tugged free a stained leather-bound journal. "It had water," he said. "And bones."

He fished into his jeans pocket and spilled a cascade of glinting gold coins into Royce's open hands.

Royce's curiosity soared. "Holy hell…" The coins gleamed a soft gold, his fingers trembling as he turned one over. "Where—?"

"At the bottom," Albert said, pushing his reading glasses up and flipping the journal open under the beam of a flashlight. "Next to what used to be Henry Stallings."

He started reading, lips moving silently, eyes scanning the smeared ink. Most of the pages bled together, but pencil entries had survived.

"Tally sheets," he murmured. "Looks like a ledger. Bottles bought and sold. Names. Quantities. Pretty organized until the end."

Albert held it open for Royce to see. The handwriting turned erratic, like the writer's hand had been trembling. On the last page, the pencil lines were smudged but still legible.

"Stallings?" Royce mused, still rubbing the gold coins. "I don't recall any Stallings around here. Got any dates on the pages?"

"April 14, 1932," Albert read aloud. "The last few pages are a letter. Written after he got hurt, I think. Says—"

He paused, squinting. Somewhere in the distance, an owl screeched. The forest had gone still. He read out loud.

My Dearest Lydia,

If this letter ever reaches you, it means someone found me, or what's left of me. I'm writing by the last light of a match and praying the good Lord guides this note into the right hands.

I reckon this is the end for me, sweetheart.

Two nights back, while moving a few crates down into my hidey hole in the old stone well in Harrowood, I slipped. Fell clean down to the bottom. The drop broke my lantern and my damn hip. Ain't no one passed by close enough since, and my voice is near gone from hollering. I've tried climbing, but the walls are slick and I'm too weak. There's no getting out.

I ain't afraid to meet my Maker, Lydia. But the thought of leaving you alone—so far off in Boston, with a child in your belly and worry in your heart—that's more than I can stomach.

I'm sorry, darling. Sorry for leaving you to chase dollars in these backwoods. Sorry for missing the swell of your belly, and sorry for every night you went to bed wondering if I'd ever come home. You've always been the best of me, and if I could swap places with any man to give you peace, I would.

I got a little something on my lap here, gold coins wrapped in oilcloth and stuffed in my satchel. If you're reading this, please take them to her. Her name is Mrs. Lydia Stallings, care of Aunt Mae Whitfield, 14 Dorchester Ave, Boston, Massachusetts.

That money's for the baby. For whatever he or she needs. Tell our child I loved 'em and I always will.

And you, Lydia, know that every step I took out here, risky and rough as it was, I took to build something better for us. I never meant to leave you alone, not like this.

I'm tired now. Cold's creeping in. But I'll be thinking of your face and that little one until the last.

With all the love in this sad heart, Henry

P.S. Whoever finds this—God bless you. Please get this to her. It's all I got left in this world.

Albert fell silent, the journal resting heavily on his lap.

"1932," Royce murmured, eyes on the shadows beyond the truck. "Nearly a century. Lots of moonshining back then with Prohibition."

"I bet they never knew what happened to old Henry," Albert released a lungful of air and took the coins back, slipping them into his pocket. "When we find the kids, and Reed and Chloe, after we figure out what's next, I'm gonna make a trip to Boston. I want to see if there's anyone left.

Someone who deserves to know the truth. That Henry didn't just vanish."

Royce lowered his gaze briefly. "Even if his wife and kid are long gone, someone might still care. Someone ought to."

Neither spoke for several minutes while they contemplated Henry's fate.

Then Albert turned to face him. "Your house, the farm, even the town—they're gone now. Absorbed up by another damn quake." He looked at Royce. "You thinking about what comes next?"

Royce adjusted his weight, stretching out stiff legs. "First thing is getting our people back. Then I'm checking on the county—who's left, what they need. Some will run, while others will want to dig in. But with the west already buried from those May quakes, I doubt we'll see supply trucks or infrastructure repairs out here anytime soon. Food is going to be a problem. I don't know how many crop fields were flooded, but the farm belt will suffer for the next several years." He shook his head grimly. "Levee's gone. Roads are torn to hell. There's too much wrecked to fix in one lifetime."

Albert gave a slow nod. He knew the truth in those words. Then, casually—too casually—he asked, "Ever been to the Blue Ridge Mountains?"

Royce glanced at him. "Can't say I have. Heard they're beautiful, though."

"They are," Albert said, then hesitated, like he was bracing for something. "I've got a place there. Bought it for my late wife, Stella, back when she got homesick for her roots. It's sat empty for five years now. I got a good caretaker, but it needs work… It's big enough for us. I figured that when this is over, we could go east. Stay there awhile. Regroup. Make a new plan."

Royce gave him a long, low look. Albert rarely talked about his past. Royce had the idea that the man must have some money put away, between the dollars he contributed to the household these last few months and the offer for a clinic, but he was not one to press. He gave a quick nod in the darkness. "Okay… sounds like a good plan. I'll bring it up with the others. Can't speak for them, but I think it's worth talking about."

"Alright." Albert's voice was sharp, almost too loud. He cleared his throat and looked away. "Think I'll get some rest."

Royce watched him for a beat, then reached down and scratched behind Stella's ears. The dog leaned into him with a sigh.

He wished morning would hurry up and dawn.

Chapter Seventeen
St. Louis, MO: Sunday, August 16, 7 a.m.

The sky peeled itself open slowly—gray first, then tinged with rust. Dawn after a disaster didn't bring peace; it brought light enough to see the destruction.

Ash-colored clouds trailed low across the horizon; the storm had limped east overnight. The world it had left behind was piled here and scattered there. Trees leaned at unnatural angles. Power lines hung like snapped strings. The scent of wet plaster, oil, and splintered wood clung to the air. It looked like the apocalypse it was.

Tau stepped over the remains of a streetlight, its cover twisted and scratched. They'd crossed the last of the fairway, now a swamp of sand traps and cratered turf. They were back out on the devastated streets. Not a single structure had survived whole. Cinder blocks spilled in a waterfall of concrete; storefronts sheared off clean to their foundations.

They picked their way through, clambering over streets choked with broken infrastructure, struggling with every step. No cars drove these streets, but sirens still screamed in the distance. The sad note of despair followed them.

Emmet led. They were disheveled and exhausted, but he looked particularly worn down, his clothes rumpled and his eyes bloodshot. However, he didn't let it slow him down.

"I know a guy. Stitch Stavo. I worked on his plane in the Air Force, back when that still meant something. Best damn pilot I ever knew." He paused, nudging aside a leaning fence post. "We kept in touch over the years. He's got a setup near the fairgrounds."

Walter didn't respond. His eyes darted to the sky, then to the trembling horizon. His fingers tapped at his thigh in some unconscious rhythm.

Tau noticed his nerves. "We're going as fast as we can, Walter. The data could have changed. There may not be another earthquake—"

"I know," Walter snapped. "It's just like the West Coast. We need to get out of here."

Emmet turned slightly, frowning, but didn't argue. "Stavo's place might still be standing. Either way, he'll be there."

Another aftershock rolled beneath them, subtle but unmistakable—a moan through the bones of the earth.

Only parts of Stavo's place still stood. The front of the house had collapsed. The back roof sagged in one corner, and a section of fencing lay scattered like matchsticks across the road, but the garage behind the house remained mostly intact. A rust-streaked weather vane spun lazily above it, creaking in the wind.

And there he was—Stavo himself—lean, sharp-eyed, and still wearing his flight jacket like the past two decades hadn't happened. He stood in the churned-up muck of what used to be his front yard, arms folded, one boot resting on the bumper of a wrecked truck. His gray hair was wild in the wind, but his gaze was fixed, like he'd been waiting for something to come down the road.

Or someone.

He blinked once, then again when he recognized Emmet limping toward him.

"Well, I'll be damned," he mumbled.

The two men shared a quick hug. "I sure didn't expect to see you in this mess," Stavo told him with a grin. "You're generally smart enough to know how to avoid trouble."

"Hate to come asking for favors, Stitch, but that's why we're here," Emmet told him. He didn't waste time. Mud-splattered and with a labored voice, he launched into it fast—earthquakes, aftershocks, the collapse of the cities, the possible triggers, the danger still coming. It said a lot about their friendship that Stavo's face didn't change. Just a slow squint, jaw working as he processed every word.

Tau and Walter hung back, watching as the old friends communicated.

"You think that will be us one day?" Tau whispered.

Startled, Walter gave him a look. "What do you mean?"

"Old friends on the same wavelength. Anybody else would think Emmet showing up like this after a major earthquake is insane, but this guy is taking him seriously." Tau patted Walter's back. "It's nice. I want someone to trust my words, no matter how outrageous the situation."

Finally, Emmet stopped, the flow of words tapering off. The silence between them was heavy, interrupted only by the crackle of something burning in the distance.

Stavo sniffed, then glanced at the corkscrews of black smoke on the horizon. "You always did bring the crazy, Em."

"Yeah," Emmet said. "And I'm usually right."

Stavo gave him a long look, then agreed. "Alright."

He stepped off the bumper and cracked his knuckles. "What's the plan?"

"A balloon," Emmet said, dead serious, pointing toward the old garage. "We want you to fly us out east or northeast if we can. Maybe Cincinnati."

Stavo raised an eyebrow. "One of the balloons?" He scratched his stubble, then gave a slow, considering nod. "Haven't used 'em for long-haul in years."

"Wait. What?" Walter blinked, his voice rising an octave. "Fly out on *what*?"

Tau stepped in, calming him with a hand on his shoulder. "Let them think it through. It's not as irrational as it sounds."

Walter's laugh was abrupt and panicked. "Not irrational? You want to put us in a *balloon* after a mega-quake and fly over a state-wide disaster zone? You think after that storm we went through last night, the tornadoes it spawned, that the air is any safer than the ground right now?"

But Emmet and Stavo were already in motion— walking briskly toward the garage's side door, planning like old pilots preparing a combat drop.

"Winds are out of the west," Emmet said. "We'll catch a push if we aim northeast."

Stavo confirmed. "Thirty gallons an hour, minimum. For that distance, call it… one-fifty. Less if we take one of the smaller rigs. Less lift, less weight. Riskier landing."

"We'll burn lighter if we climb early," Emmet added, scanning the sky before they crossed into the garage. "If the storms hold, we've got a window."

Stavo popped the lock on a dented steel cabinet and started pulling out a weather-beaten map and an old aviation calculator. "We'll need a few hours to move a balloon to the fairgrounds—set up in the clearing. There wasn't much damage from the quakes over there, and the tornadoes didn't come this way."

Walter paced like a trapped animal, arms crossed tight. "This is insane."

"No, staying here is insane," Tau said. He appealed to Walter's fear and commitment. "You want to ride out a magnitude 9.0 in what's left of this city? We need to get you back to Reston. The lab. The equipment. We're the ones who can figure out what's coming next."

Walter sputtered and looked at his shoes. He hated this plan. He walked a few feet away and tried to think of another escape plan, but no other idea surfaced.

Tau, on the other hand, was grinning like a kid sneaking onto a rollercoaster.

"I've never been in a balloon," he whispered to Emmet. "This is gonna be wild."

The ground rumbled underneath, but the skies above were calm for now. Emmet and Stavo got to work, dragging out the gear.

They had a few hours to make it happen.

And one shot to ride the wind out of hell.

Kentucky: Sunday, August 16, 8 a.m.

Since first light cracked the horizon, Chloe and Reed pushed the UTV through the country, threading it through shattered service roads, crumbling overpasses, and raw terrain where pavement had split open and fallen away. The engine growled, tires spitting muck and gravel as they weaved around sinkholes and flood zones, steering wide of the Mississippi's swollen reach.

Watson sat in the back, ears perked for threats in the silence. No birdsong broke the morning, no distant hum of traffic. Only wind. And water.

Every few miles, they hit another obstacle: a collapsed bridge, a submerged junction, a jagged rift running straight through the road, too big to cross. Chloe clutched the laminated maps with one hand, though half the time the area they displayed had changed completely or fallen into one of the many holes pocketing the area. Reed drove, shoulders tight, eyes scanning the terrain, picking their way home, one mile at a time.

The sun rose higher, pale and cold behind a veil of haze. Finally, they crossed I-94 and knew exactly where they were.

Harrowood was at the end of the Interstate.

Or what was left of it.

The town was ripped open. A massive rift cleaved through its heart, swallowing buildings, and the Mississippi River breached the offshoot. Where Harrowood had stood for more than one hundred years was now a canal off the Mississippi River.

Chloe dropped the map she was holding. "No…"

The ground trembled beneath them, a subtle but steady roll. On the torn edges of the rift, clumps of soil and rock fell into the water with a splash, widening the breach. Not done yet.

"It's still growing," she said in horrible fascination.

"We've got to get home," Reed said, fear bleeding through his words. "Now."

He gunned the engine. Watson barked once, sensing the urgency. They turned west, heading across the terrain, trying to get to the house.

They left the shattered highway behind and cut cross-country, the UTV bouncing over bent fields and grassy ridges. It was rough going, but faster—no smashed asphalt, no collapsed overpasses to detour around. Simply open country and wreckage left behind by the quake. The sun broke weakly through the haze as they passed upended cornfields and scattered livestock wandering loose through downed fences.

At each plume of smoke, Reed slowed. If they spotted movement or signs of life, they stopped, climbing out to talk, gather news, and ask if anyone had seen the kids. Most folks were dazed, sleep-deprived, clinging to whatever hadn't collapsed. One woman sat with her goats in the ruins of her barn, shotgun across her lap. Another waved them off with a wary glance, eyes wide, like she hadn't figured out what happened yet.

The land itself looked raw, like it had been twisted and dropped. Earth mounded up in places, torn wide open in others. Trees leaned at odd angles. Fences had snapped like matchsticks. Every step of recovery out here would take time.

They followed an old trail where the fields grew wild on either side, Chloe squinting against the wind as they rolled past a familiar mailbox leaning on a splintered post at the end of a long driveway.

"Wait—this is Pete's place," she said. "Matthias's scout leader."

Reed cut the engine.

The front porch was cracked but still standing. Before Chloe raised a hand to knock, the screen door creaked open.

Pete stood on the threshold—grimy, shirt half-buttoned, a faded thermos tucked under one arm and the other outstretched in greeting. Scratches lined his forearms like maps. He blinked at them, then grinned.

"Well, I'll be damned. Royce said you two were still out there. You look like hell."

Chloe didn't waste time. "Matthias—do you have him?"

Pete's grin faded. He patted her shoulder. "No. But he's alive." His voice sharpened. "They all are. Your dad and Albert, too, Reed."

Relief hit Chloe so fast her knees buckled, but Pete was already talking.

"It's a mess," he said, stepping back to let them in. "After the quake, the levee at your place failed. Water came through like the weight of the ocean unleashed. House, barn, fields were all washed away."

Reed froze in the doorway. "What?"

"The kids were there," Chloe whispered, voice cracking.

"They got out," Pete said quickly. "They used your dad's old boat. Floated out with the dogs, too. At the camp, when the water came, Matthias and two boys climbed an oak. I tried to join them, but I got washed away. They found one of those Yamaha-type watercraft drifting in. Your other three floated downriver until they met up. Jamie and Pedro, the other two boys, came back on the water bike to tell us, but your kids wound up heading downstream after one of your dogs that got separated."

Reed ran a hand through his hair. "You're serious. All of this just since yesterday?"

"Ty Patterson flew search runs in his crop duster late afternoon, looking for them. But there's a complication. Some guy—Dan—was tailing Matthias at camp. No one noticed until after the quake. Claimed he was after money or gems, some crazy story. They got split up. We found Dan later; he hitched a ride on the same boat that hauled me out."

Pete's voice dropped. "We let him borrow Ty's second crop duster to help. He never came back. Ty found the plane abandoned near Darnall Point, thirty miles from here. Your dad and Albert went after him. Think he's tracking the kids."

Reed's back clenched. "Dan Clark," he muttered. He looked at Chloe. "It keeps piling on."

"We're going after them," Chloe said, her tone steely.

Reed agreed. "You know what road they took?"

"Highway 12. Ty said there was less damage." Pete pointed to a battered pickup next to a downed oak. "Take my truck. Fuel's low, but it'll get you close."

Reed eyed the landscape. "We'll make better time with the UTV—cut through the backfields. Got any gas?"

"Three cans in the barn," Pete said. They moved fast, metal clanging and sloshing as they loaded the fuel. Pete gave a short wave as they drove away.

"Let me know!" He yelled after them.

Wind sliced past the UTV as Reed pushed the throttle. Chloe held tight, her thoughts a tangle of faces and names. She pressed a hand to her chest and whispered a prayer.

"Please. Keep them safe."

Darnall Point, TN: Sunday, August 16, 9 a.m.

The fire Matthias built still hissed at the cave's entrance; branches collapsed into glowing coals. Smoke curled out and mixed with the damp air. The dogs stirred first, shaking off the chill, their bodies warm against the kids at night. Rain had passed, but the sky still looked wrong—low-hanging clouds smeared with the red light of a dusty sunrise. The world hadn't settled after the quake. The ground felt...off, like it hadn't decided whether to be still.

They ate what little was left of the energy bars, sharing halves. The last water rationed to swish and swallow. Then they moved, ducking beneath shattered branches and stepping over fallen trees. The forest had turned into a maze of splintered trunks and hanging limbs.

Matthias led with careful eyes, eyes on his compass. Natural navigation aids like animal trails and tree moss helped a little. Luis brought up the rear and kept them steady, recalling landmarks he'd passed yesterday.

No one talked much. Winnie wore her knapsack and carried Charlie, humming a little. Piper kept a close eye on her. She had whispered her conversation with Winnie to Brett when they returned, and they were both committed to getting their siblings home safely.

A few hours later, they stumbled onto cracked pavement—Pea Ridge Road, or what was left of it. Asphalt was split like dried clay, and a washed-out culvert gaped on one side. Still, it was a road, and that felt like progress.

Piper stopped so suddenly that Matthias nearly bumped into her.

"What is that?" she whispered, squinting into the glare. She raised a hand to block the sickly light bleeding through the clouds.

Something crouched in the distance—low, wide, and out of place on the fractured road.

"Looks like a plane," Brett said, uncertain. "Did it crash?"

Matthias picked up the pace, moving closer. "Or it landed hard after the quake."

Luis murmured a question in Spanish, eyes sharp on the silhouette. Piper shrugged, then translated for Brett.

"He says, be careful. Could be a cartel drug plane or something."

Brett gave her a look. "In a crop duster that old? Come on."

"Be careful anyway," she said. Then she repeated the warning to Luis in Spanish. A motion of understanding passed between them. He unslung his rifle, and loosened the knife on his belt.

The plane loomed larger as they approached—a weather-beaten crop duster parked awkwardly at the edge of the beat-up road. Mud clung to its wheels, and specks of vegetation stuck to the wings. There was no movement inside, and no figure was in the cockpit. The propeller was motionless, gleaming dully in the steely light.

The kids slowed, with no need to speak. Even the dogs dropped low, ears forward, tails stiff.

They spread out and circled the aircraft. Coco barked once, short and sharp. Duke snuffled at the ground, tail twitching. The faint impression of tire tracks marked what was left of the road. Luis crouched, fingers brushing the damp pavement.

Then Bella growled—a low warning sound.

From the tree line, a figure emerged.

A man stumbled out of the underbrush a dozen yards away, clothes smeared with filth and leaves. Jacket open, t-shirt torn, jeans stained. He looked like he hadn't slept in days. His voice cracked as he called out.

"Brett!"

The kids froze. Luis whirled, gun pointing.

It took a second to register the voice.

"Dad?" Brett said, shocked.

Their father looked nothing like the man they were used to. His hair was wild. He had a big, swollen bump on his forehead and scruff on his face. Eyes hollow and darting, his skin was pocked with red marks.

Matthias yanked Coco back by the collar. Piper tightened her grip on Duke's scruff. Luis snapped out a command to Bella, sharp and low. She whined but obeyed, dropping to a sit with her hackles still raised. He kept the gun up, trusting the stranger wouldn't know about their lack of bullets.

Brett stared, unmoving. "What are you doing here?"

"You know why I'm here," Dan snarled, stepping closer, face twisted with anger. His clothes were soaked, hair plastered to his forehead. "I've been chasing you brats for days. I want what's mine."

Winnie didn't flinch. She lifted her chin, eyes wounded. "They're not yours. They're Nadia's. I was keeping them safe for her."

Dan's sneer deepened. "Whatever. Just tell me they didn't get washed away with that dump you were hiding in. Where are they?"

Before Winnie could answer, Piper stepped between them, dropping a protective hand on her sister's shoulder.

"Go on," she murmured.

Winnie, with wordless agreement, gently setting Charlie on the ground. The dog stayed close, ears back, watching Dan with unblinking focus, his chest rumbling angrily. Winnie slipped the knapsack from her shoulders, her small hands trembling only a little. She looked at Brett and then handed the bag to her brother.

Luis didn't move. The rifle in his arms remained steady, eyes locked on Dan. He murmured something in Spanish, low and tense.

"It's okay, *está bien*," Piper said quietly, touching his elbow. "We've got this."

As Brett unzipped the bag, a rumble echoed down the road—low at first, then rising into a mechanical roar.

Tires growled on broken pavement.

Everyone turned.

An old pickup roared over a rise in the distance, suspension screaming as it bucked and bounced across the shattered road. It flew like whoever was driving didn't care about the damage or the danger. Dust and loose rock spun in its wake.

Luis leaned right, raising the barrel a few inches.

"Someone's coming," Brett said, tightening his grip on the knapsack.

Dan stepped back, suddenly less sure of himself.

Piper peered at the oncoming truck. "Let's hope they're on our side," she said.

The truck skidded to a halt in a spray of grit. Royce leapt out first, boots hitting the ground. Albert wasn't far behind, his wrinkled shirt clinging, his eyes wild with worry. Both men looked like they'd spent the night in the car—clothes rumpled, faces streaked with dust and exhaustion.

Shadow and Stella launched from the cab, barking like sirens. They hit the ground running, Shadow, an arrow, throwing herself into Matthias. He held her tight, fighting back the tears. The chaos set off a chain reaction—Duke spun, barking back, Coco followed suit, and the entire pack erupted into pandemonium.

Except Bella.

The shepherd held her ground, tail rigid, dark eyes locked on Luis. A low growl curled up from her throat—low, menacing, not aimed at the man with the rifle, but at the figure beyond him.

Dan flinched as the sound reached him.

"Look!" he shouted, waving a hand, drawing every eye back to him. "Give me back what's mine! That kid stole from me—I want it back. Now!"

Royce and Albert reached the kids, slowing only slightly when they saw Luis and the gun he held. Royce lifted a brow at Brett, voice taut. "Everyone okay?"

"We're fine," Brett said, stepping in front of his sisters. "Just settling some old business."

His eyes slid to Winnie. She met his gaze, eyes big and wet, and slipped her free hand into Piper's.

That was all he needed.

Brett hoisted the knapsack. He stepped forward, one pace, two—then suddenly swung his arm and hurled the bag with everything he had.

It spun through the air, arcing end over end.

Dan lunged.

He hit the ground hard, chips of dirt and twigs pinging off his face as he struggled for the pack. He tore open the zipper, hands diving in. For a second, no one moved.

Then his body sagged. His face slackened with relief.

The bottom of the bag held Nadia's jewelry. He ran his fingers through the pieces, examining them as if he were a connoisseur.

Royce moved to Brett's side. "Is that your dad?" he asked quietly.

Brett signaled yes; his face unreadable. "Yeah. That's him."

Behind them, Piper finally got Charlie and Duke to sit. Matthias looped a vine around Coco's collar, rubbing her ears to keep her calm, and then pulled Shadow close, vowing inside to never leave her behind again. Stella returned to sit at Albert's feet, licking her paw. The whole time, Dan ignored them, his attention on the stones.

When he stood, his posture was loose and careless. No apology in his eyes. No flicker of guilt. Just the flat indifference of a man who had what he wanted.

Royce stepped forward, voice firm. "Are you done?"

"The kids stay with us," Albert added, planting himself like a wall between Dan and the others.

Dan shrugged the knapsack over one shoulder, a sneer turning down the corner of his mouth. "Fine. But don't follow me."

Without another word, he melted back into the woods. Leaves folded around him. He was gone.

Piper and Brett stood frozen a beat too long, their eyes tracking the place he'd vanished. They didn't speak. What could they say? Instead, they turned to Royce and Albert, throwing their arms around them and hugging the men who truly cared.

"This is Luis," Brett said, as he gestured to the man beside them.

"He helped us," Piper added quickly. "Last night, a wild pig attacked Bella, and he killed it. Then he stayed with us, to make sure we got home."

Voices overlapped, rising in a flood of relief and adrenaline. Questions, laughter, explanations. Luis stood a little shyly until Albert reached out and clasped his hand.

"*Gracias*," Albert said with a nod.

Luis smiled. "*De nada*."

Their conversation bloomed in a mix of halting Spanish and eager gestures as Albert listened to his story. Piper filled in the parts he missed.

"Still good people in the world," Albert said, rubbing Stella's head. "I didn't use to think so, but I was wrong. We can help you get home, too."

"Another engine," Matthias said, head snapping toward the distant rumble. Pebbles crunched under his sneakers as he stepped onto the edge of the cracked roadside. "It's a four-wheeler."

Dust billowed behind them. As they watched, the vehicle grew closer. It was Winnie's sharp eyes that saw them first. She shrieked with glee. "It's Reed and Chloe!" She bolted forward, arms pumping, laughter bubbling from her lips. "It's really them!"

The UTV skidded to a halt, and before it fully stopped, Reed leapt down, Chloe right behind him. In a rush of footsteps and tangled limbs, they collided in a jumble of hugs and cries of relief. Laughter echoed across the barren landscape—raw, giddy, almost disbelieving.

"I knew you were alive!" Piper choked out, gripping Chloe's arms.

"We were worried about you guys," Brett began, then stopped, grinning.

"We were worried about you," Reed said, clapping Matthias on the back. "It took forever to get here."

Voices overlapped—stories tumbling out in sputters. Flooded waters. The house sweeping away. Collapsed bridges and docks. Sinkholes and rifts. Near-misses with barges and storms. Every tale lit eyes wider, bringing more laughter and awe. For a moment, it felt like they had outrun every shadow.

And then, out of nowhere, the world lurched.

At first, it was merely a shudder beneath their feet— hardly enough to stir the dust. But in the next instant, the earth roared. A deep, growling crack like thunder rolled up through the ground. Asphalt rippled and curled, buckling like scorched parchment.

Chloe screamed, "Earthquake!" just before she dropped, drawing Piper and Matthias with her arms thrown over their heads.

"Down! Get down!" Albert's voice cut through the pandemonium like a whip crack.

The ground lurched sideways. Metal screamed as the crop duster twisted off its landing gear and cartwheeled into the air before slamming upside down in a crumpled heap. Trees thrashed wildly, trunks snapping with shotgun cracks. A hailstorm of branches tore through the air. Stones jumped from the ground, missiles in a deadly cascade. The UTV bounced and twisted, its tires sliding sideways as the cracked earth attempted to guzzle it whole.

Reed hit the pavement hard, pain flaring in his elbow. The world spun and shattered. The few large pieces of asphalt beneath them fractured again—cracks racing outward like the world's largest web. He gaped as a chasm tore open right in front of them.

Brett lunged—arms locking around Winnie just as the road under her vanished, the pavement crumbling away into a ravine that hadn't been there seconds before.

"Hang on!" he yelled, straining, sneakers scraping against the splintering edge.

The fissure shot through the dirt, grinding terribly as the rift widened.

They clung to the ground, battered by the heavy blows and choking dust. One minute passed. Then two. The earth continued to heave and roll, an endless wave of energy. Timber bent at sickening angles, rocks danced and tumbled like dice across the shattered road, and the noise was like a thousand missiles ripping into the ground all at once.

It was as if the planet had decided to shrug them off.

Chapter Eighteen
St. Louis, MO: Sunday, August 16, 10 a.m.

The balloon surged upward with a loud *whoosh*, the red-and-white envelope billowing against the streaked sky. Walter's stomach dropped, so nauseated he thought he would retch. Rain-slicked wind sheared past them, catching the basket and nudging it eastward like a toy in a bath.

He looped one of the hanging ropes around his forearm, his knuckles stretched as he clutched the laptop to his chest with the other hand. The gondola swayed, creaking under their weight. He fought to suppress his nerves. The moment they reached steady air, he planned to hit the floor and bury himself in data—anything to chase off the roiling queasiness that clawed at his gut.

Beside him, Tau and Emmet gripped the edge of the basket, faces tight with focus. Stavo, calm and methodical, leaned into the burner controls, releasing another burst of flame. The balloon climbed higher, slicing through mist and low clouds. Below them, the ground fell away. They passed the height of a six-story building. Then seven. Still climbing.

Walter was catching his breath when the world below heaved.

A low, subsonic growl rolled through the air, vibrating up through the balloon's frame. Then came the rupture.

From their vantage, they watched hell unspool in real-time.

The ground convulsed—massive, rolling waves rippling through west St. Louis like a rug being snapped by invisible hands. Walter saw what was left of the airport collapse in on itself, the few standing hangars folding like paper, runways vanishing into a widening sinkhole that seemed to draw the horizon downward.

"Magnitude nine," the words fell from his lips, barely a whisper over the roaring wind. His fingers locked tighter on the laptop. *The model was right. Again.*

The balloon lurched as an updraft welled up, the hot air reacting violently to the quake's atmospheric shockwaves. The basket tilted. Tau shouted something, but the wind stole the words away.

Below them, the city was vanishing—chunks of earth breaking loose, entire blocks engulfed as the land itself fractured and fell.

Walter's pulse thundered in his ears. This wasn't just tectonic movement.

It was annihilation.

Walter gripped the edge of the basket, heart hammering, his knuckles blanched against the rough weave of the rope.

Below, the NGB site was a chaos of motion and collapse. Tents flattened like paper under invisible hands. People—hundreds of them—were scattered like matchsticks, scrambling, falling, vanishing beneath waves of dust and suffocating clouds. A thick haze of powdered concrete and ash rolled over the camp, mercifully veiling the carnage.

His mind flashed to Edgar. Cindy. Eric. Jabo. *Please let them be safe,* he thought, the prayer sharp and hot in his chest. *Please let them make it out.*

Further downtown, yellow earth blasted from deep fissures, geysers of ancient sand erupting across the city's shattered spine. Flooded streets twisted and frothed, steaming like a witch's cauldron as the underground pressure blasted water and sludge skyward.

The balloon continued its ascent, rising in uneven bounces as it caught the swirling updrafts, drifting east toward the swollen river.

And then Walter saw it—the Arch.

The Gateway to the West, shining silver even in ruin, thrashed in terrible distress. Waters below it, already swollen and turbulent, rushed higher, the waves battering its legs with relentless force. The entire structure swayed with the tremors—left, right, then back again, faster with each sway until—

CRACK.

With a deafening shudder, one leg snapped clean through. Then the other. The Arch twisted, twisted—and fell.

The river caught it with a towering splash, swallowing the monument whole. A wall of brown water exploded skyward, the shockwave slamming outward like a cannon blast. The Mississippi was recoiling, pushed north by the quake's violent surface waves, the current reversing course like a river possessed.

Walter stood frozen, lips parted, consciousness caught somewhere between awe and horror.

"Oh my God, the Arch, the Arch!" Tau shouted, clinging to the basket's rim.

Emmet and Stavo locked eyes, duel expressions carved from stone.

Stavo grabbed Emmet's arm, squinting into the wind. "Guess you were right."

Emmet didn't answer. He couldn't. He stared at a city being undone in real-time, praying the wind would carry them faster, anywhere but back there.

They drifted across the river in silence, mouths slack, eyes wide. Below, the Mississippi looked like a dying thing—drained and battered, its once-mighty current reduced to a shuddering, shallow thread. In places where the muddy bottom was fully exposed, shattered beams, cars half-buried in silt, and the bent remains of the bridges were visible.

But it was the earth itself that defied comprehension.

The land pulsed. Waves of seismic energy rippled outward, warping the ground in slow, monstrous undulations. Entire sections of terrain split apart, massive slabs buckling upward while deep hollows opened beside them, as if the land was being crushed and torn by invisible fists.

On the far bank, East St. Louis disintegrated under the assault. Whatever had survived the first quake was no match for this one.

More holes opened—vast, smoking abysses in the earth—engulfing cars, trees, and entire blocks in a heartbeat. Walter could barely watch.

He gripped the rope and his laptop so tight his fingers ached, chest rising and falling in shallow, panicked bursts. Nothing he'd modeled in his notebook had prepared him for this. Not the simulations. Not the risk reports, nor the endless calculations.

This wasn't a natural disaster.

This was *desolation*.

"This…" he whispered, voice raw. "This is what the end looks like."

The balloon drifted east, leaving the ruined skyline behind and gliding low over a burning industrial zone. Most of the wreckage below on fire.

Then the first explosion pounded the air.

A fireball erupted beneath them, blooming from a row of corrugated metal warehouses. The blast sent a shockwave up through the sky, jarring the gondola. Below, the chemical plants were going up one by one—resin, paint, gas cylinders, pallets soaked in accelerants—igniting like dominoes in a chain of catastrophe.

Flames tore through rows of stacked containers. Tanks burst like popcorn kernels, and rivers of burning liquid flowed through the complex, merging into an inferno.

"Hang on!" Stavo yelled, wrestling with the burner controls as the rising heat warped the balloon's envelope. Turbulence smacked the basket from every side, the air itself rippling like a furnace. The balloon lurched.

Walter didn't have time to brace.

One savage pitch, and he was airborne—flipped over the side like a ragdoll.

He screamed.

The wind howled in his ears. Heat blistered his skin. And then—*snap*—the rope coiled around his arm, yanked tight, stopping his fall with a brutal jolt that nearly dislocated his shoulder.

He hung there, dangling twenty feet below the basket, legs swinging over the hellfire below. The laptop, torn from his grasp, tumbled end over end into the smoke and flames, vanishing like it had never existed.

His arm throbbed. His chest heaved. He clutched the rope with both hands, his skin already seared from the heat rising in suffocating waves.

"Walter!" Tau shouted, leaning dangerously over the edge.

Emmet was already grabbing rope. "He's alive—*pull!*"

Together, they heaved, muscles laboring, giving it everything they had. Walter's body swung toward the flames with each sway.

Stavo cursed and worked the burner harder, forcing more heat into the envelope to keep them aloft. Sweat poured down his face, but his focus was absolute—keep the balloon steady, or they'd end up in the fire.

Emmet and Tau heaved again—one foot higher, then two.

Walter gritted his teeth and clung to the rope, terrified, disoriented, and praying.

Hand over hand, they dragged him toward safety.

The rope burned in Walter's palms. Every pull from above sent pain lancing through his shoulder, but he refused to let go. Below him, the inferno writhed, flames licking higher, smoke twisting into nightmarish shapes. The heat scorched his face and hurt his lungs.

"A little more!" Emmet shouted, his arms shaking with the effort.

Tau braced himself against the railing, feet slipping on the trembling floor, sweat streaming down his brow. "Don't let him swing—pull straight!"

The gondola swayed violently as another explosion thundered below them, sending a pillar of flame skyward.

Walter screamed as it roared toward him, close enough to singe his pants.

Hands grabbed him.

Tau caught the rope with one hand and Walter's belt with the other. Emmet hauled with a last surge of strength. They hauled him over the rim and into the basket.

Walter collapsed on the floor, coughing, arms wrapped tight around himself. His skin was blistered, and his shoulder was badly injured. But he was breathing. Alive!

Emmet dropped beside him, gasping. "What the hell, Walter. Stay *in* the basket!" he said, sucking in air.

"I don't—" Walter coughed again, his voice raw, "want to ride in a balloon."

They laughed, a short, stunned bark of relief, before turning grim again. Stavo glanced at them and then returned to managing the balloon, guiding them higher and steering away from the firestorm.

Below them, hell raged.

The industrial zone had become a war zone. Storage tanks exploded in rapid succession, bright blooms of fire launching debris high into the air. Forklifts, trucks, and steel shipping containers were flung like toys. A tower crane collapsed in a slow-motion tumble, its arm cleaving through a burning warehouse like a guillotine.

Black smoke funneled into the sky, thick and oily, choking out the clouds. The ground itself, ruptured and torn from the earlier quake, roared as the last standing buildings buckled and gave way. A river of molten chemicals slithered across the cracked pavement, igniting everything it touched.

Somewhere deeper in the industrial yard, a tank labeled *Ammonia—Hazardous* teetered on its broken legs, one side already burning.

It wavered in the heat like a mirage, flames licking its lower half where chemicals had already breached. The metal screeched and buckled. A geyser of white vapor burst from a fractured seam, venting upward in a blinding jet.

And then—*detonation.*

A high-pitched shriek pierced the air like a blade. The tank went up in a searing flash of white-blue fire, brighter than lightning and twice as fast. For one terrifying second, the entire industrial zone was bathed in unnatural daylight.

Next came the shockwave.

It slammed outward with bone-crushing force, flipping cement mixers onto their backs and crushing them. Miles away, the few windows left intact, shattered. A concussive blast of wind tore through the smoke, flinging scrap metal, pipes, and barrels like shrapnel in every direction.

A mushroom cloud of toxic gas billowed upward, thick and pale green, swirling like a ghost rising from a grave. It rolled low and fast, blanketing everything beneath it in a choking, eye-watering fog that made the skin crawl and the lungs seize.

The flames changed color, burning with a fierce chemical intensity—no longer orange and red but sickly blues and greens. The heat was unbearable, melting street signs, warping guard rails, and setting everything flammable alight in an instant.

Up in the balloon, even at a safe distance, the basket rocked violently from the blast, ropes creaking, canvas straining. Tau shielded his eyes from the flash; Stavo fought the controls. Below them, the ground where the tank rested disappeared—a blackened crater ringed in flame.

Where the chemical plant stood, there was now only smoke, ruin, and the deep, ominous booms of more devastation in the fire's wake.

The balloon drifted eastward, away from the industrial park, its canvas stretched taut against the thinning wind. Stavo never let go of the burner controls, eyes scanning the horizon. Below, the scorched skeleton of St. Louis finally shrank into the haze, consumed by smoke and distance.

Walter lay curled on the floor of the gondola, his arm wrapped in a temporary sling made from Emmet's shirt, his face blistered and gray. Tau wrapped a damp cloth around his neck, wiping soot and sweat away, murmuring steady reassurances, even though Walter hadn't said a word in nearly an hour.

Emmet kept watch from the edge, eyes fixed on the land unfolding below them. It didn't look real—whole highways consumed by landslides, forests snapped like toothpicks, farmlands flooded with ruptured levees, and scattered livestock. A church steeple jutted up from a cracked lakebed. Smoke curled from hills where fires burned unchecked.

The balloon drifted through it all.

Hour by hour, the destruction gave way to damage, and damage faded to scars. Then, finally, fields.

Golden fields, some unnatural furrows, and bent trees rolled beneath them like a worn blanket. The sky had turned pale. Ash still streaked the clouds, but the wind had eased, and for the first time, the air didn't taste like smoke.

Stavo exhaled slowly. "Fuel's low," he said.

"See anything?" Emmet asked, shielding his eyes. His voice was weary from hours of shouting and heat.

"There," Tau pointed—barely more than a speck of green between two tree lines. "Clearing. Looks flat. There's a road next to it. Maybe we can catch a ride to a doctor."

"Good enough."

Stavo eased the burner, feathering the descent. The balloon sank, ropes twanging, fabric fluttering. Walter stirred, blinking at the sound of wind whipping past the basket's edge.

They clipped the top of a tree, spun once, and then hit. The basket slammed into the earth, bounced, and rolled through brittle weeds. Emmet was thrown against the side. Tau nearly went overboard. Stavo braced, teeth grinding, as the whole contraption finally came to a halt on its side, half-buried in a meadow.

The four men lay in a tangle of limbs, rope, and grass, blinking at the cloudy, gray sky overhead.

Walter wheezed out a laugh that sounded more like a deflating tire. "I officially hate balloons," he croaked, still sprawled on his back, his coat half-singed and his hair sticking out in wild directions.

Tau rolled over beside him and lifted both fists like a boxer on his last leg. "Ohio, baby," he said, voice hoarse. "Sweet flat ground. I'm never leaving you again." He leaned down and kissed the dirt. "Tastes like freedom… and cow crap."

Stavo groaned and pushed himself up from the tangle of charred nylon ropes. His knees cracked like popcorn as he staggered to his feet. "We're down," he muttered, glancing over at Emmet, who sat in his undershirt, doubled over with his hands on his thighs, his pulse starting to slow. "You dragged my ass through the fire, again, Em, and I gotta say it was a hell of a ride. Nothing is ever boring around you."

Emmet raised a thumb without lifting his head. "Glad to accommodate."

Behind them, the balloon sagged and collapsed, the last gust of heat escaping with a faint sigh. A low, almost pitiful squeal hissed out of a leaking valve, as if the balloon was sighing in relief.

Walter sat up and squinted in the direction of the road. "Uh… guys?"

Tau shaded his eyes and followed his gaze. Beyond a thin line of trees, a battered green highway sign leaned at an awkward angle.

"CINCINNATI, OHIO! WELCOME TO THE HEART OF IT ALL."

They stood there for a moment, beaten, bruised, and blackened, staring at the sign like it was a miracle. Then Emmet said what they were all thinking.

"Anybody else really need a bathroom and a burger?"

Tau perked up. "I'm hungry!"

Walter coughed a laugh. "And it's just another Sunday."

Together, limping, they turned toward the road, leaving behind the wreckage of the wildest ride of their lives.

Epilogue
White House Situation Room: August 23

The hum of fluorescent lights barely cut through the stillness. Papers rustled, muted, like dry leaves in a crypt. The air was thick with fatigue and the sour tang of unwashed suits and stale coffee.

President Avery Wallace sat at the head of the table, not so much seated as collapsed into the chair. Her blazer hung loose over slumped shoulders, a ghost of the woman who commanded the room with a glance. Sweat-matted stray strands of silver hair clung to her temples.

Across from her, General Willard Q. Brown, Chairman of the Joint Chiefs, leaned on both elbows, knuckles tight around a pen he hadn't used. His uniform was rumpled, tie undone.

On the screen, Nancy Arnold, FEMA Administrator, was halfway through a bottle of antacids, the white chalk dust smudged on the sleeve of her wrinkled blouse. She'd been running emergency ops for eight days straight with barely a moment to rest.

The screen behind them still flickered with satellite imagery: a churning river of mud and crushed cities. Memphis—gone. Greenville, Vicksburg—underwater. Chicago and Indianapolis—wrecked and overwhelmed.

Nancy reported first. Her voice cracked. "We've confirmed near-total destruction along the Mississippi River corridor. Most of the dams in the north failed or were compromised. The swollen river is now flowing along its own path. From south St. Louis down to Louisiana, the country's flattened, flooded, or burned. It's a war zone without a war. With the Old River Control Structure destroyed, the

Mississippi River shifted into the Atchafalaya River, away from New Orleans and Baton Rouge. That area will face significant economic and environmental consequences going forward."

"Levees ruptured all the way to the Gulf," Willard added, voice deep. "We lost entire towns overnight. Natchez and Jackson, to name a few, are no longer there. We're building a list now. What wasn't shaken apart was consumed in the flood. No comms. No infrastructure. We haven't been able to reach some zones in over a week."

Nancy picked up again. "We estimate fifty to sixty million dead or unaccounted for in the Midwest. That's not including the May quakes—another fifty million were lost out west." Her eyes dropped to the table. "Most evacuees who fled the West ended up in the Midwest. A lot of them didn't stand a chance."

Avery didn't flinch. She stared at the darkened map in silence, eyes studying the disaster zones marked in red.

"And now they're coming here," Nancy's voice dropped an octave. "Millions of survivors. On foot, by bus, by anything that moves. The eastern seaboard wasn't built for this kind of migration. We're past capacity. There isn't enough food, water, or power. Our grids are collapsing. Sanitation's going. People are rioting in Philadelphia. There was looting in Boston. New York's already declared martial law in three boroughs."

Willard leaned forward. "We're close to a total system collapse, Madam President. Civil unrest is growing. If we lose the East—"

"We won't," Avery said quietly.

They stopped. Even though she was tired, her voice carried weight.

The President closed her eyes for a moment. When she opened them again, the spark was faint, but it was there.

"I need strategies," she said. "No more estimates. No more projections. I want action. Shelter, supply lines, triage, relocation. I want an outline on my desk in two hours. We did it in the West; we'll do it again. You understand?"

They both confirmed. Slow. Hollow. But it was a start.

Avery pushed up from the table like a soldier rising from a battlefield. Her legs shook. She didn't care.

"If we're standing," she said, "we're still fighting."

Then she turned and left them in the artificial glow of the screens.

Condon, Montana: August 28

Dan upended the knapsack with a grunt, letting the weight of two weeks on the road fall out in a glittering cascade. Rubies clinked against emeralds. Sapphires spun over Nadia's thighs. Gems pooled like spilled fire, ocean, and blood. Her eyes lit up. Her breath caught. She touched a golden chain reverently, as though it might vanish.

A smile returned to her lips for the first time since the quake gutted Sweet Home. Not the thin, polite curve she'd worn since they landed in Montana. A genuine smile. Sharp and predatory.

She began sorting, fingers nimble and precise—no tremble, no wasted motion. The jewels clicked and clinked as she laid them in neat rows across her lap.

Dan stood across from her, exhaustion written in every line of his face. Dirt caked his sleeves. One boot was split at the sole. His shirt was slashed across the chest, blood dried in a pattern like rusted lace. But his grin—his grin was triumphant.

"We're in the clover, baby," he said. "This is our ticket. Once we fence it, we'll have enough to set up the operation. Solar, water, meds—hell, we'll rebuild it all."

Nadia's smile didn't falter, but her hands stopped moving. She blinked once, slowly. Then drew the jewelry into her lap.

"I'm not selling these," she said.

Dan chuckled. "What?"

She didn't repeat herself, just stared at him—cool, unreadable, amused.

"These are *mine*," she said at last, running her fingers across a sapphire the size of a thumbprint.

Dan's jaw tightened. "You knew what I was going for. Said it yourself—there's no use for memories. Said we needed assets. I damn near died in the Midwest, finding this stuff and getting it away from the kids. They had two freaking major earthquakes!" His voice rose as he finished.

"And you did a fine job, baby," she said. "But I never said I'd sell them."

"You lied to me?"

"No," she said sweetly. "I *let* you lie to yourself."

His hands curled into fists. "I risked everything for *us*."

"There is no 'us,'" she said lightly, brushing a speck of dust from an earring. "Just you, me, and the poor decisions you made."

Before he could reply, the cabin's front door creaked open. A tall and confident man stepped inside, wearing a pressed coat and a smile with too many teeth. He tipped his head toward Dan and glanced at Nadia with something far warmer.

Gathering the gems, she rose, smooth as a queen leaving court, and walked past Dan without looking at him. A go-bag waited near the door—neatly packed, zipped, ready. The man picked it up, slung it over one shoulder, and offered Nadia his arm. She took it without hesitation.

At the threshold, she turned. "No honor among thieves, darling. You know that."

The door shut behind them with a soft *click*.

Dan stood frozen in the wreckage of his dreams. Slowly, his legs gave out, and he slumped into her chair. Her perfume lingered—vanilla and blood oranges.
He didn't cry right away. But when he did, it was pitiful and bitter.

Washington, D.C.: August 31

The hum of fluorescent lights buzzed faintly overhead in the half-lit USGS lab, casting pale blue shadows across stacked monitors and scattered printouts. Tau leaned over a console, his fingers flying across the keyboard, while Walter stood by the whiteboard, marker in hand, drawing angular fault lines over a map of the continental U.S.

Miguel stepped into the lab, still wearing his field vest, eyes tired but sharp. "Talk to me. What do we have?"

Tau exhaled and leaned back in his chair. "Nothing. That's the problem. The model shut down again. It's like the system told us what it had, and once it completed the sequence, it turned off."

"No predictions. No anomalies. Just static," Walter added, shaking his head. Most of the red on his face had faded, but his skin still had the glossy look of a burn victim. "It will review everything to date. I can go through the parameters, use the data anyway I want to, but when asked to predict future activity, it says nada."

Miguel crossed his arms. "We've hit a wall in the algorithm."

Walter's phone buzzed. He glanced at it, then smiled faintly. "Emmet."

Miguel perked up. "He okay?"

"Yeah," Walter said. "Says Jabo, Eric, and Cindy got airlifted out before the big one hit St. Louis. They're recuperating in Florida. Edgar and his family left that same night, heading west like Emmet told them. They were clear of the epicenter when it triggered." He held up the phone. "Edgar sends his thanks."

Tau gave a low whistle. "I'm glad he listened. There's not much left of St. Louis."

Miguel frowned. "Where is Emmet now?"

"Gone," Walter replied. "Left D.C. two days ago. Took Stavo with him. He's chasing down another theory about the earthquake swarm—his words, not mine."

Miguel raised an eyebrow. "Earthquake swarm?"

"Yeah. He thinks what we're seeing isn't a series of random quakes—it's something coordinated. Patterned. Like a chain reaction."

"He's probably checking with the animals and meteorologists," Tau said, trying to be funny, but careful not to sound too condescending.

He turned the monitor toward Miguel. "We've been digging into the seismic echoes—backlogged sensor data.

There are signatures that don't match any historical quake profiles. Something's off."

Miguel walked closer, eyes narrowing at the jagged lines on the screen. "And the model?"

"It won't tell us anything we don't already know," Tau said, frustrated. "It's like the system processed what happened. But there is nothing predictive in what it is giving us now. Maybe the inputs broke the math."

Walter set the marker down and looked at both men. "Whatever happened out there, it didn't follow the rules. However, that doesn't mean we give up trying to figure out why the quakes occurred. Someday, this scenario could happen again."

Miguel nodded. "Then we rewrite the inputs. Try again."

Tau gave a tired grin. "Yeah. Reverse engineer what was almost the end of the world. No pressure."

Walter's voice steadied. "We figure out what broke the country, and maybe someday it will help someone else stop it from breaking again."

"Let's hope that's in the far-flung future and somebody else's problem," Miguel said, rolling his eyes with a smile.

Blue Ridge Mountains, North Carolina: September 1

It took two weeks to reach North Carolina, but the Walkers finally had a place to call home again.

The roads were wrecked—splintered highways, dust choking every mile. Entire bridges sagged into rivers that no longer followed maps. The Mississippi had carved a new course—wide, wild, and utterly unrecognizable—swallowing towns and farmland to reach the gulf. It would never be the same. The Midwest was battered by aftershocks, covered in sinkholes, and washed-out furrows. The cities were worse. In too many cases, there was just nothing left.

Ty's airfield in Kentucky became their first refuge, the rickety hangar a dry place to heal and recuperate. Reed limped out each morning, hand pressed to his elbow, scanning the wreckage, thinking how lucky they were. They were together, and they were moving to a safe place. Thanks to Albert.

To everyone's surprise, Albert wasn't just an Oregon farmer with a roadside stand. He'd spent a career developing contacts, networks, and investments, building a multinational corporation. After his wife died, he retreated to work the produce stand in mourning, but his empire hadn't stopped growing. Behind that produce stand, a web of farmers, processors, distributors, and logistics crews kept moving under his name.

With the heartland and the West Coast in shambles, people needed food. He knew what to do. After all, Albert had been sending semis filled with food to the West Coast since May.

Now, he spent every waking hour on the satellite phone with federal liaisons and ag suppliers. He struck deals, redirected convoys, and fed people everywhere. He didn't brag, and he didn't sleep much, either.

Last week, he handed Royce Walker a set of keys. "Take everybody home," he told his friend. Black Mountain, North Carolina, was a fresh start for all of them. The Walkers had a new place to call home.

As for the town of Harrowood, it was gone. Royce didn't wait for orders to help his people; he wasn't the type who needed direction. The morning after they arrived in Black

Mountain, he was on his feet with a map spread across the table, marking names and tracing roads through northwestern Kentucky. Some would go and some would stay. He was going to help anywhere he could.

Pete Deller stayed, along with Jamie and Pedro's families. They were rebuilding their farms by hand, crops, livestock, and homesteads. Royce made sure they didn't do it empty-handed. He coordinated crates of seed and sacks of feed, solar batteries, and spare parts. Ty and Albert even managed to convince a grounded freight company to release a cargo plane for Ty to use.

The plane's belly was loaded with crates of fertilizer, toolkits, water purifiers—anything and everything. Ty flew at dawn and touched down at dusk every day, muttering about air traffic ghosts and how the radios never worked right anymore. He became the lifeline for those who stayed.

Albert didn't slow down, either. He got Luis back to Waukegan in less than three days—by convoy, by flight, and the last stretch by borrowed motorbike. Luis's wife had survived, shaken but healthy. She ran out of the house barefoot when she saw him. They cried for a long time. The next morning, they packed what was left and headed home to Mexico. Albert covered everything—paperwork, finances, and new gear for the road.

"Come back if you want," he told them. "But if you don't, build something better down there."

At the Walkers' new home, the world was quieter.

The dogs tore across the property like sentries on patrol—Coco loping wide arcs, Shadow staying close, ears twitching at every breeze. The house creaked like old ships do—settling—but it felt solid under their feet. Chloe stood with Reed by the fence, arms folded, the sun warming her shoulders.

Reed watched the dogs chase a squirrel under the porch, then cleared his throat like he was preparing a speech. "What would you think about a picnic?"

She turned to him, brow raised. "Are we bringing the whole crew?"

"Actually…" He hesitated, rubbing the back of his neck. "I was hoping it'd just be us. A date."

Chloe smiled, slow and wide, slipping her hand through his arm. "I'd love to. But only if we leave soon. Life's short. We've seen how fast it can change."

Reed agreed, looking out over the hills. "Someone once said the secret to a good life is to have more beginnings than endings."

She squeezed his arm gently. "Then let's start again. Right now."

He looked down at her, the bruises and dust of the past months still faint on their skin, but something brighter stirring in their eyes.

Chloe held up her hand and slapped his palm in a crisp high-five. Then, softer, she drew him close. "Together," she whispered.

And this time, they didn't have to run.

Boston, MA: September 2

Stella darted up the crumbling porch steps like a shot, her paws clicking on the concrete. Albert paid the cabbie with one eye on her and one on the street. The road was busy, and the sidewalk crowded. Boston was overflowing with survivors like every other East Coast city these days.

"Stay out of the road, Stella!" he called, straightening his coat as the taxi rumbled away.

The neighborhood had a worn, bruised look. Brick buildings sagged under the weight of time and tremors that had reached here from the Midwest. Mortar spilled like sand between the cracks, and several windows bore split panes. The earthquakes had left their mark even here, hundreds of miles from the epicenter.

He climbed the concrete stairs, steadying himself on the rusted railing. A breeze stirred dust from the gutter and carried it across the stoop. Boston had felt it too—he'd heard how the church bells tolled by themselves as far east as Beacon Hill.

At the top, Albert scanned the splintered name panel until his finger landed on *Stallings*. He pressed the button.

The buzzer bleated through the stillness like an alarm in an abandoned building.
Stella turned to look back at him, her head tilted.

Albert waited.

The buzzer clanked, and the door below clicked open. Albert nudged it forward and stepped into the musty hallway. The old building smelled like dust and radiator heat, its silence interrupted only by the creak of his shoes on the worn linoleum. He climbed slowly, gripping the chipped wooden banister as he ascended to the third floor.

Apartment 3 B. A thin line ran like a vein through the door's old paint job. He knocked.

It swung open, revealing a young woman with dark braids caught back from her face. Her blouse fluttered gently with her movement, and one hand rested protectively on the curve of her swollen belly.

"Mr. Frost?" she asked with a smile.

Albert tipped his head. "Elizabeth Stallings?"

"Yes—please, come in." She stepped aside.

Inside, the apartment was small but neat. The couch sagged in the middle, and a mobile of paper stars hung above a bassinet tucked into the corner. A few textbooks lined the windowsill, corners curled and marked with notes.

"I know how hard it is to travel now," she said, easing herself onto the couch with practiced care. "I have to admit, I was curious when I got your call. What brings you to Boston?"

Albert sat gently in the armchair across from her. He set his satchel on his knees, rested his hands on it, and said, "I came to talk to you about your great-grandfather. Henry Stallings."

Her eyebrows lifted. "Henry Stallings? My great-grandfather, who disappeared like a hundred years ago?"

Albert affirmed. "I found him."

She blinked, her chest rising. "You—found him?"

He gave a slow nod. "He had a fatal accident back in 1932. But his last thoughts were of his wife Lydia and their baby."

She stared at the floor, absorbing that.

"My great-grandma Lydia used to tell me stories about him when I was little," she said, her voice softening. "Said he was gallant. Dashing. She knew he hadn't abandoned them. Even when no one else believed it."

Albert opened the satchel and removed a velvet pouch. It clinked faintly. He passed it to her.

"What's this?"

"Something he wanted you to have. His legacy."

She opened it slowly. Gold coins tumbled into her palm—gleaming, solid, weighty with time. Her mouth fell open.

"I—are these real?"

He nodded again, then drew out a second item—a worn leather ledger tied shut with a string. He handed it to her, too.

"There's a letter inside. His last entry. For your family."

She looked down at the coins, then at the ledger, then back to Albert—eyes welling with sudden, silent tears.

"He remembered her," she whispered, clutching the book. "Great-Grandma Lydia would've... this would've meant the world to her."

Albert didn't speak. He just waited, letting her have the moment.

After a long silence, she wiped at her cheeks. "I've been on my own a while now. My mom and dad have both passed. My husband's a corporal—stationed out west with the Army, helping with the recovery. It's been hard. But... I've been trying to stay hopeful. Finish school after the baby comes. I want to teach."

Albert smiled faintly. "Those coins are worth a lot. Hopefully, they'll help you get what you need. Your baby will carry Henry's legacy forward. I think he'd like that."

The mobile above the bassinet spun slowly in a draft, casting gentle shadows on the wall. The past and the present met, and they took the next step toward the future together.

****

Thank you for reading Wreckage River. I hope you enjoyed this story.

Please visit my website bewaretheend.com and sign up for my mailing list for updates and new release information.

Your support is invaluable to me. I welcome and respond to your feedback. Please feel free to email me at bb.bewareauthor@gmail.com.